Praise for The Enlightenment

The action is non-stop, with child's play, schoolwork, and danger all churned together. Lamplighter introduces many imaginative elements in her world that will delight...
—*VOYA*

The British boarding school mystery meets the best imagined of fantasies at breakneck speed and with fully realized characters.
—Sarah A. Hoyt, author of *Darkship Thieves*

L. Jagi Lamplighter, a fantastic new voice and a fabulous new world in the YA market! Rachel Griffin is a hero who never gives up! I cheered her all the way!
—Faith Hunter, author of the *Skinwalker* series

The Unexpected Enlightenment of Rachel Griffin, a plucky band of children join forces to fight evil, despite the best efforts of incompetent adults, at a school for wizards. YA fiction really doesn't get better than that.
—Jonathan Moeller, author of *The Ghosts* series

Rachel Griffin is curious, eager and smart, and ready to begin her new life at Roanoke Academy for the Sorcerous Arts, but she didn't expect to be faced with a mystery as soon as she got there. Fortunately she's up to the task. Take all the best of the classic girl detective, throw in a good dose of magic and surround it all with entertaining, likeable friends and an intriguing conundrum, and you'll have *The Unexpected Enlightenment of Rachel Griffin*, a thrilling adventure tailor-made for the folks who've been missing Harry Potter. Exciting, fantastical events draw readers into Rachel's world and solid storytelling keeps them there.
—Misty Massey, author of *Mad Kestrel*

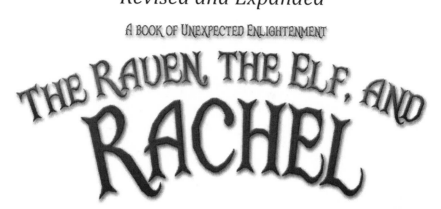

Revised and Expanded

A BOOK OF UNEXPECTED ENLIGHTENMENT

THE RAVEN, THE ELF, AND RACHEL

L. JAGI LAMPLIGHTER

Based on the works of Mark A. Whipple

Illustrations by John C. Wright

Published by:
Wisecraft Publishing
A publishing company of the Wise

This is a work of fiction. All of the characters and events portrayed in this book are fictional, and any resemblance to real people or events is purely coincidental or an Act of God.

ISBN: 978-0-9976460-2-3 (print)
ASIN: B01FYDZO3K
Second edition

First edition, 2014

Edited by Jim Frenkel

Cover art by Dan Lawlis
https://danlawlis.wordpress.com

Interior illustrations by John C. Wright

Typeset by Joel C. Salomon

Cover design by Danielle McPhail
Sidhe na Daire Multimedia
http://sidhenadaire.com

Table of Contents

Chapter 1: The Unforeseen Difficulties of Retrieving a Broom.............1

Chapter 2: The Elusive Sparks of Truth....................12

Chapter 3: The Balmy Surface of the Sun....................20

Chapter 4: Conversation with the Cutest of Boys....................28

Chapter 5: The Perfect Memory of Rachel Griffin 36

Chapter 6: The Unparalleled Advantage of Curious Friends....48

Chapter 7: The Prince of Foul Play 62

Chapter 8: The Grim General of Verhängnisburg....................72

Chapter 9: A Farewell to Innocence 86

Chapter 10: The Unlikely Proposal of Ivan Romanov 97

Chapter 11: Rachel Gets Valiant....................110

Chapter 12: The Beggar King   120

Chapter 13: Dread Versus Valiant....................136

Chapter 14: Weeping over Sheep 149

Chapter 15: The Cold Lair of Dread 163

Chapter 16: Waylaying Peter....................172

Chapter 17: Conversations in the Storm King Café....................185

Chapter 18: Sigfried the Puddle-Slayer and the Rose-ambush....................199

Chapter 19: The Magnificent Tree of Roanoke Island 211

Chapter 20: The Exiled Daughter of Idunn....................221

Chapter 21: The Raven and the Elf 231

Chapter 22: Of Brooms and Iron Filings....................244

Chapter 23: Adventures with Elf Herbs....................260

Chapter 24: Unrecognized Murder Weapons....................274

Chapter 25: Yeti vs. Wookiees....................284

Chapter 26: The Fortress That Is Dread 296

Chapter 27: Dragonsmith's Patented Crush Crusher....................309

Chapter 28: Saving the World Before Dinner, After All 322

Chapter 29: The Unfortunate Wife of Mortimer Egg....................334

Chapter 30: I Don't Remember That Cup....................343

Chapter 31: Leaving on a Jet Plane 353

Chapter 32: Hiding in the Couch....................367

Chapter 33: Held by the Collar While Everyone Else Fights....................375

Chapter 34: Tearing Down the Walls of the World....................387

Dedication

To William E. Burns III
who suffered the most

A better godfather no four children have ever had!

Author's Note:

This is a revised edition.
Some things have been changed from the original.
Most notably, Valerie Foxx is now Valerie Hunt.

Once there was a world that seemed at first glance much like other worlds you may have *lived in* or read about, but it *wasn't*...

Chapter 1:
The Unforeseen Difficulties of Retrieving a Broom

"No one's looking!" Rachel Griffin grabbed Siggy's arm and tugged. "Let's go!"

They dashed past the *No Students Allowed* sign and raced up the spiral staircase, their footsteps echoing against the stone steps of the Watch Tower. Siggy's legs were significantly longer. He soon raced past her.

"Do you think the proctors will find us up here?" she gasped.

"We have a few minutes," Sigfried Smith called over his shoulder. He took two steps at a time. He also spoke with an English accent, though his lacked Rachel's educated crispness. "They have to interrogate the princess. Think she'll break under torture? Of course, she blabbed about your boyfriend with no provocation. They hadn't even made her go without food for a week, or used a thumb screw. How long will it take to get your broom?"

"Gaius Valiant is *not* my boyfriend!"

"Shhh!" Siggy hissed. "They'll hear you!"

Embarrassed, Rachel clamped her hand over her mouth. She murmured, "They don't torture students at Roanoke Academy, Siggy. It's just not done. Did they torture you at the Unwary orphanage where you grew up?"

Siggy's voice became hard as flint. "It's not something a girl would want to hear about."

"I want to hear," Rachel responded seriously. "I want to know *everything*."

They continued pelting up the staircase, which spiraled through the middle of the tower. Through open doors, glimpses could be seen of cabinets filled with materials for warding away the supernatural. Rachel noted chalk, rock salt, stones with a hole in the middle, red thread, and a barrel overflowing with dried daisy chains. A bag of weed killer rested beside the barrel.

Plunging through an opening in the ceiling, they burst into the belfry. The air was damp and smelled of the straw that covered the rock slabs of the floor. Huge tubular chimes hung from the ceiling. Beneath them stood an obscuration lantern—a brass contraption as large as a lighthouse lamp with an enormous cut-crystal globe. It stood taller than Rachel.

The outer wall of the belfry had eight tall arches set into its thick stone. Half of them were open, containing no glass. Outside, to the north and east, stretched a forest of virgin hemlocks. The afternoon sun shone in the west, gleaming off the central lantern's brass. To the south lay the campus.

The other four arches contained mirrors, each with a hint of color to the glass—green, blue, golden, and purple. All four mirrors reflected the two young students. Both wore muddy and ripped academic robes of matte black, the kind that had been worn by scholars since medieval days, but which mundane Americans now wore only for graduations. The first student was a tall, handsome boy with golden curls and bare feet. When he smiled, the gleam of his teeth was bright enough to blind passing geese. Behind him ran a panting, tiny Asian girl, far younger-looking than her thirteen years. Black, shoulder-length locks flew wildly about her face.

Patting the back of her head, Rachel found nothing but hair. Somewhere—perhaps when she crashed through a classroom window just over an hour ago to save her science tutor—she had lost her black-and-white, polka-dotted bow. In the mirror, her reflection simultaneously patted the back of its head, seeking its lost bow. Girl and reflection sighed in unison.

"Quick," Sigfried urged, peering back down the stairs, "we only have a little time before they notice we're missing. Get your broom!"

"Right!"

Crossing to the south window, Rachel threw herself onto the sill, still panting. The campus of Roanoke Academy for the Sorcerous Arts stretched before her. An area of stumps and saplings separated the Watch Tower from the castle-like building that housed the college and the upper school. Beyond its many spires and towers, she could see bits of the reflecting lake and the long green lawns of the campus commons. Paths led from the commons to the seven dormitories, three to the west and four to the east. Farther yet, she caught glimpses of monuments and fountains, the lily pond, and the Oriental gardens.

The bells in the six domed bell towers atop Roanoke Hall rang four times, marking the end of classes. On the commons, students rushed to and fro. Proctors rounded up wrongdoers. Tutors—as Roanoke Academy called its professors—helped the injured. Rachel looked around, hoping for a glimpse of Gaius Valiant. There was no sign of him, but she caught a glimpse of Nurse Moth astride her orange Ouroboros Industries Flycycle—a device that had as much in common with an old-fashioned broom as an automobile has with a horse-drawn carriage. The nurse's hands were raised in a cantrip as she floated a patient toward the infirmary.

"I see the nurse!" Rachel leaned forward. "On her own bristleless. She's not on mine!"

Sigfried peered down the staircase. "The coast is clear! Go for it."

Rachel stretched out her hand. "*Varenga*, Vroomie!"

Siggy came to join her. He gazed out over her shoulder. "Is it coming?"

"Can't see it yet. It can take a minute or two. It's possible Nurse Moth shut it in the infirmary—in which case, it won't come." She glanced warily toward the stairs. "Can we wait?"

"Sure. What's the worst that will happen? Expelled for sneaking into the forbidden tower?" Siggy paused, cocking his head. "What's that noise?"

Behind them, the giant lantern rattled. A chill slithered up Rachel's spine. She and Sigfried exchanged glances. They both spun around.

"Why is it...doing that?" she whispered.

"I'll look." Sigfried absentmindedly touched his chest where his all-seeing amulet hung under his black academic robe. "It's an animal. A rat, maybe? Brown and ugly."

Rachel crept across the straw, close to the mossy wall. She craned her neck. A small, brown animal with a long slick tail came into view. It worried at the brass pedestal of the lantern.

"Looks like a muskrat," she whispered.

"What's it doing?" he asked.

"Don't know. Rather cheeky of it, isn't it? Maybe there is food inside."

"Probably someone's familiar."

"No." Rachel shook her head. "The pads of its paws would be silver."

The lantern flared, multi-colored flames flickering and leaping within the crystal globe. Glints of red, blue, and green danced over the hanging chimes, the straw, and the mossy walls. They transformed the drab stone belfry into a wonderland.

Rachel's lips parted in delight. "How beautiful! But we should..." Her voice died.

The muskrat's eyes were the same milky color as those of the students who had been under the control of their wicked math tutor, Dr. Mordeau. Rachel thought back several seconds, replaying her memory of what she had just experienced. In her perfect memory, a tall, black shape hunched over the little animal—like the shades from Dr. Mordeau's cloak.

"Siggy!" Rachel shrieked. "Stop that muskrat!"

Fixing her gaze on it, she whistled. A tingle of energy welled up in her body, running from her toes and fingers, through her limbs, to her lips. Excitement and giddiness gripped her, but she kept her face as calm as a mask. Silver sparkles of light flew from her mouth, forming a brisk breeze. This wind pushed the muskrat across the straw. It traveled nearly three feet.

Rachel grinned and clapped her hands. She had only been at school for five days, yet she had improved so much. She could now push something the size of a muskrat with a breeze she summoned with sorcery. Her hours of practicing were paying off.

Sigfried pulled out his trumpet from a voluminous pocket in his robe and blew. A wind, swirling with the same silver sparkles, picked up the muskrat and swept it another twenty feet—across the belfry and out the open window. Rachel sighed.

It had taken her hours of practice to be able to push that creature a few feet. Siggy was a natural.

Running to the western window, Rachel shaded her eyes against the glare of the sun and peered at the falling muskrat as it tumbled through the air. She thought back recalling everything that had happened from the moment she pushed the creature back. In her memory, she could see the shade from Mordeau's cloak. It abandoned the muskrat in mid-air and took off for the south. The little brown animal still tumbled through the air. Rachel tried a *tiathelu* cantrip, hoping to slow its fall, but it was beyond her range. Sadly, she averted her gaze, not wishing to see the poor thing splat on the stump-filled field below.

The muskrat never hit the ground.

Out of the hemlocks to the north shot a serpentine shape, about twelve feet long and covered with golden fur. Its long whiskers, the mane that ran along the length of its back, and the tuft on the end of its tail were all flame-red. Ruby scales coated its underside. Short horns curled above its vaguely wolf-like head.

"Go, Lucky!" Siggy cheered his familiar and best friend. "Get it!"

Fire shot from the dragon's mouth. It struck the falling creature, which let out a horrible screech. Lucky swallowed the muskrat whole. Rachel cringed, feeling sorry for the poor beastie: abused by Mordeau's shade, tossed out a window, and then charbroiled in mid-air.

Siggy whooped.

Rachel turned away with a sigh of sad amusement. Chiding Sigfried for lack of sympathy was like scolding the wind for blowing. Boys were like that—Siggy more than most.

Looking to the south after the departing cloak-fragment, Rachel recalled the blank faces of her fellow students as, possessed by the shades from Mordeau's cloak, they had raised their wands and tried to kill her. Mordeau had been captured, but her master was still at large.

Her hands curled into fists. "We must stop Mortimer Egg."

"Of course!" Sigfried agreed fiercely. "He tried to kill my girlfriend. He must be destroyed."

Rachel smiled, pleased and touched by her friend's enthusiasm. Anyone else would have said, "We can't stop him. We're just kids."—anyone except Sigfried the Dragonslayer.

Crossing to the great lantern, Rachel knelt before the large brass key that controlled the flame. Tipping her head back, she watched the dancing colors—red, blue, purple, green—as she searched her mental library, calling up from her photographic memory any information she might have encountered about such devices. She recalled a manual she had glanced at once on how to refill the oil in an Aladdin lamp, an encyclopedia entry on the history of chandeliers, a book on lighthouses and how they worked, the time she had come upon...

Ah! That was what she needed!

She recalled the time she had come upon her father lighting the obscuration lantern in the small turret atop her grandfather's tower at Gryphon Park, her home back in England. The spirits that the lamp commanded had loomed about him in a circle. The moment she had come bursting up onto the tower roof, he had dismissed them. She played back the memory twice, frowning. He had sent her back downstairs before turning off the lantern. That was no help.

"Which way do I turn it?" she murmured.

"Righty tighty, lefty loosey?" Siggy offered, squatting beside her.

"Does that apply to obscuration lanterns, too?"

"Is that what this is?"

Rachel nodded.

"No idea what that means." Sigfried shrugged. "Remember, I didn't grow up in your World of the Wise. I'm unwary even for an Unwary."

Rachel giggled at that. "Okay..." She paused, thinking how best to explain the lantern and its purpose. "Let me see if I can give you a proper description. You know we're on the Island of Roanoke, right?"

"Are we?"

"Yes..." She eyed him skeptically. "Remember the 'lost' colony of English sorcerers uprooted this island and made it float? So they could escape from persecution in England?"

"No."

"They sailed it around the world for several centuries. Then, it became grounded here in the Hudson River. You remember that, right?"

"No."

"But..." Rachel made a noise of frustration. An uncomfortable tingling sensation spread across her shoulders. The very notion of forgetting disturbed her. "Mr. Gideon told us. In true history class."

Sigfried looked as if he were so bored that it was causing him pain. "You mean true napping? If it doesn't teach us how to brew death or throw fireballs, what good is it? I plan to learn a cantrip that will allow me to sleep with my eyes open."

Rachel let out a long breath. "Okay...Um...The short version. We are on Roanoke Island. Only the Unwary, the mundane folks—if they look from the bank of the Hudson River or an aeroplane—they see Bannerman Island. This fake image is kept in place by a sorcerous Art called obscuration. Got it so far?"

"Maybe." Siggy tossed his Bowie knife and caught it. It gleamed in the afternoon sun. Glints of blue and green and purple flickered across the blade. "Is there going to be a test?"

Rachel threw up her hands. "*Eecks! Eegrec! Zed!* You must remember something!"

"Really? Why is that?" Sigfried scowled at her. Something painful burning behind his eyes, like glimpsing the scorching sun through the clouds on an otherwise pleasantly overcast sky. "Everything I had been taught before this week is wrong. Every fact I learned about the world. Every law of physics. Every historical event. All lies. Even the things that the Wise Guys are telling me are apparently wrong—at least if my Metaplutonian theory is correct: that there is another secret world manipulating our world the way we manipulate the Unscary—the Wiser than the Wise. If everything I've learned is wrong, what's the point of remembering any of it?"

Rachel sat extremely still, her heart thumping unexpectedly. The concept of not remembering disturbed her, partially because she was not exactly sure what people meant by it. She occasionally neglected to check her memory and thus missed an appointment or did not do something she had promised to do. That was a temporary oversight.

But forgetting? She tried to picture what that might feel like but failed.

"Magic shock." She shook herself, continuing solemnly, "Can't tell reality from fairytales. It happens sometimes, when sorcerers have been raised in the mundane world."

Siggy shrugged again. He gestured at the giant lantern, burning away merrily. Glints of red and purple and blue danced over their faces. "So...what is this thing again? Is it important?"

"Okay...even shorter version. This lantern casts magic shadows. These shadows—these servants of the lantern—can be instructed to create illusions, called obscurations. The enormous chimes above us are part of the obscuration magic, too."

"I don't understand. It does...what?"

Rachel paused, collecting her thoughts. "You turn on the lantern and call up its servants. Then, you instruct them to create the kind of illusion you want."

"The muskrat switched on the lantern...why? Did it think there was food inside? That, I could understand! It might be a great place to hide a stash. Adults would never look there."

"No! It was possessed! By one of those horrid shades that came out of Mordeau's cloak. It was using the muskrat to try and turn off the illusions and wards protecting the school."

"You mean the protections that keep out wraiths—like the one we fought? And evil teachers—like the one we fought?"

In spite of the seriousness of the subject, Rachel could not help but giggle at the aptness of his insight. "Er, yeah. Only that was one wraith and one evil tutor, and they snuck inside. Beyond the wards, there are a whole lot more waiting. If the wards ever fail, they could all rush in. *And*, the Unwary would see us."

Sigfried glanced eagerly out the western window—where Storm King Mountain rose in the distance, above the trees—as if he expected to see a horde of specters and malevolent instructors waiting to rush the campus. Seeing the gleam in his eye, she suspected he was already imagining Lucky charbroiling them all.

Rachel rubbed her temples, which were threatening to ache. "We need to turn this lantern off without calling the..." she formed the gesture for the *taflu* cantrip—middle fingers curled, outer fingers straight, thumb across the middle fingers—with both hands and crossed her arms in front of her, so that the repelling gestures blocked her mouth, "*tenebrous obscurii*, the obscuration spirits. One way turns it off. The other way, if you turn it the whole rotation...calls them. Which we don't want to do."

"Why not?"

"Because we are not their master."

"Will these *tenebrous obscurii* know we're not in charge?"

"Don't call their name!" Rachel cried.

"You did."

"No! This gesture—*taflu*—makes it so that supernatural creatures can't hear me! Please don't say their names. We don't want them to come!"

Like the whispering in the tombs of the dead on All Hallow's Eve, there came a soft sound. Dark shapes rose from the floor to loom above the lantern. Solemn, cloaked figures with deep hoods, they seemed to be made of solid darkness. Standing near the walls, they stared inward, forming a circle around Rachel, Sigfried, and the lantern.

Cold fingers of terror touched the back of Rachel's neck. She clutched Sigfried's arm.

"What's that?" he hissed. "Are they what possessed the muskrat?"

Putting her finger to her lips, Rachel shook her head wordlessly.

Ignoring her warning, Sigfried turned toward the nearest figure and made a shooing gesture. "Hey, obsceney-thingy or whatever. Stop what you are doing and go! Scat! Vamoose!"

All the shadowy hoods all turned toward him at the same time. A dozen sibilant voices spoke in unison, "Master Warder, we hear and obey. Everything we do, we shall stop."

No. No. This was bad!

Rachel threw up her hands, palms out flat, and shouted, "Maintain! Maintain!"

The *tenebrous obscurii* turned their many hoods toward her and paused, as if puzzled.

She raised her hands and held them exactly as she remembered her father had, when he had dismissed them at Gryphon Park.

"*Oyarsa! Taflu!*" cried Rachel, which she knew meant: *return to your duties, depart.*

The shadowy cloaks shivered. Silent as black moths under a new moon, they sank into the stones of the floor. The instant they were gone, Rachel raised the index finger of her right hand—the gesture for the Word of Ending cantrip—and spun in a circle, shouting over and over.

"*Obé! Obé! Obé!*"

They did not reappear. Rachel drew a ragged breath. Then, she turned to Siggy and glared at him, tapping her foot.

"What? Why was that a problem?" Siggy asked innocently.

"You told them to stop protecting the school!"

"Oh." Siggy rubbed his jaw, considering this. He shrugged once more. "It would have been exciting if wraiths and black magicians had rushed the campus."

"Not today, Sigfried," Rachel said solemnly. "We just got done fighting geased proctors, possessed students, and a math-teaching dragon. People got hurt. I think," her voice trembled, "your roommate might be dead."

Siggy's face turned pale. "Ian MacDannan? Or Enoch the Wuss?"

"The *wuss*, as you call him." Her voice felt too thick to obey her. "He threw himself in front of our alchemy tutor."

Sigfried scowled. "Who hurt him? I'll have Lucky burn his face."

"It was a crazy, possessed girl."

Siggy threw up his arms. "Why does it *always* have to be a girl?"

"Okay..." Rachel turned back to the obscuration lantern and pulled up her long sleeves. She took a deep breath. "Here goes...something!"

Lunging forward, she turned the lantern key all the way to the left. The flame sputtered and died away. The multi-colored lights dancing around the tower flickered and winked out. They stood, again surrounded by drab straw, without the wonder lent by the lantern-light. With a sigh of relief, Rachel slumped forward and rested her forehead against the lantern's column. She drew back with a yelp. The brass was hot.

Whoosh.

Through the southern window flew Vroomie, obedient to Rachel's call. Shouting for joy, she grabbed her steeplechaser, a marvel of polished dark wood and brass, and hugged it to her. It was the most beautiful bristleless flying broom in the world.

"Mission accomplished!" She flourished the broom victoriously, dashing for the stairs. "Let's go tell the proctors that shades from Mordeau's cloak are on the loose!"

Chapter 2:
The Elusive Sparks of Truth

Rachel and Sigfried clattered down three flights of stairs, her broom bouncing on her shoulder. At the bottom, they threw open the door to the disenchanting chamber, where they had left their fellow freshman, Nastasia Romanov, the Princess of Magical Australia, to be questioned by the proctors. Within, bagpipes blared an eerie tune. The air smelled newly-washed, as if it had rained in that chamber and nowhere else.

Rachel charged in and skidded to an abrupt stop. Above her, the supernaturally lovely princess hung in mid-air, surrounded by a whirlwind of golden sparkles. Her arms were spread, her head thrown back. Her black robes swirled around her. Her fair hair flowed upward, surrounded by the glints of twinkling light, as if she were twirling underwater amidst a thousand, thousand fireflies.

Siggy raised his trumpet, an expression of intense concentration on his face.

"Stop!" Rachel cried. "What are you doing?"

"Saving the princess!"

"She doesn't need saving." Rachel grabbed his arm with her free hand, yanking the instrument away from his mouth. He was much stronger, but her action had taken him by surprise. His arm dipped.

"That's the *Spell of True Recitation*," she continued. "It's supposed to do that. Though why they bother using it on the princess, I don't know. Not sure she could lie, if she wanted to."

"Sorcerers can force people to tell the truth?" Sigfried's brilliant blue eyes filled with horror. "Is evidence extracted that way admissible in courts?"

"Yes," Rachel replied solemnly. "The justice of the Wise is swift and terrible."

She wanted to charge forward and report about the muskrat and Dr. Mordeau's cloak, but she knew better than to interrupt a spell. She looked around her, impatiently tapping her foot.

The disenchanting chamber was a round room with stone benches against the walls. The heavy flagstones were painted with arcane symbols. Oak cabinets held bags of salt, sacks of flower, and piles of horseshoes, all useful for disenchanting spells. The central area was open. It was here the princess floated.

They had left their friend with campus proctors, but now she floated before an Agent of the Wisecraft. Agent MacDannan, an intelligent-looking woman with bushy red hair, played a set of green bagpipes. The tiny golden sparkles issued from it. She wore a black Inverness cloak, large glasses, and high black boots. A ribbon attempted to restrain her bushy ginger locks. A black-and-white rat sat on her shoulder. Her tricorne hat lay discarded on a nearby stone bench. On her fingers glittered seven rings of mastery inset with arcane runes and bright gems.

Rachel noted the mastery rings. Most students at Roanoke were awarded one or two rings of mastery upon graduation. Earning three was rare. Four was extraordinary. The number of people who had earned five rings was less than a dozen; one of them was Rachel's older sister, Sandra Griffin. In the history of Roanoke, only one person had earned rings of mastery in all seven of the Sorcerous Arts—Scarlett Mallory MacDannan.

"We have to wait for her to finish." Rachel bounced up and down on the balls of her feet. She hated waiting. "Then we tell her about Mordeau's cloak. After that, I guess it's our turn." She pointed at where Nastasia spun in mid-air.

"You mean she's going to cast that truth magic on me?" Sigfried scowled. "I'm gonna attack her, after all."

"You can't attack her! She's on our side!"

"Not if she's going to use truth magic on me!"

"Sigfried! She's an Agent of the Wisecraft—the law enforcement arm of the Parliament of the Wise. They're the best trained sorcerers in the world."

"I'm a sorcerer, too."

"You're hardly a proper sorcerer! You've been studying magic for five whole days!"

"So? She doesn't look so tough."

Rachel waved her arms. Her steeplechaser swished to and fro. "That's Scarlett Mallory MacDannan, one of the Six Musketeers who defeated the Veltdammerung during the Terrible Years. They don't come better than her."

"Is that supposed to scare someone? All the more glory for me when I defeat her!" Sigfried put his hand under his robe for his knife. "I think I can take her."

Rachel rolled her eyes in exasperation. "She's your roommate Ian's mother."

"Oh." The orphan boy looked woebegone. "Can't mug someone's mother. Wouldn't be knightly. What would Arthur say when he gets back?"

"Arthur who?"

"King Arthur."

Rachel blinked twice. "You literally believe King Arthur is coming back from the dead?"

"If someone other than a magical girl, going to a magical school, to study magic, asked me that question, I'd dignify it with an answer."

They stood a moment longer, watching Nastasia twirl amidst golden sparkles. Watching her friend thus, Rachel felt uplifted yet torn. Nastasia was her second-ever real friend, a kindred spirit, someone who understood the difficulties of aristocratic life—a rare quality in this egalitarian age. Also, the princess had stood up for her against the bully-girls from Drake Hall, for which Rachel was extremely grateful.

Until today, however, Rachel had been an obedient child. She had liked pleasing adults, especially great heroines such as Roanoke's dean. Dean Moth was one of the most respected sorceresses alive, and she had been kind to Rachel. Defying the dean had been tremendously difficult, but she had done it to protect the boy who had so helped her, Gaius Valiant.

The princess betrayed Gaius to the dean. Rachel did not know how she felt about this.

The bagpipe music rose to a crescendo and then grew quiet. The sparkly light issuing from the instrument slowed and swirled downward. The princess floated to the ground. Her golden locks settled around her utterly-beautiful face. As Agent MacDannan led her to the bench and began asking questions, a door opened on the far side of the disenchanting chamber.

Two men in black tricorne hats strode in, their Inverness cloaks swirling around them. Each one wore an Agent's medallion, a circle of pewter showing a lantern surrounded by stars, and each carried a fulgurator's staff—a length of polished wood topped with a gem the size of a man's fist. As the men advanced, the staffs clanked against the stone.

The first had skin the color of dark coffee, thick dark hair that fell to his shoulders in tight, oiled curls, and a neatly-trimmed beard. His boots were a deep forest green. A cheetah stalked at his side. The great cat surveyed the chamber and then sat regally beside the door, like a guardian from an Egyptian tomb. The second man had pale skin, short dark hair, and an impish gleam in his blue eyes. A tortoiseshell cat padded beside him. At the sight of his familiar face, Rachel's heart leapt.

Finally, someone who would answer her questions.

She started across the floor, but Sigfried grabbed her shoulder.

"What about those two?" He turned his back to them and covered his mouth with his hand. "Real Agents? Or imposters—like that creep who tried to kill my girlfriend?"

Rachel squeezed Siggy's arm in delight. "That's Dorian Standish and James Darling! They're as real as Agents come. Agent Darling used to be my father's partner."

Rachel refrained from adding that her father was now the head of a secret department called the Shadow Agency. Nor did she explain that she had not known this until a couple days ago—when she had been told by a certain intriguing, yet possibly dangerous, older upperclassman whom the princess had recently betrayed to the dean.

Siggy interrupted her reverie. "You mean James Darling, Agent? The guy from the comic books? The guy our alchemy tutor told us about?"

"That's him."

"Huh." Sticking his trumpet back in his enormous pocket, Sigfried crossed his arms, unimpressed. "I don't see why Darling gets all the credit, when it was Mr. Fisher who defeated that horrible death guy. What was his name? Cost-Eye the Death-less?"

"Oh, you! Enough rubbish!" Rachel ran across the room, skidding to a stop before the two men, her broom clutched tightly in her right hand. "Mr. Standish! Mr. Darling!"

James Darling bent down onto one knee, so that he and Rachel were eye-to-eye. His hair was thinning. Otherwise, he looked like the youthful version of himself in the painting of the Six Musketeers that hung in the Wisecraft offices at Old Scotland Yard, where her father and sister worked—a handsome young man with intense blue eyes, spiky black hair, and a cocky grin.

He also looked a great deal like his son, John, a senior at the upper school along with Gaius and Rachel's brother Peter. John Darling had been Rachel's crush from afar for three years running, ever since he paused to admire her pony at a Yule Party at Gryphon Park. She had glimpsed John a few times since coming to school but had not found the courage to speak to him.

Agent James Darling leaned back and gave Rachel a charming smile. His familiar, Pyewacket, rubbed against her leg, purring. Rachel bent down and pet the cat. "Well, what have we here? Little Rachel Griffin. All grown up."

"I must disagree with you, Darling. She has not yet grown much *up*." Agent Standish prodded her fondly with the butt of his staff. His voice was rich and deep with a touch of an accent that Rachel knew was from Sub-Saharan Africa, a country of the Wise known as Prester John's Kingdom. His dark brown eyes were wise and compassionate, but there was an air of danger about him. "Why is this, Lady Rachel? Fourteen-years-old and no bigger than a radish?"

Rachel smiled at his use of her formal title. Few people realized that, as the daughter of the Duke of Devon, she was technically Lady Rachel Griffin. "I'm only thirteen. I was invited to come to school a year early."

"Ah! That explains all." He laughed, a deep, jovial sound. "By next year, I expect you to be as tall as trees. As tall as mountains. As tall as the Dragonslayer here." He extended his staff toward Sigfried, who was still standing on the far side of the room.

Beaming, Sigfried crossed the chamber and joined them. "You've heard of me?"

"Everyone's heard of you, boy. You are the most famous young man in the World of the Wise. How many orphans kill dragons and make off with their hoards?"

A huge grin crossed Siggy's face. "Wicked!"

Rachel was dying to ask the thousands of questions she had gathered over the last five days, but she restrained herself. First, she had a report to make.

"The shadows from Dr. Mordeau's cloak!" she blurted out, gesturing wildly in the direction of the belfry. "One possessed a muskrat and switched on the obscuration lantern."

Both men stared at her, their smiles frozen on their faces.

Still kneeling, Agent Darling searched her face carefully. "And this shade came from Mordeau's cloak?"

Rachel nodded.

He glanced up at Standish. Agent Standish nodded once and took off at a run, his cheetah loping ahead of him. Outside, his footsteps rang against the stone steps.

"Your Master Warder, Nighthawk, rounded up quite a few of the shades. We had hoped that was all of them." Agent Darling drummed his fingers thoughtfully on his knee. "If only we had some way of discovering how many there are."

Rachel thought back to the basement of Drake Hall, the moment when Mordeau threw down her cloak and it dissolved into shadows. She froze that memory and counted.

"Twenty-four."

"What?" Agent Darling glanced up.

"There were twenty-four shadows, sir."

"Are you sure?"

Rachel examined the moments after that, as the shadows rushed away down the corridor. She counted twice more. "Yes, sir."

"Well, that's...very useful." Agent Darling blinked. "Thank you, Rachel." He reached into his pocket and pulled out a green-tinted, mirrored business card. When he passed his hands over it, the image changed to show the Wisecraft's lantern surrounded by stars. He spoke to the card, "People. Darling here. Six of Mordeau's shades are on the loose. Keep a sharp eye out."

"Whoa! I want one of those mirrors!" Sigfried exclaimed. "It would have been useful to be able to talk to each other when we got separated today. And in this crazy place of yours, phones don't work. What about those? Do I have to be a spy to have one?"

"They're calling cards," Rachel told him. "You can buy them at alchemy shops."

"Will you order some? That would be wicked cool!"

"They're very expensive," Rachel began, but Siggy cut her off.

"Expensive for you? Or expensive for me?"

"Oh, right. I'll order some."

Agent Darling gestured at where Agent MacDannan questioned the princess. "Anything I can do for you, while you wait your turn?"

Rachel gazed at him, questions burning her tongue like hot embers. She wanted to learn the answers so much. Not knowing was nigh unbearable. *Who was Mortimer Egg? Why did he try to kill Valerie Hunt? Where was Valerie's missing father? What about the Raven? Was their world the one whose doom the Raven foretold? Or another? Were there really other worlds? Where did the princess go during her visions? Why did Dr. Mordeau think it was possible to resurrect the dead? Could it be done? If so, could they bring back her beloved Grandfather?*

Dr. Mordeau had mentioned a tragedy related to her grandfather. Rachel desperately wanted to know more about that. Yet the idea that some harm might have befallen him was so horrifying, she could hardly find her voice to ask.

Misinterpreting her distress as shyness, Agent Darling gave Rachel an encouraging smile. "It's been some time since I took you for that broom ride, Miss Griffin. I see you ride yourself now." As he glanced at Vroomie, his eyebrows arched. "A steeple-chaser! Impressive. I didn't know anyone rode those anymore."

"A few people do," she replied with pride.

"I knew another little girl once who rode a steeplechaser." He chuckled, "She used to tilt her head to one side and say, 'James, what is a steeple anyway? And why should I chase it?'"

"Who was she?" Rachel twisted her broom between her hands. "Does she still ride?"

Agent Darling's face became very still. His gaze took on a faraway look mingled with something else Rachel could not place. Weariness? Sorrow? Despair?

Rising, he brushed off his hands. "I...I had better go see if Standish needs a hand. Scarlett...uh...Agent MacDannan will see to you two."

He walked abruptly from the chamber, his tortoiseshell cat padding silently behind him.

Chapter 3:
The Balmy Surface of the Sun

"Miss Griffin, Mr. Smith," called Agent MacDannan. "Your turn."

Rachel crossed to stand before the ginger-headed Agent and curtsied. The rat on the woman's shoulder sniffed at her inquisitively. Rachel held out her finger and smiled as the little beast snuffled her. Behind her, Sigfried approached more warily.

"Our turn for...what?" he asked suspiciously.

Agent MacDannan replied, "We have a method for undoing the new geases—the spell your math tutor used to control your fellow students and make them attack each other. We want to ask you about what happened today. First, we must make certain you are not under her influence. We don't know how many students she ensorcelled."

"What's the process for ending the spell?" Sigfried squinted at the Agent through one eye. The other eye was squeezed shut. "What exactly will happen to us?"

"A fair question. First, I'll use the Word of Ending cantrip. It stops any active effects of the geas. After that, I will play a song—an enchantment that compels the listener to tell the truth. It has other side effects—such as to remove the geas itself. Which is why we are using it here."

"But we are not geased," Rachel objected.

"We cannot know that for certain," replied the Agent. "Best to be careful."

Sigfried took three steps backwards. "Tell the truth for how long?"

Agent MacDannan snorted with amusement. "The effect is temporary, Mr. Smith. Once the music stops, it only lingers briefly. This is not like being questioned by the Grand Inquisitor. I shall not take advantage of the fact that you are under the influence of my spell to ask you your life history and every wrong thing you have ever done. I only plan to ask one question: 'Do you remember anything that you did not remember a minute ago?'"

"That doesn't sound...so bad," Siggy said uncertainly. "Will it hurt?"

"Not at all. Right, Miss Romanov?" Agent MacDannan gestured at the princess.

"It was not uncomfortable in the least, Mr. Smith." Nastasia nodded her head graciously from where she sat on the stone bench. "It felt cool and refreshing. I am already myself again."

"I guess that's okay," Sigfried spoke reluctantly.

"Not that anyone should need compulsion to tell the truth," the princess added.

Siggy rolled his eyes.

Agent MacDannan instructed Rachel and Sigfried to stand side-by-side. She raised the index finger of her right hand and moved it horizontally, the gesture for the Word of Ending.

"*Obé*," she commanded. "There, the first part is done. Very well, Miss Griffin first. Now, where did I put my bagpipes? Oh. Still wearing them. Right."

Rachel leaned her broom against the wall. Stepping into the center of the disenchanting chamber, she took a deep breath. Despite how nonchalant she had been when describing the *Spell of True Recitation* to Sigfried, her stomach felt as if it had been tied into knots. She favored telling the truth. As someone who normally hid her reactions and chose her words carefully, however, the idea of having no control over how she might answer filled her with dread.

Agent MacDannan raised her bagpipes and began to play. Music flowed from the instrument, along with sparkles of golden lights and the fresh scent of newly-fallen rain. The tiny stars twirled around Rachel, lifting her off the floor. Her hair flew up above her. A wonderful sensation bore her upwards, as if she were resting upon a bed of warm wind. It felt so wonderful. She let go of her trepidations and shouted in delight.

The glinting lights felt refreshing, like a crisp autumn breeze. As they brushed against her skin, one or two pricked with uncomfortable heat. Rachel twitched and shimmied in mid-air. A gleam caught in her hair. It hung above her, a star stuck in a cascade of satiny blackness. The sight filled her with unexpected joy.

The rousing music caused images of recent events to flash through her mind. She vividly recalled the duel she had won the previous night and how Gaius had smiled at her, right before he leaned in and kissed her. The memory sent a shiver of anticipation throughout her body. He was so cute, so intriguing...

But did she want him to be her boyfriend?

Her feelings for him were so fierce, so pure, so new. She was not certain she wished to risk adding volatile romantic emotions. What she felt toward him seemed sacred, exalted above ordinary things, like one of these tiny sparks that danced around her. She wanted to catch it in her hands and protect the precious thing, in the hope that, if nurtured, it might grow into a blazing fire. She did not want to take any chances that it might get extinguished.

She would have liked to dwell on Gaius, but the music compelled her mind to move forward. The events of this day, the first Friday of her first week at Roanoke Academy, rushed past. Everything was as she had experienced it the first time, except for one thing.

While she and Gaius had been watching the duel between the dean and the math-teaching dragon, they had not been alone. Perched in a nearby tree had been a raven the size of an eagle with eyes as red as blood.

A frisson of fear crept up her spine. No. The Raven had not been watching Mordeau. It had been watching *her*.

The music rose, reached a crescendo, and faded. Her feet touched the stone floor. Her hair settled around her shoulders. She tried to catch the last gleaming spark but it had vanished. She gazed sadly at her empty hands.

"Miss Griffin. Do you remember anything now that you did not remember before?"

Images of the Raven crowded into the foreground of her thoughts. Rachel's fears came rushing back. She thought panic would close up her throat, but her mouth opened and answered without consulting her.

"That horrid Raven was watching me. The one that is the omen of the doom of worlds."

"Raven, doom of worlds?" Agent MacDannan blinked.

"That's what Master Warder Nighthawk called it."

"Interesting. Anything else?"

Rachel shook her head, but, to her dismay, she could not keep herself from continuing to speak. "The Wisecraft does know the world's in danger, right?"

"The *world's* in danger, Miss Griffin? How so?"

"Didn't you hear me?" Rachel cried. Then she cringed. She never would have spoken so rudely to one of the Six Musketeers if she could have controlled her response. "That horrid Raven signifies the *doom of worlds*, and he's here. On our world. Looking at people! Something's terribly wrong. I know it!"

Agent MacDannan stared at her, her expression unreadable. "An interesting theory, Miss Griffin. Please wait with Miss Romanov. Your turn, Mr. Smith?"

Rachel wanted to explain how she had heard Dr. Mordeau *admit* that she worked for Veltdammerung, an organization devoted to ending the world, but Agent MacDannan had already turned to Sigfried. Sighing, Rachel stepped to the side and sat down on the bench.

She smiled cheerfully at Nastasia, but, underneath, she felt shaken. First she had blurted out things against her will—a disturbing experience for anyone, but doubly so for someone who usually masked her emotions—and now, when she wanted to talk, no one would listen!

Some days, it was hard being so tiny.

It made it easy to get overlooked.

Then there was the disquieting thing she had just recalled. Why had the Raven been watching her? Was she doomed personally? If an omen intended to be invisible, and you saw through its disguise, did it count as having seen it?

What if the world really were in danger, and none of the adults believed her?

Sigfried stepped into the center of the floor, scowling. The bagpipe music swelled, sparks swirled. He soared up into the air, an extremely handsome boy amidst glinting golden sparkles, like a young Adonis surrounded by fairy dust.

"Ouch! Hot! Hot! Hot!" Sigfried shouted.

Hot?

"I'll save you, Boss!" The door banged open, and Lucky swooped into the disenchanting chamber. He flashed toward Sigfried and wrapped his long sinuous body around him and yanked him out of the swirl of bright gold sparks. Huge gouts of red-orange flame shot out of his mouth. The tiny sparkles burst and dissolved in the dragon fire.

Rachel cringed. So much for keeping Lucky's ability to talk a secret. Agent MacDannan was staring in open astonishment.

Lucky and Sigfried spun across the floor, somersaulting, limbs flailing. Rachel heard a muffled "Ooch! Ouch! Ooch! Ouch!" but could not tell which one of them made the sound.

"Oww! Ow! Owww!" Sigfried rolled up onto his feet. The long, sinuous dragon still wrapped around him like a furry golden boa. "That hurt!"

"Sorry," Lucky mumbled.

"No, not you, though my elbow smarts something fierce from where it clonked against the stone. I meant those sparks. They burned!"

Agent MacDannan lowered her bagpipes. "If a person habitually lies, this spell can feel a bit warm."

Rachel thought of the two sparks that had burned when the others felt cool. She recalled the moment she chose to lie to Mortimer Egg—possibly her first serious real lie. That decision might have saved Valerie Hunt's life. Hot sparks or no, she was glad she had done it.

"Warm?" Siggy cried. "I suppose you'd call the surface of the sun warm. I'm covered with burns!" He pulled up his sleeve and looked at his arm, but there were no marks. "Huh. Was that like that spell the Starkadder rotter used on the princess? The one with the black fire that made her scream but didn't leave burns?"

"He did...*what*?" Agent MacDannan gasped.

"Phantom fire," Rachel answered without even meaning to. She shivered and hugged her arms. Blurting things out without forethought was so disturbing!

"Please, it is no matter. Let us not talk about it." The princess flushed.

"That's...black magic!" Agent MacDannan cried in shock. "That's illegal. He could go to jail for that. Which prince did this? Was he over eighteen? Oh, please tell me it wasn't the crown prince. That's a political mess no one wants to have to face."

"Remus. He's number two in line," said Rachel.

"Thank goodness." Agent MacDannan rubbed her face. "Oh! Quickly, before the enchantment wears off: Mr. Smith, do you remember anything you had forgotten?"

Sigfried's eyes grew huge. His jaw flapped up and down like a flag in the wind.

"Hundreds of things! Blimey!" he cried, waving his arms expansively. "The skies of London are filled with people on brooms. And giant flying umbrellas with platforms at the bottom of their handles, large enough for families to stand on. And flying ships. Huge clipper ships with massive sails that fly through the air! And buildings! Whole buildings I didn't remember! The Temple to Apollo at Westminster has an additional wing I had never noticed. How could we Unwary fail to notice a whole third of a public building? Oh, and men in Inverness cloaks with staffs! Are those staffs like the wands the Drake kids use, only bigger? Wicked! Oh and horse-drawn carriages! And an aardvark the size of a house! How could I have I not noticed all this?"

Aardvark the size of a house? That was new. Perhaps Siggy made it up. But wasn't he still under the sway of the *Spell of True Recitation*?

Agent MacDannan nodded calmly. "Obscuration causes people to forget what they see."

A cold tingle ran up Rachel's spine. For her, remembering back broke the illusion of an obscuration, but she had not realized that obscurations worked by interfering with memory.

The thought made her queasy.

"That's not very nice." Sigfried scowled. "Why do you hide things from the Unwary? How can they be anything but unwary, if they have no way to grow wise to what you're up to?"

"Many reasons," Agent MacDannan replied briskly. "They can be summed up as: if the Unwary knew about us, we would have to rule them."

"But...why?" Sigfried exploded, stomping forward. "That doesn't make any sense!"

The Agent ran a hand over her bushy hair, a crackle of impatience in her voice. "Because those without power are envious of those with it. Even if this were not true of many, it takes only a few rogues to ruin things. Our treaties with the fey world—the Five Elf Lords, the Pixy Claves, the King Beneath the Mountain, the Gnomes, etc.—are very delicate. They only protect the Unwary as long as the Unwary do not interact with the supernatural world.

"The instant mundane folk find out about magic, they invariably rush off and make deals with the magical entities, in the hopes of gaining powers like ours for themselves—and these deals *always* go badly. It is better they remain unaware. It is their only chance at freedom and a good life."

Siggy scowled. "Doesn't seem fair. Lucky! Did you know that the skies are filled with flying sorcerers on brooms and floaty ships and stuff."

"Yeah."

"Wh-why didn't you tell me?"

"Uh...don't know." The dragon shrugged, a process that caused a wave to travel down the length of its body. "Didn't know you didn't see them."

"Huh," muttered Sigfried. He started to say something more, but then he stopped. He and Lucky looked at each other silently for a time. Rachel suspected they were talking to each other mind-to-mind.

Agent MacDannan addressed Sigfried and Rachel. "Now that we know you were not under a geas, we'd like to hear what happened today, from each of you. We already heard what Miss Romanov remembers. Mr. Smith?"

She tried to ask Sigfried questions, but his answers were so disconnected that she was not able to follow his story. Rachel stepped forward and tugged on Agent MacDannan's sleeve.

"Ma'am, there's a thinking glass in the belfry. Sigfried could show you his memories."

Siggy threw Rachel a dark look, but Agent MacDannan's face lit up. Eager to take advantage of Rachel's suggestion, she shepherded the three students out the door.

Chapter 4:
Conversation with the Cutest of Boys

The foyer of the Watch Tower was now crowded with students. Proctors herded more through the door. As Agent MacDannan led them toward the stairs, Rachel recognized those from Drake Hall with whom she had recently fought. Their eyes were no longer cloudy. Rachel hoped that this meant these students were no longer under the control of the geas Dr. Mordeau had cast to compel them to fight their fellow students at the evil tutor's behest.

A visiting nurse from the Halls of Healing in New York City stood by the front door, playing the flute. She was dressed in the white habit and wimple of the Order of Asclepius. Green sparkles swirled from her instrument. The air near her smelled of freshly-baked bread as the magic swirled around the entering students, healing their cuts and bruises.

Most of the young people crowding into the foyer were dressed in subfusc, the least formal of the three uniforms allowed at Roanoke Academy. The girls wore white blouses, black skirts or slacks, and thin, black velvet neck ribbons, almost like ties. The boys wore dark suits. Over this, both wore half capes that fell from their shoulders to their upper thighs. A few wore their square mortarboard caps, but most had lost their hats in the recent tussle.

Only three of these students were dressed in the full academic style—long black robes from neck to ankle. Two towered above everyone else in the foyer, including the adults. William Locke was a serious-looking young man with dark hair and a wry, sardonic expression. Detached yet curious, he surveyed the room around him as if he were viewing a fascinating scientific experiment. He wore his fulgurator's wand attached to his wrist in a spring-loaded device that could release it into his hand with the click of a switch.

Even taller stood the impossibly-handsome Prince Vladimir Von Dread. He was exquisitely built, with piercing dark eyes and wavy black hair with red highlights. His robes bore a golden royal crest on the left breast. The Crown Prince of Bavaria clenched and unclenched his thick black leather dueling gloves and frowned at the other students from Drake, as if each had personally disappointed him. Perhaps they agreed—most could not meet his gaze.

Next to Locke and Dread, a much shorter boy lounged against a pillar. He regarded the proceedings around him with amusement, as if he enjoyed watching life's little dramas. His chestnut hair was pulled back into a short ponytail. His robes were worn and patched. A fulgurator's wand, a length of teak and brass tipped with a sapphire, hung from a loop at his hip.

When he saw Rachel, he straightened, and his eyes lit up. The ember of affection Rachel guarded so vigilantly within her heart blazed anew.

Gaius Valiant was the cutest of boys.

Resting her broom against the wall, Rachel broke away from the others, as they headed up the stairs, and ran through the crowd. She slid to a stop before Gaius.

He grinned down at her with a familiar big smile. "Hey, Rachel."

"Mr. Valiant," she murmured.

Then she paused, unexpectedly tongue-tied. She had so much she wanted to say, yet she did not know where to begin.

"Please. Call me Gaius." He reached out and brushed his finger against her sore cheek.

Rachel's breath caught. A tingle that had nothing to do with soreness spread through her.

"That ugly gash is gone." His voice rose in surprise, sounding more British than usual. "Your cheek's only a little red!"

Rachel gestured toward the flute-playing nurse by the door. "One of the visiting nurses played a proper healing song for me. Took care of my cuts and bruises, too. On my ear—from where the whip hit me; my back—from where I somersaulted across the gravel; and on my leg and shoulder—from where I smashed through the window. She also summoned all the shards of broken glass out of my clothing."

"You had quite a day, didn't you?" he drawled. "I hadn't heard about the gravel."

"A boy made my broom freeze in mid-air. I flew off."

Gaius's eyebrows leapt upward. "Wait! You fell off, and you managed a somersault before you hit the ground?"

A pleased little smile darted across Rachel's lips. "And I paralyzed him on the way down. Thanks to our practice session."

"You..." the older boy paused, his brow creased as he worked through what she had just said. "You mean, you paralyzed him *while falling?* And then you somersaulted?" He blinked. "That shows an amazing presence of mind!"

Gaius gazed at her, awed.

Rachel drank in his admiration like wine.

"I haven't told anyone about you helping to save the dean, since you asked me not to." Gaius said, his voice low. "Even though I am at least eighty-five percent sure that if I did tell, only good things would come from it. Are you sure you don't want the world to know? You might get a commendation or something."

Rachel envisioned the public scrutiny that would accompany the revelation that she had helped save the dean. It was bad enough that people knew she had saved her science tutor, Mr. Fisher. She hated being the center of the attention. It gave her a claustrophobic feeling, as if her surroundings were closing in on her.

"Please don't tell anyone," Rachel begged fervently. "Hopefully, no one other than you and I will ever know. Oh, and..." she glanced to the right and left and then leaned toward him, whispering intently, "remember the horrid Raven I told you about?"

"The one that is the omen of the doom of worlds, right?"

"Right. It was watching us while the dean fought the dragon."

"It watched the fight?"

"No. It watched us. You and me." A shiver ran along her spine.

"Oh." He blinked. "That's...rather disturbing."

"I'm scared, Gaius." She stepped closer to him and grabbed his shoulder, suddenly frightened. "My father told me to stay away from the Raven, but it's watching me. It knows I can see it. What if it doesn't like that? What if it..."

He moved toward her until they stood very close together, gazing at one another. He was short for his age, but to her, he seemed so tall and solid. He lay his hand on her arm.

"I'll protect you," Gaius promised gravely.

The fingers of fear clutching at her chest loosened a tiny bit. She whispered, "Thank you."

He squeezed her arm. Such happiness flowed through her that she forgot to breathe. She felt as if a bright star had left its place in heaven and come down to drive back the dark and cold. It reminded her of the previous night, when he had leaned in and kissed her. She wondered hopefully if he might kiss her again. But he merely took a step back, still smiling.

"How do I find you? I mean, should there be another emergency where I need protecting," Rachel said as casually as she could manage. She feared she sounded a bit breathless. "Should we exchange schedules?"

"I had been wondering the same thing." He pulled his schedule out of a pocket and showed it to her. Rachel glanced at it, memorizing it instantly. Reaching into her pocket, she handed him her schedule. She had glanced at it once. She did not need it anymore.

He had been thinking about finding her!

Inside, she was aglow.

She looked around at the growing crowd. "So. What are you all doing here?"

"They want to ask us some questions. I'm assuming they know the three of us weren't working for Dr. Mordeau." He gestured from himself to Locke and Von Dread. "I would hate to get expelled for having fought to save my fellow students."

"They know you weren't with the baddies. The princess shared her vision with them. She saw you all facing down Mordeau." Rachel smirked. "The dean was properly impressed."

She did not add that it was Von Dread's unyielding resolve that had so impressed Dean Moth. By that point in the princess's vision, Gaius and William Locke had both been killed, something Rachel was extraordinarily glad had not come to pass.

She glanced surreptitiously at the Bavarian crown prince, as he brushed a speck off the sleeve of his black poplin robe. He glanced up at the same moment, and their eyes met. His gaze was cold and imperious, yet Rachel held it, undaunted. Adrenaline rushed through her, as if she were afraid. Only it did not feel like fear. It felt like...

Salome Iscariot sauntered between them, blocking Rachel's view. The blonde glanced provocatively over her shoulder, fluttering her lashes at one of the proctors. Her white blouse had been tailored to show her curves to best advantage. Catching sight of Rachel, she winked and gave her a thumbs-up. Watching the other girl as she swayed away, Rachel recalled that Salome was probably the one who had told Valerie Hunt...

Rachel put her hands on her hips and cocked her head. As archly as was possible to girl-kind, she asked, "Gaius Valiant, did you tell people you were my boyfriend?"

Gaius took two quick steps backward. "No, I...No!"

"Someone spread that rumor." She narrowed her eyes. "People have asked me about it."

"It wasn't me!"

"Are you certain?" she teased. "Rather cheeky of you to tell other people when you haven't even asked me."

He looked so cute when he was flustered. His cheeks were growing a bit red.

Then, he leaned toward her, his eyes bright. "Do you want to be my girlfriend?"

Her heart leapt, expanding to fill her chest, the tower, the whole universe.

Then his exact wording filtered through her consciousness.

Oh, no, no, no.

This kind of question was a set up for humiliation. If she said "yes", he could laugh and say, "Oh, how cute, the little girl likes me. She wants to be my girlfriend." No Griffin girl worthy of the name would allow herself to be maneuvered into such a position. It would be undignified, worse than being caught with one's pants down.

That had happened once to her brother Peter. Two years ago, when he was a sophomore, some stupid bully had used a cantrip to yank her brother's pants down in public. Peter had been totally humiliated. It was the same beastly boy who blackened Peter's eye by deliberately botching a spell in class. Rachel hated that boy. She surreptitiously glanced around at the snooty Drake students, wondering if any of them were her brother's unknown rival.

Turning back to Gaius, Rachel narrowed her eyes until they were mere slits. "Are you asking if I *desire to* be your girlfriend? Or are you asking me *to be* your girlfriend?"

Gaius considered this, rocking back on his heels. His face betrayed an internal struggle.

"Do you want to be?" he blurted out finally. "I think I like the idea of having you as my girlfriend."

Had he truly asked her?

Rachel's jaw dropped. She gawked back at him, too flustered to speak. He leaned down, so that their heads were close together again, and peered at her.

"Yes? No?" Gaius asked. "Am I too old for you? Should I come back next year? The year after?"

Gaius was so cute. Talking with him made her feel so happy, so grown up.

What girl in her right mind would not want to be his girl-friend?

Yet was she ready for a boyfriend? True, her feelings for him were growing, but they were like a newly-sprouted seed. What if she agreed to date him and the pressures of daily life pulled up the seedlings of her affection before they had a chance to take root?

"I...um...it's like..." She struggled to express what she felt. "Im-imagine m-my feelings for you are a spark I'm protecting from the wind and the elements." Cupping her hands, as if holding something precious, she blew several short breaths into her palms. "Nurturing it and blowing on it, patiently waiting for it to grow into a proper fire." She spread her fingers. "If I open my hands too quickly, it may go out."

"What? Was that a *yes* or a *no*? I don't understand. Oh, wait..." Gaius rubbed his temples, his voice suddenly unenthusiastic. "That was an analogy, wasn't it?"

He did not understand.

She had felt certain that he must be experiencing something akin to the pure, almost sacred feeling inside of her. She had forgotten how practical and unpoetic boys were.

She felt suddenly lonely.

Other objections began to crowd her thoughts.

Gaius Valiant was three years older than she was. He was a Thaumaturge. He was a commoner—her family might not approve. He had not asked permission of her brother. She was very young. None of her sisters had dated at this age. Nor was she entirely sure he was the boy for her. After all, she had not even had a single conversation with John Darling, the boy she had crushed on for the last three years.

Oh, and then there were the things that an older boy would want from a girl—things Rachel *knew* she was not ready for.

"I've heard sixteen-year-olds..." Rachel struggled to gasp out such a mature and embarrassing word. Her face burned. If she had dunked it in a lake of lava, it could not have been hotter. "...that sixteen-year-olds *snog*."

She gazed at him, waiting for him to reassure her, but Gaius just looked hugely amused.

"Yes." He struggled not to laugh. "Sixteen-year-olds *do* sometimes snog."

Rachel lowered her eyes, embarrassed. "I-I don't believe I'm ready to have a boyfriend."

Now it was Gaius whose face looked as if it had visited the lava baths.

"Right. Got it. See you later."

Locke and Von Dread had moved across the foyer. Gaius stomped off after them, glowering. Rachel bit her lip and gazed down. She had not meant to upset him. Did this mean he would not want to talk to her any more? That would be terrible.

Sighing, she reluctantly set out after the others.

Part way up the staircase, she glanced back. Locke and Von Dread were deep in conversation. When Gaius trudged up to them, they paused and looked him over, inquiringly. Locke raised an eyebrow. Von Dread frowned and leaned toward Gaius, perhaps asking him what was the matter. Gaius shook his head and gave no answer. Crossing his arms, he stared across the foyer, glowering, his brow beetled and his face dark.

Rachel bit her lip.

Should she have said "yes"?

Chapter 5:
The Perfect Memory of Rachel Griffin

Reaching the top of the stairs, Rachel burst out into the belfry. Sigfried and the three Agents were gathered in front of the stone arch that contained the mirror with a golden hue. Lucky hunched beside his master. Siggy rested one hand on the dragon's flame-red mane. The other was pressed against the thinking glass. Behind them, Agent Standish's cheetah stalked straight-legged around the belfry, carefully sniffing the straw. The princess was there, too, but she stood with her back to the others. Her chin was raised, her expression prim.

Rachel tromped across the straw to join them. Stretching her hand over her head, she tried to jiggle one of the giant chimes, but she was not tall enough. Reaching the others, she examined the thinking glass. Only the golden edges still reflected the staircase and the lantern. The rest of it showed the dining room in Roanoke Hall—or rather a fuzzy dining room, where everything—chairs, tables, the ceiling, the fountain—was out of focus.

Rachel started in horror. Surely, this impressionistic collection of mess and murk could not be Sigfried's memory. No one's memory could be that bad.

But it was.

Rachel swallowed, feeling faintly dizzy.

Peering closer, she saw that not everything was blurry. The sandwiches, muffins, and yogurt on the table were clear, even larger than life. The cutlery was crisp, too, especially the sharp serrated edge of a steak knife. A gold coin lying next to the plate, probably a piece of Siggy's hoard, looked so realistic that Rachel felt as if she could have reached in and touched it.

One other thing stood out vividly amid the fog of indistinct images. Faces were blurry, and clothing indistinct, but the curvy chests and rounded hips of the school girls appeared in all their voluptuous glory. The heat, which had departed when Rachel pulled her face from the lava lake of embarrassment, crept back into her cheeks. No wonder the princess had turned her back.

Did Valerie Hunt have such a womanly figure? Rachel had not noticed. Here, Miss Hunt looked as if creamy peaches had been tucked under her white blouse. Worse, the image rested upon this viewpoint for an uncomfortably long time. And Salome: true, Miss Iscariot went out of her way to draw attention to her charms—but her eye-catching curves appeared illuminated by their own spotlight. Beside her, Zoë leaned over to adjust her shoe. Her brightly-colored hair and her legs were indistinct, but her derriere was unmistakable, like a glorious moon.

Rachel raised her hand to block the image. She would have been mortified to be caught in such a position. An exposed rear end was a matter at which to poke fun.

Did boys truly ogle girls' backsides?

Rachel peeked down at herself with some trepidation. She knew one day she would look like the other women in her family. She had never seen women as pretty as the Griffin Family women. Even Salome was not as voluptuous as Rachel's sisters, much less her mother. Currently, however, Rachel looked like a child, straight and boyish.

If the images in the thinking glass reflected what the other girls at school looked like, why in the world did Gaius Valiant want to date *her?*

Gaius's interest in her must be a trick. He must be up to something. The princess had warned her that Gaius was a wicked boy. Maybe it was true. He had given Rachel information to pass on to her father. Maybe he hoped that, if he won her trust, she would spill Wisecraft secrets.

A lot of good it would do him.

Her father told her nothing.

In the thinking glass, another figure burst onto the scene, a little dark-haired girl as pretty as a porcelain China doll. She was quick and vivacious, her almond-shaped eyes sparkling with laughter. Just seeing this pretty figure lifted Rachel's spirits and made her want to laugh. This girl must be someone who mattered a great deal to Sigfried, because his memory of her was sharp and clear. Only Lucky and Siggy's girlfriend, Valerie, appeared more vividly. Rachel wondered who it might be. Perhaps, their tiny classmate Magdalene Chase?

Peering closer, Rachel noticed two things: the girl Sigfried was recalling was Asian, and she was wearing a black and white bow in her hair.

That was *her*!

Rachel leaned forward, amazed. Was that how she looked to others? She might not be as womanly as her classmates, but as much as she was reluctant to admit it, she looked adorable.

Maybe Gaius *really did* want to date her.

• • •

"That's all, Mr. Smith? Very good." Agent Darling stretched, leaning to the side. "Rachel, your turn."

Sigfried took several steps backward, away from the glass and wiped his forehead. "Phew! That was hard, Lucky! Good thing my superlative master-control of my own intellect allowed me to suppress all memory of the thousands of murders, acts of arson and vandalism, not to mention looting the Crown Jewels from the Tower of London, for which I am solely responsible. Oh, and the Hindenburg Disaster, World War One, and the extinction of the dinosaurs. I did that, too. It was quite a strain to hold those things out of my otherwise perfect eidetic memory." He paused and then asked vaguely, "Who are you people, again?"

"Move over, Sigfried Smith." Rachel pantomimed rolling up her sleeves. "Let me show you how it's done."

She stepped up next to the mossy stone wall. Agent Standish drew a magical connection between her and the thinking glass with the *oré* cantrip. Rachel's lips curled into an eager, impish smile. She would show them everything in crisp and perfect order.

In gratitude, they would answer her questions.

She had so many questions. They swirled in her mind like a tornado of embers, scorching her. It was because of this ceaseless yearning for answers that she had chosen her goal of wishing to know everything.

Not knowing was too painful.

"Ready?" Agent Standish crossed his arms, his voluminous cloak and half cape nearly brushing the ground.

She laid her hand against the cold, smooth glass and closed her eyes. The noise of Siggy's feet scuffing the straw that covered the stone of the floor seemed suddenly loud. A warm breeze blew against her face. Perhaps it had been there all along, but she only noticed it now.

"What do you wish to see?" she asked, her eyes squeezed shut.

"Why not begin at the beginning?" Agent Standish suggested, his voice deep and sonorous.

Rachel chewed on her lip thoughtfully. She recalled Mortimer Egg, a mild-mannered man with his hair drawn into a pony-tail who was dressed in an Inverness cloak with his false Agent's medallion around his neck. He stood on the dock at the foot of the staircase that led to Frances Bannerman's castle, behind which lay the path to Roanoke Academy.

Gasps rang out in the belfry. Rachel's eyes flew open. The gathered company was staring intently at the image on the glass.

"It's so clear!" the princess declared, a hand pressed against her chest.

"Amazing!" Agent Standish breathed. Clicking the heels of his green boots together, he bowed toward Rachel. "You have your mother's gift."

"Is that a memory?" Agent MacDannan tapped the mirror. From her shoulder, her rat sniffed the mirror, peering at itself sideways. "Are we sure this isn't a looking glass?"

"It's my memory," Rachel replied simply. She stabbed a finger at the thinking glass. "That's the man who tried to kill Valerie Hunt."

"But that's—" Agent MacDannan bit off her comment, unwilling to reveal more.

"Mortimer Egg, a clerk at the Wisecraft offices in New York City," Rachel finished, a note of censure creeping into her voice.

"We cannot comment on the identity of suspects," Agent MacDannan replied coolly.

Anger seized Rachel. It offended her that the Agents knew the identity of the villain and did not immediately rush off to warn as many people as possible. What if Mortimer Egg tried to kill someone else, and they were not on notice to avoid him?

Taking a deep breath, Rachel made herself calm and returned to the matter at hand. Proceeding in order, she recalled Mr. Egg's attempt to give Valerie the hexed scarab brooch, Sigfried and Lucky's attempts to save Valerie, and the brooch's eventual destruction by the imposing Prince of Bavaria. Jumping ahead, she remembered how the princess had touched Lucky, been transported into a vision, and physically brought water and cherry petals back from a Japanese landscape.

Later, the princess had explained how, after touching upperclassman Joshua March, she met a creature of incomparable beauty with wings of smoke called the Lightbringer. In the vision to which Nastasia had been transported, the Lightbringer had been torturing an older version of Joshua March. Aided by the red-eyed Raven, this Lightbringer had visited the princess's dreams. Since Mordeau and the students in Drake Hall already knew this secret, Rachel also showed them Zoë Forrest walking out of nowhere as she stepped out of the dreamland in her silver-soled sandals.

Rachel then showed them the infirmary, where—after no adult would believe them—she and Sigfried had faced the wraith that had been consuming an older girl. She showed them how Lucky had become a dumb animal when the Raven flew by, but how he had remembered himself and returned in time to defeat the wraith, with the help of the Dare Vampire Hunter's Club.

Next, Rachel leapt to earlier this very afternoon, when she found Valerie Hunt in the girl's bathroom, bleeding from the effort of fighting a geas. She recalled everything that followed, except her private conversation with Gaius in the infirmary.

The Agents watched as, warned by the princess's vision, Rachel and Sigfried stopped the young proctor, Mr. Fuentes, from killing Valerie Hunt, while he was under the control of the geas. Then, the four of them—herself, Sigfried, Nastasia, and their fellow student Joy O'Keefe—stopped the events depicted in the princess's second vision—which had included the victory of Dr. Mordeau and the deaths of Gaius Valiant, William Locke, and Vladimir Von Dread.

In the thinking glass, Sigfried saved the P.E. teacher, Mr. Chanson, from being killed by an invisible Dr. Mordeau; Rachel crashed through the window of the alchemy classroom to rescue Mr. Fisher from a geased girl wielding a bloody whip; and Mordeau's creepy student assistant, Jonah Strega, was prevented from stabbing Joy O'Keefe with his huge cruel knife when Lucky breathed fire on him, burning his face.

Finally, she recalled the end: the fight between Dread and Prince Remus Starkadder in the summoning chambers below Drake Hall, how Dread brought the incoming flood of moat water to life, and the final battle behind Roanoke Hall between Dean Moth and Dr. Mordeau, who had transformed herself into a dragon.

"And that was the end of the battle," Rachel concluded. The image of Dr. Mordeau's unconscious body lying partially under the conjured meteor that struck her larger dragon form appeared both in the thinking glass and in her mind. "Anything else?"

"Thank you, Miss Griffin. That was a great deal of information." Agent MacDannan blinked and ran a hand through her bushy ginger hair. Her black-and-white rat chattered and scuttled up onto her head. She brushed at it absently. "If we have questions about what we saw, we will be certain to ask."

"Glad to be of service." Rachel bobbed up and down, curtseying.

She loved having an opportunity to put her perfect memory to use. Helping the agents was almost as satisfying as reporting to her father had been—before he rejected her help, ordering her to stop noticing things and be an ordinary student.

Only, ordinary students did not get spied on by giant ravens with blood-red eyes. They were not led to bleeding friends by miniature talking lions. They seldom came upon china dolls dragging the unconscious bodies of the girls who owned them to the infirmary. Ordinary students did not remember everything in such detail that they felt their lives were wasted if there was no one with whom to share their recollections.

"I must say, I am impressed." Agent Standish bowed low. "The three of you and Miss O'Keefe saved the lives of Mr. Chanson and Mr. Fisher, as well as those of a number of students. The Dean should declare a holiday in your honor."

The princess inclined her head regally. "No reward is required. We did as duty dictated."

Siggy snorted. "Duty, smooty! We fought the bad guy and won! We deserve to be heroes. I'm thinking a national monument, but a holiday in our honor is okay. Maybe a park named after Lucky. Or a dormitory here at school! Kids could live in Dragonslayer Hall! That'd be a good start!"

Rachel, meanwhile, blushed and shyly lowered her gaze. She hated having to take credit for good works. It made her feel unpleasantly exposed—as if, without doubt, the next thing she did would be the wrong one. Perhaps, if she stared at that particular piece of straw hard enough, everyone would forget she was there.

"You three did an excellent job." James Darling knelt down and scratched Pyewacket behind her ear. The cat purred. "That was astonishing work! As impressive as anything the members of the Young Sorcerers League did in my day! And we were much older. College students, for the most part."

"And after only a week of school." Agent MacDannan looked grudgingly impressed. "Many freshmen can't cast even single spell until well into their second or third month."

"First saving a young woman from a wraith, then saving the whole school from Dr. Mordeau and her geased henchmen." Darling turned to Sigfried. "And you, Mr. Smith. I hear that only a day or two before, you saved a group of students from a flying, flaming skunk. Seems you are quite the hero."

Siggy merely grinned and bowed, accepting his accolades with gracious aplomb. Rachel yanked her hand away from the thinking glass, lest a more accurate version of that particular event be displayed from her memory. Watching Sigfried, it took all the dissembling training she had received from her mother to keep her face expressionless. It amazed her that he could accept praise so unabashedly, when he himself had conjured the skunk, lit it on fire, and sent it flying.

"It's time we deal with the students in the foyer." Agent MacDannan started toward the stairs. "Some of them are still under the geas."

"Before you go!" Rachel grabbed her sleeve. "You said we did rather well and we deserved a heroes reward. We don't need all that, but you can repay us by answering our questions! I am sure Siggy and the princess must have some, too, but to start—" She drew a deep breath and plunged, speaking rapidly in her excitement. "Do you know why Mr. Egg wanted to kill Valerie? Is he the secret boss Mordeau spoke of? Did you know Mordeau's boss was from Outside—from another world? Who is the Lightbringer? Have you heard of him? Is it true that he captured the princess's father? If so, can anything be done?"

"I am sorry, Miss Griffin," Agent MacDannan dismissed her questions with a crisp shake of her head. "We aren't able to answer questions about an ongoing investigation."

"But...I showed you so much! Everything I know." With tremendous effort, Rachel kept her voice calm. "We're not yet safe here. We need to know more!"

"You can leave the investigation to us."

"B-but..." she repeated, stuttering. She glanced at the other two Agents, begging. "You said we should receive a proper reward! There must be something you can tell us!"

Agent MacDannan shook her head. "I am sorry, Miss Griffin. Good day."

It was going to be like her father all over again.

It was so unfair. Were they really going to rob her of her carefully-gathered secrets and give her nothing in return? The Agents were not facing the Raven of Doom and the evil fire-breathing dragons. They were not the ones whose lives were at stake, whose future might depend upon being properly informed. She and her friends were the ones who were, to quote her alchemy tutor, *on the front lines.*

Only Mr. Fisher had not been referring to Rachel and her
friends when he used that phrase. He had been speaking of
another group of students who had faced terrible odds—
students led by an intrepid boy who had understood that
sometimes the young were called upon to fight evil where adults
could not. That boy had grown up to be an Agent.

As if a heavy yoke had been removed from her, Rachel's
heart lifted. Her shoulders relaxed, and she breathed more
easily. James Darling understood what it meant to be young and
on the front lines of the battle. He was the one adult she could
trust.

The ginger-haired Agent headed down the stairs, her footsteps a series of quick beats. Agent Standish tousled Rachel's
hair fondly and then strode off after MacDannan, his cheetah at
his heels. As Agent Darling rose to follow, Rachel stepped in front
of him.

"Please, Agent Darling. May I speak with you privately?" she
asked.

It was always wise to speak to people privately about
important things, especially people in any position of authority.

"Of course, Rachel." He gestured at the far side of the belfry.
"How about there?"

The two of them circled around the giant lantern. Agent
Darling's tricorne hat brushed against the lowest of the giant
chimes, setting them jangling. They had a deep sound, deeper
than the bells that marked the change of classes, more like those
rung at the temples of Osiris in London.

They crossed to the North window, between the blue
walking glass and the cracked purple mirror. Rachel sat on the
sill of the arch, her hand resting on the moistness of the moss on
the stone wall. She breathed in the damp earthy scent and gazed
out at the forest beyond. The dark green of hemlocks stretched
away like a jagged carpet. Beyond, in the distance, rose the bare
peak of Stony Tor, where the storm goblin, the Heer of
Dunderberg, and his lightning imps were imprisoned. The tor
had been rumbling with thunder all afternoon. Rachel wondered
if the Heer could sense the chaos Mordeau had caused.

Agent Darling leaned against the stone wall, one hand on his tall fulgurator's staff. "What can I do for you, Rachel?"

Rachel's courage faltered. Looking at him, as he smiled down at her so kindly, she was reminded of the young man with the cocky smile in the painting of the Six Musketeers. This was that James Darling, the hero. The tension in her throat eased.

"Mr. Darling," she addressed him without his title, as she did when he was a guest at Gryphon Park, "you know better than anyone what it is like to be the ones on the front lines."

The smile disappeared from his face. "I do."

"My friends and I—we are the ones facing the dangers. The Lightbringer and the Raven are still out there. Mordeau and Egg may have more allies. We cannot defend ourselves if we are not informed. We need answers."

An expression of pain crossed his handsome features. "I am sorry, Rachel. But this is an official investigation—involving members of the Wisecraft. My hands are tied."

She leaned forward, her eyes intent upon his face. "No one will know. Just answer a few of my questions. Even one? There must be questions you can answer without...Please!"

He shook his head.

Oh! If only she had refused to answer questions until they agreed to answer hers.

Rachel reined in her impatience and tried another tack. "Don't you want our help figuring things out?"

He looked at her sharply. "Do you know something you didn't tell us?"

"No."

"Then, we know everything you know. You'll have to trust us to take it from here."

Rachel's questions burned so fiercely that not receiving answers was causing her physical pain. As she rubbed her temples, it occurred to her that the question she most wanted answered was unrelated to this matter. Relief flowed through her.

She blurted out, "You can answer questions that are not about this current matter, right?"

"Of course, Rachel." He smiled at her very kindly.

Rachel drew a ragged breath. "Okay...during her fight with the dean, Mordeau said something about my gra—"

He held up his hand, cutting her off. "I am sorry, Rachel. Anything to do with Dr. Mordeau is related to this matter. You must understand that."

"But this wasn't! I just wanted to know—"

He shook his head firmly. "I cannot help you."

Rachel cringed. She hated feeling pathetic.

And to think that she had feared that Gaius would be the one to humiliate her.

"But...I...I showed you everything! I could have kept secrets back—the Raven, the Lion, the vision the Lion showed me of the great tree—but I didn't!" Her voice rose piteously. "You, of all people..."

He flinched as if she had struck him. She saw it in his face, the moment he remembered—remembered what it had been like, remembered being the boy on the front lines, with no one to protect him, remembered being the last defense against the coming of the night. He had been where she was now. He knew it.

A light shone in his eyes, mischievous and fierce. It made him look younger, as if the youthful James Darling lived again, the troublemaker who had inspired the comics and saved so many lives. He leaned toward her with a conspiratorial grin. The motion made the Agent's medallion on his chest jangle.

He paused.

Lifting the medallion, he traced his thumb over the lantern and stars, the symbol of the Wisecraft—of his current life, of the promises he had made, the oaths he had sworn, the duties he had undertaken. Closing his eyes, his body bent like an old man's, he leaned on his fulgurator's staff, as if he could not stand without its support.

When his eyes opened again, the light was gone.

He put his hand on her shoulder. "I do understand. I do. But I can't."

Rachel nodded, not trusting herself to speak. She swallowed convulsively. Agent Darling gave her a last, apologetic smile and hurried down the stairs after his companions.

Several steps down, he paused, looking up at her across the straw-strewn floor. "Rachel, the paralysis spell that helped Dean Moth capture Dr. Mordeau—it seemed to come from the forest near where you were standing. Did you notice who cast it?"

Rachel stared at him.

He had refused to answer a single question. He had not even let her ask about her beloved grandfather. *Now he wanted her help?* Even if he had not been asking about a matter she wished to keep a secret, she would never have told him.

The sheer audacity of his request outraged her.

"No," she lied.

Chapter 6:
The Unparalleled Advantage of Curious Friends

Rachel stared out the north window, stunned. She felt betrayed, worse than betrayed. She felt as if her secrets had been stolen, leaving her bereft.

Without secrets, she felt powerless.

Knowing things no one else knew made her useful. She was not a great sorcerer, like Sigfried and Nastasia, or even Joy and their fellow student Wulfgang Starkadder. Those four were the best freshmen sorcerers the school had seen in generations. While she could barely manage any magic. Only with hours and hours of practice—all by herself while everyone else was off having fun—had she been able to work any spells at all.

She felt so lost here.

It had not been so bad at first. Everything had been exciting and new. Her long letters to her father had kept her grounded. Reporting to her father had helped her make sense of the disorienting events around her. Even when terrible things had happened—like someone trying to kill Valerie, or mean girls from Drake Hall paralyzing her and distorting her body, or a wraith sucking out her life essence—she had been able to bear up, because she felt as if she were part of something greater, as if she were the youngest member of the Wisecraft's information gathering service, giving Agent Griffin valuable information that he would not have otherwise. In her mind, as she wrote each letter, she had pictured him smiling with pride.

Foolish little girl that she was.

When her father had instructed her to stop writing to him, everything fell apart. Intellectually, she understood his reasoning. He wanted her to enjoy her time at school, to stop seeking out trouble, to be an ordinary girl.

Being an ordinary girl was not an option.

The world was in terrible danger, and nobody believed her. She knew there was nothing she could do. How could a thirteen-year-old girl save the world? And yet, she felt compelled to try, as if—even though she did not have the slightest chance to stop whatever was coming—if she gave up, gave in, or even slowed down, everything would be lost.

Maybe she was wrong. Maybe *Everything* would not be lost if she stopped, but, without question, *she* would fall apart. When she slowed down, the terrible things that had happened during the last week came rushing back, like an avalanche. With her perfect memory, she experienced each horror as vividly as she had the first time. Every time she closed her eyes, she hit the window of her science lab again. The pain of breaking through the wooden muntins, of glass cutting her cheek, returned— striking her so hard that it sucked away her breath. She saw again the drops of blood spattered across Mr. Fisher's discarded glasses, the unblinking form of Enoch Smithwyck lying across their alchemy tutor's bloody body. She experienced again the humiliation of running through the darkness, one side of her body swollen and distorted, as she tried to hide from the laughter of Cydney Graves and her friends. She relived finding Valerie Hunt crying on the floor of the girl's bathroom, blood running from her eyes and nose and more blood dying the toilet water red.

Only when she acted, when she stayed focused, could she stave off the terror, the panic, the fear.

Rachel gripped the rough stone and laid her cheek against the cool, mossy wall. She missed Gryphon Park. She missed being in a place of comfort and familiarity. She missed the long empty hallways and tall towers with no one to bully or humiliate her.

She wanted to go home.

But going home meant giving up, and she did not want to give up, not yet.

The one thing that she had to contribute was what she had learned, what she *knew*.

Secrets.

Secrets were her native atmosphere. She breathed them in the way mermaids breathed water. With secrets, she had some- thing that drew the attention of people like Gaius—who otherwise would hardly care to spend time with a little girl who did not even have a figure yet. And she needed to gather as much knowledge as quickly as possible, because if the world was going to be saved, no one knew ahead of time which secret might be the one that mattered.

So she had gathered secrets to offer in return for more secrets. But the Agents of the Wisecraft had violated that bargain. They had taken what she knew and given her nothing in return. It was as if she had brought them her most precious possession—and they had stolen it.

Without secrets, she was worthless, unnecessary, marginal, as her conversation with Agent Darling had proven.

Without secrets, she felt mundane.

The feeling of betrayal stole her breath. Her thoughts seemed slow, heavy. She had never felt this way before. So flat, so empty. The trick she had learned recently, of thinking quickly, as if all the gears in her mind were engaged simultaneously, failed. If Mr. A. Square had visited his friend the cube in the world of three-dimensions and then been dropped back into Flatland, he might have felt as she did now.

It was as if her magic had been stripped away.

That was silly. She was a sorceress from a long line of sorcerers, descended from the ancient Arimaspians and from some kind of *tian*—Asian sky fairy—on her mother's side. She had not possessed any particular secrets when she arrived at school. Secrets were not the source of some unknown power. Eager to prove this, Rachel whistled.

Her lips felt wooden. No sparkles filled the air. No wind came.

A cold tremor ran up her spine. She dismissed it. She was nervous. Sorcerers could not lose their magic powers because their secrets were stolen by Agents. Agents were the people who solved supernatural crimes. They were not allowed to share the information they were gathering with civilians. She could not blame them.

A tremor of fear went through her. No one else had a memory like hers, except her mother. Rachel knew her mother would never allow anyone to take all her secrets. Though Ellen Griffin was quiet and very sweet, she always kept a part of herself private, apart from others.

Trembling, Rachel pursed her lips again and concentrated.

Caw.

The sound came from the south. Spinning, she looked through the southern window. She saw nothing of note. Then, she thought back two seconds.

Atop the highest bell tower of Roanoke Hall, a giant, jet-black raven with eyes as red as newly-pooled blood sat watching her.

Rachel grew weak with fear. Then unexpectedly, relief rushed through her.

She still had *one* secret.

She had not thought to tell the Agents that her perfect memory allowed her to see the Raven without the help of the *Spell of True Recitation*.

Suddenly, the gears of her thoughts engaged again, whirling. Her mind sprang into vibrant three-dimensions. Experimentally, she whistled. Silvery sparks left her lips and blew straw across the stones.

Lightheaded with relief, Rachel slumped against the mossy stone wall and breathed.

• • •

Rachel crossed the belfry to the southern window where Nastasia, Sigfried and Lucky stood looking out at the campus. Siggy was leaning over the sill with a maniacal grin on his face, aiming a gold coin he held between his fingers.

"Do you think if we throw hard enough we could stick this into someone's skull?" Siggy asked Lucky in the same enthusiastic tone he always used when he spoke about killing and blowing things up.

"Good gracious, Sigfried! We don't kill our fellow students here at Roanoke!" Rachel waved her hands. She stomped up beside him. "Really, I shouldn't have to keep telling you."

Lucky flew to Sigfried's hand and kissed the coin repeatedly. "Are you crazy! That's part of our hoard! I know every piece—by name. That one's..." the dragon peered closely with one huge jade green eye, "Alfred Pennywiggle the Three Hundred and Forty-Second! I can't believe you would throw away our gold, Boss. Would you defenestrate an infant? Toss your own flesh and blood out the window?"

"Oh, good point." Siggy polished the coin against his shoulder and stuck it in his pocket. He pulled out an apple core, brown and covered with lint. "How about this?"

Nastasia pinched her nose shut. "That's most unsanitary, Mr. Smith."

"Hmm." Lucky curled through the air like a dancer's ribbon. "Something to eat later, versus the havoc of pelting the unsuspecting from above. Pelt, I say, pelt! Pelt!"

Siggy drew back his arm and threw.

"Siggy!" Rachel lunged forward but failed to catch his arm. From below came a thump and a hoarse cry. Rachel winced in sympathy for the victim.

"Really, Mr. Smith, that is most unbecoming." The lovely princess frowned sternly. "Not the behavior expected of a knight in service to a princess."

"Oh! Right! I'm your knight now!" Sigfried straightened and bowed. "Your highness. What can I do for you?"

"You can stop throwing objects at innocent bystanders," Nastasia said severely.

"That wasn't an innocent bystander," objected Sigfried, "that was Remus Starkadder."

"Oh." The princess blinked, perhaps recalling the pain of the phantom fire Remus had used to torture her. "In that case...No! Wait! It is still not becoming behavior, despite what I may have suffered. After all, the poor young man was under the control of a geas. He is not responsible for what he did while under a spell."

"No, he wasn't," Rachel stated forcefully. "His eyes were clear. He and his brother Fenris participated on purpose. Just like Jonah Strega."

Nastasia inclined her head toward Sigfried. "Carry on, Sir Knight."

"He's gone inside." Sigfried scowled in disappointment. He had not turned back to look out the window. Rachel started to ask him how he knew but then remembered. His magic amulet let him see all around him without moving. "Besides, I'm out of apple cores."

Stretching, Sigfried left the window and began meandering around the belfry. His long, sinewy red and gold dragon snaked after him. Rachel leaned over the sill they had vacated and stared out at the twilit campus. The feeling of powerlessness that had gripped her earlier had receded, but the ache of betrayal still pained her. True, she had not technically been betrayed, as nothing had been promised. And yet, she could not shake the feeling of bitterness.

It *was* like what happened with her father all over again.

She could have been such a useful ally, both to her father and to the Agents. It was their loss. She would find the answers to her questions. Of that, she was certain. When she did, she would not be so quick to share what she discovered.

Ching-Chang-Chong. Lucky weaved back and forth between the chimes, setting them ringing. Their deep tones resonated throughout the belfry. Rachel grabbed her ears.

"Don't do that!" she called. "Those maintain the obscuration protecting Roanoke Island."

Lucky paused and looked at Siggy, who shrugged.

"Probably better not to call up those shadowy thingamy-whatsits again," said Siggy. "Not to mention that we don't want to draw the Agents' attention to the fact that they left us up here."

"Oh, good point." The dragon dropped to the ground and began slithering on the ruby scales of its belly around the huge brass cylinder of the lantern.

Sigfried looked at the colored mirrors. "So, what are these? Are they all for thinking at?"

Rachel left the window and joined him. She shook her head, her dark locks flying hither and thither. "No. Only the golden one. The green is a talking glass—a big version of the calling cards Agent Darling used to speak to the other Agents—the ones you want me to order for you. Talking glasses allow you to talk to other talking glasses in distant places."

"Wicked!" Siggy's eyes glittered. He peered at the green mirror. "And the blue one? Is this a smoking glass for making fires? Or a scratching glass for hard-to-reach places that itch?"

Rachel snorted in amusement. "No, that's a walking glass. Only it isn't working."

"How do you know?"

"Walking glasses and travel glasses—which is a fancy name for the really big walking glasses—are always paired," Rachel explained as they peered into the blue mirror. "When you look through one, you see the other side of the far glass. This one just reflects us, like a regular mirror. That means there is no second mirror somewhere else to which it is tied."

The princess glided across the belfry to join them as well. Tilting her head, she regarded the blue-tinted walking glass. "Perhaps the second glass has been broken."

"Perhaps," Rachel nodded, "or the wards that keep walking glasses from working on campus have disrupted the consanguinity between the two halves."

"Con-sane-guinea-piggies?" Siggy yawned, patting his mouth. "Is there going to be a test? I assume that's what Alice-In-Wonderland actually fell through—a walking glass?"

"Alice Liddell was a famous sorceress," Rachel said. "Her great granddaughter goes to the Lower School. She'll be a freshman here next year."

Siggy shrugged, uninterested. "What about this purple one?"

They stopped before the cracked mirror.

"I don't know," Rachel admitted.

Siggy pulled his robe away from his chest and peeked underneath. He glanced back and forth between something under his clothing and the mirror. "Whatever it is, it is the same dark purple color as the center of my all-seeing amulet."

"Really?" Rachel's eyes grew larger by the second. "Could it..." She reached out and touched a smooth section of broken mirror. Under the cracked glass, she could see the antique silver of the backing. "Do you think it could be a *looking glass*?"

Lucky slithered through the straw until he reached the purple mirror, then he straightened his legs and raised his head, sniffing the cracked mirror. "That's a looking glass, all right."

"Walking and talking glasses are real, but looking glasses, real ones, only exist in fairytales," the princess objected.

"Isn't 'looking glass' just another term for a regular mirror?" Sigfried asked.

Rachel shook her head. "The Unwary use our term, but they do not understand what it means. I mean a *proper* looking glass—the kind that can look *anywhere*."

Nastasia peered at the cracked mirror with interest. "In fairytales, looking glasses are used for seeing far away. Such as when the wombat is spying on the kookaburra so as to fulfill its wager with the dingo. Or when the merchant's daughter wanted to see her father, and the beast let her use his magic mirror."

"Do you mean Belle?" Sigfried scratched his head. "Isn't she an inventor's daughter?"

"Certainly not," Rachel corrected him absently, as she ran her fingertips over this object of wonder out of legend. "Her father is a merchant coming back from a far land with presents for everyone except his youngest daughter who wanted a rose. That's why he takes the rose from the Beast's garden."

"I don't remember that from the cartoon."

Rachel paused and squinted at him. "Cartoon? It's a fairy-tale."

The princess made a dismissive gesture. "The particulars are of no import. Looking glasses are legendary. This one is broken, but the one around Mr. Smith's neck still works."

"So, your amulet is a looking glass!" Rachel said, impressed. "That's smashing!"

"I can see all around me in a sphere—up and down as well," replied Sigfried. "And, by the way, never, ever again suggest that adults look at my memory! Do you know how difficult it was not to remember having looked through walls and behind closed doors?"

Rachel pressed her hands against her mouth in dismay. No wonder his memories seemed so disjointed. He must have felt as awful as she did when she was forced to blurt things out without discretion. "Oh! Sorry!"

"How far up and down?" The princess asked.

"Well, for instance, right now," Sigfried paused, apparently examining the lower floors, "the Agents are interrogating Rachel's boyfriend."

"He's not my boyfriend!" Rachel squeaked, outraged.

Sigfried grinned. The princess sighed, as if the whole topic pained her.

"Wait!" Rachel cried. "They're talking to Gaius?"

An idea seized her—an idea so marvelous that her whole body went rigid with anticipation. If the Agents would not answer her questions willingly, might she be able to glean some information from them anyway? After all, they owed her.

"Sigfried!" she cried. "Show us in the thinking glass! You should still be attuned."

They sprinted back to the thinking glass. As soon as Sigfried placed his hand on its golden surface, a picture sprang up. Unlike his long-term memory, the images of what he was actively seeing with his amulet were crisp and clear. In the disenchanting chamber below, Gaius landed on his feet as the glittery motes of the *Spell of True Recitation* faded away. Upon seeing him, Rachel's heart did a dance of joy. She felt a pang of disappointment, though. She would so have liked to see him in mid-air with sparkles in his hair.

"How did you find that, Mr. Valiant?" Agent MacDannan lowered her bagpipes and wiped the sweat from her forehead. Her tone was light, but her eyes glinted with interest.

"Very cold." Gaius shivered and chafed his arms.

The Agent's brows arched in surprise, and the princess nodded in approval. So Gaius was an honest boy. Rachel grinned. That was good news.

"Do you work for Dr. Mordeau?" the Agent asked.

"No, I don't work for Dr. Mordeau." Gaius's voice lacked its normal casual drawl. Rachel guessed that the uncharacteristic flatness was the result of the truth-compelling magic. Also, he sounded more Cornish. "I work for Vladimir Von Dread."

Rachel grabbed the crimson mane that ran the length of Lucky's serpentine body. It was much fluffier than she had expected. Embarrassed, she let go of the dragon and picked up her broom. Downstairs, MacDannan's exclamation of surprise spooked her rat. It scuttled under the wide collar of her Inverness cloak. The smile the Agent had begun to give Gaius froze on her face.

"Why?" asked the Agent.

Gaius answered without hesitation. "I respect Vlad more than I respect any of the tutors."

"And why is this?"

"Dread does not let anything pass without investigating it," Gaius answered. "He's dedicated to protecting the school, to the Knights, and to the rule of law. Plus, he is smart, powerful...and kind of scary."

Rachel listened intently, twisting the polished shaft of her steeplechaser between her hands. Rogue strands of her hair floated in her face, tickling her cheeks. She batted them aside. Several things occurred to her to say, but she said nothing. The excitement of spying on the Agents and her desire to hear what Gaius truly thought was too great.

The princess frowned disapprovingly. Her hand strayed to touch her forehead, her expression thoughtful, as if she were remembering something. "I told you that boy was not to be trusted. Von Dread certainly is untrustworthy."

"Really?" Siggy asked. "I thought you were going to marry him."

"Von Dread! Certainly not." The princess looked uncharacteristically irate. "My father said to stay away from him. Only Von Dread..." Her voice trailed off.

She touched her forehead once more and frowned, clearly dismayed.

"Shh!" Rachel hissed, leaning forward to hear better. "We can argue about how evil Dread is later. I want to hear what they are saying!"

Below, in the disenchanting chamber, Agent MacDannan was asking, "And do you recall anything from the last three days that you did not before?"

"No. Yes!" Gaius's eyes grew wide with astonishment. "That little lion, the one from the infirmary? When we were trying to find a way back into Drake Hall, it was as big as a house! Bigger! It was as big as..." He spread his arms. "It was huge! Enormous. Bigger than the universe." He gave his head a hard shake. "Which doesn't make any sense at all."

"No. It doesn't." Agent MacDannan shot a wary look toward the other two Agents.

They stood in identical poses, leaning against the wall with their arms crossed. Standish gave a little shrug. Darling shook his head, indicating that he did not know, either.

Upstairs, Rachel swallowed convulsively. Gaius had seen the Lion during the moment when it was greater than the universe and holding the world on his paw? She had thought that was a vision. A shiver crept down her spine. What did it mean that someone else had seen it, too?

More intriguing, what did it mean that *the little lion was a deception and the bigger-than-the-universes one was real?*

Below, Agent MacDannan asked, "One last question: how did you know about the geas?"

Gaius blinked in surprise, but his voice answered obediently. "Vlad told me."

The Agents dismissed Gaius and called William Locke. Rachel would have liked to ask Sigfried to follow Gaius out into the foyer and see what he said or did, but she was too shy. Instead, she watched as bagpipe music raised the tall, lanky college junior into the air. Rachel marveled that Locke managed to keep his calm, detached, scientific demeanor even when floating and surrounded with sparkles. A couple of times, he twitched and looked at his arm or leg curiously; perhaps a spark or two had burnt him.

When William Locke had landed on his feet again, Agent MacDannan lowered her instrument. "What do you remember from the past week that you did not previously?"

William Locke shook his head. His dark hair flopped into his eyes. "Nothing."

"Do you work for Dr. Mordeau?"

"No."

"Do you work for Vladimir Von Dread?"

"Yes."

"What do you do for him?"

"I work with Dread to discover the secrets of the universe."

"Interesting. Tell me about your father's company: Ouroboros Industries. It is one of the largest corporations in the world. It caters to both the Wise and the Unwary. Is it dangerous?"

"No." He paused and seemed to struggle slightly. Absentmindedly, he brushed the hair from his forehead. "I do not believe your jurisdiction extends to asking questions about my father's company. How is that related to the matter at hand?"

The Agents exchanged glances, looking disappointed but impressed.

"So, nothing they are doing is a danger to this school?"

Locke paused again. "I am not one-hundred-percent sure."

"That's creepy!" Sigfried muttered.

The Agents must have agreed, for they eyed each other warily, but MacDannan did not ask any follow-up questions. She released him and asked that he send in Mr. Von Dread. Siggy's viewpoint followed Locke as he walked back into the foyer, where he spoke to the Bavarian prince and then went to stand by Gaius. They spoke to each other in an unknown language.

"I wonder what they are saying," Rachel murmured wistfully.

The princess looked faintly surprised. "I can understand them."

"What language are they speaking?" asked Lucky, cocking his head, his long golden tail with its tuft of flame-red at the end snaking back and forth. "I can't understand a word."

The princess shook her head. "I do not know, Sir Dragon. I was not even aware that they were not speaking English. I understand all languages. It is called the Gift of Moira. According to my father, this talent was a gift from my grandmother."

"Wicked brilliant!" Siggy peered at the picture eagerly. "What's Valiant saying?"

Nastasia inclined her head, listening. "He just said: 'I would really, really like to be a fly on the wall while they interview Vlad.'"

Siggy grinned. "He can't...but we can."

The viewpoint returned to the disenchanting chamber. Von Dread hung in mid-air, his arms crossed, his face impassive. If the sparkles felt cold or hot to him, he gave no indication.

When his feet were on the floor again, Agent MacDannan lowered her bagpipes. Von Dread gazed down at her imperiously. He towered over the short Agent. He was half a head taller than Standish and Darling as well.

Agent MacDannan took a nervous step backward, but her voice was calm. "What do you remember that you did not before?"

"I am a citizen of the sovereign nation of Bavaria." Von Dread's voice was even, but his brows drew together into a fearsome scowl. "To question me, you need permission from my embassy and my father, the King."

"He...didn't answer the question," said Sigfried, his mouth agape. "When it was my turn, stuff poured out of my mouth without consulting me!"

Below, the Agents looked equally startled. Rachel's mouth hung open, too. She remembered what it had felt like. She had answered without being able to stop herself. Von Dread could resist that? Even Nastasia looked grudgingly impressed.

In the thinking glass, Von Dread spoke. "Go ahead. Ask your questions. I am not afraid of them."

"Do you work for Dr. Mordeau?" Agent MacDannan's voice only wavered slightly.

"No."

"Do you work for anyone else...other than your father?"

"No."

"How did you know about the geas?"

"My father's intelligence agents informed me that such a danger might exist, and that I should be wary. You need not bother asking me how they learned of it. They did not tell me."

"Do you mean harm to this school or anyone in it?"

"Certainly not. This school and its students are under my protection."

The Agents exchanged glances. "Do you remember anything that you did not before?"

Von Dread flexed his heavy dueling gloves. "Nothing that bears on the matter at hand."

Agent MacDannan frowned, again clearly surprised at his ability to resist the *Spell of True Recitation*. She glanced at the other two Agents. They exchanged looks and shrugged.

Turning back to the prince, she said, "Very well, Mr. Von Dread. That is all at this time."

Vladimir Von Dread inclined his head and strode from the chamber.

Chapter 7:
The Prince of Foul Play

"It may be less than polite of us to eavesdrop." Nastasia Romanov turned away from the thinking glass, a thoughtful frown creasing her lovely brow.

A breeze blew through the Watch Tower, carrying the scent of pine smoke. It stirred the princess's pale locks; they curled around her head like a shining cloud. She looked so beautiful, like a fairytale princess. Of course, Nastasia *was* a princess and a magical one at that. Sometimes, it was difficult to comprehend that real life was now as marvelous as stories.

Siggy stuck his pinky finger into his ear and turned it back and forth as if to clean it. Then, he leaned that ear toward the princess, cupping his hand around his ear. "What's that crazy moon language coming out of your mouth? I understand the individual words. But, grouped together, they fail to convey any discernible meaning."

Rachel giggled, but she clapped her hands over her mouth when she caught a glimpse of the princess's sour expression.

Nastasia stated crisply. "We would not want people to spy upon us."

"I think we should listen in." Rachel jumped to Sigfried's defense. "They stole our secrets and gave us rubbish in return. This is our chance to find out the proper truth."

Lucky nodded along in agreement.

"They *stole*?" The crease in the princess's forehead grew deeper. "*They* who?"

"The Agents."

"It is our duty to help those who enforce the law." Nastasia touched her forehead, the same spot as before, adding darkly, "At least, the Agents are on our side."

Rachel did not answer immediately. She had to acknowledge the wisdom of the princess's words; however, it did not lessen her feeling of having been ill-used. She decided to try a new tack. "But the whole world may be at stake! Dr. Mordeau admitted she was a member of Veltdammerung. The word means *Twilight of the World!*"

"We must save the world at any price," declared Sigfried. "Today, the price is spying!"

Princess Nastasia drew herself up, eyes flashing. "The ends never justify the means. We must always do what is right. No matter the threat."

"That's just stupid," Siggy snorted. "If there's a threat, we should eliminate it. No matter what the cost." He slipped his hand under his robes—presumably grabbing the handle of his knife—and looked right and left, as if expecting an attack.

Rachel nodded in agreement. That was the kind of thing her grandfather would have said. Defeating the powers of evil required terrible sacrifices. Only a general who did not flinch when called upon to make the difficult decisions could hope for victory.

"That is a very unknightly attitude, Mr. Smith." The princess's voice was low with warning. "Virtue must be our first concern."

"Watch if you want to. Leave if you don't." Sigfried turned away with a shrug. "I'm watching either way."

From the pocket of his scholar's robe, he pulled a pancake he had stolen from the dining hall during breakfast. It was covered with lint and stained with something red, possibly jam. He broke off a piece and offered it to the two girls. They held up their hands and shook their heads firmly. Siggy shrugged and began eating the pancake.

His mouth still full, he mumbled, "You can't trust adults. They're out to get you. They take away your food and lock you in closets. If anything is going to be solved, we're going to have to do it on our own."

Rachel frowned uneasily. Siggy's attitude was not helping. If he kept this up, the princess would leave.

But would that be such a bad thing?

The idea shocked her, but she paused to consider it. She felt so overwhelmed after all that had happened. On top of it all, did she really need a friend who could not grasp the importance of what was at stake? Something terrible was afoot, yet the princess still seemed to think that their efforts to stop it were the actions of a social club.

Nastasia was so blessed. She was immensely talented, astonishingly beautiful, widely popular. Yet, during an emergency, when Rachel—who could barely manage even simple cantrips—had cast a spell Nastasia did not know, the princess had responded by pouting with envy.

Never mind that Rachel had learned that spell because another girl used it to attack her!

Then there was the question of a friend who had betrayed the most important person in Rachel's life. True, the dean knowing that Gaius knew about the geases was not going to get him in trouble now, but the princess had no way of knowing that when she tattled. Recalling Gaius's look of surprise when the Agents asked him how he knew about the geas, Rachel's stomach knotted. *What if he thought that she, Rachel, had told on him?*

Maybe it would be better if the princess left.

Then a thought stopped her, a very ungenerous thought: No princess, no visions; no visions, no new secrets to replace those stolen. The thought of someone else befriending the princess and becoming privy to her visions frightened her. How could Rachel help save the world, if she did not have enough information to figure out what the threat was? How could she keep Gaius's attention if she did not have secrets to reveal?

These thoughts embarrassed her. Wanting something from a person was not a very good reason to be their friend. There was even a term for that, and it wasn't a pleasant one. And yet, she could not shake the thought: No visions, no secrets. She tried to swallow but could not.

If she wanted the benefits of the princess's friendship, she would have to be a good friend to her. If Rachel were willing to do the difficult things, then one of those difficult things was to be a real friend.

She should be grateful to have a friend at all. Her first efforts to make friends here at Roanoke had gone horribly, and she continued to make blunders. Having spent so much of her life by herself, reading, riding, flying, she had not developed the skills other people had that let them interact with one another so easily. Everyone liked Nastasia. Everyone looked up to her. While she, Rachel, continued to rub others the wrong way, and she had no idea what she did wrong. She felt lost.

Carefully, she recalled what she knew about Nastasia, searching for good traits. She thought of the kindness the princess had shown to students who came to her for aid, how she had protected Rachel from the teasing of the Drake girls, how many common experiences the two of them shared, one having been raised as royalty and the other as nobility.

Besides, she liked Nastasia.

Resolving to overlook the princess's past actions, Rachel drew herself together and returned to the conversation. "We do all agree that we must stop Mortimer Egg, right?"

"The guy who tried to kill my G.F.?" Siggy's eyes flashed, and Lucky opened his mouth, belching a huge gout of dragon-flame. "Yes! Without question! He goes down!"

"Egg must be stopped." The princess nodded firmly. "I agree absolutely."

"Wonderful." Rachel sighed happily. "We are agreed on something."

"Not by us, of course," added Nastasia. "We are but children. So, there is no need for us to spy. Wiser minds, such as my father and the dean, will tell us what we need to know."

"But..." cried Rachel. "Nastasia, we students are the ones in danger. What if I had not known that Mr. Egg was not an Agent when I met him on the docks? Valerie Hunt might be dead. Don't you think we need to know as much as possible?"

"Ah," Nastasia mused. "That is an important argument."

The princess crossed to the window and tapped her fingers pensively on the stone sill, looking out over the campus. Rachel came and stood beside her. Together, they stared down at scurrying students; fallen trees, knocked over by Dr. Mordeau the Dragon; and burning pines—the fires of which glowed brightly in the deepening twilight.

To the southeast, through the trees, stood the imposing edifice of Drake Hall. A crack ran through the granite of the dormitory, from its roof to its foundation. It had been damaged during the battle between the dean and Dr. Mordeau. Ordinarily, the building was surrounded by a moat. Now, the water spilled down into a chasm in the earth, leaving an empty muddy channel.

"You make a good point, Rachel." Nastasia's voice sounded as weary as Rachel felt, but her gaze was firm. "It is the responsibility of royalty to look out for the commoners. To that end, we must be prepared. I do not know why I am having visions, but I must take responsibility for them. If I am to help those who appear in my visions, I need to understand the situation."

"*Rah*-ther!" Rachel nodded emphatically.

"Besides," the princess continued, her voice lighter, "my father always says that nothing is as valuable as good intel. He would greatly admire Sigfried's amulet. He is always complaining about the poor quality of his spies."

Opening her purse, the princess pulled out some needlepoint and a straight-backed chair from the house that Rachel knew was hidden inside. She placed the chair over by the thinking glass, sat down on it, and placed the needlework on her lap.

"Yes. You mentioned that before." Rachel came up beside her. "Something about fruit bats and kookaburras?"

"So, I did." Nastasia nodded in sad agreement, as she picked up her frame and needle. "It is entirely possible that my father chose his intelligence staff by randomly glancing out the window into the garden and appointing whatever happened to be in sight. It wouldn't be the first time he had done something like that. He does govern in his own style.

"Very well, Sigfried." The princess inclined her head regally. "Show us more."

• • •

Sigfried touched the thinking glass again. The golden glass swirled and cleared, so that it looked as if they were peering through a window into the disenchanting chamber below. Agent MacDannan had slung her green plaid bagpipes onto the stone bench. She plopped down beside her instrument and then jumped up again. Retrieving her now-crushed tricorne hat from where it had rested on the bench, she sighed and touched her forehead to its battered felt.

"This poor hat. It's the third time I've sat on it this week." She ran her hand over her frizzy ginger hair and sighed again. Tossing the hat on the bench, she sat down beside it and shot her fellow Agents a wry smile. "It's good I'm not the gambling kind."

"How so?" Darling squatted down and put his hand out for his cat to sniff.

MacDannan pushed her round, owlish glasses up on her nose. "I would have wagered my left arm that Von Dread was mixed up in this Mordeau matter."

Darling chuckled. "Scarlett, I would've been fleeced—or disarmed—right beside you."

Rachel's breath escaped softly. MacDannan and Darling were two of the Six Musketeers, still friends and working together decades after they had saved the world from the Veltdammerung. She glanced surreptitiously at Sigfried and Nastasia. Would facing the dangers before them be enough to forge such a bond between the three of them? Could they still be friends twenty years from now? She dearly hoped so.

Agent Standish watched his cheetah stalk around the room. Periodically, the great cat froze, its head cocked to the side, its round ears twitching. Then, it would begin pacing again. Standish leaned on his fulgurator's staff and spoke in his deep sonorous voice. "The young crown prince handled himself well. I have never heard tell of anyone showing such extraordinary presence of mind under the influence of the *Spell of True Recitation*."

"Think he used magic to interfere with the enchantment?" asked Agent MacDannan.

Standish shrugged. "I don't know."

Leaning forward, MacDannan lowered her voice, "Just between the three of us: he scares the living daylights out of me."

Standish's dark lips twitched with mirth. "You handled yourself very well for a woman with no daylights."

"What I wouldn't have given to have been able to ask him other questions," she sighed.

"You mean, questions not related to the matter at hand?" Agent Standish stroked his short-trimmed beard. "Such as the real story of what led his father to destroy the country of Syria? Or whether Bavaria was behind the nefarious happenings at the Budapest Convention—though I'd place my bet on either Transylvania or China. Or, whether there is any truth to the rumor that his father offers sanctuary to surviving members of the Morthbrood in return for them teaching their black magic to the Bavarian Army."

"Those among many others, yes." Agent MacDannan's eyes flashed with eagerness.

"The person I was dying to question was Locke." Agent Darling looked up from where he squatted beside Pyewacket. He had pulled a plumb bob from his pocket and was dangling it for the tortoiseshell cat to bat. "What is O.I. doing in their facility in Toronto? What led them to abandon the Miyagi Plant? The survivors we found were encased in a caramel-colored crystal we could not make sense of. We couldn't even tell if it was magic or technology. Boy, I'd like to know more..." He sighed. "But it was not to be."

"Because we obey the rules," MacDannan said fiercely, "even if everyone else does not."

Upstairs, the princess murmured, "Commendable."

"Because we are the good guys, Scarlett." Darling gave her an encouraging smile. "Always have been. Always will be."

Despite the ache in her heart, Rachel could not help nodding. *Good for him.*

Standish intoned in his deep voice, "At least that potential political nightmare's behind us. I would not care to have ended up on the wrong side of King Ludwig IV of Bavaria."

Agent MacDannan sighed. She pulled her rat off her shoulder and held it. "We still have a Transylvanian prince who used phantom fire on the Princess of Magical Australia."

Both men blanched. Darling shot to his feet. They looked at each other warily.

"The king of Magical Australia is a strange bird," Standish offered hopefully, "but he is not unreasonable. He'll understand that the boy was geased."

MacDannan's voice was grim. "Unless he wasn't."

"The Drake students were clearly geased." James Darling shifted his weight to the balls of his feet. "Who says otherwise?"

Agent MacDannan pursed her lips and blew. "Rachel Griffin."

"Oi!" Standish struck his forehead with the palm of his hand. "Why couldn't the claim have come from someone more likely to be mistaken? Perhaps, the memory-less kid?"

Upstairs, Sigfried muttered, "Great. Make fun of the orphan boy."

Scarlett MacDannan deposited her rat on her battered tricorne hat and rose to her feet. "Might as well get to it."

• • •

In the thinking glass, Remus Starkadder swaggered into the disenchanting chamber. The Transylvanian prince was tall and blond with rugged, Germanic good looks, and a smug leer.

"Hey, it's the guy who burned the princess." Putting his elbow against the thinking glass, Sigfried began playing with his knife, twirling it and passing it between his fingers.

Lucky swooped down and landed beside his master, his immensely long scarlet whiskers trailing behind him. "Also, the guy you pelted with the apple."

"Enjoyable, but a waste of perfectly fine food," Sigfried replied.

"I'll go down and find it. Someone should eat it." Lucky flew out the window, diving downwards. He returned a few seconds later, looking happily smug.

Rachel and the others waited impatiently while the Agents disenchanted the Transylvanian prince amidst bagpipe music and sparkles. Finally, his feet were back on the floor. Agent MacDannan swung off her bagpipes and mopped her forehead.

"Do you work for Mordeau?" she asked, resting her instrument on the bench. Her rat ran over and sat on the bagpipes, zealously guarding them with his fat little body, nose twitching.

Remus's voice had that odd distant sound of someone under the *Spell of True Recitation*. Even so, he managed to sound smug. "I like to think of it more as a partnership."

"Oh? How so?"

"We help them. They help us."

Agent MacDannan glanced significantly at her companions. James Darling pulled out a notebook and raised his pen.

"You say 'we.'" She asked, "'We', who?"

"Myself and my younger brother, Fenris."

Upstairs, Rachel murmured, "That's nice to know."

Nastasia shot her a puzzled look. "What is?"

"That the brothers are working together," Rachel explained. "The Starkadders are famous for fighting bitterly amongst themselves. Valerie mentioned that this generation—here at school—is the first that has ever shown signs of getting along with each other. Valerie's info must be true, if he admits under the *Spell of True Recitation* to cooperating with his brother."

"Indeed. But cooperating to do what?" the princess asked darkly.

In the glass, Agent MacDannan asked, "What did Mordeau want?"

"A secret base. We gave Mr. Egg and his confederates access to Beaumont Castle."

Rachel made a soft noise, deep in her throat. The other two looked at her.

"Sorry," she whispered, chafed her arms against the sudden chill. Her steeplechaser, which she held between her thumb and forefinger, swung around wildly, nearly hitting Lucky. "I think of Beaumont as a place of ill-omen. My hero, 'Daring' Northwest, died there."

"Recently?" Siggy asked. "Maybe it was these guys."

"No. Well over a hundred years ago."

"Hmm." Sigfried shrugged. "That lead might be a bit cold. Even for my daughter-of-a-detective G.F."

Nastasia smoothed her needlework. "Do you mean Darius Northwest, the author of *The Not-So-Long-Ago Dream Time: A Comprehensive Study of the Bunyip*?"

"Yes. That is he!" Rachel grinned with delight. "My hero!"

"Hero?" Siggy perked up at the word. "What did he do? Kill dragons?"

"No. He was a librarian," Rachel announced proudly.

"Oh." Siggy looked so uninterested it was painful to see.

"An adventurer librarian," Rachel explained rapidly. "Not like Unwary librarians. He went out in the field and hunted down the things people came to his library to ask about."

"Huh. That sounds okay, I guess." Siggy shrugged again. "Or at least, it doesn't make me so bored that I want to shoot myself."

"I want to be just like him when I grow up," cried Rachel. Her eyes shone as she opened her heart and shared her hidden dreams with her two friends, because that was what friends were for, right? "Traveling to unexplored places, seeing things no one has ever seen before, and then coming back and telling people about them."

"Shhh." The princess shushed her. "We're missing the questions."

Below, Remus was saying, "...in the deep countryside, away from prying eyes. Besides, it's mine. No one was using it."

"Your highness, you mentioned a *quid pro quo*." Agent Darling looked up from his notebook. "What were Egg and his friends to do for you in return?"

Remus's grin faltered. He struggled not to answer. His face contorted from the effort, but the power of the *Spell of True Recitation* was too great.

He blurted out, "They were to kill my brother Romulus, the crown prince."

Chapter 8:
The Grim General of Verhängnisburg

A flurry of activity followed, ending with the two guilty Starkadder princes being led away under guard. Upstairs in the belfry, the three students whooped with glee. Sigfried high-fived Lucky. With a triumphant little smile, the princess lifted her robes as if they were skirts and danced victoriously in the straw.

Clickity-clack, tap, clickity-clack. Nastasia's legs flashed, her heels clicked. Her motions were vigorous but orderly. Her long locks bounced about her like a fringed shawl of spun gold. Straw flew through the air, filling the belfry with the scent of hay.

"Stone the crows!" Siggy exclaimed. He took three steps backwards away from the dancing princess, waving his hands before his face. "What in Zeus's name is that?"

"Something I learned during dance class." The princess panted, her cheeks shone pink with animation. She looked even prettier when she was smiling brightly.

"That's from Riverdance. I know that one, too!" Rachel ran forward and stood beside Nastasia, lifting her own robes. She had not practiced that particular routine, but she had seen the princess do it. Now, she would never forget.

Side by side, the two girls performed the Irish step dance, legs kicking, feet stamping. Their faces glowed as they moved in perfect synchronization. Rachel's heart swelled with happiness until she feared it would burst. Keeping the princess as her friend had been the right decision. Nothing could come between them now! In twenty years, they would surely still be close, like James Darling and Scarlett MacDannan.

Siggy watched them, eyes agog. Then he grabbed his head, twirled three times in a circle, and began hitting his forehead against the stone wall.

"Boss, what are you doing?" Lucky watched him with puzzlement.

"Girls. Too cute!" he cried, banging his head with a *thunk*. "Can't endure the cuteness!"

"Stop that, Boss!" Lucky urged, his voice faint and muffled. "You don't damage your head when females are desirable. You bite them on the neck and put them in your lava nest, adding them to your harem. Boss? Stop that! You'll damage the few brain cells you have!"

The dragon darted between the young man and the wall, opening its mouth wide enough to grab Sigfried's entire head and wrestle it away from the hard surface.

The two girls looked at each other and burst into laughter.

"Look at us." Nastasia pressed her hands against her lips, her eyes sparkling, "Giggling like school girls."

"We *are* school girls." Rachel spun around, her robes flaring about her. Dark wisps of hair went everywhere. "If we cannot behave this way, who can?"

"Good point." The princess's eyes danced. Then, the humor in them faded. She moved back to her chair and sat down, smoothing her robes. "You know, I've never been in pain before. Not like today. Normally, if I stumbled or grew ill, my father's servants fixed it right away. We had excellent nuns and monks from the Order of Asclepius on staff. What Prince Remus did...was quite painful," she finished with quiet dignity.

"I'm so sorry," Rachel whispered.

"'Tis no matter. I am happy he was apprehended before he could commit worse crimes. He used black magic on children, and he was willing to commit fratricide."

"A total rotter," Sigfried swore, holding his aching forehead. "What will become of him now? What do you Wise guys do with criminals? Do you torture them? Hang them upside-down from racks? Rip off their fingernails and feed them to their children? Force them to eat their own toes? Make them watch while the lower half of their body is consumed by fire ants? Do you all have special fire ants that actually burst into flame? Flaming ants! Wicked!"

"Bet they're tasty, too!" Lucky licked his furry dragon-lips.

"He's a citizen of Transylvania." Rachel knelt down and pulled a piece of straw out of her shoe. "He'll be handed over to their king."

"They should turn him over to the Grand Inquisitor." The princess *tsked* disapprovingly. "Not his own father. Whatever punishment he receives, it will be too lenient."

"Transylvania is rather old-fashioned." Rachel stood up. Her eyes snapped with gleeful spite. "Maybe they'll clap him in irons and toss things at him. That could be rather horrid."

"Do you think they'll invite Nastasia to go throw things?" Siggy asked. "Are there spells that make really foul-smelling stuff? Putrid?"

"You could always conjure another skunk."

"Oh, yeah. Come here, Lucky." Siggy began making the gesture for drawing down a conjured object.

"Not now!" Rachel squeaked in exasperation. "Later. Do that later, Siggy. We still want to see what's going on downstairs."

"Where are my manners?" The princess jumped up and pulled two more straight-backed chairs from her purse, the mouth of which seemed quite elastic. "Here. Have a chair."

Sigfried turned his chair around, sat on it backwards, and put his hand on the thinking glass. Rachel sat on the third chair. Downstairs, the Agents interviewed students who had been under Mordeau's geas, one after the other. Each student seemed shocked when the *Spell of True Recitation* revealed hidden memories of having been told a command word that would force them to obey the speaker. Some had been given simple orders: carry a message or deliver a package. None recalled having been asked to do anything violent before today—when Mordeau instructed them to kill all the students who had no wands.

Rachel sat on the edge of her chair, eager to hear more. Learning things by spying on the adults was even better than having them volunteer information. It was like a secret within a secret. *And she wanted to know everything!*

It was not merely her burning curiosity that drove her. The wonder of learning, the excitement when unconnected facts came together to form a pattern—making order out of chaos—filled her with a delight that she could not put into words.

It was as if she lived in an enormous dark mansion, of which she could only see a tiny portion. As she explored, candle in hand, occasionally she would come upon a lamp. Each time she lit a new lamp of knowledge with the fire of her curiosity, whole chambers, previously dark, became illuminated. Here was a drawing room of fascinating facts. There a hallway hung with breathtaking landscapes and paintings of faraway places she longed to visit. And over here was a ballroom filled with dancing hopes and dreams that she would not even have known to yearn for if she had not sought out the forgotten things that others overlooked.

However, not everyone matched her enthusiasm. As the bells tolled five o'clock, the interviews downstairs became repetitive. Siggy grew bored and began falling asleep, causing the image to go blank. Rachel poked his shoulder repeatedly. She did not blame him. Her eyes kept closing as well. When they did, however, sleep brought nightmares. She dreamt she was back in the hallway under Drake Hall, paralyzed with Dr. Mordeau's eared snake slithering toward her, preparing to bite. Only this time, the princess did not arrive to rescue her.

This time, the snake's sharp white fangs bore down upon...

Rachel sat up and shook Siggy's shoulder again. She must keep watching, learning. It staved off the darkness.

The only unexpected bit during the next hour was their friend Joy O'Keefe, who had finally been released from the infirmary. Joy remembered, as a child, coming upon her father talking with a black Raven the size of an eagle, with blood red eyes. Rachel also liked the part where her senior resident, Yolanda Debussy, admitted to having kissed an Agent named Jack Oliver, but Sigfried pulled his hand off the mirror before Yolanda finished. He claimed that the "boy-girl" stuff was so revolting it made him physically ill.

By the time she got Siggy to put his hand back on the mirror, Yolanda had departed. Agent Darling stood looking off into the distance with a thoughtful expression on his face.

"Scarlett, that kid who helped Finn when he was injured, after his duel with Aleister Crowley...wasn't that Mortimer Egg?"

Agent MacDannan had put down her bagpipes and was searching for something. She tipped back her head, thinking. "The quiet one with the funny felt hat?"

"That's him."

"Yes. It was."

"Huh."

A shiver traveled up Rachel's spine. *Crowley*. Mordeau had mentioned him. He had helped Rachel's grandfather defeat Bismarck's sorcerers in the 1880s. After that, Crowley had gone bad. Very bad. He had been one of the Terrible Five who caused the Terrible Years. What did it mean that the man who had tried to kill Valerie, who might be Mordeau's secret boss, was present at the death of this horrible sorcerer?

And what about her grandfather? What was this mysterious tragedy he suffered?

"Who's Finn?" asked Sigfried.

"Finvarra MacDannan, Scarlett's husband and James Darling's best friend. He was one of the Six Musketeers Mr. Fisher told us about," Rachel reminded him. "He's also thought to be the best Enchanter alive today. He's so good, he is even a hit with the Unwary. He's the lead singer of a band called Bogus."

"Nowadays, he is one of the Peers on the Parliament of the Wise," said the Princess.

"Which means?" asked Siggy, looking bored.

"It's like being a Member of Parliament or an American senator," replied Nastasia.

"He helps run the world," laughed Rachel.

• • •

Downstairs, Scarlett MacDannan continued her search. She checked under the bench and along the edge of the room. Then she groaned and rested her forehead against the wall. Turning toward the others, she sighed, "Drat my absentmindedness! I left my staff upstairs."

Glancing around, Rachel saw a fulgurator's staff lying to one side among the straw.

Standish bowed. "I'll go fetch it. I'm not needed to play the enchantments."

As Agent Standish strode from the disenchanting chamber, Siggy sauntered away from the thinking glass. He leaned casually against the sill of the western window, whistling—as if he had been sitting there, minding his own business all along.

"See!" He waved his hand at Nastasia. "It was a good thing we were watching, or we would not know that he was coming."

A tiny quirk of amusement flickered across the princess's lips, as she gathered the chairs and put them back into her purse. "True, Mr. Smith. But if we were not doing anything wrong, we would not have needed prior notice of his arrival."

Sigfried blinked, puzzled. He looked at Lucky and scratched his head.

Lucky shrugged. "Dunno either, Boss."

Turning back toward Nastasia, Siggy spread his arms in puzzlement. "What is this 'not doing anything wrong' of which you speak?"

• • •

The bells in the six bell towers atop Roanoke Hall tolled six o'clock as Agent Standish jogged up the stairs. Reaching the belfry, he nodded to the three students, where they lounged by the southern window, attempting to look casual. Golden rays of late afternoon sun illuminated the chimes and the lantern with a fiery glow. As he crossed the straw-covered stone, and bent to retrieve the dropped staff, Rachel recalled the *No Students Allowed* sign at the bottom of the stairs.

Should she stay quiet? Or distract him with questions?

Staff in hand, he turned toward them and smiled. It was too late to hope they would be overlooked. Rachel's heart rate sped up. Running forward, she tugged on the half-cape of his cloak like a little child. "Agent Standish. Did you know my grandfather?"

"General Griffin? Indeed I did. Indeed I did. He was…" The Agent pursed his dark lips as he searched for the right words. "Quite an impressive man."

"Imposing?" Rachel offered with only the faintest hint of a smirk.

"Very imposing," Agent Standish admitted, smiling down at her. "Also the most brilliant cryptomancer I have ever had the honor to meet."

"What's that?" Sigfried asked. "Magic from Krypton? Does it involve Krypto the Superdog? I think you can lick 'im, Lucky!"

Agent Standish chuckled, "Cryptomancy is a very difficult branch of magic. It involves casting spells in such a fashion that they can be recast by repeating a single masterword."

"It's almost like inventing one's own private cantrip," contributed Rachel. "Geases are usually cast using cryptomancy...so the caster can re-activate the geas merely by saying a word. We saw Dr. Mordeau do that to the kids in Drake—in the princess's vision."

She glanced cautiously at Agent Standish. Careful not to mention Mordeau again, she asked, "Do you know if anything happened to my grandfather during the Eighteen Eighties?"

"Eighteen Eighties?" The Agent's eyebrows shot up. He shook his head slowly. "No. I do not believe I do. I know about his exploits in World War II—how he put an end to Hitler's dreams of a German victory by black magic. He was a superb general. He lost fewer men than any other cadre of sorcerers."

Despite her disappointment at his inability to resolve the mystery of her grandfather's tragedy, Rachel grinned with pride, her head bobbing up and down with enthusiastic agreement.

Turning to Siggy and the princess, Standish said, "General Griffin was a most amazing man. Brilliant. An incredible sorcerer. But a more intimidating man I have never met. During my Agent training, General Griffin came to speak to us. I remember he said that a true man should be—" He dropped his voice and made it deeper and more gravelly. Rachel repeated the words along with him, bouncing up and down. "*Fierce as a tiger. Calm as a lake in August. And cool as ice—when you are not as fiery as a furnace.*"

Standish ruffled her hair fondly. "I see you know that one."

"Grandfather repeated it often," replied Rachel.

As a little girl, Rachel had taken those words to heart. Fierce as a tiger and fiery as a furnace had been easy enough to master.

But at the tender age of four, she had not been capable of calmness. Eager to please the irascible man who doted on her, she had substituted her mother's art, learning to make herself appear calm to outside observers.

Cool as ice was still a work in progress.

With an expansive wave of his hand, Standish continued. "We had this fellow in our group who was a clown and a complainer. He started cracking jokes while General Griffin was speaking. The general turned on him—he had the most impressive set of eyebrows—and he glared. Just glared, until the poor fellow was literally shaking in his boots. Wasn't just him either, to tell you the truth. I was doing a bit of shaking myself.

"General Griffin leaned toward the joker and said 'Boo!' Just like that. That fellow ran. Right out of the compound. I never saw him again."

Rachel's lips quirked. "You mean, like this?"

She reached out and touched the thinking glass. A picture appeared, but, oddly, the color of the glass did not change. The image remained tinted golden, as if they were glimpsing something antique and supremely precious. Amidst the glow, a slender feminine figure loomed, reaching forward, face wild and menacing.

The princess sniffed in disapproval. "Who is that undisciplined rapscallion?"

"My middle sister Laurel," Rachel murmured, for once in complete agreement with Nastasia. "Age seven."

The tormentor was an Asian girl, her hair flying free from her barrettes. Only it was a seven-year-old as seen from the point of view of a much smaller child, so she loomed huge and ominous.

From the thinking glass, little Laurel taunted, "I can so pull your hair! I can pull it anytime I want!" Reaching forward, she yanked. There was a screech, the sound of a little child in agony.

A deep voice interrupted her. "What's all this, hmm?"

A man stepped into view. He was white-haired with thick sideburns, dressed in a scarlet smoking jacket and carrying a pipe. He towered over the seven-year-old, and scowled, his gaze fierce and flashing. Rachel's tormentor quaked. Blaise Griffin, the Duke of Devon, drew himself up. His face grew stormy and wrathful. His bushy white eyebrows drew together like two advancing avalanches. Laurel quivered in terror and took two steps backward.

The duke leaned forward. "Boo!"

Screaming, her arms waving above her head, Laurel ran from the hallway.

The imposing duke turned and regarded something before him. Caught up in the memory, Rachel acted along with her tiny, three-year-old self. Her face scowled, imitating what his had just done. Her dove-wing eyebrows drew together. At the precise moment that the tiny voice sounded from the glass, Rachel shouted along with it.

"Boo!"

In the glass, her grandfather glared down at where Rachel's tiny past self must have stood. Then, deep and glorious laughter boomed from his chest. He swooped forward and leaned down. The view then showed what was over his shoulder, a hallway with paintings and urns.

Lost in the memory, Rachel recalled the feeling of his arms closing around her, his rough bristly cheek against hers. She loved remembering this moment.

It was the first time she had ever felt important.

With a sudden crushing wave of longing, Rachel missed her grandfather. He would never have dismissed her, telling her to try to be an ordinary girl. He had required her to watch, to observe, to report. He had required her to be extraordinary. Without him, there was an empty place inside of her that she could not fill.

She had tried to fill it with her father, but Sandra was Father's special person. She, Rachel, would always be second best. Now, she was trying to fill it with Gaius, but she had no idea if he was capable of fulfilling such a role, much less if he were worthy.

If only her grandfather had lived a few short years longer.

"Ah!" Standish stroked his beard, his dark eyes twinkling. "Another mystery explained."

"What mystery?" Siggy asked.

"How a tiny thistle-puff of a girl, not yet even pint-sized—so small her mother had to wash her in a teacup—won the heart of the grim general of the Battle of Verhängnisburg. I have often wondered how they came to be so fond of each other."

"After that, we were friends," Rachel replied gravely.

"How old were you?" Standish asked.

"Three and a half."

He clicked his heels and bowed again. "Thank you for sharing this memory with me, Rachel Griffin."

She nodded seriously and then gave him a tiny smile.

Wishing them all a good day, Agent Standish turned and jogged down the stairs, Agent MacDannan's fulgurator's staff swinging in his hand. As he disappeared, Rachel's smile grew.

He might not have been able to shed any light on the mystery of what Mordeau knew about her grandfather, but he had forgotten to ask them to leave.

• • •

"Quick!" Sigfried ran back to the thinking glass. "This is what's going on downstairs."

An image appeared. It was the proper color, not golden, like Rachel's memory. A commotion had broken out by the door to the Watch Tower. Tiny Magdalene Chase, the only person at Roanoke Academy smaller than Rachel, stumbled into the foyer, her eyes bloodshot, her face ghastly pale. She clutched her China doll.

Rachel eyed the doll carefully. When Magdalene was unconscious, it had talked. Now, it showed no sign of life.

Nurses fluttered around Magdalene, insisting she return to the infirmary. The tiny girl shook her head fiercely. Leaves from when her doll had dragged her through the forest, trying to save her, flew from her hair. She ducked under the nurses' arms and ran into the disenchanting chamber, where the Agents were interviewing another student.

"Please," Magdalene cried imploringly, grabbing James Darling's arm. "I heard you could remove the geas spell. Help me!"

"Certainly," Agent Darling smiled kindly at the little girl. "Here you go."

He cast the Word of Ending cantrip on her and then sent her to stand before Agent MacDannan. Magdalene's eyes grew large when she noticed the cheetah prowling around the chamber, but she did not twitch a muscle. She waited motionlessly, clutching her dolly, while the ginger-haired Agent dismissed the other student and began to play for her.

Sparkles spun Magdalene into the air. She cried out in terror. When nothing bad happened, a look of tremendous joy came over her little face. She twirled her arms, until she and her doll spun in mid-air, amidst the twinkling lights. Rachel smiled. She wished she had thought of spinning in the sparkles. She felt glad that she and Gaius had been able to help the doll get her tiny mistress to safety.

Agent Standish entered the room and placed MacDannan's staff beside the bench next to her hat. She nodded at him in thanks but did not pause in her playing.

When Magdalene eventually landed, Agent MacDannan asked, "What do you remember that you did not before?"

Magdalene blinked three times. Then she spoke in the flat monotone imposed by the *Spell of True Recitation*. "Dr. Mordeau came to our house with three other people. They spoke to my parents. My parents offered me for the ritual, but the man said my parents—who are really my aunt and uncle—didn't care about me enough for the ritual to work."

Rachel pressed her hand against her mouth in horror.

Magdelene's family did not love her?

"What ritual, child?" Agent MacDannan pressed. "What did it do?"

"I don't know." Magdalene clutched her doll tighter. "The man said they should use Eunice, but our parents refused."

"Do you know what your part would have been in the ritual?"

"The sacrifice," the tiny girl said flatly. "They were going to kill me."

Agent MacDannan nearly dropped her bagpipes. "Holy Zeus! Were your parents relieved—that you would be spared?"

"No. They were very angry with me. My mother shouted, 'Why are we housing the ungrateful wretch, if she can't help us with the spell?'"

Agent MacDannan pushed her owlish glasses up on her nose with a no-nonsense look, but her voice shook. "What happened next?"

"They locked me in my room for a week. Twice, they forgot to feed me all day. I was very confused because I could not remember, until just now, why they had put me there."

Magdalene was trembling, her slim limbs shaking. James Darling leaned down and gently embraced her. She made no sound as he hugged her, but tears—still tinged pink from the residual blood that had run from her eyes when she fought to break the geas—stained her cheeks.

"Can you tell us anything else about the other three people with Dr. Mordeau?" Agent MacDannan asked with some reluctance. On her face, the need to know more warred with her desire to protect Magdalene.

"There was a British gentleman, a red-headed woman, and a man with a ponytail."

Upstairs, Rachel whispered, "That last one is Mortimer Egg!"

Below, Agent MacDannan asked, "Do you remember their names?"

Magdalene shook her head. She looked up imploringly. "The geas? Is it gone now? It's not going to make me kill anyone anymore?"

"It's gone," Darling assured her. "You are all right."

Magdalene's whole body sagged. She sobbed soundlessly against his chest. Darling lifted her into his arms and carried her back to the foyer, where he gently handed her to the worried-looking nurses.

Turning, Darling called out, "Eunice Chase. You're next."

• • •

Under the influence of the truth magic, Magdalene's older sister, Eunice, described the visit of the same four people.

"My parents wanted them to kill Magdalene," Eunice said flatly, "but Mr. Egg said the spell would not work. Next, he wanted them to kill me, but my parents refused. They love me. They were very angry that they had taken care of Magdalene all this time, even though she's a sniveling weakling, and it wasn't going to do them any good."

"Do you know the names of the four visitors?" Agent MacDannan asked tensely.

"Dr. Mordeau, Mr. Egg, a woman I don't know, and Mr. Browne."

"What did this Mr. Browne look like?"

Eunice smiled, remembering. "Blond. Very handsome, very strong."

The Agents exchanged horrified glances.

Agent MacDannan asked, her voice tight, "Not...Daniel Hanson Browne?"

"Mother called him Daniel. Yes."

Agent MacDannan shooed Eunice Chase out of the disenchanting chamber and came back to join her two companions. Her face was pale. Darling's hand shook slightly as he pulled out his calling card. "Agent Carlson, Agent Briars, encrypted message to follow."

He performed a cantrip over the mirror and then said something that made no sense.

"What is he saying?" Siggy asked Nastasia.

"He said: 'We have been infiltrated,'" the princess replied. "'Agent Browne of Wisecraft, Scotland Yard is working for the enemy.'"

Rachel gasped and clutched her neck. She knew Agent Browne. He once showed her a trick where he hid an egg and pulled it out of Peter's ear. He had taken Sandra under his wing when she started with the Wisecraft this summer. He and Sandra were friends.

"I don't know Browne," murmured Agent MacDannan.

"I do." Darling's voice cracked. "Served with him back when Griffin and I were partners—when I was posted to London. Good Agent in those days, Browne. Hard worker."

"I know him well." Standish's face contorted with wrath. "We've worked together. I did not realize he was the kind of man who asks a family to kill their own children."

An odd expression crossed Agent MacDannan's face. She sat down and began rubbing her temples, her face screwed up in concentration.

Darling watched her carefully. "Scarlett, I know that look. You're onto something?"

"There's something familiar about all this, James. Families...mass deaths..." With a clap of her hands, she leapt to her feet, startling her rat who scuttled off, squeaking "Hunt's list!"

"Who...what?" Standish asked, his voice still bearing a dangerous edge.

"The list of names Kenneth Hunt gave Kyle Iscariot the morning before he disappeared."

Upstairs, Rachel grabbed Siggy's arm. "They mean Valerie's father. That's the list Valerie said she asked her friend Wally, back home, to send to her! It was a list of names from the case her father—a police detective—was working on."

Agent Darling looked at MacDannan without comprehension. Suddenly, he pulled out his card again. "People, we may be onto something big. Bring me the students whose families were on Hunt's list." He tilted his head back, as if thinking. "Sakura Suzuki and Misty Lark."

Upstairs, Siggy perked up at Valerie's name. He asked, "Who are these other people?"

"Freshmen like us." Rachel's voice was barely a whisper.

"What do they have in common?" asked Sigfried.

"Their entire families were murdered before their eyes."

Chapter 9:
A Farewell to Innocence

"I don't get it." Siggy took his hand off the mirror. "What does this have to do with Goldilocks's father?"

The long day had slid into evening. The sun had disappeared beneath the horizon. It was getting harder to see one another's faces. Nastasia had brought out her chairs again and returned to her needlework.

"Detective Hunt was working on a rather controversial case when he vanished," Rachel explained. "The people in her town thought he ran out on her family. But Valerie is convinced he was investigating this case, and something bad happened. Sounds as if he shared some clues with Salome's dad before he disappeared, and Salome's father gave the information to the Agents. If Detective Hunt's investigation was related to this ritual Mordeau wanted to perform, maybe that's why Mortimer Egg tried to kill Valerie."

"But why be so obvious about it?" the princess asked. "If the brooch had killed Valerie, we all would have been able to identify him."

"I have no idea." Rachel shrugged. "Maybe he hoped we'd never figure out who he was."

"Maybe the brooch was supposed to alter our memories of what happen…only Lucky and Dread destroyed it before it could perform its expected function. Do you think he and Mordeau ever performed that ritual?" Nastasia asked. "Did someone die because of them?"

"Let's hope not," replied Rachel. "Let's hope that the deaths of Sakura and Misty's families are not related to this. But…"

"But what…" prompted Siggy.

"It just doesn't bode well that Mr. Darling called for these other girls right after Detective Hunt's list was mentioned," Rachel said. "If the names of those girls are on Hunt's list…the deaths of their families might be related to Mortimer Egg and his cohorts."

The image in the thinking glass followed Eunice Chase as she left the disenchanting chamber and walked back into the foyer. Valerie Hunt sat outside the door, spinning a pencil back and forth between her fingers the way one might spin a knife, as she waited her turn to be de-geased. Sigfried's girlfriend was pretty with short flaxen hair, a squarish jaw, and bright blue eyes. An old-fashioned camera with a huge zoom lens hung from her shoulder on a red strap. Last time Rachel had seen her, she had been in a bed in the infirmary, recovering from the trauma caused by attempting to overcome the geas spell by sheer effort of will. She looked better than she had, but her face was still unusually pale. One of the visiting nurses stood beside her.

As Eunice walked by, Valerie stood up, stepped in front of her, and crossed her arms. "Who's the snitch, Eunice? Who betrayed our secrets to you?"

In that same flat tone that the *Spell of True Recitation* inspired, the words spilled out of Eunice's mouth. "You are. Dr. Mordeau spoke a secret code, and you told us everything."

Eunice's face betrayed shock and annoyance at the words spilling from her mouth. Glaring, she struggled to regain control of her voice and stalked off. Smirking, Valerie sat down.

"Woohoo!" Siggy punched the air. "Go, Goldilocks!"

"That's one mystery solved." Rachel gave a little ironic smile.

While the other Agents waited for Sakura Suzuki and Misty Lark, Agent Darling stepped out into the foyer. Instantly, he was mobbed by students asking for autographs. A few, hearing he was on campus, even brought copies of *James Darling, Agent* comics and novels. They pressed around him, clamoring for his attention, asking questions, and shouting comments. He seemed embarrassed, but he spoke to each student graciously.

Another Agent came up and whispered to him that, with the help of Master Warder Nighthawk, they had caught the rest of the shadows that had escaped from Mordeau's cloak. Rachel and Siggy grinned at each other and exchanged high-fives.

Agent Darling's son approached him. The Darlings, father and son, moved to one side. John Darling wore a dagger with a bone handle and a copper blade on his hip. He also carried a silver flute. From the look of him, he had been in a fight.

Rachel's heart skipped a beat. In addition to being her crush-from-afar, John Darling was the captain of the upper school's flying polo team and a standout athlete in Track and Broom. He looked so cute with his dark hair all disarrayed and his suit and half-cape disheveled. The memory of how he had laughed at her, the time she dropped her breakfast tray in the kitchen, produced a funny fluttering in her stomach.

"Hey, Siggy, can you move us closer to those two?" Rachel asked.

"Zoom in," Siggy said, adding, "Cool copper knife!"

"Is it an athame of some sort?" asked the princess. "For drawing wards?"

Rachel said, "It's a symbol of membership in the Brotherhood of the White Hart." When they both looked blank, she added uncomfortably, for she was not certain if this was a secret, "A secret organization devoted to the safety of the World of the Wise. There are several members on campus. Your brother Ivan is a member, Nastasia."

Downstairs, John leaned close to Agent Darling. "Father, what's really going on?"

Agent Darling winced. "I am sorry, son. I can't tell you."

"Please, Dad? Anything? I don't even know why we are here. Or what the problem is. Or what we were just fighting over."

Agent Darling shook his head, sadly but firmly. His son's shoulders slumped. He looked dejected.

Sympathy for John filled Rachel's heart. He and she really were alike! They both yearned to know secrets James Darling refused to tell them. Still, it made her feel a tiny bit better that, after telling her nothing, the Agent had not shared information with his own son. The thought that she knew more about what was going on than John Darling gave her a delicious sensation of secret pleasure.

Agent Darling lowered his voice and whispered to his son, "How about you? Have you learned anything?"

"No." John said sadly. "I was completely taken by surprise. I didn't even know anything was wrong, until Mr. Tuck came and got me out of class."

James Darling looked disappointed. "I'd always assumed my children would be in the thick of any adventure, as your mother and I were." His eyes twinkled. "There is still time. You have five more years here."

"I'll do my best, Dad. Being a White Hart helps. The tutors occasionally tell us things they don't tell the regular students."

Oh! Rachel had not realized being a member of the White Hart meant knowing secrets! Now she wanted to join, too. If she did, she could spend time with hunky John Darling, who, in the words of her sister Laurel, was "definitely snog-worthy." Rachel wondered how old a person had to be to join, and if her parents could make her a member.

"And the Tarn Helm?" Agent Darling asked. "Making use of it? Keeping it secret, I assume."

A shiver ran across Rachel's shoulders. The *Tarn Helm*!

John Darling grinned. "I've used it a little. But only for frivolous things. Liam and Oonagh know I have it, of course. But no one else. And Wendy, of course."

"Not Conan?" his father asked.

"Heck no! Conan's one of those vampire hunters who follow Abraham Van Helsing. If I told him, they'd be pestering me for it day and night. And that would come to no good end!"

"No," laughed his father. "That would most certainly go badly."

As the father and son parted, Siggy asked, "Who are those people he just mentioned?"

Rachel replied, "Oonagh, Liam, and Conan are Scarlett Mac-Dannan's children. Your roommate Ian's older siblings. They're John Darling's cousins. Wendy is his sister. She's in our class... and our dorm."

"What's the Tarn Helm?" he persisted.

"One of the great talismans Mr. Fisher fashioned for the Six Musketeers, back during the Terrible Years. He based it on the one made by the Nibelung—the dwarves of the North. It turns the wearer invisible."

"Cool!" Siggy grinned at Lucky. "If I were invisible, we could sneak around together."

"And both drink tutors' coffee unseen," crowed Lucky.

"Er...yeah." Siggy scrunched up his nose at the thought of coffee, possibly the only food he did not adore.

• • •

The two girls Agent Darling requested did not show up immediately. The Agents went back to interviewing the remaining students from Drake. As these students knew very little, the Agents picked up the speed of the interviews. Standish and Darling interviewed one student while Scarlett MacDannan disenchanted the next one.

Siggy took his hand off the mirror. "This is boring. It's easier for me to watch on my own. I'll keep an eye on the proceedings and let you know if something interesting happens."

Rachel crossed to the northern window and stared out at the forest. The light was fading. Night was nearly upon them.

Had it only been last night that she had dueled her rival, Cydney Graves, at the Knights of Walpurgis meeting? She still felt a rush of pleasure when she recalled how, thanks to Gaius's training, she had won the duel. Was it only last night that he had walked her home and kissed her? Only this afternoon that the Lion had led her to where Valerie sat slumped on the floor of the girl's bathroom, blood running from her eyes and nose, as she fought the geas spell?

It seemed a universe ago, another lifetime.

What should they make of the news that Mortimer Egg and his cronies had planned to kill Romulus Starkadder? The crown prince of Transylvania was a bit of a prig, but that was hardly a crime punishable by death. Nor was that the strangest part. A second son wanting to displace his elder brother was alarming, but common enough throughout history to not be utterly shocking. No. What disturbed her most was Magdalene and Eunice Chase.

Who refused to kill a girl because her family did *not* love her *enough*? Was there a connection between Magdalene and the other two girls whose families had been murdered? Most of all, what was the purpose of the ritual Mordeau and her partners-in-evil wanted to perform?

Resurrection of the dead.

That was what Mordeau had promised the dean. What had the math-teaching dragon said? *What are a few traumatized infants, a few lost worlds, compared to what we seek to achieve?* Were Sakura and Misty among the *traumatized infants* to whom Mordeau referred?

And what of these *lost worlds*?

Was this world, her world, to be one of the casualties?

Rachel wrestled with these ideas but did not have enough pieces to form a picture. After a time, her thoughts drifted dreamily toward Gaius. She gazed out over the hemlocks at the tor, its rocky silhouette still visible against the darkening sky, and remembered the lazy way he smiled at her. She recalled the admiration in his eyes when she impressed him, the feel of his lips brushing against hers as he kissed her. Then, she remembered watching him stomp away from her after she turned him down. At the time, she had wondered why the two standoffish upperclassmen had showed such concern for Gaius when he joined them. Now she understood.

Gaius worked for Dread.

Puzzle pieces suddenly clicked together. In the infirmary, when she had asked him where he had learned about the geas, he had replied: *"I am almost a hundred percent sure the person who told me did so because he is trying to figure out if anyone was under it. I do not think he knows how to cast it. I also don't think he would cast it, if he did...Well, I hope he wouldn't..."*

Then, the time she had accused him of leaking her secrets, Gaius had protested that he told no one. She recalled that he blurted out, *"I didn't even tell..."* before his voice trailed off.

Both times, he must have been referring to the crown prince of Bavaria.

She mentally replayed Gaius stomping off to join Locke and Dread one last time. Suddenly, she felt oddly light, as if her feet did not quite reach the ground. Gaius had looked so upset. Would he have been so distressed if he had been turned down by a girl he was merely toying with?

Maybe he really did like her!

If only there were someone whom she could talk to about Gaius. Not her older brother Peter. He would be outraged that his baby sister even contemplated dating boys, and Laurel would laugh at her. But her oldest sister Sandra was wise about many things. She would kneel down—Sandra was tall, like their father—and listen carefully, with her complete attention, giving due consideration to everything Rachel had to say. Sandra was back in London, working at her new job with the Wisecraft. Sighing, Rachel resolved to write her a letter.

The princess crossed to stand beside Rachel, where she stood staring out the window. "We have learned many interesting things today. Disturbing things."

"Yes, we have."

Nastasia glanced over, as if to make sure that Sigfried was otherwise occupied. She spoke in a low voice, "I hope you will have nothing more to do with that boy."

"Who, Gaius?" Rachel's heart skipped a beat. "I thought he did rather well before the Agents."

"He *admitted* he works for Von Dread," objected Nastasia.

"Is that so bad?"

"Dread is wicked. Remember how he asked me..." Nastasia touched her forehead again, frowning. "No, I won't speak of that yet."

From across the chamber, Sigfried, who was apparently paying attention after all, called, "At least, Valiant did not say: 'I was sent to seduce Rachel Griffin to win access to her father the Agent.'"

This made Rachel giggle. She threw Siggy an appreciative smile.

He shrugged. "Besides, I think Dread is wicked excellent!"

The princess began pacing the belfry. Rachel fell in beside her. "He asked me to be his girlfriend—Gaius, I mean. Not Dread."

"You said no, I presume," Nastasia said.

"Yes. I did." Rachel bit at her lip. "He had not asked my brother's permission. Also, I am not sure a thirteen-year-old girl should have a boyfriend. Especially an older boy. Older boys...expect things." She faltered, her cheeks heading for lava territory again.

"Of course not. We are far too young." The princess nodded in approval. "Very wise."

"But..." Rachel began, eager to speak of the struggle in her heart, even if the princess were not the ideal audience for the matter.

"Whoa. They're here!" Siggy interrupted, rushing back to the mirror. "The two girls."

Rachel and Nastasia rushed back to the mirror. Siggy's hand rested on the thinking glass, which showed two girls being escorted into the foyer. Sakura Suzuki was a tall girl with glasses and long pig tails into which she had tied bells that looked like tiny versions of the ones in the Oriental gardens. She came from an ancient line of sorcerers who could trace their lineage back to the Japanese sun goddess. She had been orphaned at the age of five and raised by her aunt and uncle.

Misty Lark's straw-colored hair stuck out like hay. Her familiar, a tiny unicorn, trotted beside her. Her face bore a dull, almost lifeless, expression—which did not surprise Rachel. Her parents and three siblings had been murdered before her eyes less than a year before.

The Agents interviewed the two girls separately. Misty's feet had hardly left the ground before she began to keen, a low, painful sound. When she landed, she seemed disoriented. In a dazed monotone, she told the Agents the details of the death of her family, which she had not been able to remember until now. The same four people that the Chase girls had described had come into her house, tied her to a couch, and forced her to watch their ritual. She hesitated at times, and her words were jumbled.

Rachel was not entirely certain of the order of events. But the gist of it was clear: her father, her mother, her twin younger sisters, and her two-year-old baby brother had been murdered.

The nurses took Misty away to the infirmary, and the Agents spoke with Sakura. She recalled watching a smoke-winged entity with burning eyes kill her parents and come after her. It had cast a cantrip at her and had become enraged when the spell failed to work. It moved to attack but had been stopped by their true history teacher, Mr. Gideon. A friend of her parents, he had been invited to dinner that night and had arrived in time to save her.

The Agents asked Sakura a series of questions about the creature who slaughtered her parents. As she was answering, a dark shadow passed by the window of the belfry. *Caw.* Lucky darted out the east window and flew away to the south.

"Lucky! No!" Siggy grabbed his head. "He's gone dumb again! Like an ordinary animal! His last cogent thought was about the menagerie. Something about ducks. I think he's gone to eat someone's familiars!"

"It's the Raven!" Rachel ran to the window and watched the giant, coal-black bird with its eerie blood-red eyes wing off to the north. "It had this horrid effect on Lucky before! Turning him into an unintelligent animal."

Like a streak of furry lightning, Lucky shot through the gloom of the evening straight at Drake Hall, which was the opposite direction from the menagerie. He soared over the damaged dormitory and disappeared behind it.

"Weren't there a lot of animals in cages behind Drake?" Siggy leaned on the windowsill beside Rachel.

"Doves and chickens and goats. Offerings to be used as sacrifices by the thaumaturgy students." Rachel could not quite keep the disdain out of her voice. She and her family strongly disapproved of any magic that required a living sacrifice.

"Oops." Siggy shrugged.

Under his nonchalance, he looked worried and kept peering out the way Lucky had gone.

Eventually, Siggy returned to the thinking glass. The Agents had wrapped up their conversation with Sakura and were interviewing Valerie Hunt. She was pale but smiling. She snapped a picture of the Agents before MacDannan began to play. Up in the air, surrounded by twinkling gold, she kept swatting at the little sparkles and saying, "Ow! Ow! Ow!"

Siggy grinned with obvious adoration, as if the fact that his beloved was a liar, like him, made her dearer to him.

He pointed at her. "Isn't Goldilocks adorable?"

Rachel grinned back, her body trembling with excitement. Finally, they would find out what had happened to Valerie at the Wisecraft offices!

• • •

When Valerie landed on her feet again, Agent MacDannan took a deep breath. "Now, Miss Hunt. What do you remember that you had not?"

Valerie's eyes grew wide with distress. Whatever she was remembering horrified her.

"I went to the Wisecraft offices. The man behind the counter was a guy with a pony-tail. I remember being surprised. I had seen him before. The day my father disappeared!" Her voice rose. "The last time I saw my father, he was talking to Mortimer Egg!"

The Agents looked back and forth among one another.

"I approached and introduced myself," Valerie continued, her fingers fidgeting. She wiggled her fingers as if spinning her pencil, even though she was no longer holding it. "I asked what he and my father had been talking about and whether my father had mentioned where he was going next. Mr. Egg said, 'Oh, no. This is not good. Come with me.' I thought that a bit odd, but I went. I thought maybe he hadn't known my father was missing until I told him. He brought me into a break room. There was a pump—an old fashioned one with a handle—and a self-heating tea kettle. He made me a glass of tea. Then, he pointed a wand at me. There was a burst of purple sparks. He told me to forget about seeing him and go on my way..." Valerie's voice broke. "And I did."

"Was that the only time the geas was used on you?"

"No." Valerie frowned and rubbed her temples. "Dr. Mordeau called me over several times and asked me questions in front of a group of other students, including Eunice Chase and Cydney Graves and other kids whose names I don't know. But I could pick them out of a line-up. Afterwards, she would say a word and tell me to forget the questions. And I did."

"Remember any of Mordeau's questions?" asked Agent MacDannan.

"Certainly!" The Fearless Reporter Girl counted off the questions. "Dr. Mordeau asked: How much did my father know? Could someone called Adam Kadmon resurrect the dead? Did my boyfriend know his father's name? Had Miss Griffin's father told her the secret of the moon glass? Did the princess know her father's origins?"

The three students spoke simultaneously:

"Moon glass?" Rachel asked in awe. "What could that be?"

"My father?" The princess exclaimed, "He's from Magical Australia. Wait? Could Father be from another world, too...like Lucky and all these people about whom I have had visions?"

"What do I care who my father was," Siggy scowled. "Who cares about the kind of parents who throw their son away?"

"Interesting," Scarlett MacDannan said below, in the mirror. "Is there anything else?"

Valerie's face grew entirely pale. "Then she..." Her voice failed. She closed her eyes. Then, she opened them again, her expression grim. "She told her assistant, Jonah Strega...told him to do whatever he wanted."

"Jonah Strega? The boy whose face got burned? What did he choose to do?"

Valerie did not answer; her whole body trembled like a branch in a gale.

"Miss Hunt," Agent MacDannan asked in her no-nonsense fashion, "did Mr. Strega take advantage of you?"

Valerie could not get her voice to work.

Silently, she nodded.

Chapter 10:
The Unlikely Proposal of Ivan Romanov

Screaming in inarticulate fury, Sigfried punched the glass with the hand holding his knife. *Scrack!* Cracks spread like dark spider-webs through the golden glass, and the picture vanished. Small shards rained down with a sound like cracking icicles. Blood dripped from his knuckles.

"Oops." Rachel's lips moved, but her voice caught in her throat.

Unconcerned with either the fractures spreading through the talking glass or the abrasions on his hand, Sigfried tore down the stairs from the belfry, jumping three steps at a time. Rachel and Nastasia stood as if rooted, watching him go.

Then, very deliberately, Nastasia began to pack the chairs back into her purse.

• • •

The dining room at Roanoke Hall was an enormous chamber, shaped like a plus sign, with a vaulted ceiling. To one side were the kitchens and the feeding stations for familiars. A fountain stood at the center, where the four wings met. The table nearest the fountain was the domain of Vladimir Von Dread and his cronies. The rest were either associated with a specific Sorcerous Art or free for anyone to use. Rachel and her friends had gathered around one of these, though there was no sign of Sigfried. Rachel hoped he was comforting his girlfriend.

It was after seven, but, due to the commotion, the kitchens were still serving food. Many of the students had already left. Most of those still present had been embroiled in the day's events. There was an air of excitement and relief, as those who had participated in the fighting told their battle stories.

Rachel sat in front of her dinner tray, stunned. She had been tremendously hungry. Now, she stared at her food but neither saw nor smelled it. Instead her mind spun over and over, stuck. Something so unimaginable had happened to Valerie. How should she feel about it? She could not even bring herself to think about it properly. Something inside her felt torn, wrenched.

Could there be things she did not want to know, after all?

Not wanting to know everything was too alien a concept to properly contemplate. Yet, Rachel could not help wishing that it was last week again, before something so horrible had happened. Lifting her head sluggishly, she gazed around her. True, there were lots of excited conversations as people shared their experiences from the afternoon's adventures, and plenty of students looked unsettled. Other than that, though, it seemed like a perfectly normal evening. People chatted. Familiars barked. Dishes clattered. Silverware clanked. Chairs squeaked along the floor.

How could such terrible things occur, and everything not be transformed?

Breaded fish and potato salad sat on her plate, but Rachel could not bring herself to eat. She had misplaced her stomach. The rest of her seemed to be there, but there was no spot inside her for food to fill. With Herculean efforts, she took a couple of sips of grape juice.

Was this how her grandfather had felt when he suffered his tragedy?

• • •

"*Psst.* Nastasia." Zoë Forrest leaned over. Her hair, short except for one long braid, was bright green. The narrow braid hung in front of her right shoulder. It had a large mottled brown and white feather stuck in it. "Even royalty are allowed to eat fish sticks with their hands."

Nastasia appeared unusually pale. Yet, she calmly ate her strips of breaded fish with a knife and fork. "In times of trauma, it is best to maintain discipline. Even when eating fish fingers."

Rachel forced herself to take another sip of grape juice. "That's a bit like what my grandfather used to say."

"Oh?" Zoë asked, tipping her chair back. "What was that?"

Rachel was so weary that she could hardly hold her fork, but she forced herself to rally. Deepening her voice to match the intonations of her grandfather's voice, she tapped first her temple and then her heart in imitation of his gestures. *"'Think now, Child. Feel later. There will be time enough to mourn when you bury the dead. If you think first and mourn later, you might not have as many dead to bury.'"*

Rachel blinked with surprise. Wasn't that how she had comported herself today, during the fight against Dr. Mordeau? In fact, wasn't that what she was doing right now? Her grandfather would have been proud of her.

The thought almost made her smile.

"That's rather creepy." Zoë made a face, scrunching up one eye.

"I approve." The princess nodded regally. "You were lucky to have known your grandfather." She pierced a piece of fish with her fork, looking thoughtful.

The princess remained quiet until Zoë started talking with Joy O'Keefe, a cheerful young woman with mouse-brown hair and a heart-shaped face. Joy recited her adventures of that afternoon, describing with great excitement how the princess saved her life when Jonah Strega tried to stab her. The others at the table listened to her recitation, enthralled.

Nastasia spoke softly to Rachel, "I have never met my grandfather...unless the older man, whom I remembered when Agent MacDannan played her music, was him. The gentleman looked a good deal like my father, but..."

"Yes?" Rachel inclined her head toward Nastasia so she could hear better.

"If my grandfather were alive, wouldn't he still be king?"

"Oh." Rachel blinked. "Maybe this man was a different relative, like a great uncle?"

"Perhaps," the princess mused. "But why could I not remember him before today? I remembered coming into a room and finding him speaking with my father. Nothing more. Why was I made to forget that? More importantly, why did Mordeau ask Valerie questions that implied that she thought my father might come from...elsewhere?"

"I don't know." Rachel forced herself to try a bite of the fish. To her surprise, it tasted good. She was even able to swallow it.

"Maybe that gentleman is your grandfather, and he is from Outside. Maybe, King of Magical Australia is a courtesy title."

"Courtesy title?"

"You know, when a father has more than one title, so he fobs one off on his son? My brother Peter is the Earl of Falconridge, but my father isn't dead. His title is Duke of Devon."

"You mean like the Prince of Wales? Wouldn't my father be a prince then?"

Rachel shrugged. "Maybe your grandfather is an even higher rank. Grand Imperial Majesty? Only, wouldn't you have had a vision of your father, if he were from Outside?"

"I only have visions the very first time I touch someone. Or they touch me," she added darkly, brushing the back of her hand across that same spot on her forehead again. "If I had a vision the first time I touched my father, as a newborn, I would not remember it."

Rachel nodded. "Even I only remember events from after I learned to speak."

Thinking of her childhood reminded her of her grandfather yet again. After he died, Rachel had taken over his tower. It was the highest part of the Old Castle, the original edifice of Gryphon Park built in 1452. At the top of the tower was a library. If she bent close to the shaft of her bristleless, she could fly her steeple-chaser straight up through the center of the spiral staircase, directly into the top chamber with its wonderful scent of old books.

Shelves covered the walls from floor to ceiling, except for the high, round windows. A cavernous fireplace kept the room warm and cheery. Wing-backed chairs provided comfortable places to curl up and read. In three small alcoves, three eternal flames burned—one before a portrait of Alfred the Great, the king who had bestowed the original land grant for Gryphon Park; one before a painting of a Victorian woman surrounded by five happy children; and one in front of a likeness of the Second Duke of Devon, the builder of the Old Castle. Those things and thousands of books made Grandfather's Library the most wonderful place in her world.

Because it was his tower, filled with his journals and his memoirs, she felt close to him there. She would curl up in one of the big chairs and pore through his thoughts and experiences, fascinated by the parts of his life that had happened before she met him. Yet, in the dozens and dozens of journals she had read, there had been no mention of a terrible tragedy.

How could he have suffered as terribly as Dr. Mordeau and Dean Moth implied and never mentioned it?

A wave of homesickness swept over her. She missed Gryphon Park. She loved their tenant farmers, the forests, the fields, the ruins on Gryphon Tor. She loved the great mansion itself, as if it were a dear friend. For her, living there was like dwelling in paradise. Yet, she was always aware that it was a paradise from which, ultimately, she would be expelled. Even from a tiny age, she had understood this. Someday, Gryphon Park would belong to her brother Peter. Upon her marriage, she would depart to join the world of her new husband.

Rachel shot a cautious glance across the dining hall at where Gaius sat at Von Dread's table, laughing with William and a perky dark-haired upperclassman whose name, Rachel recalled, was Jenny Dare. Gaius was adorably cute, but he was a farmer's son who wanted to be a scientist. If Rachel married a commoner, like Gaius, she would have to leave the aristocratic World of the Wise—the great manors and noble castles that so sang to her.

She would be cast out of paradise.

Across the room, Rachel could see the princess's siblings heading purposefully toward their table. The oldest brother, Ivan, the crown prince of Magical Australia, looked both furious and concerned. Rachel guessed that he had only just heard what befell his sister at the hands of the Transylvanian prince.

As she regarded Ivan, an unexpected sensation of mirth took hold of her. She felt too solemn to laugh, but, leaning close to the princess, she confided with a wan smile, "You realize if I married your brother Ivan. I would be your sister..." Her smile grew slightly more robust. "When he becomes king, I would outrank you."

The princess touched Rachel's arm. "I would be honored to have such a sister."

Rachel looked down shyly, pleased.

The first bite had made it down her throat. Rachel tried some of the potato salad, which she had to admit tasted quite good. Sighing, she resigned herself to eating another fish finger.

• • •

The princess's siblings descended upon her, expressing great concern. Rachel slipped from her chair and headed back to the kitchens, to give the Romanovs some room. As she refilled her glass of grape juice, she caught a glimpse of John Darling talking intently with Marta Fisher and Oonagh MacDannan, perhaps telling them of his part in the events. He looked so handsome that Rachel stumbled. Catching herself, so that she did not spill her juice all over herself for a second time in front of him, she jerked her head away. Then, thinking back three seconds, she examined him in her perfect memory, where there was no danger of being caught staring.

He leaned against a pillar, so lanky and athletic, so intelligent and so tousled. His dark hair stuck up. His suit and half-cape bore rips from his recent tussle against the geased students from Drake. Even seeing him in her memory made her knees feel wobbly.

Three years of yearning, while she watched him from afar at Yule parties and Wisecraft picnics, welled up inside her. John was a senior at the upper school, the same as Peter and Gaius.

If Gaius could like her, why not John?

Should she walk over and talk to him?

They had so many things in common. They were both expert flyers. They both wanted to protect the school and their fellow students. As of today, they had something more in common. They had both been given the brush-off by his father. Rachel imagined the two of them grumbling good-naturedly about the Agents, sharing stories about how they had been denied information. She could confess to him the secret things she had learned, tell him about her struggle with his father, share with him the strange events of the past week. How pleased

James Darling would be that his son was finally in the thick of things. How pleased John would be that she had taken him into her confidence. She pictured John's expression of amazement and concern, as he listened to her exploits, him reaching out to brush a hair from her face, his fingers lingering on her cheek.

Snapping herself out of that daydream, she glanced again at where he laughed with the two girls, his cousin Oonagh and Mr. Fisher's daughter—all three of them were children of the Six Musketeers. What would she say in front of the two older girls? What if she froze up? Made a fool of herself again?

No. Better not to talk to him now.

But she should speak to him before she made up her mind about Gaius Valiant. Quietly, she resolved that, if she could catch him alone, she would find the courage to approach him.

• • •

As Rachel returned to the table, she came face to face with the princess's eldest brother, as he departed, a tray in his hand. Ivan stood over six feet tall with dirty blond hair and very dark brown eyes. Like the princess, his robes had a golden crest on the left breast that showed an emu. He was dressed in half-academic, which meant that his sleeveless robes revealed his white shirt sleeves. While he was neither muscle-bound nor as supernaturally beautiful as his sister, he was solidly built and rather handsome. Rachel noted that he still wore his copper White Hart knife hanging from a loop at his hip.

Glancing thoughtfully at Nastasia, who sat primly eating her dinner with her knife and fork, Rachel approached the older boy. "You're Ivan Romanov."

"I am. And who are you?"

"Rachel Griffin."

"Laurel's little sister?" Ivan looked intrigued. "You helped my brother Alex and his crazy friends fight a wraith?"

"Actually, he helped me fight a wraith, but yes."

He leaned down until he was closer to her height. "That was very brave of you."

His cheerful grin dispelled some of the gloom that had fallen over her. Rachel smiled. Tilting her head to gaze up at him, she wondered what kind of a person he was. She decided the bold approach would be best.

"Are you stiff and proper like your sister?"

He looked amused. "Not in the least."

"And neither is Alex," Rachel mused. "He runs around with Abraham Van Helsing and Conan MacDannan chasing non-existent vampires. What about your sister Alexis and your mother? Are they like Nastasia?"

Ivan glanced over at where pretty, blond Alexis spoke quietly with her friends, scholarly girls wearing glasses. "Alexis is the most normal of us, I would say. Cheerful but level-headed. Mother is calm and serious...but not like Nastasia. No one is like Nastasia."

"How did Nastasia come to be the way she is?"

"We don't know." Ivan sighed and put down the tray he had been returning to the kitchen on an empty table nearby. "We think she may be overcompensating for Father's lack of..." he waved a hand, "er...decorum."

"I gather your father is..." Rachel searched for a polite word for daft. "Absentminded?"

"Absentminded? Father?" Ivan's voice rose in amazement. "Not in the least. I'd say he's the sharpest mind I know!"

"But...doesn't he confuse crocodiles with swimmers and kookaburras with spies?"

"Confuse..." Ivan made an involuntary noise, perhaps a gasp of laughter. "You think he did all that by mistake? Oh, not at all! That sort of thing is Father's..." Now Ivan was the one searching for a word. "Let's call it his sense of humor."

"So he knows he's being absolutely outrageous? Using pink Monopoly money for your national currency and all that."

"Without a doubt."

Rachel was not sure what to make of that.

The events of the afternoon played through Rachel's memory. She lowered her voice so that they would not be overheard. "Your highness, your sister is a very powerful sorceress, yet I could not help noticing that during the battle...She hesitates to act. This could lead her to harm."

Her news disturbed him, but he gave her a kind smile. "Thank you for telling me."

Rachel asked, "Can I do anything to help you keep her safe?"

"Besides coming to get me?" Ivan shrugged his shoulders, causing his sleeveless robes to ripple across his broad chest. "You could call a tutor, or a proctor. Or even a senior resident."

Rachel shook her head fiercely. Her hair went flying, numerous strands ending up in her face. "Adults are not always practical."

"Oh?"

"Either they don't believe us, or they aren't there when we need them." Rachel wrestled the stray locks away from her face.

"Hmm." He nodded with complete seriousness. "I can see how that would be a problem."

"So, we need a proper way to protect ourselves."

"Hopefully," Ivan said kindly, "these last few days will turn out to be the rocky start of what will be an otherwise extremely dull year."

"A nice hope but...Um...What if it isn't...extremely dull, I mean."

Ivan stroked his jaw, which had a rather attractive amount of five-o'clock shadow stubble on it. Finally, he nodded. "I think you are correct. She needs some training. I will speak with our siblings and arrange for some private instruction for her from Alex, Alexis, and me."

"An excellent idea," Rachel replied, pleased and the tiniest bit envious. She wished her siblings would take more of an interest in training her.

Rachel gazed up at him, examining the young man who would someday be king of a country that put kangaroos on its Olympic team and used pink Monopoly money for its currency. He did not seem as goofy as his father or as strait-laced as his sister. What kind of a man was he? Would he make a good king? Was he the sort of man she might wish to marry?

For that matter, what sort of person would she want to marry? An intriguing scientist like Gaius? An athletic sports hero like John Darling? A good-natured prince? In the best of universes, she would marry someone who lived in the world of castles and noble obligations—the world she currently inhabited and loved. She was not sure Magical Australia, with its kookaburra spies and emu heraldic crest, was such a place.

"What are your plans for after graduation?" she inquired curiously, tilting her head to one side. "What does a future king do before he takes the throne?"

"I hope to be assigned as our ambassador to America. I have my fingers crossed. My hope is that I will have a long and tedious career ahead of me before the day when I need to become king. My father is rather young—especially for a sorcerer."

"Do you want to be king?" Rachel's curiosity got the better of her. "Or is that a bit of a dodgy question to ask a crown prince? Are you forbidden from answering?"

"My wish to be king is slightly greater than my fear that I may do something horrible and destroy my kingdom. So, yes." Ivan leaned against the table, balancing his tray on his hand. "There are other choices I might have made, had I been someone else. As it is, being king sounds much more fun."

"Fun?" Rachel surprised herself by laughing with delight. "If you think that, then you are the proper man for the job." Gazing up into his handsome, animated face, she scrutinized him again. She found kindness and intelligence, and he clearly had an excellent sense of humor. After regarding him a bit longer, she concluded, "I think you will be a good king."

"I appreciate your confidence." He gave her a relaxed smile. "What are you planning to do when you graduate? Work for the Wisecraft, like your father and Sandra?"

"No. I want to be like Daring Northwest," Rachel replied fiercely, her mind's eye gazing upon the distant places she wished to visit. "Someone who searches out the hidden and forgotten things that other people overlook. It's a bit like being an Agent but with no boss."

"Interesting."

"Once you are king, should you need someone to investigate hidden and forgotten things in Magical Australia, I hope you will keep me in mind."

He nodded, solemnly. "I will."

With an over-boldness only possible to thirteen-year-olds, Rachel looked Ivan straight in the eye. "Is it true that if I married you, I would be queen someday and outrank the princess?"

Ivan must have faced overly-bold thirteen-year-olds before. He did not so much as flinch. "Yes, you would outrank my sister. Why? Would you like me to ask my father to speak to yours?"

Was he proposing?

Rachel felt a blush of heat travel up and down her body. It certainly sounded as if he were. Most likely, it was a joke. On the other hand, there were only so many girls in the World of the Wise of appropriate rank to marry a prince. As a noblewoman, the daughter of a duke, Rachel qualified. Nor was she just any aristocrat. Her family was the oldest noble line in existence, extending back over two thousand years. Griffin women had married royalty for generations, usually younger sons, but at least three of her ancestors had been queens.

She looked carefully at his face. He was smiling, but she could discern no trace of mockery. She should give him the benefit of the doubt and consider his offer carefully.

Did she want to be a queen?

As she considered the question, she suffered an epiphany. Or rather a series of epiphanies.

The first realization was that queens needed to be stately and gracious, like Rachel's oldest sister, Sandra. Rachel, on the other hand, was socially awkward. She said the wrong things, made enemies of girls who might have been friends, made people burst into tears when she had not meant to upset them.

The second was that a girl who did not enjoy public scrutiny, who wanted her accomplishments to go unnoticed, was not a good candidate for a head of state. Queens must appear in public before the gaze of thousands. The third was that people who suffered from wanderlust were not well-suited for remaining in one place, as a ruler must.

Finally, she desired wisdom, not power. She would rather grow up to be a wise adviser to the throne than to sit on it. All this took an instant, but it was a pivotal moment for her. Before it, she dwelt in the ignorance of childhood, unaware of her strengths and flaws. Afterward, she perceived herself with much greater clarity.

The effect was disturbing and yet exhilarating.

Rachel shook her head slowly. "You appear to be a very upstanding young man, Prince Ivan, and I would love to be the princess's older sister. But I fear that I am unsuited to be queen.

"But don't be sad." She patted the light-brown hairs along his nicely-formed forearm. "Girls like handsome, powerful boys. You won't have any trouble finding a wife."

"Ah..." His dark eyes danced with good-humor. "Kind of you to look out for me."

As she turned away, Rachel's eyes fell on her sister Laurel, who stood far across the dining hall waving her arms energetically, as she recited a story to an audience of admiring boys. Laurel was much more mature than she had been at seven, but she still had the same wild look in her huge, dark eyes. Unlike Rachel, she dressed in the subfusc style, with a well-tailored white blouse, a split ribbon like a narrow tie, a black skirt, and a half-cape falling from her shoulders. With her velvet neck ribbons flying every which way and her half-cape askew, she looked both tempestuous and utterly adorable. At home, the farm boys who worked their tenant farms had a special whistle they used to alert each other when she was coming, so that they could line up along the fences and watch her walk past.

"You could marry my sister Laurel." Rachel leaned toward Ivan. "Then I would still be Nastasia's sister by marriage, but I would not outrank her, which would be perfect."

Ivan glanced over at Rachel's sister. A bright, roguish grin lit his face, making him even more handsome. "Laurel's really cute. I'll run the idea by her and see what she thinks."

Rachel smiled, feeling very pleased. How wonderful it would be if her sister became a princess. Even if Laurel used to pull her hair and torture her stuffed penguin, Rachel loved her dearly.

• • •

Heading to her seat, she saw John Darling leaning over to adjust his shoe, his foot resting on a chair. He looked so charming and tousled. All her past affection for him came rushing back.

He was alone.

Heart hammering, Rachel approached him. She considered her words carefully, though that did not stop them from escaping her mouth in one quick rush.

"I must say, Mr. Darling, I am rather disappointed with your father," she said with sad humor. "I thought if anyone would understand what we were up against here and secretly help us, it would be him...but, alas, he did not." She sighed dramatically. "Does he tell you anything at home? Or is he as exasperating as my father, who tells me nothing at all?"

John Darling straightened and regarded her for an uncomfortably long time. When he spoke, his voice reverberated loudly throughout the entire dining hall.

"Yeah, I've heard the bad things you and your dragon boyfriend said about my dad," he glowered. "Why don't you and your friends just shut up?"

Chapter 11:
Rachel Gets Valiant

Rachel took a stumbling step backwards.

"I don't care if you're disappointed in him!" John Darling pointed a finger at her. "But I do care if you insult him in front of my sister Wendy."

"But...I didn't..."

"It's pretty crappy," his voice cracked with fury, "if your father's nice to my dad's face, and then talks trash behind his back."

Rachel shrank back, horrified. Unfamiliar eyes stared at her from all directions, trapping her like a bizarre curiosity on display in a broken shop window. A strange buzzing in her ears threatened to drown out John Darling's voice. She tried to swallow, to clear her hearing, but fear and embarrassment had swollen her throat closed.

Surely this had to be a nightmare.

She pinched her forearm, hoping to discover that this was a dream. The pinch stung.

"Leave my little sister alone!" a soprano voice rang out like a trumpet.

A tall figured swooped down on her, squeezing her tightly. Long dark hair covered Rachel's face, getting in her mouth. Rachel coughed and struggled to breathe, but she was grateful that her sister's presence shielded her from the eyes of the crowd.

It broke the mesmerizing terror.

Ordinary sound came rushing back.

Only then did the strangeness of the situation register. Laurel was defending her? Laurel? Her "wild child" sister's avowed purpose in life was "to stir up chaos to liven up the dull lives of their parents." Usually, Laurel was the person from whom Rachel needed defending.

School was definitely a strange place.

"Okay, Griffin. Whatever." John shrugged. "I'll leave her alone. Just make her do the same to my sister."

John Darling stalked off. Rachel's sister hugged her tightly. Laurel Griffin hugged tighter than anyone else Rachel knew. She wondered if that cracking sensation were her ribs.

Their brother Peter appeared and laid a protective hand on Rachel's shoulder. He arched an aristocratic eyebrow and frowned at the still-gawking onlookers with a severity possible only to future dukes. "As you were, everyone. Nothing to see here."

Quickly, the diners looked away, returning to their meals. Relief flooded through Rachel, who was thankful to no longer be the center of attention. Some of the wobbliness left her legs. She smiled gratefully at him.

Peter gave her an affectionate nod. Slender and bookish, his features were a perfect mix of their mother's striking Asian features and their father's handsome looks. It had always been assumed, due to his short stature, that he had inherited his height from their tiny mother. Over this last summer, however, he had grown four inches.

Perhaps he would attain their father's height after all.

Peter peered down at her. "Why was Dash yelling at you, Rach?"

"Dash?"

"Fastest boy in our class." Peter shrugged. "No one wants to call another boy Darling."

"He thought I had insulted his father," Rachel's voice sounded unnaturally high in her ears, "b-but it wasn't I. It was a friend of mine, and even then, this friend didn't mean any harm. He's Unwary. He doesn't understand what Agent Darling did for us all."

"Ah." Peter blinked. "Well, that doesn't sound too bad. I'm sure it can be sorted out."

Laurel leaned down and peered into Rachel's face from two inches away. "I heard you crashed through a window."

"I saved Mr. Fisher." Rachel stepped backward until she could make out her sister's face.

She felt so young and small surrounded by her siblings. The idea that she was old enough to face the terrible things that had recently occurred suddenly seemed laughable. A desire seized her to throw herself into their arms and burst into tears.

"You shouldn't do such dangerous things." Peter put a protective hand on her shoulder, frowning furiously at her. "You should have called a proctor."

"There wasn't time," Rachel objected.

Peter straightened and massaged his temples. He sighed. "I am proud to have such a brave sister. But...please, be more careful."

Rachel stared at him. She did not answer. She did not even nod. To do so would be to imply that she had agreed. But *careful* implied *stay away from danger.* If she did not move toward danger, how could she stop the bad things from occurring?

Peter peered at her closely. "You're sure you're all right?"

She straightened and gave him a firm nod. "I am."

"Good." He ruffled her hair and whispered hoarsely, "Keep it that way."

Peter strode off in pursuit of John Darling. The moment their brother was gone, Laurel leaned over and regarded Rachel with a bright, conspiratorial smile.

"Is Gaius Valiant your boyfriend?" Laurel teased, grinning as if Rachel were still three.

"Um..." Rachel glanced over at the central table by the fountain where Gaius sat chatting with William in an animated fashion and looking stomach-churningly cute. She thought of the moment on the steps of Dare Hall, when he had kissed her. "Um...Kind of?"

"Kind of?" Laurel asked, her interest piqued.

"He asked me to be his girlfriend. But I said 'no.'"

"Really?" Laurel's eyes bulged. She recovered quickly, her surprise turning to a self-satisfied grin. "You mean he fancies you? Trust my little sister to pick a cute one." She paused and then leaned even closer, whispering, "Does Peter know?"

Rachel shook her head solemnly. "I doubt he would approve."

Laurel smirked, her dark eyes gleaming with amusement. "If you change your mind and say 'yes,' I'd like to be there when Peter finds out." She kissed Rachel's forehead and left.

Rachel blinked after her in astonishment. Was she mistaken, or did Laurel *approve* of her being Gaius Valiant's girlfriend? Laurel? Who never approved of anything? Rachel had assumed her entire family would be against the idea.

Her sister's support made her feel unexpectedly good, as if a tiny star blazed inside her.

• • •

Rachel returned to where her friends were engaged in energetic conversations; however, their words failed to penetrate the whirlwind of her thoughts. Her mind reviewed her conversation with Ivan, John Darling, and Laurel. Contemplating this kept her thoughts from returning to the horrors they had faced today.

A few minutes ago, the knowledge that the boy she had adored for the last three years had the nickname Dash would have thrilled her. Now, she felt empty. John Darling was a horrid boy.

What a rotter!

With young Darling in disgrace, the floodgates restraining her feelings for Gaius Valiant burst asunder. A tidal wave of longing swept over her. Gaius was suddenly more impressive and much less like second best. The nagging little voice warning her that she still might discover someone she preferred more was drowned in these floodwaters. She could not imagine ever liking any boy more than she currently liked Gaius Valiant.

And Laurel called Gaius a "cute one"!

Rachel glanced toward the center of the dining hall. Gaius sat on the side of Dread's table nearer to the fountain. He tilted his chair back, reached behind him, filled his cup from the rushing water, rocked forward again, and drank, without so much as turning his head.

Impetuously, Rachel shot to her feet and raced across the room. As she stopped beside Gaius's shoulder, he looked up with obvious surprise. He had taken his hair out of its short ponytail, and drops from the spray of the fountain glistened in his silky chestnut locks.

"Hello, Rachel Griffin." Gaius had to speak somewhat loudly to be heard over the rush of the water. He gave her a most engaging grin. "What can I do for you?"

Rachel clasped her hands behind her and went up on her toes. She was so short that she was hardly taller than he was even when he was seated. Her heart beat so rapidly that she felt it might lift her body off the ground. She leaned toward him.

Gaius's pupils widened as if mesmerized.

Before she could speak, however, a young man interrupted them. He was slender and blond, his gray eyes filled with regret. Rachel recognized him instantly. He was the boy who had stopped her broom in mid-air, causing her to tumble across the gravel. The nurses had healed her bruises, but she flinched as she remembered her previous discomfort.

"Excuse me," he said, "I've come to apologize."

"Ah, Mark Williams. Man of many failings," Gaius drawled, tipping his chair back. "Exactly what are you apologizing for today?"

"Stopping this young woman's broom. When I was possess-ed."

"Wait." Gaius leaned forward, looking tremendously amused. His chair legs struck the floor with a *clunk*. "You're the one who stopped her in mid-air? You? Mark Williams the..." He did not finish his statement. From his expression, Rachel sus-pected that he had planned to say something he deemed inappropriate to repeat in front of young ladies.

"Yes. That was me," the young man replied, shame-faced.

"It's all right," Rachel said, eager for him to be gone. Her heart still raced, but the delay was causing her courage to ebb. "You were geased. Please. Don't think of it again."

"Whoa!" Gaius held up his hand. "Not so quickly. I rather think a crime of this severity demands a penalty, don't you, Mr. Williams? As penance for your assault on this lovely young lady, you should share with the rest of us the story of how ably this freshman recovered from your attack. And by the rest of us, I mean..."

Rising to his feet, Gaius pointed his wand over his shoulder. Silver sparkles with a scent like a winter's day burst from its sapphire tip. The leaping sprays of the fountain turned to ice. The cessation of the roar of rushing water was almost as jarring as a loud noise. Heads turned in their direction. Jumping onto his chair, Gaius struck his glass with a spoon. A chiming noise reverberated across the dining hall. People looked at him.

"Attention! Attention," he called. "Mr. Marcus Williams has something to tell us."

Gaius jumped down and gestured toward Mr. Williams, making a "come along now" motion with his hands. Nervously, the other young man climbed onto the chair. In a tight voice that grew louder, Mark Williams told the story of how he had stalled Miss Griffin's broom in mid-air with a cantrip; how she had fallen, called for her broom, somersaulted, bounded up again, caught her broom, flipped onto it, and flown away.

He finished with, "Oh, and before she left, she relieved me of my wand."

"A tiny freshman grabbed a wand from a big guy like you... how?" Gaius asked loudly.

Mark Williams's face fell. "I was paralyzed."

"Who paralyzed you?" Gaius waved a hand airily. "A symphony of adult sorcerers standing nearby with oboe and saxophone?"

"No. Miss Griffin whistled."

"A freshman paralyzed you—without an instrument or a wand—while she was falling through mid-air? She paralyzed you *by whistling*? Then, she somersaulted, grabbed her broom, snatched your wand, and flew away?"

Murmurs of astonishment rippled through the crowd.

"Yeah. And when she got back on her broom—" Mark Williams cried, his eyes great with enthusiasm. "You should have seen her fly! It was amazing! She's a broom goddess."

All eyes in the dining hall focused on Rachel again. She glanced rapidly left and right, but there was nowhere to hide. At that moment, she would have done extraordinary things to gain possession of John Darling's tarn helm and turn invisible.

Gaius cupped his hands around his mouth. "Three cheers for the Broom Goddess."

"Hip, hip, hurray!" shouted the entire gathered company of students in the dining hall.

Rachel stood immobilized, her face as hot as the interior of the sun. Her vision blurred. She counted this as a good thing. It kept her from seeing the sea of faces turning toward her again—strangers' faces. Nonetheless, her head was growing light. Air did not seem to be reaching her lungs. She wondered abstractly if she would faint.

Gaius's smile saved her. His warm eyes glowed with encouragement and delight. He was proud of her. That knowledge steadied her like an anchor against the hurricane. If public acknowledgement of her prowess on a broom pleased this boy she so admired, then maybe it was not so terrible. With this thought comforting her, she was able to draw a single ragged breath.

At the head of the table, Von Dread clapped dryly. That small gesture brought her back to herself. Regaining her aplomb, Rachel curtsied. With a flourish, she reached into her pocket and presented the wands she had picked up during the fight. Sheepishly, Mr. Williams took his, a length of birch and brass tipped with a ruby. He held it up for all to see.

A fury of applause and shouts of "Broom Goddess! Broom Goddess!" rocked the dining hall. Rachel held her breath. Eventually, the fervor died down, and Mark Williams departed. Gaius sat back down in his chair. Rachel held out the rest of the wands she had collected, lengths of wood and precious metals with gems set into the tips. "What should I do with these?"

"Where are they from?" he asked.

"Drake students who were geased. I collected them during the fight."

"Give them to Vlad. He'll know who they belong to." Gaius gestured at Von Dread, who regarded her with the slightest hint of approval on his otherwise impassive face.

She stepped around Gaius and held out the wands with only a hint of uncertainty. "Mr. Von Dread, these belong to students from your hall."

Dread stood and accepted them. "Thank you, Miss Griffin. I will see they are returned."

Vladimir Von Dread was tremendously imposing and so handsome it almost hurt to look at him, like staring directly at the sun. But he seemed almost like a normal human being as he nodded graciously. She felt secretly pleased to be the object of his calm attention.

Dread sat again, and Rachel went back to Gaius, determined to speak to him before they could be interrupted again. She hovered beside his shoulder.

"That offer you made me?" she spoke rapidly. "Is it still open?"

"Which offer? Oh, if you mean..." Gaius half stood up. "Yes!"

"I accept."

"That's great! You won't be sorry!"

They shone enormous smiles at each other. Rachel wondered if he would kiss her or even hug her. He had carried her when they were running from the meteor that Dean Moth had conjured to strike Mordeau the dragon, and he had swung her around afterward, in joyous adulation. Both those occasions, however, had been fleeting. They had never hugged properly, not the kind of embrace in which his arms surrounded her, and she leaned against him.

She waited, but he did not rise. He just gave her a knee-liquefying smile. She ached to touch his shoulder, or run her fingers through his glistening chestnut hair, but she was too shy.

Still, she had a boyfriend!

The thought made her giddy.

"Rachel! Rachel!" The princess and a gaggle of their girlfriends poured around her, exclaiming over Mark Williams's tale. Joy hugged her exuberantly. Zoë gave her shoulder a friendly punch. Kitten Fabian, one of Rachel's three roommates, and their dorm-mate Brunhilda Winters both gave her big smiles. The princess stood by graciously, nodding her approval.

"Your courage becomes you, Rachel," Nastasia said simply.

"That was amazing!" Joy cried. "All I did was nearly get stabbed!"

"I had hoped to be the Broom Goddess," sighed Brunhilda, who preferred to be called Hildy. The cheerful, blond cheerleader from California was a newcomer to the World of the Wise. She had fallen in love with brooms, however, during her first flying class. She flew very well for a beginner. "But if it had to be anyone else, then it should be you: our teachy-weachy. Or is it teachy-witchy?"

When Gaius and Von Dread looked at her blankly, Zoë explained in her light New Zealand accent, "Rachel's Mr. Chanson's student assistant."

"Ah." Dread nodded in approval. "The P.E. teacher."

Rising again, Dread stood before the princess. "I would like to thank you and your companions. It has been told to me that you took steps to save the lives of my comrades and myself. If there is any service I may perform on your behalf, please do not hesitate to ask."

"I only did as duty dictated, Mr. Von Dread."

"Nonetheless, Miss Romanov, the debt remains. I shall honor it." Dread clasped his hands behind his back. He cleared his throat. "Earlier today. Did you have a vision of me?"

"I did, Mr. Von Dread," Nastasia replied stiffly, brushing the same spot on her forehead she had been touching all evening. "But I am not inclined to share it with you, as you would thereby benefit from your flagrant violation of my father's orders."

"Ah. I see." He bowed and returned to his seat.

The others stared at this exchange, puzzled, but Rachel played back her memory of Von Dread's rescue of Nastasia and Joy from the moat waters flooding the summoning vault beneath Drake Hall. He had removed his right glove before he cast the cantrip to wake the water and turn it into a sentient creature. As he reached around the princess to grab Joy, her memory showed that the back of his bare hand had trailed across the princess's forehead.

That would have been enough to cause Nastasia to have one of her strange visions that apparently sent her into other worlds. It also would have caused her to disobey her father's order never to touch the naked skin of Vladimir Von Dread.

Kitten Fabian peered at the frozen fountain. She was a short girl, fierce and sweet, with straight brown hair and a mess of freckles. The tiny Lion who had warned Rachel that Valerie needed help—the Lion that Gaius had seen as bigger than the universe—was Kitten's familiar.

"May I ask you what you did to the fountain?" Kitten asked Gaius. Her lovely English accent sounded delightfully familiar to Rachel's ears.

"Froze it." Gaius tipped his chair back and tapped on the ice. A frozen arc of spray fell to the ground with a chime-like tinkling. "So people could hear over the noise. It'll melt."

"Jolly good." Kitten touched the frozen fountain experimentally. More ice cascaded to the ground with more chime-like tinkling. "Rather smashing of you, really."

Nastasia took Rachel's arm. "Are you coming with us?"

Rachel wanted to stay with Gaius, but if she went with the girls, perhaps Nastasia would share her vision. She sympathized with the princess's desire not to let the Bavarian prince profit from his perfidy. Yet, she yearned to know who Von Dread had been before he came to Earth.

With a sigh, Rachel let the princess lead her away. The other girls followed.

It saddened her to leave without a kiss goodbye. She had not even had a chance to introduce her new boyfriend to her friends. She threw him a lingering glance goodbye.

Gaius winked at her.

Chapter 12:
The Beggar King

The night was chilly. The first stars were rising. A breeze sent the early autumn leaves rustling across the gravel paths as the girls crossed the bridge that arched over the reflecting lake and headed across the lawns to visit Valerie Hunt.

The infirmary, a brick building with white marble columns, stood between the eastern dorms and the gymnasium. The floors were green marble veined with black. Blue tiles, painted with silver arcane symbols, covered the walls. Overhead, puffy white clouds decorated a domed ceiling of periwinkle blue. From it hung a clockwork orrery. Each heavenly body rotated independently, allowing the nurse to alter the celestial influences that had been imbued by alchemy into the tiny sun and planets, so as to create, within the chamber, the date and time most propitious for the healing needed. In the center of the chamber, a fountain gurgled.

Flame-orange curtains separated the cots from one another. Four beds were in use, the curtains around them pulled closed. Rachel pushed one curtain back with her broom. Inside, Misty Lark lay asleep, curled around her tiny unicorn. Siggy's friend and sparring buddy, Seth Peregrine, sat beside her in a chair, head lolled to one side. His mouth hung open, snoring. Rachel quickly let the curtain fall shut.

"Siggy?" she called softly.

"Over here," he answered from behind another curtain.

Rachel and the other girls from Dare Hall crowded around Valerie's bed, where she rested, recovering from the severe blood loss she had suffered earlier in the day when she had tried to break the geas she was under by sheer effort of will. She sat holding Sigfried's hand, looking wan but resolved. Her Norwegian elk hound, Payback, lay stretched across the bed on her other side. The dog's black nose was pressed against Valerie's cheek.

A breeze from the open window stirred the chimes that hung over the bed. Their light tones rang out cheerfully. Tiny green sparkles formed around them and drifted toward the patient. Above the headboard hovered a glass ball that burned with green health-giving fire. In the corner, Siggy sat beside a tall, antique mirror with a golden hue—the dean's thinking glass.

"I offered to kill Strega, but she said 'no,'" pouted Siggy. Under his breath, he muttered, "I shouldn't have asked her first."

Valerie flashed them a brave smile. She held Siggy's hand in both of hers. "Can't have you going off to the slammer. A jailbird boyfriend would be most embarrassing for the daughter of a cop. Besides, didn't Lucky already burn his face off? I hear he's at the Healing Halls of Asclepius in New York. They've sent Agents to arrest him."

"What happened?" asked Joy.

"Dr. Mordeau's assistant, Jonah Strega, hurt her," Rachel said quickly, before Siggy or the princess could blurt out anything more distressing.

Valerie shot her a grateful glance.

"You mean the same guy who nearly stabbed me?" Joy cried. "What a creep! The princess saved me. She's the most amazing girl in the whole universe." She grabbed Nastasia's arm, beaming. The princess looked pained, but she did not push Joy away. Joy continued, "If it weren't for the princess, birds would not sing, and fireflies would not glow."

"Please," the princess murmured, dismayed, "such exaggeration is not becoming."

Joy ignored her and continued praising.

Siggy fetched some more chairs. The girls found places around the bed to put them and made way for Beauregard, the princess's Tasmanian tiger familiar, who had stalked up beside her. They all chatted cheerfully, describing their day. Valerie listened but did not say much. She seemed grateful for the distraction but also weary. Rachel smiled and chatted, but her thoughts were on Gaius and her new status as a *girlfriend*.

Part of her wanted to shout this out loud, telling everyone. Why have friends, if she could not share such important news? But she held back. The princess had expressed such disapproval of Gaius Valiant that Rachel felt reluctant to tell her.

Eventually, Kitten and Hildy took their leave, and Zoë went to visit with Scott and Misty, who were now awake. That left Rachel, Siggy, Nastasia, Valerie, and Joy.

The moment the others were gone, Rachel leaned forward, her eyes shining. "Valerie, what you did to that beastly Eunice, that was excellent!"

"Oh, you saw that, did you? I hated finding out that I was the snitch, but we'd already guessed that." Valerie chuckled maliciously. She picked up her camera, adjusted the lens, and snapped a picture of the orrery above them. "It felt so good to bring Eunice down a few pegs. She's a huge bully. Have you seen the way she treats her little sister? She's such a bi—" Valerie's voice cut off as the nurse walked by.

"Her behavior toward Magdalene has been deplorable!" Nastasia agreed firmly. "I hope the authorities find some appropriate penalty."

Valerie adjusted her camera again and snapped another picture of the ceiling. "We're just the Inner Circle here now, right? Sigfried's been telling me everything. Have we learned anything new?"

Ah. A good opening to ask about the thing she left Gaius in hopes of hearing.

"Von Dread touched the princess while he was rescuing her." Rachel traced with her toe the swirls of the pattern on the section of Valerie's comforter that hung down over the side of the bed. "He wanted to know about her vision, but she wouldn't tell him."

All eyes turned to Nastasia, who sat petting her Tasmanian tiger.

"Can you tell us what you saw?" Sigfried asked.

"Or show us?" Valerie gestured at the thinking glass with the hand that held her camera. Beside her, Payback's curly tail thumped. She stroked the dog's head and ears with her free hand. "Siggy tried to use this one. But neither of us knows the attunement spell. But you used it earlier, Nastasia. Attunement spells last till midnight, right?"

"I believe so," said the princess.

Rising, Nastasia moved to the antique mirror. Beauregard rose and stood protectively at her side. Nastasia placed her hand against the thinking glass's surface, and a picture formed. Portions were blurry. The perspective looked wrong. Still, the main scene was clear, except during the moment when the flash from Valerie's camera reflected off the glass.

Knights in brightly-colored armor and spangled-robed magicians gathered in a semi-circle on a hilltop, facing a domed temple or shrine. Each knight wore armor of a single color that shone like a gem: ruby, amethyst, emerald—except for one who wore a golden helmet along with his sapphire armor. Over this, they wore long surcoats emblazoned with heraldic symbols. The knights and their steeds were gathered in two groups that eyed each other warily. A huge green ogre, carrying a tree trunk for a club, stood between the two groups.

To the left of the knights stood the magicians. Tall sorcerers in starry robes and pointed hats leaned on their jewel-tipped staffs. In their midst, three enchantresses in gowns of rich brocade and velvet stood together, holding the rail of a chariot pulled by winged serpents. One wore white, one red, one black.

To the right of the knights was a group of rag-tag men, with vests and baggy pants, wide brimmed hats and gold earrings. A few of them were mounted. They surrounded a flag, a wide strip of blue above a wide strip of green with a red, sixteen-spoked wheel in the center. Checking the library of her memory, Rachel recalled that this was the flag of the Romani people.

At the very top of the hill, in front of the domed shrine, four beings on horseback faced the gathered crowd—a gaunt figure carrying a balance on a black horse; a fierce soldier with a sword on a red horse; a kingly figure, wearing a seven-pointed crown of gold set with seven gems that twinkled like stars and carrying a bow, on a white horse; and a hooded figure with a scythe on a horse that was the pale color of the deathly ill.

"*A measly gathering to oppose the might of the Four Horsemen,*" taunted the figure in the crown. "*A few magicians, half a dozen paladins, a handful of Saracen knights, one ogre and...Oh, and a spattering of gypsies. All alone. Without their king. What's the matter? Was he too afraid to face us?"*

"He will be here!" shouted one of the mounted Romani. To Rachel's delight, this man rode a piebald Gypsy Vanner—one of the three breeds of horses her family bred at Gryphon Park. *The enormous black and white horse pranced, tossing its long mane and lifting its feathered feet.*

"We do not need the likes of the Beggar King!" called a tall, bareheaded knight, who looked to be Arabian. His armor was a shiny peacock blue. His surcoat and shield were quartered blue and silver. "Our might is more than enough to defeat you."

"That's the Swan King to you!" the gypsy shouted back.

The crowned figure laughed disdainfully. "No mortal can defeat the power of the Septentrion Crown. Kneel before me."

The picture in the thinking glass froze.

"This is what I saw when I first arrived," the princess said.

Valerie's flash lit the mirror again. Then, she turned it off and took two shots without it. "I hope at least one of these will come out. Taking pictures of mirrors is always tricky."

"Look how strong that knight carrying the anvil is, and how fast the ruby-colored one moves! Like the Flash or something!" Sigfried watched the thinking glass intently. He grinned a huge, eager grin. "These guys are amazing! They're like medieval superheroes."

"That enchantress in red." Rachel leaned forward and tapped the glass. "Doesn't she rather look like Wanda Zukov?"

"Who? Jerk-what?" Sigfried moved his head back and forth, squinting at the picture.

"Wanda Zukov," Rachel repeated. "A fellow freshman. She was my sparring partner at the Knights of Walpurgis meeting last night. She looks like that woman, only younger."

Joy pointed with great excitement at the knight with the golden helmet. "Oh! He looks familiar, doesn't he, Rachel!"

Rachel peered closer. The knight's blue armor shone like sapphires. Over it, he wore a long white surcoat. A red lower-case 't' ran the length of the garment, with the horizontal line crossing his chest. His white shield bore the same device. He was a handsome man with blue-black hair and very blue eyes. Rachel gasped.

It was Mr. Chanson, the gym teacher.

"It's my boss!" she cried. "What's he doing there?"

"I wonder if more people from the school are here somewhere?" Valerie scrutinized the scene. "People we just haven't met yet."

"Where's Dread?" Siggy asked, peering at the scene.

Rachel searched the gathered company of knights and magicians. "He's not there."

"How could you tell?" Valerie asked, amused, snapping yet another picture of the mirror. "Some of them have their face plates down."

Rachel could not say how she knew, yet she was absolutely certain.

"Maybe he looked different," Sigfried offered. "Maybe he's one of those horsemen. The skeleton? Who knows what it would look like if it had skin."

Nastasia turned her attention back to the mirror. "This is what happened next."

A shadow appeared before the rag-tag gypsies and congealed, forming a tall figure in black armor that shone like a dark mirror. His faceplate was of the same polished black as the rest of his armor. Had he not been moving, he might have been taken for a marble statue. A huge cloak of sable swan feathers billowed from his shoulders. A sword with a serpent for a hilt hung at his hip. Atop his winged helmet, he wore a crown of stars.

The gypsies cheered.

The black armored figure spread his arms and raised them, palms upward. All around, mounds formed in the hillside. They broke open to reveal automatons of stone, like statues of men at arms, that rose from the earth and stood at attention, increasing the defenders against the Four Horsemen by a hundred-fold.

A strange shiver, both wonderful and terrible, spread through Rachel. It was a sensation she had felt once before—on the commons, after the evil scarab brooch had been destroyed—the first time her gaze had met that of the prince of Bavaria.

Her mouth went dry. "That's him."

"We don't know that," the princess replied firmly. "Anything could be in that suit. And Miss Hunt is correct. The faces of quite a few of these people were obscured."

"Could be him," Valerie shrugged, beginning to turn the crank on the back of her camera. "The late queen of Bavaria was a gypsy. Dread's mother, I mean.

"Can you hold it here a moment?" she added. "I am out of film." Valerie rolled her eyes. "I feel like a character in an historical drama. Who runs out of film nowadays? Who even uses film?" She opened the back of the camera and held up the spent roll. "Do you know how much these babies cost to develop? Boy, do I miss my digital Canon."

Sigfried patted her hand sympathetically. "There, there."

Joy giggled, "Maybe Dread's the big green ogre."

"Wouldn't be surprised," Valerie quipped. "He *is* big and hulking."

"Nah, the ogre's not Dread. Dread is cool!" Siggy insisted. "He is the epitome of cool! You should have seen him destroy that jewelry thing that tried to kill you! When you and he are married, Nastasia, I hope you invite me by for royal skeet shooting, or whatever he does for fun."

"I do not plan to marry him, Mr. Smith," Nastasia replied, "unless it is my family's will."

Joy giggled again. "You're perfect for each other! All dignified and absolutely stunning."

"I would prefer not to marry a man who knowingly forced me to disobey my father." Nastasia said coldly. "I care not how 'cool' he is in other areas."

Rachel stared at the Swan King, with crown of stars and his billowing cloak of black swan feathers. "That's him."

"We can't know that," scoffed the princess. Her voice faltered. "Now, here's...where things became...uncomfortable."

At first Rachel thought that the scene was still frozen. Then she noticed that, while everyone else was immobile, the Four Horsemen still moved. *The hooded figure on the pale horse trotted forward, gazing directly toward them. He came right up, until he seemed to be looking out of the mirror.*

The view pivoted, as if the princess had glanced over her shoulder to see what the skeleton was looking at. Rachel gasped again. Farther down the hill was most beautiful building she had ever seen. It was only visible for an instant, but Rachel froze it in her memory and examined it in detail.

It was built of granite, but it was not square and solid, like most stone buildings. Instead, a wonder of arches, buttresses and spires spread behind twin towers that rose into the sky. There was not merely one statue of human forms with bird wings—like the one she had found in the forest; the one that had been wingless when she visited it the second time, with no evidence that its wings had ever existed—*but dozens of such statues adorned the walls, along with gargoyles and men with bare heads and belted robes. And the windows! Were they made of gems? They shone with brilliant color—blues, reds, greens—sparkling in the noonday sun.*

A tingle ran the length of Rachel's entire body. She could not explain the feeling the sight evoked in her. It was like catching a glimpse of the sky through an opening in heavy clouds, only to discover that, instead of an empty expanse of blue, a city hung there—a celestial city more glorious than any upon the face of the earth. Such a city would have buildings like this.

The skeleton stared out from the mirror. "What have we here?" *asked the creaky voice that spoke from the tongueless skull.* "A child. An interloper. A Wayfarer, perhaps? Let us discover what she knows."

The princess raised her hand. The golden hue returned to the thinking glass.

"What happened?" Valerie cried, her camera pointed at the mirror.

"He probed my mind," stated the princess. "It was...quite disturbing. I could feel his cold presence inside my head. My childhood, moments by the river with the koalas when I was a toddler; meals with my family, including one I had forgotten where my father had us all make crowns from tinfoil and kiwis—

the fruit, not the bird—and wear them at the table; the many classes in dance, music, comportment; the recent events here at the school. He looked at it all."

"That's horrid!" Rachel's breath caught. The notion of someone rifling through her memory left her feeling nauseous. It would be like telling everything to her father and the Agents and being told nothing in return—only a thousand times worse. "He learned all our secrets!"

"By which you mean: he knows nothing of worth," the princess stated flatly.

"But...of course, we know important things!" cried Rachel. "We know about that horrid Raven who robs Lucky of speech. We know that people here come from different worlds. We know that Egg is actually from Outside. We know..." she waved her hands, "a great deal of things!"

The princess shrugged. "That is of little consequence. Death—that was how he thought of himself. I sensed a few of his thoughts while he was examining mine—came to the conclusion that the figures in that particular place where I was were dream figments of people who had already left, and he destroyed them. But I suppose he was right, since the real Mr. Von Dread, Miss Zukov, and Mr. Chanson are here."

"Destroyed them?" Valerie's brow drew together. "I don't understand."

"There is no point in trying," the princess said glumly, "nothing makes sense."

"But—" The idea of not striving to make sense of things, not constantly searching for a pattern among the scattered pieces, shocked Rachel.

She could not think of anything else to say.

Rachel turned and stared through the darkened window. Outside, beyond the reflecting lake, the silhouette of the many bell towers and spires of Roanoke Hall rose against the nearly black sky. She could make out figures moving that seemed taller than they should have been.

The night lit up. A starburst, a phoenix, a winged horse, and a bird-of-paradise, each composed of thousands of shining, gold-white flecks, hovered in mid-air like fireworks. These shapes, along with the street-lamps that normally lit the campus, made the lawns bright.

Rachel ducked her head around the chimes and leaned out the open window, her lips parted in delight. Charmed as she was, the phenomenon was familiar to her. Her parents used will-o-wisps sculptures to illuminate evening parties and entertain at Yule. To Siggy and Valerie, however, this display was entirely unexpected. They stared slack-jawed out the window.

The figures on the commons were now visible. Rachel recognized the dean, a few tutors, and Maverick Badger, the head of campus security, along with some adults she did not know. To one side, a group of older girls and boys stood gawking at something beyond her line of sight.

The bell on the door rang. Salome Iscariot glided into the building, her hips swaying provocatively. She threw a spunky grin over her shoulder at three older boys, who had turned away from the crowd to ogle her instead. Letting the door swing shut, she crossed the infirmary to check on her best friend Valerie.

"Salome, what's going on over there?" Joy pointed at the crowd of students outside.

"Parents are arriving," Salome drawled, as she sauntered forward, hips swaying, "to check on their precious wittle ones after the big fighty-poo."

"Since when are parents gawk-worthy?" Valerie asked. "Most kids avoid adults the way perps avoid cops." She and Sigfried gave each other a knowing look.

Stopping beside Siggy, Salome leaned forward, eager to impart her juicy news. "There's one couple out there you have to see to believe! He's tall and gorgeous and ever-so-refined—looks a little like Merlin Thunderhawk from the *James Darling, Agent* comics. You know, the guy who appears and vanishes like Batman? And she's even cuter...tiny as a butterfly, but oh, so well-endowed—she makes me look positively flat!" Salome looked down at her own generous endowments, as if astonished that such a thing could be. "I've seen giant slaloms that are less curvy!"

Rachel sprinted toward the door, swinging her broom as she ran.

"Where are you going?" Joy cried.

Over her shoulder, Rachel shouted back, "Those are my parents!"

• • •

The Duke and Duchess of Devon stood on the grass talking with Laurel and Peter. Ambrose Griffin was an extraordinarily handsome, extremely tall man with dark hair and steady hazel eyes. Implacable and calm, he did not seem the least bit disturbed by the gawking young co-eds who had gathered to admire the famous Agent, but then, Rachel had seldom seen anything disturb him.

Rachel's mother was less unflappable. She hid shyly behind her husband's elbow. Her straight dark hair was held back with a clip, though some had escaped and fallen forward into her pixy-like face. She had up-tilted Asian eyes that regarded the world with a gentle, merry intelligence. Her lips were pressed slightly together, giving the impression that she was perpetually struggling not to laugh.

Rachel ran to her. Her mother might be tiny by adult standards, but she was still taller than Rachel. As the two embraced, her warmth encircled her daughter like a soft, sweet-smelling cloud, providing a safe haven against the storms of evil teachers and crazy murderers, not to mention the chill of the night air. Rachel hugged her tightly, trying not to jab her with Vroomie.

It felt wonderful to just be a little girl again. Rachel had not realized, until this moment, what terrible burdens her new life entailed.

Laurel tugged on Rachel's hair. "Look it's our sister, the Broom Goddess!"

"Are you going out for Track and Broom?" Peter asked. "If so, between you and Dash, we might actually beat Vermont E. and the Tennessee Institute of Alchemy this year."

"I don't much care for sports," Rachel murmured into her mother's shoulder. She pulled back and looked at her mother's face. "What are you doing here?"

Her mother's eyes crinkled kindly when she smiled. "Meeting of the Brotherhood of the White Hart. James Darling called us to help with the emergency."

Rachel looked around and realized that there were only about a dozen adults there.

"The King of Magical Australia is in the Brotherhood of the White Hart?" asked her brother Peter.

Her mother nodded again. Of course, thought Rachel, his son was a member, too.

Her father laid a hand on her shoulder. "I hear you've had quite an adventure. Wasn't it just yesterday that I instructed you to avoid trouble?"

Rachel looked up at him. He looked so steady, so strong. Her anger at him drained away. "Would you like to hear about what happened?"

"Yes, indeed," her father replied solemnly.

"First things first." Rachel's mother beamed at her youngest daughter, touching her cheek lightly. "You finally achieved your dream of coming to Roanoke. How are you finding it? Are you enjoying your studies? Is your dorm room acceptable? Is the food to your liking?"

"Yes! Everything is fantastic!" Rachel cried. "Classes, roommates, meals!" There was no point in telling her family that she would have preferred to be in Dee Hall. They would just be hurt. She tipped her head, thinking. "Except that there is no kimchi."

"Ugh!" Laurel cried. "How can you like that stuff? It's like eating pickled dirty socks! Even the smell is vile! Lack of kimchi is one of the highlights of this place!"

Peter laid a hand on Rachel's shoulder. "Don't worry. I keep a tub of it in my room. I usually bring some to dinner. The Americans react strangely if I bring it to breakfast. You are welcome to come by, Rach, and get some."

"Thank you, Peter."

The door to the infirmary burst open. With uncharacteristic enthusiasm, Nastasia sprinted across the lawn, her face beaming. "Father! You're all right!"

Nearby, a smiling man stood beside Ivan Romanov. The gentleman was good-looking in a rugged sort of way, with sandy hair, a mass of crow's feet around his keen and laughing eyes, and straight teeth. He wore a bright pink and blue Hawaiian shirt, a pair of green plaid Bermuda shorts, and long orange socks decorated with wombats. When Nastasia reached him, he scooped her up and hugged her tightly. For once, she did not look pained by the familiarity.

Watching the man carefully, Rachel decided that Ivan was right about his father. The King of Magical Australia did not look like a man who would mistake an emu for a track star. Rather, he looked like the kind of man who understood completely the consequences of putting his country on the pink Monopoly money standard and who found it very amusing indeed.

How exceedingly strange.

"I am, indeed. Awake even." Her father placed his daughter on the ground. "That silly old Lightbringer couldn't get the best of me."

Nastasia smiled gratefully. She looked so pretty, so endearing, that Rachel's heart swelled. Ivan must have agreed that his sister looked sweet, for he was gazing at her with an expression of fondness and pride.

Rachel regarded him, the young man who thought it would be fun to be king someday. Had she made a mistake, picking the scientist boy instead of the prince? She could have been the princess's sister. Then, they certainly would have still been friends twenty years from now, just like Scarlett MacDannan and James Darling. She would so love for that to come true for her, too.

No. Ivan might be cheerful and amusing, but Gaius was infinitely intriguing. It was the avidness with which Gaius approached life, the interest that he showed in things, that so captivated her. It reminded her of her own desire to know *everything*.

But maybe she still could be Nastasia's sister-in-law. Rachel could not help noticing how Ivan's gaze strayed to rest admiringly on Laurel, who stood beside their father, smiling happily—an oddity in itself, as Laurel seldom saw eye-to-eye with their parents on anything.

"Just a moment." Rachel excused herself briefly from her parents. She ran over to where Ivan stood with a slight smile, as he watched his father and his sister. Tugging on his sleeve, she whispered, "Psst! Are you going to ask her?"

Ivan regarded Laurel, who watched them curiously, her half cape curled up over her head as she peeked at them from under the dark poplin. Rachel beckoned her sister to join them.

Ivan bowed to Laurel with princely grace. "Miss Griffin, may I ask my parents to speak to yours?"

Laurel blushed and giggled girlishly, but she held her head high. "I would be honored."

The Prince of Magical Australia nodded, his own cheeks growing pink. Rachel jumped up and down in delight. *Laurel really was going to be a princess.*

Ivan glanced from his father to Rachel's father. He muttered under his breath, "Better wait for Mother. If Father handles it, one of us might end up betrothed to an emu."

Blushing even more, Laurel took Rachel's hand firmly and led her back to their waiting parents. Partway there, she paused and looked at Ivan over her shoulder, fluttering her dark eyelashes. Ivan watched her, entirely captivated. Laurel pursed her lips and blew him a kiss.

Returning to her parents, Rachel pulled her father aside. He leaned down, inclining his ear toward her. She whispered, "Have they caught Egg?"

"Egg?" Her unflappable father showed no change in expression.

Rachel rolled her eyes. "I *saw* him. I am the one who lied to him to save Valerie's life. The Wisecraft is telling people, right? Warning them about Mortimer Egg?"

"We cannot reveal the name of suspects during an investigation, honey."

"*But…!*" Rachel exploded. "What if he comes to kill someone else? Why aren't they circulating his photo? Urging people to report sightings of him?"

"I am sorry, Rachel. I cannot discuss this matter."

"If someone else dies," Rachel cried fiercely, "it will be the Wisecraft's fault!"

Her father nodded, a hint of weariness in his steady hazel eyes. He knelt down, bringing himself closer to his daughter in height. "I can't tell you anything about that, but I can tell you one thing: an expert in dreams is coming from New Zealand—to help the tutors and proctors protect the campus from attacks from that quarter—such as what happened to your friend the princess when the creature called the Lightbringer visited her dreams."

"Thank you, Father." Rachel rested her forehead on his shoulder. Sternly, she reminded herself that it was not her father's fault that he had to obey his superiors. It was foolish to be too angry. "I'm ready to tell you what happened."

Her father gestured her mother over. Opening her mouth, Rachel recited everything she could remember, starting with the appearance of Mr. Egg on the dock. After the first minute, her father's eyes glazed over. He blinked twice.

"Too much information, too quickly. Tell your mother. She'll tell me later, more slowly." Kissing Rachel on her forehead, he went to speak with Peter and Laurel.

Rachel turned to her mother. Her words sped up, until she spoke extremely rapidly, the way she and her mother did when they talked exclusively to each other. Ellen Griffin listened avidly. Rachel told her every pertinent detail from Mortimer Egg's appearance until the defeat of Dr. Mordeau. She did not say anything about Siggy's amulet or what came after.

When she finished, her mother hugged her. She explained that she and Rachel's father would be joining the tutors' efforts to repair Drake Hall. A work like that required many experienced sorcerers. Rachel hugged her one last time.

Halfway back to the infirmary, she called to her mother, "Oh, and I have a boyfriend!"

Only she shouted it too loudly. The look of horror on the face of her usually unflappable father was almost comical. Glancing over her shoulder, she saw Laurel speaking rapidly, her expression a riot of delight. Peter's expression, on the other hand—like a massive thunderstorm gathering over a once-lazy river—went in a quarter-second from dismay to outrage.

Rachel ran.

Chapter 13:
Dread Versus Valiant

"Wait, Rachel!" Laurel sprinted after her, her straight dark hair flying behind her like a banner. "Daddy wants to talk to you. He's horribly angry. I had no idea he'd take it so hard."

"Sorry. Busy," Rachel shouted over her shoulder. "Must go."

She jumped on her steeplechaser and shot off into the night.

Rachel soared high into the sky and then dove toward the infirmary. Ducking low over the broom, she shot through an open window. Her shoulder brushed the chime that hung there, setting it jingling and sending out a cloud of green sparkles.

Landing on an unoccupied bed, she watched through the window as Laurel walked back to their parents. She waited, her body tense, for her father to come after her. He did not. When she saw him walk toward Drake Hall with the other adults, Rachel let out a breath of relief.

She also felt unexpectedly disappointed.

Hopping off the bed, she grabbed her broom and ran to where Valerie and Siggy still sat.

"The princess and I are going to Roanoke Hall to practice." Joy rose to her feet. "After how lousy we were today, we figure we need all the practice we can get! Wanna come?"

An unpleasant feeling of fear and dismay spread through Rachel. She was eager to practice. If her friends watched her efforts, however, they could not but feel superior to her. She was not nearly as good as them. Her best attempt at a wind had pushed the possessed muskrat a few feet. Siggy's had thrown it from the belfry. If she went, she would be deliberately exposing herself to humiliation. She shook her head, and Joy departed with a shrug.

Rachel sat down on a chair next to Siggy and said hello to a sleepy Valerie. As she smiled at the other girl, she caught sight of a flash of gold and red outside. Lucky flew in the open window, wobbling unsteadily. He flopped onto the floor with a squishy *thud*, the sides of his furry golden belly bloated, like a serpent that had swallowed a mouse.

"Soooo stuffed. Ate too many chickens!" Lucky rested his head on Sigfried's lap. He wiggled his extremely long, flame-red whiskers. "Sorry, Boss. Don't know what came over me."

Valerie snapped a picture of him.

"What did you eat?" Siggy asked.

"Chickens. Doves. A goat, I think."

"A goat?" Valerie perked up.

"They were in these convenient 'to go' boxes."

"Those are called cages." Rachel rolled her eyes.

"Cages, where?" Valerie asked. "Oh, wait! Don't tell me. I don't want to end up as an accessory to your crime."

"Behind Drake Hall," Rachel explained. "He has been eating the sacrificial animals."

"Oh...well." Valerie blinked. She lowered her camera and put the lens cap on again "They were just going to kill them anyway, right?"

"Yeah. Better eaten than wasted, I say." Lucky's eyelids drooped. He started to snore.

"That's what happens to them most of the time, anyway. They are eaten by some supernatural beast." Rachel sighed. "I hope you don't get in trouble, Siggy."

Sigfried shrugged. "For what? My familiar eating livestock? Nothing gold can't fix."

"Gold!" Lucky's eyes flew open. He moaned as if having a tooth pulled. "Tell me you aren't going to give away our precious, round, shiny babies for chickens I already ate!"

"You have to stop doing that," chided Sigfried. "They weren't our chickens."

"I can't help it. I can't think when I can't think."

"That does make sense," Valerie stated wryly.

"I am going to blast that blasted Raven!" Siggy announced savagely. "I'm tired of that stupid bird messing with Lucky."

"Isn't it the Doom of Worlds?" cautioned Valerie, as she leaned back against her pillows. "Blasting it might not be an easy job."

"Is it? I can't remember." Siggy shrugged. "I can't be expected to remember every little thing we find out. That's Griffin's job."

Rachel gawked. Everything about the Raven frightened and fascinated her. She could not imagine not paying attention—especially to details that had to do with *the safety of the whole world*. The notion of not paying attention to it was almost as disturbing as Nastasia's comment about not bothering to make sense of the clues.

What was wrong with her friends?

Didn't they love learning? As clue came together with clue, forming a mental puzzle, didn't their hearts burn within them with joy? She could not understand them. It made her feel as if there were a gaping chasm between herself and them, a gulf she did not know how to bridge.

Gazing out the window, Rachel recalled the beauty of sunlight glinting off lavender in bloom; the majesty of a storm-filled sky; the hush of a deep forest of tall trees. She thought of foals gamboling across a newly-mowed field; of children laughing as they chased each other beside rushing waters; of scholars in the vast libraries of mankind, spellbound by the knowledge they were discovering. She pictured the pyramids of Egypt, the Great Wall of China, the vast cities of Europe, Asia, America. All this, and so much more, would be lost if the world ended.

She could not bear to lose even a single lavender sprig, a single spotted filly. How it was that others did not see what she saw, how it was that they did not burn with the same longing to protect all that was so sacred and beautiful, so unique, she did not understand.

It was a very lonely business, this wanting to save the world. She felt lost, misunderstood. If only someone else believed her.

"Do you even know any blasting spells?" Valerie asked Siggy.

"Oh, rub that in my face, will you?" Siggy crossed his arms in mock outrage.

Rising, Valerie knelt on her bed and peered out the window. Payback leapt to her feet and bounded up beside her mistress, panting happily. Valerie gave her an affectionate nuzzle and then asked, "What's going on out there?"

Rachel looked. A large number of people had gathered in front of Drake Hall.

"They're repairing the dormitory," Rachel replied.

"You mean the place where the fight between our dean and a dragon caused an earthquake and split the stone?" Valerie asked, amazed. "Magic can fix that?"

"Yes, it can." Rachel smiled. "Watch."

In the light of the will-o-wisp sculptures, they could see the tutors, proctors, and parents who had gathered along with some older students in front of Drake Hall. Even at this distance—Dee and Raleigh lay between the infirmary and Drake—Rachel could make out her father and Vladimir Von Dread. The two of them towered over everybody else.

It took the group a long time to get everyone into position, as they moved to circle the august granite building. Rachel and her friends leaned against the windowsill, waiting. A cool breeze ruffled their hair. Rachel gazed up at the phoenix and the bird-of-paradise in the sky. The tail of the latter trailed across the campus. A few of the will-o-wisps danced in and out of formation, flickering like fireflies. It was beautiful and hypnotic.

Eventually, the gathered company of sorcerers was ready. They grasped hands, spread out, and then dropped their arms. Someone called out, possibly the dean. They all raised their hands, preparing. Valerie grabbed her camera again, yanked off the lens cap, and began snapping pictures.

"*Legaralqué!*" they shouted in unison.

They were too far away for Rachel to make out what they were saying, but she knew what cantrip they were using. With a resounding *clap*, the crack in the stone snapped closed. The granite wall was whole again. No crack remained.

They chanted again. This time, the break in the stone of the moat healed itself. The water from the stream that fed the moat had been pouring into the chasm in the earth and flooding the basement of the dorm. Now, it began to flow through the moat again. The adults then broke into groups and went inside to repair damage to internal walls.

"Wow!" Valerie snapped one last picture. "Why don't they do repairs this way after storms and earthquakes? That would speed up disaster recovery more than ten thousand percent."

"The Unwary would notice the magic," Rachel said. "Though, occasionally, we do sneak in and do repairs. Whenever you heard reports that some major undertaking turned out not to be as difficult as first predicted? That was probably us."

"But...why? Why hide? Why not tell everyone?" Valerie plopped back down onto the bed. Payback turned in a circle twice and then put her head in her mistress's lap.

Rachel shrugged. "That's the way it's done."

"That's stupid," Sigfried complained over his shoulder. "What if we start telling people?"

"The Wisecraft sends out Obscurers to alter their memories." Rachel shivered.

"My mother's a reporter. What if I had her put it on the evening news?" Valerie asked. "Telling millions of people all at once."

"Numbers don't matter," Rachel replied. "Back in the last century, there was that astronaut who married a genie. It was reported all over the mundane press. Nowadays, the Unwary remember the events as if they had occurred on a television show."

"You're kidding, right?" Valerie stared at her. "You're...not kidding."

Rachel shook her head. "And if you kept on trying to tell the Unwary, you'd be turned over to the Grand Inquisitor."

"Is that bad?"

"Very bad." Rachel shuddered. "Do you remember being under the *Spell of True Recitation*, where we blurted out everything? When the Grand Inquisitor questions you, he does it while you are under the influence of that spell, and he asks you about *everything*. If you have so much as stolen a cucumber sandwich off a tea tray, that's it for you. He claps you in irons."

Sigfried was still leaning on the windowsill, staring at the happenings over at Drake Hall.

"Just that?" Sigfried objected. "Aren't they going to blast something? Boring. Maybe a skunk would liven things up."

"Flaming skunk." Lucky perked up. "That was fun. Stank though."

"What did we do last time?" Sigfried raised his hand, fingertips pressed together, forming a beak with his fingers.

"Sigfried," Valerie warned, straightening up. "Don't!"

Sigfried's brow furrowed in concentration.

"I can see it." Lucky announced, his eyes tracking something Rachel could not follow.

Rachel opened her mouth, intending to speak words of caution—to act as a breakwater against the riptide of the headstrong boy. She paused. Two nights ago, here in the infirmary, she had sworn to herself that she would stick by Sigfried—that she would help him to feel less alone in the world. Living up to that vow meant proving to him that she was on his side—come disaster or detention. She closed her mouth on her objections.

Instead, she leaned forward, her eyes glittering. "Go for it!"

Siggy brought his hand down, fingers still pressed together. "*Muria.*"

"Incoming!" shouted Lucky, batting at an invisible something with the silver palm of his taloned hand.

A black animal with a long white stripe running the length of its body waddled across the green and black floor. Valerie shrieked, but this did not stop her from snapping a picture.

"Aw." She lowered her camera and tilted her head to one side, gazing down at the fluffy black and white creature. "It's cute!"

The striped tail lifted. Then, the stench hit. The pungent odor stung Rachel's eyes.

"Get it out of here!" Valerie shouted. "Pronto!"

Siggy cast a *ti* cantrip and gestured. The skunk floated into the air and out the window. Terrified, the creature fired its foul-smelling spray.

"Now, Lucky!" Sigfried commanded.

It took Lucky two tries to get off the floor. He was so stuffed that his huge tummy dragged him backward. Finally, he made it to the window sill. Before he slid down again, he opened his mouth and breathed. A plume of fire shot out, igniting the creature. The skunk let out a horrible squeal. Siggy floated it up the pathway away from the infirmary, flaming spray trailing behind it like a comet's tail.

"Look at it burn!" Siggy leaned on the windowsill directing the skunky inferno and grinning like a fiend. "Wicked!"

"The poor thing!" Valerie cried.

"It's not a proper skunk. It's conjured," Rachel pointed out. "It only appears real."

"It is absolutely brilliant!" Sigfried laughed.

Valerie plugged her nose and hid her eyes with her other hand. "I *so* don't know you."

The fiery skunk continued to wobble up the gravel path, shedding a bright glare. As it passed the forest glade between Dee and Raleigh Halls, Vladimir Von Dread leaned out from behind a tree and blasted the skunk with a bolt of lightning from his wand.

The black and white creature dissolved into mist. The flaming comet's tail behind it briefly burned in mid-air, and then it sputtered and vanished. Von Dread calmly disappeared behind the tree again, returning to whatever he had been doing.

"Aw! He blasted my skunk!" Siggy cried. "Though he's as cool as a cucumber, isn't he? As cool as the iceberg that took out the Titanic. Maybe I could get him to blast the Raven!"

"What's he up to back there?" Rachel asked curiously, wondering what Siggy could see with his amulet.

Sigfried sat back down in his chair. "He's talking to that kid with the ponytail."

"Truly!" Rachel jerked as if she had been electrocuted. "What are they saying?"

"His name is Gaius, right?" Valerie asked. "You two are friends or something?"

Rachel's cheeks turned pink. "He's my boyfriend."

"I knew it!" Valerie smirked. "You said he wasn't this morning."

"He hadn't asked me yet."

Valerie grinned a huge grin and gave Rachel a thumbs up.

"Well, he's not going to be your boyfriend for long," Sigfried announced. "Dread is ordering him to dump you."

"*What?*" Rachel jumped to her feet again. "Wh-why?"

"Dread's saying: '*...affection for a child of her young age is unbecoming in a sixteen-year-old, no matter how high her station. You will inform her that you cannot court her.*'"

A lump formed in Rachel's throat the size of one of the moons of Mars. And after she had defied her family for him. Ah, well. It had been nice having a boyfriend for the hour it lasted. At least, she had not embarrassed herself by telling Nastasia.

"Oh, ho!" Sigfried's eyebrows flew upward. "Valiant just replied: '*I will not.*'"

"He defied Dread?" Rachel cried in astonishment.

Valerie gave Rachel a second thumbs up. "This Valiant guy must *like* you."

Sigfried continued, "Now Dread's saying, '*If you persist in romantically pursuing a thirteen-year-old, you will be thrown out of the Knights.*'"

Rachel recalled how proud Gaius had been of having been asked to join the Knights of Walpurgis. The lump in her throat grew larger, perhaps to the size of Earth's moon.

"Ooh! Valiant's cheeky!" Sigfried crowed. "He laughed! He told Dread, '*Good luck finding someone who can defeat me.*'"

"Oh, my!" Rachel grabbed the headboard, her nails biting into the oak. A strange giddy sensation was taking hold of her, as if her blood had been replaced with wine.

She asked breathlessly, "What's happening now?"

"Dread's pointing his wand." Sigfried reported excitedly. "A stream of blue sparkles hit Valiant. He's not moving—standing motionless with a dumb look on his face. Okay, just kidding about the dumb look. Dread is saying, '*I leave you here to contemplate the matter.*'"

Through the window, Rachel could see Vladimir Von Dread
tucking his wand back into his sleeve as he stalked across the
lawn toward Roanoke Hall.

Gaius had stood up for her.

Her heart expanded, until it encompassed the whole solar
system. She thought she had cared about Gaius before. That had
been nothing to what she felt now. When the dean had
questioned her, she had chosen to be loyal to him, even though
defying Dean Moth had been the hardest thing she had ever
done. Now, he had paid her back. He had stood up to the person
who he had admitted, under the *Spell of True Recitation*, he
admired more than any other.

"So, Gaius told his boss about asking you out, and his boss
just turned on him? Bummer," said Valerie.

"Valiant seemed surprised that Dread knew." Siggy stroked
Lucky's fluffy, flame-red mane. "I don't think he's the one who
told him."

"How'd he find out?" Rachel cried. "We only just…"

She suddenly recalled the two tall silhouettes towering
above the others gathering to repair Drake Hall.

Her father.

The floor dropped out from beneath her feet. It took a
moment before she realized that this had not actually happened.
She just felt as if it had. Her father had not bothered to come
after her to talk to her.

Instead, he had gone to Dread.

"I should do something." Rachel's fingers were white where
she grasped the headboard. She stared toward the darkened
trees, behind which stood the frozen Gaius. "I should help."

"You should do something," agreed Valerie. "A girl's gotta
help her man."

"I'll free him."

Leaping on her broom, she ducked low and shot through an
open window toward the trees. The glowing phoenix and starburst had moved to hover over Drake Hall. Shadows gathered
here thick and dark. Luckily, Rachel had been in this forest
earlier that afternoon, when she helped the living porcelain doll

bring tiny Magdalene Chase to the infirmary. Thinking back, she searched her memory, noting the location of every tree. Using the technique she used for gauging distances when flying, she rapidly built a model of the forest in her mind. Relying on this, she darted around the near-invisible trunks as easily as if it had been daytime.

As she grew closer to the place from which Von Dread had emerged, she slowed. She wanted to approach without Gaius seeing her. It pleased her to set him free, but she preferred nobody know. A boy mysteriously breaking free of a spell was impressive. A boy being freed by his girlfriend—his much younger freshman girlfriend—might seem embarrassing. Beside, she did not necessarily want him to know she had overheard his argument with Dread.

Drake Hall had been repaired. Once freed, he could go back to his dorm. She imagined Von Dread returning to find the younger boy there before him. The thought made her feel smug.

Gaius stood in a small clearing, as motionless as the first time she had kissed him. His back was to her. She thought of slipping off her steeplechaser and kissing him again. Instead, she landed behind a large oak and pressed her back to the rough bark. Peering around quickly, she cast the Word of Ending.

"*Obé!*"

Gaius started. He looked around wildly. Rachel ducked behind the oak. Pulling out his wand, Gaius ran through the trees. As he raced toward Roanoke Hall, he repeatedly touched the sapphire tip of his fulgurator's wand to his chest. Each time, a silvery sheen coated his body. Rachel recognized this as the mirror spell he had used to protect her earlier that afternoon.

Jumping on her steeplechaser, she slipped through the forest after him. She hung back, not wanting to reveal her presence. Gaius sprinted across the lawn. He caught up with Von Dread just as the older boy entered the main hall.

Gaius pointed his wand at him. Rachel tensed. Was he going to attack his friend? Freeze him, perhaps?

"Vladimir!" he shouted.

The older boy turned. Gaius fired off a stream of blue sparkles. Rachel's heart skipped a beat. Gaius had not attacked Von Dread from behind, even though that would have given him a huge advantage. A happy, bubbly feeling spread through her.

Young Mr. Valiant was chivalrous.

Von Dread parried the spell with a *taflu* cantrip. He trained his own wand on the younger boy. "We cannot duel out here. The tutors will interfere. Come inside."

Gaius nodded, and the two young men disappeared into Roanoke Hall. Rachel flew up to the great oak doors, which bore the Roanoke heraldry of a seven-branched tree growing from a floating island with wings. She performed the cantrip for opening. One door wiggled slightly. The other did not even budge. Grinding her teeth in annoyance, she zipped sideways, flying from one great window to another, looking for Gaius.

By the time she found them, the two boys had left the dining hall. They were running down a hallway, firing spells at each other. Scarlet and blue sparks danced in the air, scattered from hexes that ricocheted off walls and staircases. Trumpet flourishes and the trill of a flute rang out, accompanying the enchantments. Silver glints dashed against a landscape painting, leaving a coat of frost over the picturesque pumpkins. Twisting vines and glowing golden bands that had failed to ensnare their target littered the hallway.

Rachel pressed her forehead and palm against the cold window pane and gazed in wonder. The two young men fought as Thaumaturges did, using their fulgurator's wands to cast spells stored in the gems on the wand's tips. Rachel was more familiar with Enchanters, who used musical instruments for their magic—as the young vampire-hunters from Dare Hall had, during the fight against the wraith. The Thaumaturge method allowed for much more magic to be cast much more quickly. She winced as she thought of how long it must have taken them to painstakingly cast and store the spellwork they currently were expending at high speed.

Most of their spells were enchantments, which burst forth from the wands with sparkling lights and notes of music. Some, however, were cantrips, which were invisible until they struck. Yet, both young men parried them. Rachel wondered how they knew the cantrips were coming.

Nastasia, Joy, and Sigfried's roommate, Ian MacDannan, a mischievous, round-faced, red-haired boy with freckles, emerged from a classroom. They forgot their practicing and stood wide-eyed, gawking at the duel. Ian ventured too close and found himself constricted by a golden Glepnir bond. Emerging from another classroom, Salome Iscariot whooped with delight. She cheered Gaius on, jumping up and down in her excitement.

They stood like fencers, facing each other sideways. Dread shot and parried calmly, performing his task with extreme precision. His broad shoulders and towering height gave a distinct impression of power and grace. Gaius fought back fearlessly, firing off enchantments one after another. He spent less time parrying, preferring to rely on his mirror spells to repel Von Dread's spells.

Gaius was short for his age, wiry and slight, but he was holding his own, fierce concentration blazing in his eyes. Rachel's heart beat with the motion of his wand arm, a feeling of glee running through her body.

He was doing this for her.

The two kept firing. Spells volleyed back and forth. Then, a swirl of red mist broke through Gaius's mirror spell, striking him without bouncing back. Mist billowed around him, until she could no longer see him. When it cleared, he was gone. In his place stood a four-legged animal with a thick coat of curly white wool.

Gaius Valiant was a sheep.

Chapter 14:
Weeping over Sheep

Gaius's wand clattered to the ground. Dread pointed his own wand at it. Lightning crackled through the air, striking the length of teak and brass. The other students jumped back, alarmed. Ian's red hair stood up from his head. The sheep *baaed* in terror and scampered backward into a wall. Dread crossed the intervening distance and stepped on the now-burnt wand, crushing the sapphire at the tip—the repository of all the stored spells—beneath the heel of his boot.

Then he strode away without a backward glance.

Flying to the nearest door, Rachel leapt from her broom and wrestled it open. Once inside, she jumped on Vroomie and flew at top speed, whipping around corners until she came to where the princess and the others had gathered around the sheep. She soared over the heads of the other students and leapt off. The sheep had backed into a corner, the white showing around its terrified eyes. Rachel knelt before it and spoke to Gaius, looking into its face.

There was no recognition, no sign of intelligence. Terror seized her, her heart swelling and contracting painfully. Had Dread *killed* Gaius?

• • •

Rachel's friends helped her get the sheep to the infirmary. Nurse Moth met them. She was a nervous, quick, bird-like woman with a large nose, dressed in the white habit and wimple of the nuns of the Order of Asclepius. *Tsking* over the sheep, she pulled out her flute and played a song. Green sparkles came from her instrument and danced around the sheep, but Gaius did not revert to his normal form. Frowning, she tried several others, to no effect. Shaking her head, she departed for the back room.

Rachel sat with her arm around the terrified animal, her fingers sinking into its soft, fluffy fleece. Twice it bolted, stepping on her with sharp hooves. Her left hand and her right thigh throbbed. Her whole body shook. She gazed after the departing nurse with confusion and growing fear. Why had the nurse not been able to restore him to his proper shape?

"Psst," she whispered, waving Nastasia over to where she knelt, hugging the sheep.

"Yes, Rachel?"

"Your magic school book—the one that opens to any textbook you desire," Rachel asked fervently. "Can we try it? Maybe it will open to the spell that will fix Gaius."

The princess frowned disapprovingly. "We could not cast such a complicated spell."

"We don't need to," insisted Rachel. "We can show it to Nurse Moth."

"I think not," was the princess's only reply.

If Nastasia had taken out a knife and cut her, it could not have hurt as much as this. The pain was so great, her body went numb. Rachel forced her numb body to breathe. Couldn't Nastasia see how important Gaius was to her?

No, of course she could not. The princess thought Gaius was some wicked boy they should avoid, and no one had explained that he was fighting over Rachel.

She pressed her face into the sheep's wooly fleece, trying to smother her fear. What if he stayed this way? What if the process of changing the sheep brain back into a human brain went awry, and he never recovered his intelligence? He had been such a bright boy—that had been one of the things she had found most attractive about him. She knew of people who had been damaged by spells and never recovered.

Oh, please let him get better!

Rachel stayed there, hugging the frightened beast until nurses arrived to take him to the Halls of Healing in New York City. As the visiting nurses departed, floating the terrified, bawling animal through the air, Rachel asked them if Gaius would be okay.

She received no answer.

• • •

The next hour passed in a blur. Rachel was aware of her friends talking and laughing in voices made overly-excited by the day's events. But she could not seem to participate in the conversation. Everything around her seemed muted and far away. She wanted to go to sleep, but she was too tired to drag herself to bed. Eventually, a conversation caught her attention.

"The assistant dean called me to his office," the princess informed Sigfried and Rachel as they finally walked back to Dare Hall, Lucky zigzagging beside them. It was nearly midnight, way after their normal ten o'clock curfew. The night had grown quite chilly.

"Assistant dean?" asked Siggy, "What is that? Is it related to Jimmy Dean? Do we have an office here just for sausages?"

"I'd like a sausage," chimed Lucky. "I'd even be willing to eat a sausage officer."

"Mr. Gideon, our true history tutor," Nastasia explained patiently. "He is one of the two assistant deans. He explained this to us in class. Several times."

"Did he?" Siggy yawned. "I wasn't listening. What does he teach again? True Snoring?"

The princess ignored him. "Mr. Gideon informed me that we are to report for detention tomorrow afternoon. Apparently, since we board here, detention can be held on weekends."

"Detention?" Rachel's eyelids were barely open. "For what?" Only after she spoke did she remember the broken thinking glass in the belfry of the Watch Tower and the skunk.

Sigfried shrugged, uninterested. "Adults are always punishing you for something."

"For disobeying the dean and leaving the infirmary, of course," the princess replied.

The fog cleared from Rachel's mind. "What? They're giving us detention for *saving the world?*"

"We did not save the world," Nastasia scoffed. Her hand rested on the back of her Tasmanian tiger. "Exaggeration is unbecoming. We saved a few lives. This is no small thing, though, especially to those whom we helped."

"But..." Rachel tripped over the uneven gravel. Her arms windmilled in an effort to keep her balance. Righting herself, she cried, "We're fighting *Veltdammerung*! Dr. Mordeau said her boss was from Outside. And there are all these new magics, and your visions, and the Omen of the Doom of Worlds Raven. You don't think the whole world is at risk?"

"True, there is disturbing magic from outside the world, but I see no evidence of Veltdammerung," the princess replied firmly. "They were bad people, certainly, but, like our proctors, I grow tired of the claim that every rogue is the Morthbrood come again."

"But Dr. Mordeau *said*—" Rachel began.

Siggy interrupted her. "The Velt-who-ha now?"

"Veltdammerung." Rachel sighed patiently. "It's an organization that consisted of the Terrible Five and their servants. By their servants, I mean several groups: Unseelie monsters, thugs, cultists, supernatural monstrosities, and an ancient organization of witches and warlocks who practice black magic called the Morthbrood."

"The Horrible Who?" Siggy took an apple from his pocket and tossed it in the air. He took three huge bites and then threw the rest to Lucky, who downed it in a single gulp.

"Not a sausage or an officer," crowed Lucky, "but still tasty!"

"We don't eat people," Sigfried reminded him.

"Oh! Right!" agreed Lucky.

"The Terrible Five," repeated Rachel. "The evil sorcerers who terrorized the world when my parents were in college? You know, the guys that Mr. Fisher told you about?"

"Oh yeah, that guy who wore nothing but his own hair Mr. Fisher beat, and some other guys who fought some other unimportant people."

"Sigfried, you shouldn't go around saying that. You upset Wendy Darling."

"Who?"

"Wendy...You know, the girl in our dorm? The girl whose father we talked to today?"

"We talked to someone's father?" Siggy said blithely. "When?"

"Argh!!!" Rachel grabbed her head. "Your memory cannot actually be this faulty!"

Sigfried shrugged. "What do I care about these things?"

"We can't save the world, if we aren't tracking the clues."

"We were not saving the world," Nastasia repeated again, firmly. "As to detention, justice requires that we be reprimanded for disobedience—no matter what the justification. Our later actions may have been commendable. But we disobeyed and must face the consequences."

They reached the doors of Dare Hall and separated. Sigfried headed across the foyer for the arch that led to the boys' side. Rachel and the princess climbed the sweeping staircase to their room on the fourth floor. Kitten and Astrid, their roommates, were already asleep. Rachel tried to get undressed without summoning the will-o-wisps out of their nighthoods. With her new familiar sense, she could feel her cat Mistletoe curled up under the bed. She thought of climbing under there and getting him—it would be nice, to have something warm and cuddly to hug—but the effort involved was too great.

As she fumbled in the semi-darkness, trying to find her nightgown, Nastasia approached. She pressed something into Rachel's hand "I picked this up earlier. You might wish to return it."

Rachel felt a hard, narrow object. The odor of charred wood assailed her. Moving to the hallway, she held the thing in the faint triangle of light that came through the partially-opened door. In her hands lay a burnt, blackened fulgurator's wand, with only the jagged base of a sapphire tip.

Rachel's stomach did a triple flip. She touched the scorched wood tentatively, recalling how Gaius had used it to cast the mirror spell that had allowed her to defeat Remus Starkadder, earlier that very afternoon. She gazed at it and thought of how much work he must have put into maintaining it, of how difficult it must have been for a poor farm boy to afford such an object, and of what a good duelist he had become. She recalled how, during the Knights of Walpurgis meeting the night before, Gaius had handily defeated the boasting braggart, Seymour Almeida.

If he did turn back into a boy, the loss of his wand was going to break his heart.

A wave of nausea spread through her. Smelling the smoky odor of the damaged wood struck her much harder than even seeing the sheep had. Tossing the charred wand onto her bunk, she ran to the bathroom and threw up into the toilet.

• • •

She sat on the stall floor, her arms wrapped around her head and her forehead resting on her knees. Her skin was clammy. The square tiles were cold and hard beneath her backside, but she felt too weak to rise.

Her father had set this in motion. He had spoken to Von Dread, and it had led to this.

Her father.

Two days ago, he had been the center of her world. Then, he had deserted her. In the midst of a crisis of loyalty, she had chosen Gaius as her guiding star. And now, her father may have killed—or at least erased—the charming, outgoing, brilliant boy who had been Gaius Valiant.

There had been no recognition in the eyes of the sheep, no intelligence as human beings used the word. Had her father's actions destroyed the only person entirely on her side, the boy she loved?

She loved him.

The realization jolted her, as thoroughly as if she had put her hand into the path of the lightning bolt that had destroyed Gaius's wand. If she had not loved him before, she surely loved him now.

She sat there, on the cold bathroom floor. Her hand throbbed painfully where the sheep's hard hoof had trampled it. Sorrow and wrath warred within her, trampling her heart in their battle. She had never felt emotions like this before. It was like getting caught in a thunderstorm, after having only ever encountered mild drizzles. She did not know how to weather such a tempest.

Of one thing, however, she was deadly certain. If Gaius died—if he was not restored to his brilliant, life-loving self—she would never speak to her father again. Never. Ever. Not if she lived to be a thousand.

She loved Gaius. Loved him so much that she wanted to spend the rest of her life with him. She wanted to marry him. As she wept on the bathroom floor, their future unfolded before her—almost like a vision. He worked as a sorcerer-scientist for William Locke's Ouroboros Industries. She was a librarian-adventurer, visiting unknown places and coming home to write books about them. Their six children—destined to be five great sorcerers and a librarian—were all students here at Roanoke Academy.

What a happy life they might have lived.

Instead, the future was dark and bleak. She had nothing to look forward to but decades of living alone and childless, perhaps with a pet sheep.

• • •

Hours went by. She remained on the cold tile floor. Sometimes, she sat curled in near delirium. Sometimes, she wept.

She wished she were at home, curled up in her room within the safety of the pink curtains of her canopy bed—rather than sitting on the cold floor of a public bathroom. She wished she could hug her stuffed animals: Mr. Muffin, Splashdown the Dolphin, and Torture the Penguin. When she was little, Laurel used to grab this last toy and run about the house shouting, "Torture the penguin! Torture the penguin." Tiny Rachel had thought that was its name. The moniker had stuck.

She wished Sandra were nearby. Neither Peter nor Laurel would sympathize with her agony. Peter would be stuffy about her liking a boy—he still thought she was eight, and Laurel was unsympathetic in general, though she could be very good company when one was cheerful.

Sandra, however, would understand. Rachel was sure of it. She imagined her older sister kneeling beside her, her dark eyes alight with love. Sandra would gaze at her with concern, the same way she had the time she had found Rachel stretched out on the floor by the servant's staircase, cradling her broken arm, her steeplechaser impaled in the grandfather clock. This was the second time that Rachel failed to make this turn and had flown into the clock. Sandra was the only member of the family who did not chide her for having tried the maneuver again.

When Rachel finally mastered the staircase and could take that turn at full speed, Sandra was the only person she had invited to witness her success. She remembered how her sister had clapped and laughed, the air of the hallway fragrant with her sweet honeysuckle perfume.

But her sister was far away in London. Thinking of Sandra's compassion only made her feel lonelier. She began crying again.

The horror of the whole day hit her, and she wept for her friends: for Valerie who suffered so horribly; for Nastasia who was tortured with phantom fire by Remus Starkadder; for Joy who had stood paralyzed while Johan Strega's cruel knife sped toward her back; for Misty and Sakura, and all that they had lost; for tiny Magdalene Chase, whose life was far worse than Rachel could have imagined. She wept until her whole body shook, curled up on the cold black-and-white tile, till she was sick with weakness from crying.

A knock sounded on the stall door.

"Rachel?" Zoë Forrest's voice asked. "Are you okay?"

"No," Rachel whispered very softly.

Zoë opened the stall door and knelt down beside Rachel, patting her on the back. She wore a pair of purple and blue pajamas sporting a bashful Eeyore. Rachel shrank away from the other girl, embarrassed. She feared the smell of vomit still lingered.

"So, is this from the excitement of the day?" Zoë's hair was bright orange now. The neon-orange braid swung down beside Rachel, the feather tied into it tickling her cheek. "Or are you coming down with something?"

"Zoë," Rachel's voice hiccupped when she tried to speak. "I- If someone gets t-transformed into an animal—a dumb animal... A-are they dead?"

Zoë shook her head firmly. "My uncle got turned into a sea tortoise. They lost him in the bay for months. Eventually, they found him and changed him back. Afterward, he was fine. Except for the weird things he did at the beach..."

"Lost him!" Rachel laughed in spite of her inner agony, hiccupping. She pressed her hand against her mouth and then winced at the pain in her bruised hand. "I'm glad you got him back!"

It was as if a great weight had been removed from the burden oppressing her. So, a person could be transformed into a dumb animal and recover his intelligence.

Zoë rubbed her back some more.

"See? It won't be so bad." Zoë's drawl, which was normally dry, had a cheerful, encouraging tone. "You're worried about that boy who got turned into a sheep, aren't you? Don't worry. They'll fix him. Things like that happen in duels."

Rachel took a shaky breath and nodded wordlessly. She felt like a plucked viola string. Much as she appreciated sympathy, right now she wanted to be alone. Otherwise, everything she was thinking would come spilling out. *On the other hand, maybe that would not be such a bad thing.*

"Um…Zoë?" Rachel's voice squeaked. "I really need to talk to someone. But I-I might break down in the middle. That's a lot to ask of someone I only recently met. If you want to go away and pretend you didn't see me, that's okay."

Zoë looked at her thoughtfully. She shrugged. "You can talk to me. I don't mind if you break down. I'm feeling rather useless. It would be nice if I could help someone." She looked around. "But maybe you would be more comfortable talking somewhere else."

Zoë helped Rachel stand up and got her a glass of water. Rachel drank it slowly. She leaned against the black marble counter. In the mirror, her tear-stained reflection looked woeful.

"Something is wrong—seriously wrong—with our world." Rachel closed her eyes, searching for words to express the thoughts tormenting her. As her personal fear for Gaius ebbed, the greater fears, brought on by events of the day, were catching up with her. "Magic that's not supposed to work does. People are here who aren't supposed to be. And I keep seeing this Raven, whose presence supposedly signifies the Doom of Worlds. No one knows what's causing all this, and no one seems to be taking it seriously.

"Even my friends, who have vowed to help, aren't serious. Siggy's very brave, but he's like a small boat suddenly adrift on a large sea. Everything is so different from the restrictive atmosphere of the orphanage that he doesn't know how to control himself. How to choose what to say or do. Sometimes, he's helpful. Other times, he's totally crackers.

"And the Princess—she's so sweet. But she doesn't understand we're trying to protect the world. When we talked about it earlier this afternoon, before everything went crazy, she thought we were forming a social club! She's too concerned with rules and politeness, to tackle the real problems."

Zoë leaned against the tiled wall, twirling the tip of her neon orange braid. She did not say anything, but she listened intently. Drawing an uneven breath, Rachel forged ahead.

"And the adults!" she continued. "You'd think they'd be properly serious, but they're not! Like the princess, they're too concerned about rules and regulations to put the resources they have—knowledge—where the problem is: with us.

"You'd think James Darling, at least, would understand," cried Rachel. "Can you imagine how much easier his life would have been had the Parliament of the Wise supported him, instead of trying to placate the Terrible Five?"

Zoë's eyebrows arched upward. Rachel noticed that they were a dark auburn. She wondered if that was the original color of Zoë's hair.

"Yeah." Zoë blinked twice. "That woulda been really different."

"I trusted the adults, but they don't trust me—because I'm thirteen." Rachel's voice took on a hard, bitter tone. "But being thirteen doesn't protect me. It hasn't kept me from being the one who had to decide what to say to Mortimer Egg. Or the one who heard that horrid Raven talk to Kitten's Lion. It won't keep me alive, if I do the wrong thing when the Raven comes. Because sooner or later, it might do more than just watch me.

"You know what I see, in my mind's eye, when I think about the Agents refusing to share information?" Rachel's voice went low and flat, her eyes glazed over. "I see Valerie dead on the grass, killed by the evil brooch. Or the princess unconscious and covered in blood. Or Siggy—forever pale and still—killed by black fire shot out of the hands of the geased Mr. Fuentes. Or you dead—because, when the danger came, the adults had failed to share the information needed for us to know to be wary of it.

"We students are the ones under attack! We are the front line!" Rachel finished fiercely. "We are the ones who need to know what's going on!"

Zoë jumped up to sit on the counter. "Doesn't anyone care? You would think..." She waved a hand as if to indicate someone out there, somewhere.

Rachel snorted ironically. "The only other person who's serious is Vladimir Von Dread."

"Dread? He's the guy who sheeped that boy, isn't he?"

"Yeah."

"The sheep kid—was that the same boy you were talking to in the dining hall? The one who stood on the chair and made that other guy tell everyone how he tried to stop your broom?"

"Yeah, Gaius Valiant." Rachel nodded. "My boyfriend."

Zoë's eyebrows shot up. "I didn't know fourteen-year-olds had boyfriends."

"I'm thirteen."

"Oh. Right. That makes it all right, I guess," Zoë drawled, rolling her eyes.

"At first, I thought being his girlfriend was a very bad idea," Rachel admitted, "even though I fancy him something fierce. He's sixteen. He's dangerous. I'm tiny. My older sister says—" Rachel's cheeks grew warm. Her words rushed out. "She says even nice boys sometimes get...um...over-exuberant when you let them date you. What could a little girl like me do to stop such behavior? So, I said 'no.'"

"I can understand that." Zoë ran her fingers down the feather tied into her braid. As she did so, it changed color, turning purple spotted with blue. It now matched her Eeyore pajamas.

Rachel gawked. "Did you...just *change the color* of the feather?"

Zoë gave her a cocky grin. She ran her hands over her hair. As they passed, her short locks changed from neon orange to a frosty lavender. As an afterthought, she passed her hand across her head once again, this time adding blue highlights.

"That's absolutely brilliant!" Rachel gaped. "I've never heard of anyone doing that! Is that a Metaplutonian power?" Her eyes widened. "That's what you did to that beastly Cydney Graves and her friends! When you made their hair spew-colored. Can they change it back?"

"No idea." Zoë grin grew even wider. "You were saying?"

"Oh, um...Right. So, at first, I wasn't going to date him, but Gaius kept impressing me. After a bit, things that had seemed like big obstacles just fell away."

Zoë nodded. "I thought that kid and Dread were friends. What went wrong?"

"Me." Rachel traced the swirls of the marbled lines on the countertop. "My father found out Gaius was my boyfriend. He told Vladimir Von Dread to order him not to date me."

Rachel shivered. Up until tonight, her family had meant everything to her. Now, she felt as if she had been ripped out of her family portrait.

"Your father?" Zoë frowned. "That's really crappy. Not that I don't think a thirteen-year-old dating a sixteen-year-old is a little weird. But still. Your father coulda at least met the guy before he decided if he's a jerk or not. Yeesh, you English!"

Zoë slipped off the counter and poured herself a glass of water. "So, what happened? Instead of talking to him, Dread turned Valiant into a sheep? That was choice!"

"Dread talked to him all right, and Gaius jolly well said 'no!'" Rachel's eyes grew large. Even thinking about it made her giddy with astonishment. "He stood up to Vladimir Von Dread—the person he most admires— rather than not be my boyfriend." Rachel blushed furiously. "I think he likes me."

"You think?" Zoë asked sardonically. "So, he dueled Dread— over you?"

Rachel's head bobbed up and down, a tiny smile curling up the corner of her lip. "He even held his own for a bit! And Gaius's only an upper school senior, while Dread's a college junior. But," she gave an exaggerated sigh, "it ended in sheepness."

"Mmm. A shame."

"Now Gaius is at the Halls of Healing, and I-I'm really scared." Rachel's voice shook. "If you're right about your uncle, though, maybe Gaius'll swim out to sheep sea and eventually be restored—to a guy who's just like the old Gaius, except that he likes to chew cud."

"Most likely." Zoë nodded. "Same old Gaius—only more likely to *baa* when he laughs."

Rachel's voice broke. "People are alive, who might be dead, were it not for the spell Gaius taught me. I didn't realize how much he had helped me this week—until he...stopped being around."

The sorrow and loss was too much for her. She covered her face and wept. Zoë did not comfort her, but she did yank a paper towel from the dispenser and hand it to her. Rachel pressed it against her eyes, sniffing. Then, she splashed cold water on her face.

"We'll get Valiant back," Zoë announced decisively. "I'll help you. I can walk through dreams, and I have a super-cool war club. That's two of us. With Valiant, that's three. We'll find other people who are trustworthy, and then we'll save the world."

Rachel felt a rush of joy, as if a weight had lifted from the burdens oppressing her. "I knew there had to be more people who were serious!"

"What the rest of us need is to learn how to cast like you," Zoë said. "Even though you're thirteen, you beat people you shouldn't have. And Valiant held his own against Dread. I bet he woulda won, if I had whacked Dread over the head with my war club in the middle of the fight."

The image of Zoë whacking Dread with her greenstone club made Rachel giggle unexpectedly. "You give me hope. I feel much better!"

"Hey!" Zoë flipped her braid over her shoulder. "I think you can save Valiant right now!"

"H-how?"

"You guys saved Dread's life, right? I heard him say he owed you. Princes take that kind of thing seriously, don't they? Tell him you want him to turn Valiant back."

Rachel's heart began to race. "You think Dread can turn him back? The nurses couldn't."

"I'll bet you good money Dread knows what spell he cast. Three-quarters of recovering from magical accidents is figuring out what went wrong. Don't skimp on it, either. Tell him to go to New York, fix Valiant, and get him a new damn wand. What a jerk face!

"Or, if you prefer," Zoë added, "I can step out of a dream into Dread's room and bash him with my club. You decide."

"Tempting, but no." Rachel chuckled. She chewed on her lip, thinking. The Prince of Bavaria intrigued her. She was angry with him for hurting Gaius, but she would not let that stand in the way of what needed to be done—like learning more, and saving people, places, and things—including the world, which was either a place or a thing. Maybe both. "I don't mind talking to Dread. I have a number of things I'd like to say to him. Thank you for the idea and for listening to me. I'll go talk to Dread now. Oh, wait. It's after curfew."

"Not if we go my way." Zoë tapped her silver sandal against the tiled floor.

"Do you think if we appear in his room, Dread will blast us?"

"Yeah, nah." Zoë tilted her head in thought. "He's evil, I'm sure. But I doubt he would blast a couple of girls. Or do you want to wait until morning?"

Rachel smiled wickedly. "Let's go!"

Chapter 15:
The Cold Lair of Dread

Zoë knelt and motioned for Rachel to hop on her back. Rachel did so, holding tightly to the other girl's shoulders.

"Good thing I'm tiny."

"You truly are." Zoë crossed her arms behind her and lifted Rachel up. "You look more like an eleven-year-old than a thirteen-year-old. People keep mistaking you and that Chase girl—What's her name? Madeline? Magdalene?—for visitors from the Lower School. No offense, but it makes your having a boyfriend even weirder."

Zoë started forward. Mist rose around them. Then, they walked through a forest of dark evergreens. It was eerily quiet. Zoë's footfalls made no sound. Overhead hung the night sky—a different night sky from the one Rachel knew. It looked like black velvet bejeweled with lopsided, five-pointed stars.

Storm King Mountain loomed to the west. A river leapt merrily down its slopes, ending in a waterfall. Next to the falls, a gigantic old woman with long braids held what looked like the moon. She wore a long tunic decorated with porcupine quills and fringed trousers of deerskin. Mentally reviewing an encyclopedia she had once read, Rachel recalled this was a costume of the *Lenni Lenape* people, the tribe that had once roamed the Hudson Highlands.

The old Native American woman placed the moon into the night sky. Then, she picked up what looked like a smaller half-moon. In the way of dreams, Rachel understood that this was yesterday's moon. With a flint knife, the old woman cut the glowing, white substance into stars. These she positioned on the velvety darkness overhead.

"Who's that?" Rachel whispered.

"The local dream warden." Zoë hefted Rachel, who had begun to slide.

"Hang on. Dreams have wardens?"

"Every area has its own. Or most places do, anyway. They kind of keep an eye on things. The good ones chase nightmares away. At least, some of the time."

"Wow. I wonder what other dream wardens are like."

"Back in New Zealand, the dream warden was the forest god, Tāne Mahuta, who is either a freaky masked guy or a seriously big tree, depending on whom you ask," replied Zoë, shrugging. "In Japan, it was this enormous, gray, teddy bear-like forest spirit. In Michigan, it's Paul Bunyan and his giant blue ox, Babe. Ah. Here we go."

Mist drifted out of the waterfall, forming tall ribbons that undulated back and forth, like pale northern lights. Zoë walked through some of these wall-like mist-ribbons. The soft fog-stuff clung to Rachel's face and hands. She caught a whiff that smelled like mingled plaster-of-Paris and lilacs, an odor she recognized. It was the scent that clung to newly-conjured things.

As Zoë and Rachel moved through the rolling mist-ribbons, each curve of the veils held a living diorama. They passed through a flying polo game where the ball was an armadillo; a chase scene in slow motion where the runners raced across a road-sized scroll of musical notation; a bedroom with large posters on the wall, where a boy whom Rachel had seen in the dining hall kissed a girl dressed in provocative red lingerie.

"What are these?" Rachel studiously averted her eyes. She tightened her hold on Zoë's shoulders.

"Private dreams," Zoë replied. "The dreams of the people asleep here at school."

"Oh!" Rachel gazed around her with interest. Overlapping images spread away from her, like waves in a pool, images of people studying, singing, kissing, arguing.

"Best not to look too closely," advised Zoë. "It can get freak-arific."

"Speaking of dreams," said Rachel, who was not entirely certain what freakarific meant. "My father did tell me one thing—which would have gone a long way toward putting him back into my good graces, if he hadn't commissioned Dread to turn my boyfriend into a sheep—does this mean our future children will have wooly hair or something? Did your uncle have children? Did they show signs of being turtle-like?—Anyway, Father told me a sorcerer is coming from New Zealand to put up dream protections here."

"It's probably Aperahama Whetu," said Zoë.

"The shaman who made your slippers?" asked Rachel.

"That's right. Good memory! He's weird but nice," said Zoë. "I am not aware of anyone else among the Wise of New Zealand who could set up dream protections on such a level."

Rachel stared around her in fascination, temporarily distracted. A tall blond boy blew a great trumpet. A red-haired girl tried to rescue a drowning puppy from a lake. Glancing to the right, she recognized her dorm mate, Brunhilda Winters. Dressed in her old red and white cheerleader outfit, Hildy rode a winged horse across an American Football field.

"Whatever he does," she murmured, "I hope it doesn't stop your sandals."

"Maybe I can talk to him first. Ask him if he can make an exception for them," Zoë said. "I'd hate to not be able to use them for the next eight years. Ugh! What a horrible thought!"

"Just in case, we should think of interesting experiments to do before he gets here. Gaius can help us with that, if we get him back. He wants to be a scientist. They're good at thinking up experiments." Rachel said. To her left, the red-head and the puppy were now zooming down some rapids on a yellow-duck raft. "Do sheep dream?"

Zoë did not answer. She had stopped to peer off into the distance, her hand shading her eyes, perhaps trying to pick one diorama from among the hundreds.

Standing amidst the curling mists, Rachel marshaled her thoughts. Despite her fear for her new boyfriend, she felt secretly eager for the upcoming confrontation. This was her chance to show Von Dread she was not just another foolish little girl. Like a general reviewing his troops before the battle, she considered which subjects might be of interest to the Prince of Bavaria.

"Ah. Here we are," said Zoë.

Zoë walked them around a curve in the mist-walls and stepped into the dreamscape beyond. The rest of the dream lands receded. They seemed to be walking down one of the underground tunnels beneath Roanoke Hall. Rachel recognized them because she had glanced down one during her initial tour of the campus, the day she arrived. Zoë opened a door marked *Custodial Office.* The janitor, Umberto Sarpento, sat behind a desk talking to a woman with bushy ginger hair—and nothing else.

The woman was not wearing a single strip of clothing.

Rachel's jaw dropped. "That's Scarlett MacDannan! Naked! But she's...married! Oh, wait. This is someone's dream, isn't it?"

"Yep. Sarpy knows where everything in the school is. But there's always a naked woman in here." Zoë sighed. "At least, this time, it's not one of the college girls—"

"Ew! Yuck!" Rachel cried, belatedly remembering to avert her gaze.

"Hey, it's a dream." Zoë shrugged. "People can't help what they dream about. I've seen a *lot* of naked people. I think I'm getting used to it." She gave a mock shudder. "Scary."

Zoë rapped the janitor on the forehead. "Sarpy! You've seen Dread's room, right?"

The janitor looked to the right. A solid oak door appeared in the previously blank wall.

"You ready, Griffin?" asked Zoë.

"I hope no one's in their underwear. Or worse," Rachel whispered back, trying very hard not to giggle. The sight of the naked Agent had discombobulated her. That, combined with the emotional roller coaster of the day's events, was beginning to make her feel punch-drunk, not a good state for facing down the imperious prince. "Hopefully, Dread sleeps in his royal pajamas."

"I don't know," Zoë drawled. "I might enjoy seeing Dread naked. Ready?"

Zoë walked through the door. The chamber snapped into focus. Rachel realized the previous version had been fuzzy, in-distinct. The air became colder. Shivering, she slid down from Zoë's back and straightened her robes.

They stood in a nice-sized chamber with three doors, each of which led to a bedroom. Pale blue curtains billowed in the chilly night breeze. In two of the bedrooms, young men lay asleep in their beds. In the third, Dread sat on his bed in a long shirt and sweatpants, reading a book. As they approached the door, his gaze flickered to the two girls.

"Forrest. Griffin. This is not an acceptable way to approach me."

Rachel's insides quivered with fear. All desire to be flippant withered away. There was an undercurrent of unbroachable authority to his calm voice. She shifted onto the balls of her feet, poised to flee. There was no way she could talk to this looming bully. He was as intimidating as if...

As if he had shouted *Boo*? Rachel nearly smiled. *He was like her grandfather.* Despite the shakiness of her legs, she straightened her backbone and walked to his doorway, looking him directly in the eye.

"Quite true." Rachel inclined her head solemnly. "But we could think of no other way of reaching you. Is there another place we can talk where no one will be disturbed?"

"Say your piece." He gestured toward the other rooms. "It is one fifty-seven a.m. My suitemates will not awaken. Just keep your voices down."

He closed his book. His wand lay on his desk, but he made no move to pick it up.

Rachel walked into his room and stood in front of his bed. "Mr. Von Dread, I believe you are aware of the princess's vision—the one that foretold your death—and of the efforts we made to save your life and those of your comrades. An effort that has earned us detention, among other things. Would you be willing to grant a request, in return for my part in saving you?"

"I've already promised you a service in return for your efforts," he replied curtly. "While I am not thoroughly convinced this vision would have come to pass, I am not so foolish as to question the direction of the occurrences of the afternoon. Make your request."

"I propose an alliance between your group and ours." Rachel continued to meet the intensity of his gaze full-on, despite her mounting desire to quail. "To share information for the purpose of discerning the current threat to our world and stopping it, along with any lesser threats we might discover. My group has access to a great deal of information. Yours has greater experience and ability.

"What is more, in my opinion," she added, "you are the only person who truly takes this danger seriously—other than myself. I believe it would be to our advantage to work together."

"Are you proposing an alliance?" He frowned. "Or making a request?"

"Both. Here is the request," Rachel plunged forward, speaking rapidly. "Before our alliance can go forward, I must ask you to return Mr. Valiant to his proper shape, provide him with a new wand, and restore him to his previous place in your esteem."

She waited, too tense to draw breath. Still, she felt particularly clever for having thought to add the last part.

"Ordinarily, I would cast aside your request, due to the nature of the offense against myself by Valiant," Dread replied. "But, considering the present danger to our reality, and my lack of reliable seers, I will agree. Before I release Valiant, however, I must have your word that we will either share our direct sources or offer assurances that our information is reliable."

Rachel drew herself up until she stood as regally as a queen. "Mr. Von Dread, I may not be a princess, but I am of the English Top Ten Thousand. The Griffins can trace our ancestors back to the time of the Roman republic, which makes my family older than any existing dynasty on earth—even the long-reigning Danish and Japanese courts. I would not dishonor my family by breaking a promise once given." Her eyes glittered intently. "I give you my word."

He nodded.

Rachel regarded him, taking in the red highlights in his dark wavy hair and his well-defined jaw line. The thin cloth of his shirt did little to conceal his broad shoulders and washboard stomach. Nor did his sweatpants hide the firm muscles of his thighs. Suddenly, she found herself uncomfortably aware of just how very masculine he was. This notion, and the accompanying unfamiliar sensations it produced in her body, alarmed her.

Quickly, she glanced away.

Von Dread's desk was well-organized. Metals, bronze, silver, and gold, hung on the wall above his trunk. Looking farther, her heart skipped a beat. In the partially-opened wardrobe, she caught a glimpse of a cloak of sable swan feathers—*just like the one the Swan King wore in the princess's vision.*

Thinking of other images she had seen in mirrors recently, she had an idea.

"Speaking of secret sources," Rachel said suddenly. "I happen to know what Valiant said to the Agents under the influence of the *Spell of True Recitation*. I will tell you, because it might make it easier for you to forgive him." Word for word, she repeated what Gaius had told the Agents about why he respected Von Dread more than anyone else.

"Interesting." Von Dread's face remained impassive.

She paused, moistening her dry lips, and marshaled her best arguments on Gaius's behalf. "My grandfather was a brilliant man, Mr. Von Dread. He fought against Hitler's dark magicians and lost fewer men during World War II than any other sorcery cadre. He may not have been as powerful as your family, but he was wise and an excellent leader of men."

"I knew General Blaise Griffin, The Tenth Duke of Devon," stated Dread. "He freed our capital from the Nazis."

Of course! Verhängnisburg, the city her grandfather had liberated, was the capital of Bavaria. Rachel had seen photos of it, a picturesque valley in the Alps with Svartschwanstein Castle towering above it on the mountainside.

"I once heard my grandfather explain why he kept stallions in his stable," Rachel continued gravely. "Stallions are harder to handle than geldings, and apt, especially when young, to chase after mares." She flushed at the implied analogy but pressed onward. "But, he said, no other horse was as effective at crossing the intervening territory to reach the enemy.

"I am sure you are too wise a prince to let anger come between yourself and someone as loyal, brave, and intelligent as Gaius—just because his head has been turned by a girl."

Von Dread nodded, indicating that he understood her words. His expression did not change. She had no idea what he was thinking.

"And, finally," she plowed ahead, "as a gesture of good faith, I will share our first secret—a secret that may be of some practical value."

"Indeed?" Von Dread crossed his arms. "Proceed."

Here was the moment for which Rachel had been waiting: the chance to share the secrets she had so painstakingly gathered. As she spoke, she watched his face carefully, searching for some sign as to whether her words were making an impresssion.

"You may have heard about the Raven, who is said to be the omen of the doom of worlds?" she said. "This Raven occasionally flies around the school grounds. When he gets near Smith's dragon, it becomes a dumb animal, like dragons on this world." Was it her imagination? Or was there the slightest glint of interest in his dark eyes.

Now for her brilliant idea. "If you could harness this power: get its help? Snag a feather? You might be able to shut off the new magic—such as Lucky the Dragon, the magic paper that ensorcelled Miss Iscariot, the extreme speed and toughness of Mr. Chanson. Maybe even Zoë's sandals."

"Thanks a lot." Zoë stuck out her tongue.

Rachel could see her in her peripheral vision; however, she did not look away from Von Dread's face. She would apologize later. "In order to investigate the Raven, you have to find it. As far as I know, I am the only person at school who can tell when it is present. I am willing to help you...so long as Valiant is with us. He has promised to protect me from it."

"Very well," replied Dread. "I may have need of the Guardian. If you can locate it, perhaps we can convince it to speak."

The Guardian?

If he had hauled off and punched her in the solar plexus, she could not have been more shocked. Von Dread knew more about the Raven than she did? More than Mr. Badger and Master Warder Nighthawk? So much for impressing him. Rachel schooled her expression, but she could not keep her pupils from widening.

"Yes, Miss Griffin, I know what the bird is," Von Dread continued grimly. "It protects this world from external threats. It seems it has been negligent in its duties. Powers have been crossing the borders into this place for decades. Some long enough for generations to pass." He looked at her long and hard.

Rachel swallowed. *Was he implying her family had come from Outside?*

"Forrest," Von Dread turned to Zoë, "you will want to bring Miss Griffin away from here. I cannot promise my suitemates will be well-mannered after I am gone." Crossing the room, he picked up his wand from the desk. He swirled it above his head. A ruby-colored mist curled about him. His shirt and sweat pants transformed into robes.

He fixed his gaze on both girls. "You will not repeat this, ladies. It is a secret between us." Raising his hands, he performed three quick gestures. "*Libra orbeathe Roanoke: venjelrian. Kalu.*"

With a flash of light, Vladimir Von Dread disappeared.

Chapter 16:
Waylaying Peter

Kataang!

Thunder cracked across the sky, jolting Rachel from her sleep. Dull gray clouds hung low over the campus. Steady drizzle pattered against her window. Her bedroom was as dim and gloomy as pre-dawn, except when a lightning bolt lit the heavens.

Peering blearily at the clock, Rachel yelped and leapt out of bed. She had overslept and was about to miss breakfast. She was up and in her robes before she remembered that it was Saturday. Breakfast ran a half an hour later. Still, she would need to hurry.

She ran down the stairs of the dormitory, holding onto her mortarboard hat to keep it from blowing off. As she reached the final staircase, her brother Peter came in the front door, chafing his arms to warm them. Rage gripped Rachel. Tossing the tassel of her cap to one side, she marched up to him and crossed her arms. The tassel fell back across her eyes.

She shouted, "You said bad stuff to Father about Gaius, didn't you?"

Ordinarily, Peter was a calm, quiet fellow who spent his free time reading stories of the Knights of King Arthur. Now, however, he visibly bristled.

"Listen, little sister." Peter stepped so close that she had to crane her head to see him. She suspected he wished to appear intimidating, but he did not have much experience. He looked about as threatening as a dachshund in a top hat. "It's my job to watch out for you. My job to make sure you don't get picked up by some idiot who's *only dating you to piss me off.*"

"No, he's not!" she objected loudly, successfully brushing the tassel aside.

"The guy's a total git! He's a *freaking Thaumaturge.* He's also too old for you. You're too young to date anyone. Also, did I mention: he's a *freaking Thaumaturge.*"

She shouted back, "Thanks to you, he spent last night in the Halls of Healing!"

"Uh, I didn't hurt him. I didn't even *see* him." Peter frowned. "And don't think I didn't try! I did speak to the foremost evil boy himself, Vladimir Von Dread. I told him to keep his toady in line, or he'd have to answer to me." Sadly for Peter, he did not look very imposing as he spoke, possibly because he shook slightly at the memory of what he had done.

"*You* did that?" Rachel cried, grabbing her head. "You? I blamed Father! Von Dread did talk to Gaius. He told him to stop dating me."

"Good for him." Peter looked so pleased.

"Gaius said, 'No.' So, Von Dread told him that if he didn't stop seeing me he'd throw him out of the Knights." Rachel's expression faltered, as she recalled how certain she had been that Gaius would drop her. Then, her face lit up. "But Gaius just said, 'Good luck finding someone who can beat me.'"

"He stood up to the Prince of Evil?" asked Peter, mildly surprised.

"They fought a duel! Zap! Bang! Pow!" Rachel jumped around, gesturing wildly. "Spells flying everywhere! Gaius held out against Von Dread for an amazingly long time. But in the end, he got turned into a shee...ram, and he had to spend the night at the Halls of Healing."

"He fought Dread?" Peter's eyes widened, impressed. Then he remembered himself. "Listen, I don't care. He hasn't even asked Father if it's okay to date you. That's extremely rude, to say the least. Not that Father would say yes. He'd also say you're *too young*. You know why? Because you're *too young*. Did I mention how *old you are not*?"

"I did explain all that to Gaius," Rachel said.

"Okay, so, fine. You're not dating him. Tell him he can wait a year. Or four. By then, you'll meet a nice Dare boy, who will make you completely forget any stupid *Thaumaturge*."

"Peter Griffin, what kind of girl would I be if I were to walk out on a boy who fought *Vladimir Von Dread* for me?"

"A *thirteen-year-old* kind of girl! I don't care if he shot down the moon and can walk and chew gum! You're too young to be dating."

"I am not!"

"Yes, you are! And you need Father's permission. Or at least mine, as his official representative for our family at school." His face suddenly took on a weird expression. "Good gods, he kissed you, didn't he?"

Rachel blushed and looked down. Lightning flashed across the sky, momentarily illuminating the wide foyer where the two Griffins faced each other.

Peter knelt down in front of her, gazing earnestly into her face. "Rachel. You shouldn't be kissing anyone. You're thirteen. And he, at sixteen, shouldn't be kissing thirteen-year-olds. I assume he is the only boy you've kissed, right?"

Rachel nodded sincerely, biting her bottom lip. Then, she blurted out, "It's not his fault. I kissed him first. He was paralyzed." She giggled slightly at the memory, even though she was aware this might not be the most appropriate reaction under the circumstances.

His jaw dropped. If it had fallen off his face, rolled out the window, and grown back a few moments later—looking ugly for a bit before it righted itself—he could not have looked more surprised. He stood up and stared blankly at the wall over her head. "Yes. Of course. He was paralyzed. Silly of me to be so concerned."

"The first time..." Rachel gazed down at her hands. Her fingers looked utterly fascinating.

"You're going to ignore me, aren't you?" Peter said. "I've known you for your entire life. I've watched out for you. One boy comes along, and I'm not worth listening to any longer? Just say it, Rachel. Say: 'I am going to keep dating him, Peter. I don't care what you say.'"

Rachel looked up at her adored brother. Even though she was angry at him, she wanted him to be proud of her. But she could not give up on Gaius.

Not after he had fought Dread.

To her tremendous embarrassment, she started to cry.

"Rach, you can't cry your way out of this." Peter knelt down again and held her at arm's reach. "A lot has happened to you in your first week of school. Probably more than has happened in the whole three years I have been here.

"I understand you're very mature for your age," he continued, "but, mature or not, you're too young to be kissing boys. I'm sorry, but, as your brother, I cannot let this continue. If you were thinking straight, you'd understand."

Rachel stood there, shaking and crying. Then she wailed softly, "But...I love him!"

Outrage and revulsion fought for control of Peter's face, leaving it rather splotchy. Pivoting, he strode off toward the boys' side without another word.

• • •

Outside, the morning was gloomy. Rain fell briskly, splashing loudly on newly-fallen leaves. Huge floating umbrellas hovered rim-to-rim over the walkways that ran between the dormitories and the main hall. The edges glowed silvery, as did the handles, the curves of which all faced the same direction, like a line of Js. The few people braving the weather rushed along, their shoulders hunched against the biting wind. They walked under the long line of umbrellas, to the right of the curved handles, in both directions.

Rachel hated fighting with Peter. Of all her siblings, she was closest to her brother. They had been at home together for a couple of years after the older girls had left for school. She and Peter had spent these early years under the tutelage of their grandparents, who had grown up during the reign of Queen Victoria. For Rachel, this period had been idyllic. For Peter, it had been less pleasant.

In the Griffin family, everyone except the wayward Laurel had a most-favorite person. Rachel had her grandfather. Her oldest sister Sandra had Father. Peter had their mother. They understood each other much the way Rachel and her gruff grandfather did. Sandra and Father shared a mutual love of the Wisecraft. Mother and son shared a gentleness and a delight in the natural world.

Unfortunately, from her grandparents' point of view, gentle and bookish were not qualities prized in an heir to a dukedom.

It was Laurel's wildness that caused the falling out between Rachel's mother and the late duke and duchess. As much as Rachel loved her grandparents, she understood their shortcomings—one of which was that they, particularly her grandmother, had trouble seeing the good qualities of Rachel's sweet and wise mother. (Rachel suspected her grandfather secretly had a soft spot for his lovely Asian daughter-in-law. She had caught him several times being uncharacteristically kind to her in the last year of his life, after his wife died.) It was never said within Rachel's hearing, but the implications were that The Duchess of Devon felt her son had been taken in by a pretty face and had unwisely married beneath his station.

Ellen Griffin had grown up in an upper middle class family, but she had not been raised to the duties of the aristocracy. The result was that her first two children, Laurel, and even Sandra, whom everyone else found utterly charming, had behaved too commonly to please the elderly Duke and Duchess of Devon— who had expected their grandchildren to live up to the rigorous standards that had been required of lords and ladies for centuries. Sandra did not gallop naked across the countryside in an attempt to impersonate Lady Godiva, or talk the tenant farmers' boys into setting fire to their entire supply of hay to "make a really big bonfire worthy of the gods" the way Laurel did; however, Sandra loved all things Unwary—to the degree that nowadays she lived in a flat in London, complete with mundane curiosities such as electricity and refrigerators. This disregard for authority and lack of respect for the traditions of the World of the Wise had disturbed Rachel's grandparents.

They had loved their granddaughters, appreciated their good qualities, and lauded their talents, especially Sandra's prowess on horseback. They had worried, however, about trusting the future of their over two-thousand-year-old family line, and the almost eight-hundred-year-old ducal title, to children who showed so little regard for their world and its traditions.

To remedy this, her grandparents, particularly their stern grandmother, had taken over the children's early education—

particularly Peter's and Rachel's, as the older daughters left for Roanoke Academy. Her grandparents had taught them to value the world to which they had been born. Rachel had flourished. The requirements upon a young girl were not overbearing. By the time she reached an age at which their tutelage would have restricted her adventurous spirit, her grandparents had passed away.

Peter had not been so lucky. The demands on a young duke-to-be were rigorous, and her grandparents had been less tolerant of weakness in a boy. He had been expected to be much fiercer and more sober than otherwise had been his nature. That, combined with the constant accusations that their gentle mother was coddling him, had made Peter's young life difficult.

Life might have been different had Father been home to mediate. During Rachel's early childhood, however, Ambrose Griffin had been away, hunting down the remnants of the Morthbrood and other servants of the Terrible Five. His wife had been left alone to bear the brunt of his parents' disapproval. Rachel realized that, due to her mother's sweet and private nature, it was unlikely Ellen had ever told her husband how she had suffered during this period.

Peter had lived up to the challenge. He had learned to carry himself as a duke ought and to perform the duties expected of him. Rachel had a wonderful memory of seeing ten-year-old Peter and their towering grandfather, their rifles resting on their shoulders, coming back from walking the boundaries of the estate together. One of the last things her grandmother had said upon her deathbed was how she could die in peace, knowing that Peter would uphold the family honor. Peter's face had shone with pride that night.

Rachel sighed, her emotions a jumble. She understood why Peter had acted as he did. Even she would have considered him derelict of his duties had he not been concerned about the safety of his little sister. Still, it pained her so to be at odds with her family.

• • •

She arrived in the dining hall, shivering and clammy. None of her friends were there. She ate hurriedly, taking advantage of the solitude to dry her tears. By the time she finished, she felt calmer, though her eyes still smarted. Putting her tray away, she ran down the spiral staircase to the basement, where she stamped the order for Sigfried's calling cards with her postal seal and slipped it into the slot for the outgoing post. Then she sat down at a table beside the mailroom and wrote a letter to Sandra.

She missed Sandra tremendously. Peter was the sibling she had spent the most time with, but Sandra was the one with whom she had the most in common, the one to whom she found it easiest to talk. They were both students of their mother's dissembling techniques and placed great value on discerning secrets and hiding their thoughts. Peter and Laurel had never picked up the dissembling arts. They wore their hearts on their sleeves. This suited rebel Laurel but was a hardship for the dignified Peter.

It was by observing the interactions between their gentle mother and their stern, overbearing grandmother—in which their mother never lost her temper, never raised her voice, never let on how much the elder duchess's disapproval hurt her—that Sandra and Rachel had first glimpsed the fine art of dissembling. They had learned both from their mother's example and from her direct tutelage: how to hide their emotions, how to appear ever calm under pressure and graceful, how to keep the world from seeing their joy or pain. They had also learned to see through such deceptions. The Griffin Girls—as Father called them—might hide their feelings from the world, but they could not hide them from one another.

Seated at the table by the mail room, Rachel's lips quirked as she penned a letter she hoped would amuse Sandra and spark her curiosity, thus increasing the odds that her sister would respond more quickly.

Dear Sandra,

How are you? How is your new job with the Wisecraft? I am at Roanoke Academy now, with Peter and Laurel. It's very exciting.

Someone has already tried to attack two friends of mine. (One on the first day of school, the other in a dream.) Also, my math teacher turned into a dragon and tried to kill us. Other than that, we're settling in and learning lots of good things.

I have a theoretical question that I thought a person of your age and experience might be able to address. Imagine there was a boy who was petrified by a cantrip during magic practice, and a girl kissed him: would that count as a first kiss? What if the girl stood still, and the boy kissed her? Would that count as a first kiss? Or do both parties need to participate?

Just wondering.

Your littlest sister,

Rachel

Upon finishing it, she sealed it, slipped it into the post slot, and ran back up the stairs.

• • •

Rachel headed for her favorite corridor between two turrets on the top floor of Roanoke Hall, her own private practice area. A suit of armor stood beside a high round window. Across from it, a wooden doorstop, a battered book, and a large rock lay on a small table. An empty trashcan stood at the end of the short hallway. Originally, the corridor had been dusty from disuse, but the wind blasts she had repeatedly whistled into existence had put an end to that.

Once there, she quickly got down to the business of practicing her spellwork. Whistling up a breeze, she strove to blow the large rock off the table. Whistling enchantments was difficult. They were meant to be played on an instrument. The tingles from the energy made her want to grimace or giggle. But the secret dissembling techniques she had learned from her mother that allowed her to mask her emotions helped her keep her face calm and still. This allowed her whistling to succeed. Still, most of the time, her little breeze, with its silver sparkles and scent of evergreens, was not strong enough to budge the stone.

Occasionally, the rock did roll off and crash to the floor. Then, she used the cantrip *tiathelu* to float it back to the tabletop.

It was hard work. The rock was too large for her current skill level, but she did not give up. Patiently, she tried again and again and again and again.

As she practiced, the sky rumbled and flashed. Rain pelted the round window above the suit of armor. The sky grew even darker, making the corridor gloomier, punctuated now and again by brilliant flashes of light. Occasionally, Rachel was quick enough to try *tur lu*, the cantrip Mark Williams had used on her broom. Its effects were inconclusive because the rock dropped straight down anyway. But if she used the doorstop, she could blast the triangular piece of wood across the room with her wind and then remove its inertia, so that it stopped moving forward, paused momentarily in mid-air, and then flopped harmlessly to the floor.

The first time this worked, a slow smile crept across her face. Then, frowning seriously, she repeated it again and again and again.

• • •

Much later, she sank down next to the suit of armor. The floor was cold, but she was too exhausted to notice. Her tremendous effort, practicing so diligently, combined with her late night and the heavy gloominess of the weather, had sapped her strength. Her eyelids fluttered shut.

She woke with a start to find herself asleep on the floor, her bruised hand and thigh aching painfully. She was curled up next to the suit of armor underneath a cozy blue comforter, her face resting on the flat square portion of her hat. The weight of the blanket brought a big smile to her face. Only one person knew she came up here. She sniffed the comforter and rubbed her cheek against it. It smelled faintly of fresh soap. Then, she stretched and looked around.

Gaius sat against the far wall of the corridor, reading. He looked up and smiled. Rachel's heart pirouetted around her chest. He looked so adorable sitting there all human-shaped and not covered with wool. She wanted to leap up and run over and hug him. Shyness held her back.

She hoped he would cross the distance to her, but he did not. He did, however, give her a huge beaming grin. Though the weather had not changed—outside the sky remained overcast, and the winds still howled— the day seemed suddenly cheery.

"You're not a sheep." Her joy lit her whole being.

"Not anymore." He held up his hands, turning them this way and that, as if to demonstrate that they were not hooves.

"I had a huge row with Peter."

"Over me, I'm guessing? Sorry about that." He paused. "Unless irking Peter is a perk?"

She shook her head. "I love my brother. I had hoped he would approve of my boyfriend."

"Ah. A pity."

"Are you...all right?"

"Yeah. Last night was...weird." He shivered. "Rather not talk about it, actually."

"Okay." Rachel paused, unsure what to say next. Running a hand across her face, she discovered there was an indentation in her cheek where she had been lying on the tassel string of her hat. "Um...did you get a new wand?"

"Vlad's away getting it right now. He promised me a higher quality sapphire this time—it will hold more spells." He winced and grabbed his head, making a masculine mock crying noise. "Ugh! So many spells lost! And I had some really good ones stored up, too."

"Yeah. That's really a shame. I imagine it will take a long time to replace them."

"Some of them I can't replace. The person who played enchantments for us graduated last year." Gaius searched her face carefully, as if anticipating a reaction. Rachel had no idea what he was expecting. She kept her head turned so that the part of her cheek bearing the impression of the tassel line was out of sight. When she did not respond, he gave her a grateful smile. "I hear you came to my defense. I rather appreciate that. There is a ninety-eight percent chance I would still be a sheep right now, were it not for you."

Rachel's cheeks grew warm. "Glad to help."

"Yeah. I just wish it hadn't been necessary."

"Some good things came from last night," offered Rachel. "I found out that Zoë Forrest is willing to help us save the world." She shook her head in astonishment. "I don't understand my friends. Siggy doesn't seem to care—or at least he doesn't keep the details straight—and the princess! She thinks we're running a social club."

Even as she spoke, Rachel realized that while Zoë had offered to help, she had showed no real interest in saving the world, asked no questions. She just wanted to be helpful. Glumly, Rachel leaned back and watched the driving rain sluice against the round window.

"I care! I want to help," cried Gaius. "William and I both. We'll do everything we can!"

A joyful little smile tugged at her lips. They were kindred spirits, she and Gaius Valiant.

"You and William?" she asked curiously. "Not Mr. Von Dread?"

Gaius's voice became lower. "Vlad's different."

"How so?" Rachel leaned forward eagerly. Did Von Dread want the world to end? Was he as wicked as Nastasia and Peter believed? The foremost evil boy? If so, the princess was right not to want to marry him.

"He thinks the world's actually under attack," Gaius said, "as in literally."

Two things happened to Rachel simultaneously. The first was crushing disappointment. If Gaius thought the danger was figurative, not an actual threat, he did not see what she saw after all. He was not her longed-for *somebody else who understood*.

The second was surprise—as startling as the thunderclap that shook the campus. Vladimir Von Dread understood the world needed saving? And he wanted it saved—not destroyed? She felt an unexpected sense of kinship with the grim older boy.

Maybe she *should marry Dread.*

Rachel straightened and briskly shook her head. *Where had that come from?* Was her heart so fickle as to flip-flop with every inconsequential thing? Refusing to give in to disloyal thoughts, she pushed away any fleeting thoughts of marrying someone other than her boyfriend.

Still, it pleased her to know Dread saw what she saw.

She felt less alone.

Glancing across the hall, Rachel peered at Gaius's book to see what he was reading. The answer gave her another jolt of surprise, this time of a joyful one. In his lap was *A Field Guide to Gryphons and their Southern Cousins.*

"Oh, you are reading a Daring Northwest book!" cried Rachel, delighted. She darted across the hall and sat down next to him.

"Yes, indeed I am. See? I pay attention." He gave her an engaging smile and scooted closer to her.

They were so close that she could feel the heat of his body. It felt very nice on such a cold, damp day.

"Here. Look!" She reached over and flipped to the chapter on Arimaspians. "This section is about my ancestors and how they stole gold from gryphons—Lucky and Siggy would like that part. And this, here, is about my direct ancestor, Abaris. He was a priest of Apollo and a famous physician. We are descended from him on my father's side."

"I've heard of him." Gaius nodded, impressed. "We talked about him in true history sophomore year. He's the guy who flew around standing on top of an arrow, right?"

"Yep. I like to think my broom-riding skill comes from him."

"Maybe it does."

"Unlikely," she laughed. "Otherwise, wouldn't all members of my family be as good?"

"Maybe you're the only one who inherited that particular trait."

"Could be," she said, amused.

Looking down at the book, her eyes were drawn to the contrast between the white page and his tanned hand. It was a well-formed hand, nicely callused, as if used to working—and so much larger than her own. Feeling suddenly delicate and demure, she lowered her lashes.

Gaius turned a page, still reading about Abaris. Without looking up, he said, "I hear you and Vlad made some kind of information-sharing pact."

"Yes. I am working on a list of information to give him. You'll be there, right?"

"Wouldn't miss it. When were you thinking of doing this?"

"As soon as I clear everything with my friends."

Gaius glanced at his watch. He closed his book and stood. "I have to go," he said regretfully. "It's almost two o'clock. We have a meeting." He shot her an apologetic grin. "You know how Bavarians are about punctuality."

"Right." Rachel rose, too.

She stood awkwardly, her hands in her pockets. She wanted to rush over to him, to hug him, but she dared not. There were words for girls who behaved too freely with boys, words her grandmother had spoken with scorn.

Gaius smiled down at her. She gave him a shy half smile. Lifting her chin with a finger, he leaned in and gave her the lightest of kisses. When he pulled back, his cheeks were a bit red. Picking up his blue comforter, he departed, stopping once to wave goodbye. She waved back. Then, he was gone.

Rachel stared after him, her fingers resting on her lips, her face aglow.

Chapter 17:
Conversations in the Storm King Café

"Our detention's been put off until the next sunny day," announced Nastasia. "Mr. Gideon says the task he has assigned us is better performed in dry weather."

She, Joy, Sigfried, and Rachel walked single file beneath the floating umbrellas as they hurried across campus to visit Valerie. The girls wore warm coats over their scholar's robes. The princess had placed a perfectly-tailored, blue Gore-Tex rain cover over the square portion of her cap. Siggy wore one of the new robes Rachel had helped him purchase. But he did not yet own a coat or shoes. His bare feet slapped against the puddles pooling on the wet gravel.

"By 'our', I assume you mean the four of us," said Joy hopefully.

"Miss Griffin, Mr. Smith, and I." Nastasia brushed water from her robes.

"Why wasn't I included?" Joy demanded. "I did the same things as the rest of you!"

"Maybe because you came in to the infirmary on your own...pretending to be ill?" Rachel said pointedly. She stomped in a puddle in her high green rain boots. Droplets flew everywhere. The princess made a noise of resigned distress.

"I was not pretending," Joy objected. "I had a stomachache."

"You admitted you were pretending," said Rachel stubbornly.

"All right, it ached from curiosity," admitted Joy. "But who could bear such curiosity?"

The princess sniffed disapprovingly. "A person concerned with the honesty of his word."

Joy's face crumbled, crestfallen, more because of the princess's censure than from concern for her integrity. "Please take me! Please! Please! You guys will have so much fun together! I hate being left behind. Are you really going outside the campus wards?"

Nastasia nodded. "The herbs we are to collect grow on the northern part of Roanoke Island." She said something else, but Rachel was no longer listening. The hair on her arms had risen.

The Tree!

The previous day, while petting the little Lion, Rachel had had her very first vision—a vast tree rising far above the others in the forest. She had received the impression that this Tree was on Roanoke Island, but she had not seen it from the Watch Tower. It must be on the far side of the tor. A slight smile curled about her lips. Could this detention have been arranged by the power that sent the vision?

As she walked along, her shoulders hunched against the cold, Rachel wondered how to broach the topic of her midnight visit to Von Dread. The princess would certainly disapprove. As Rachel recalled the previous night, she found herself haunted by some of the images she had seen. Zoë might be used to seeing people naked, but Rachel was not. Her memory of the janitor's dream office continued to disturb her. She shook her head, as if to dislodge the image, but it did not help.

As her feet crunched against the soggy gravel, her thoughts moved from Dread to Gaius. She pictured him smiling at her in the hallway and remembered, with perfect vividness, the feel of his kiss on her lips. She imagined what it would be like when he finally hugged her properly, allowing her to curl against his chest. These thoughts filled her with a happiness that made her step light.

Once or twice, her imagination strayed into bolder territory, not something as passionate as full-out snogging, but a more intimate kiss. Each time, she balked, disturbed and uncomfortable. Apparently, she was just not ready for such things, even in her fantasies. She bit her lip and hoped the older boy would prove understanding.

• • •

She had still not made up her mind how to tell Nastasia by the time they reached the infirmary. Valerie sat upright, reading one of her school books. Tiny Magdalene Chase lay curled up with her head on Valerie's lap. Payback snuggled beside her; the elk hound's circular tail curled over her back. Salome sat on the bed next to Valerie, her pretty cheeks flushed, and her eyes red, as if she had been crying.

Sitting down on a nearby chair, Rachel gently asked her, "Is something the matter?"

Salome looked away. "Someone hurt my friend. I'm angry."

Valerie hugged her. "It's okay. He's been caught. He'll go to jail. That's what is important." Valerie stroked Magdalene's hair gently. "Other people had it much worse than me."

"If you say so." Salome stared sullenly at the flame pattern of her brightly-painted nails.

Rachel looked down at Magdalene. The sight of the tiny girl clutching her porcelain doll to her chest caused Rachel's heart to ache. How horrible not to be wanted by one's family. If only she could do something to help. She recalled how Magdalene had wanted the doll to be her familiar. Everyone had laughed at her, and yet, Rachel had seen that doll move and talk and bravely attempt to drag her unconscious mistress to safety. If Magdalene were bonded to it, she would always be able to feel where it was. That might be comforting.

Rachel considered explaining this to Mr. Tuck, the tutor who presided over the Familiar Bonding Ceremony. He was cheerful and jovial and she loved his class. Then she recalled how he had ignored her when she told him about the wraith. He would not believe her. But there was someone else who was willing to look out for Magdalene who was "neither a tutor nor a fool." Rachel made a mental note to ask Gaius to tell him. Mr. Tuck might ignore her, but he would listen to Vladimir Von Dread.

• • •

The nurse came bustling over with her scrutiny sticks, two rounded lengths of wood carved with runes and set with gems of different colors. She ran them over Valerie and Magdalene. Some of the gems lit up. Others remained dark.

"You are free to go, but yes?" Nurse Moth said in her French accent. She looked down at the sleeping girl in Valerie's lap. "Miss Chase should stay."

As Nurse Moth turned away, her scrutiny sticks passed near Rachel. The amethyst lit up. Lifting Rachel's hand, the nurse *tsked* over the large bruise. Pulling out her silver flute, she played a song. Soothing music filled the room, accompanied by the smell of fresh baked cinnamon buns. Twinkling green sparkles played over Rachel's hand and thigh. They tickled and felt very good at the same time. She watched the black and blue splotch on her hand, where the sheep's hoof had stepped, shrink and fade. When she poked her thigh, there was no pain.

Rachel thanked the nurse with great enthusiasm.

• • •

Back out in the rain, they hurried along under the rim-to-rim floating umbrellas, which buffeted about in the wind. In the dimness of the gloom, the umbrellas' silver outlines and handles glowed eerily. The group seemed quiet and caught in their own thoughts. Looking at Salome's bloodshot eyes, Rachel recalled how frightened she herself had been when she had first found Valerie on the floor of the bathroom and how that fear had been dispelled by the sense of peace she had felt while hugging the little Lion.

"We should get Kitten's Lion," Rachel said. "I bet he could make everyone feel better."

"Kitten Fabian's familiar?" Valerie adjusted her camera as they walked.

"Yes, if you hug it, you feel...happier. Comforted."

"A comfort lion," giggled Joy.

"Yes! A Comfort Lion!" cried Rachel with a laugh. "Exactly!"

"It came and sat on my lap briefly yesterday," said Nastasia.

"Was it comforting?" Joy asked.

"Perhaps." The princess frowned thoughtfully. "I had this odd vision, while it was sitting there, of a great, enormous tree."

"I had that vision, too!" cried Rachel.

Walking across the foggy commons, she considered what it meant that the Lion had given both her and her best friend the same vision. Did that make it less special or more? More, Rachel decided, because she shared it with her friend.

• • •

Valerie had missed lunch, so the group made its way to the Storm King Café, located in the basement of Roanoke Hall, near the mail room. Warm wood moldings and bright brass made the place cheery. Behind the marble counter was a soda fountain. Behind that, a door that led to a kitchen with a grill for hot sandwiches and burgers. In front of the bar, tables, some round, some rectangular, stood on a black and white checkered floor.

The waitresses were a spirited dark-haired girl with a mischievous smile, and Xandra Black, the young woman who, while possessed by prophetic spirits, had warned Nastasia not to touch Joshua March—a warning Rachel now wished she had not encouraged the princess to ignore, since it had put Nastasia in the Halls of Healing. Both girls wore café uniforms, a smart, blue sailor dress and a white paper hat with blue trim. Along with her dress, Miss Black wore a hood that covered her face, except the tip of her nose and her mouth. The hood looked odd under her paper hat.

Joy gestured at the first girl. "Everyone, this is my sister Faith. The soda jerk."

"You call your sister a jerk?" Siggy asked.

"No, that's her job. Soda jerk," explained Joy. "It's what they call someone who works at a soda fountain."

"Waitress is fine with me." Faith leaned against the bar, smiling impishly.

The waitresses handed them menus. The Storm King Café served exotic teas and a variety of soft drinks: sarsaparilla, birch beer, Cheerwine, elderberry cordial, and egg creams. It also served light fare—grilled cheese, sandwiches, hamburgers, and all manner of ice cream sundaes. A case to one side held confectionery sculptures made out of maple sugar or marzipan—leaves, fruit, fanciful unicorns, and castles. Beneath these were honey cakes, sugar flowers, and other items available for purchase by those who wished to leave an offering at one of the shrines in the Memorial Garden.

The friends sat on stools by the high bar, all except the princess, who seated herself at a table. Despite Lucky's moaning, Sigfried generously pulled out a fistful of money and paid for drinks and snacks for everyone and a sandwich for his girlfriend. The princess thanked him primly but insisted on paying for herself. She pulled out her crisp, hot pink bills with drawings of wombats that looked like they could have been done by five-year-olds. The two girls behind the counter laughed and said that the Storm King Café did not accept Monopoly money. Nastasia humbly accepted Siggy's largesse.

Valerie ordered a Reuben and a Cheerwine, which turned out to be a kind of cherry soda. Siggy asked for a burger and fries with a malted milkshake. The princess picked Earl Grey tea and scones. Joy had a sarsaparilla float. Salome chose a peach sundae. Rachel ordered an egg cream, which turned out to contain neither egg nor cream. It was surprisingly good, though, frothy and chocolaty. She drank it slowly, dreaming of sharing one with Gaius, their heads close together as they sipped on their twin straws.

The princess frowned slightly. "My father seemed to recognize our P.E. teacher."

Suddenly alert, Rachel asked, "How so?"

"When we passed Mr. Chanson last night, Father looked extremely surprised to see him."

"Surprised worried or surprised happy?" Valerie paused between bites.

"Happy surprised," replied Nastasia. "Father clasped him on the shoulder and cried, 'Roland Saint-Michael! You're alive.' Mr. Chanson explained that Father must have mistaken him for another. Father nodded and apologized, but he just kept smiling. When Mr. Chanson left, he murmured something like, 'He must have been here all along. Who would have thought?'"

"What does this mean?" Joy bounced nervously on her chair.

Siggy said, "It means that the King of Smagical Mosstralia recognized Memory Lass's boss from Outside. It means our P.E. tutor is a Metaplutonian."

Valerie rolled her eyes at Siggy's mispronunciation of the princess's homeland.

"We knew that," Rachel said. "He was in the princess's vision. He is from the same world as Von Dread and the amazing building." She paused and then added wryly. "We also knew that when he survived being thrown through a stone wall and fifty yards of dirt."

"He did...what?" Salome leaned forward, her luminous eyes even wider than normal. "Our hunky gym tutor? And to think I thought he was just eye candy!"

"And it means my boss's proper name isn't Chanson." Rachel's mind raced, trying to put everything together. "It's Saint-Michael." She searched the dictionaries and name books in the library of her memory. "Does anybody know what Saint means?"

"I've never heard the word before, outside of the dog breed, St. Bernard," the princess said. "I tried to ask Father—about his being from Outside. He said some sort of foolish nonsense that didn't answer the question. Something like: '"Have a radish" said the kookaburra to the emu.'" Nastasia sighed. "Which is about what I expected."

"Your father didn't look foolish," mused Rachel. "Rather he looked very much like someone who was having a joke at the expense of the rest of us."

"Do you think his foolishness has to do with his being from Outside?" Joy asked.

"When the Raven flies by, I go dumb." Lucky wiggled his long flame-red whiskers. "If it flew past the princess's father, would he stop being goofy and insist on using real money?"

That made everyone laugh, but it was nervous laughter.

• • •

Xandra Black, her nose and mouth visible beneath her hood, gave Valerie Hunt her grilled cheese and pickle on a silver tray. Then she served the princess her Earl Gray tea with scones, Double Devon Cream, and huckleberry jam. Nastasia watched her with some interest.

"I wish to thank you for your warning, even though I did not heed it," said Nastasia. "You are...Xandra Black, if I recall?"

"That's me." The young woman's tone of voice was sardonic. "Or Flops-over-Dead-Chick. Whichever suits your fancy."

"Do you...flop over dead?" Valerie asked, snapping a picture of her. Xandra recoiled as if annoyed and then sighed wearily, as if it was not worth her time to make a fuss.

"Occasionally," Xandra drawled dryly. "Fortunately, it hasn't been permanent."

"I assume you faint or something." Salome's overly-large eyes looked even larger when she paid attention to something. "I mean, you don't actually flop over dead."

"Does enduring the burning fires of a lake of flame in the underworld sound dead enough for you?" Xandra drawled. "I flop over dead. It's the price for...a gift of mine."

"Really? Dead-dead? Can I watch?" Siggy leaned forward eagerly, his chocolate and mint sundae forgotten. "If Lucky ate you while you were dead, would you still get better?"

"Please don't let your dragon eat me." Xandra gave an exaggerated sigh. "That might turn out badly for both of us."

"I can be magnanimous! Lucky, don't eat her. Even if she looks dead," said Siggy.

"Thanks," Xandra murmured dryly, as she returned behind the counter. "Much obliged."

"Saw your boyfriend last night," Valerie smirked over her Cheerwine. "Von Dread brought him back wrapped in a pink blanket. I got a picture of it." She patted her camera. "I'll make you a copy when I get it developed."

"Oh, thank you!" Rachel grinned.

The thought of Gaius wrapped in a pink blanket filled her with a kind of bubbly delight.

"He is not her boyfriend." The princess primly defended Rachel.

"Um...actually, he is." Rachel blushed. "My boyfriend, that is."

The princess's face betrayed surprise and hurt. "But you said you had refused him?"

"I ch-changed my mind," Rachel stuttered.

Nastasia frowned with such obvious disapproval that it snuffed out quite a few of the candles on the chandelier of Rachel's happiness.

"Boyfriend?" Joy squealed. "You have a boyfriend?" Faith shot her younger sister an inquisitive glance, raising an impish eyebrow. Joy gave an exaggerated sigh. "My father doesn't allow my sisters and me to have boyfriends until we are at least sixteen."

"Valerie and Siggy are boyfriend and girlfriend," Rachel pointed out.

"That's true," Joy shot Valerie a wistful, envious look.

The sourness and anger was fading from Salome's face. She clapped her hands gleefully and began attacking her peach sundae with her long-handled spoon. "Oh, that's so exciting. Gaius Valiant's so cute. All us girls in Drake sigh over him."

"I thought you had a boyfriend, too?" Joy asked Salome.

"I do."

"Should you be sighing over some other boy?" asked the princess with a frown.

Salome shrugged. "I can window shop."

"If you're not going to eat that, Princess, Lucky and I can help you." Siggy leaned over and took a scone that the princess had slathered with cream and jam but not eaten. Nastasia sighed but did not protest. Sigfried broke it in half and tossed the rest to Lucky, who gulped it happily, despite that he was still pudgy from last night's feast behind Drake Hall.

Joy leaned forward. "So...what does Mr. Valiant think of Track and Broom? Is he an athlete? Is he going to want you to go out for the team?"

"I don't know," Rachel admitted. "I don't really know him very well yet."

"If you don't know him," Nastasia stirred her tea with a tiny silver spoon, the furrow in her brow deepening, "why are you dating him?"

"Um...because I quite fancy him, and he likes me." Rachel blew through her straw and watched her egg cream froth as it bubbled. "He fought Von Dread for me."

The princess *hmphed* dismissively. "He is a boy. He fought to defend his pride."

Rachel's heart clenched painfully. Her brother's claim, that Gaius wanted to date her only to irritate Peter, had not troubled her. This, however, shook her.

What if Nastasia were right?

Rachel knew very little about boys. What if she was fooling herself? It happened all the time in books and ballads—Girls were taken in by handsome faces and sweet words, usually to their ruin. She did not think Gaius fought just to defend his pride. But how could she be sure?

• • •

Three freshman boys came tromping down the stairs, their familiars in tow. They came up to the counter and ordered ice creams. One was pale; one had very dark skin; and the third was in between. As Xandra took their orders, Rachel thought back to the Familiar Bonding Ceremony, in which all the freshmen had been called by name. She recognized them as: Mortimer Egg, Jr., Jarius Knight, and Juma O'Malley

She glanced at the three boys and then back at her egg cream. She studied their faces as they appeared in her memory of the previous few seconds, giving particular attention to the son of the man who had tried to kill Valerie.

Mortimer Egg, Jr. was a slender boy with straw-colored hair and freckles, who dressed in the subfusc style. He struck Rachel as good-natured but a bit hapless. Under one arm, he carried his familiar, a white rabbit with black nose and ears and red, red eyes. Not blood red, like the raven, but an eerie color nonetheless. Rachel would have bet money that it was a phooka. She was good at spotting phookas.

Did he know that his father was an evil murderer?

No, Rachel decided. His face was open, and his smile genuine. If word had come that his father was wanted for murder, or even in custody, he would have had a nervousness around his eyes, a tightness around his mouth. No one had told this boy that his father was a suspect.

Rachel shivered. *That meant that they had not caught the man yet.*

Rising, she paced about the café. On a mural stretching across the wall next to the bar, Storm King Mountain rose above the Hudson. The storm goblin known as the Heer of Dunderberg stood atop its peak, arms akimbo, in his orange and green doublet and hose and his pure white sugar loaf hat. A storm brewed above and to either side of him. His lightning imps leapt through the air, their javelin-bolts sizzling. His mist sprites reached down with eager faces and long foggy fingers. Below the mountain, the artist had painted the original *Pollepel* and other famous wrecks, sunk by the fury of the Heer. The vessels were depicted as broken and sinking, their crew crying out.

One ship did not sink, or even rest on the brown waters of the Hudson. Instead, it hovered above them, its sails in tatters, except for the wing-like ones spread horizontally to either side. A man dressed in a black jacket with lace at his throat and a silver buckle on his hat stood defiantly on the prow. He played a double flute. Sparkles of gold spread from his instrument, encircling his ship and protecting it from the winds, as his sailors shot arrows and spells at the Heer.

Rachel traced her fingers over the man, exclaiming in delight, "Captain Vanderdecken!"

"You recognize that bloke?" Siggy had come up beside her, along with Valerie. He turned his head sideways as he regarded the mural.

Rachel nodded. "He is the captain of the most famous ship in the world."

"And that is?"

"*The Flying Dutchman.*"

"I thought the captain of *The Flying Dutchman* was a squid," said Sigfried.

"What? No. He's a Dutchman. Hence the name." Rachel squinted at the picture. "Why is he shown here? By Storm King Mountain?"

"I did some research on the Hudson Highlands before coming to school." Valerie slid her arm through Sigfried's, pointing at the mural with her other hand. "Even among the Unwary, there are tales of *The Flying Dutchman* sailing these waters. Washington Irving refers to it in a story. That story also mentions the Heer of Dunderberg." As if on cue, thunder rumbled from the direction of the Heer's prison, followed by a louder thunderclap from the sky.

Valerie shivered. "He can't hear us, can he? That storm goblin locked up in Stony Tor."

"No idea," Rachel murmured.

"I bet he can." Juma O'Malley's voice was as eager and infectious as his smile. He had a caramel-colored complexion and a very shaggy head of tight, kinky, coppery curls. His familiar, a tiny elephant no bigger than a cocker spaniel, stomped along beside him.

"Hey, you, Storm Goblin!" Sigfried shouted. "I'm coming for you!" He cupped his ear, but there was no answering thunder-clap. He scowled, disappointed.

"Captain Vanderdecken's granddaughter goes to school with us." Juma held a short red metal tube with a black rubber button that he pressed repeatedly. "She's in our dorm."

"She's one of my roommates," Valerie said, "Rowan Vanderdecken. She's said to be descended from a long line of sea witches."

"What are you holding?" Rachel asked, leaning over to see the red tube.

"Flashlight," said Juma.

"Torch," said Sigfried simultaneously.

"A mundane torch! Oh! I've read about them in stories!" Rachel looked at the flashlight with interest. "But it doesn't work here, does it?"

"Sometimes, I can make it turn on." Juma pressed the button and frowned. "Not now."

"Wow!" Valerie marveled, "Can you do that for my computer? Or at least my iPod?"

"Sorry," Juma hung his head. "That's beyond my ability. Mom can do stuff like that." Beside him, the tiny elephant stole the metal tube from his hand with its agile trunk and began trying to eat it. Juma grabbed it back, laughing. "Jellybean thinks he's the technomancer, too."

The third boy, Jarius Knight, joined them as well, along with his immense St. Bernard—there was that *saint* word again, Rachel noted. Jarius was tall for a freshman and distinguished-looking with glasses and nearly black skin. He was older than most of the other students in their class and already sported a mustache. Siggy eyed this dubiously, as if sizing him up for a brawl.

Taking advantage of the space between young Mr. Egg and his friends, Rachel walked up beside him. Eager to connect with this unfortunate boy, she leaned forward and whispered, "Just between you and me, is your rabbit a phooka?"

Mortimer Egg Junior's cheeks grew red. "W-what would make you say that?"

Grinning, she whispered back, "I've spent hours on the Dartmoor, learning to tell phooka and kelpies from rabbits, dogs, and horses. But it's all right. Your secret's safe with me."

His nervousness ebbed away. "Um. All right." He grinned tentatively. "Our secret!"

While Rachel grinned back at him, inwardly, she cringed. He was utterly transparent with no dissembling skills at all. If he knew anything about his father's crimes, he lacked the skill to hide it.

She smiled and extended her hand. "I'm Rachel Griffin."

"I know. Agent Griffin's daughter." Mortimer Egg, Jr. grinned and shook her hand. "My father works with your dad, you know. He's occasionally been assigned to the London office."

"I...didn't realize." Rachel blinked at this information. Valerie had met the man in the New York office, but if he worked in London, too, that must have been how he met the traitor, Agent Browne. She added casually, "How is your father?"

"Fine, thanks." He smiled so openly that a throbbing pain ripped through Rachel's heart. His father had committed horrifying crimes, and he knew nothing. How terrible.

Juma and his elephant joined them. Mortimer gestured at the other boy with the huge, infectious smile. "This is my best friend, Juma. We're roommates in Dee."

"Best friends after one week of school." Rachel smiled happily, glancing fondly from Sigfried to the princess. "That's fast work."

"Oh, no," laughed Mortimer. "We've known each other for years. We're neighbors."

"My mother and I live next door to Mort." Juma bent and fed his tiny elephant a slice of dried apple he took from his pocket. "He's the one who told me all about magic."

"Just you and your mom? Is your father dead?" Rachel inquired gently.

Juma shrugged. "Who knows. Mom hasn't seen him in years. I've never even met him."

"Oh…" Rachel murmured, stunned.

She had been told that such arrangements were common in the Unwary world, but she had never actually met someone from a broken family. All these people with family problems: fathers who were murderers, and fathers who were absent. It made her miss her father.

As if the café had suddenly grown chilly, a shiver passed through her body. She thought of the conversation between Dr. Mordeau and the dean about her grandfather. These two boys knew so little about the true natures of their fathers.

What secrets might she not know about her family?

Chapter 18:
Sigfried the Puddle-Slayer and the Rose-ambush

"You were going to go without me, weren't you?" Joy O'Keefe stood on the path ahead of them, her hands on her hips, her face blotchy from anger. It was Sunday afternoon. The sun had finally peeked from behind the cloud cover, but the air was still damp and chilly. The princess and Rachel wore sweaters under their scholar's robes.

"This is detention," Nastasia replied, unperturbed, "not a social outing."

"You promised to take me!" Joy shouted.

"That is a big, fat lie," Siggy declared loudly. "I don't make promises I don't keep. Who is this girl? And why is she yelling at us?"

Rachel shook her head. His memory could not possibly be *that* bad.

"This is Miss O'Keefe," the princess replied primly. "She is part of our Inner Circle."

Siggy shrugged. "I guess you can tag along. I mean, you are a sorceress! You can only be killed if someone stabs you through the heart with a stake in the sunlight, right?"

The princess gave him an arch look. "You are speaking of vampires, Mr. Smith. We children of the Wise have no special way to charm our lives from harm."

Siggy looked back and forth between the girls in horror. "You mean you little witch-girls can be hurt like real people? Good grief! Are you insane? You cannot go on adventures any more, none of you! You could get hurt! And then you'd cry! You're just like girls!"

"We are girls," Rachel calmly reminded him.

"Girls with arcane powers," the princess spoke icily. "Your words are most unbecoming of a young gentleman. As for myself, one of royal blood may never cower when the lives of common people are exposed to danger. Only among the Unwary is it deemed fit for leaders to stay far behind the lines of battle, instead of fighting in the forefront. And look at how low their modern world has fallen and what cowardly weapons they use, and against civilians, too."

Lucky said, "She's got you there, Boss! You can't tell the princess to stay back, because you're following her."

"Who gives people detention for acts of valor, anyway?" Sigfried stomped his foot vehemently into the next puddle, making the muddy water jump. Then he hopped around in pain. His bare foot had impaled itself on a sharp stone hidden below the waterline.

"That puddle attack you, Boss?" Lucky snaked up beside them. "Should I incinerate it?"

"Burn it, Lucky, Burn it!" Siggy yelled, hopping.

Lucky drew a large breath and breathed huge gouts of red-gold flame all over the puddle. The odor of newly-struck matches billowed from him. The water sizzled and hissed. Hot steam rose in a huge cloud. The girls jumped backwards.

"Wait! It wasn't the puddle. The culprit is that sneaky rosebush there!" Siggy shouted, still holding his sore foot with one hand and pointing a finger, shaking with rage, at a rosebush growing beside a bench. "It was a sneak attack! A booby trap! A rose-ambush! Make it pay for its craven and unknightly attack! Incinerate the miscreant!"

Lucky leapt forward. The rose bush and the wooden bench next to it erupted in roaring flame. Joy shouted in alarm. Rachel watched the red-gold fire dance. If anyone else had done such a thing, she would have strongly objected to them damaging school property. In keeping with her promise to support Sigfried Smith against the world, however, she merely grinned, amused by his audacity. She knew the proctors would be able to repair the damage.

The princess rubbed the bridge of her nose, as if soothing a headache. "Mr. Smith. Please, in the future, refrain from burning school property."

Siggy sat down in the dirt and pulled a marshmallow and a half-eaten hotdog from his pocket, impaled them both on his huge Bowie knife, and held them toward the burning bench. "Mustn't let a good fire go to waste. Lucky! Check for other suspicious-looking shrubbery!"

"Why don't you wear shoes?" The princess cast Sigfried a disapproving glance. "You are only asking for trouble, walking around barefoot."

"Only wimps wear shoes," Sigfried mumbled.

Rachel, who was swinging her broom back and forth, kept quiet. She had ordered some for him a couple of days ago. She hoped they would soon arrive.

Siggy casually drew his foot up to his face with one hand. Bending, he began licking and sucking at the tiny red mark amid the grimy coal-blackness of the dirty sole of his foot. Rachel winced inwardly, but her face showed no reaction.

"Eww!" exclaimed Joy.

"Don't worry," said Lucky. "He's not eating his own foot! He's just licking the wound."

Joy covered her head with her arms, making jerky outraged motions. "Spit is unhealthy!"

"How can that be?" Siggy looked up, surprised. "There's spit in my mouth at all times."

Lucky said, "Spit sterilizes wounds. Because of the heat. It is a scientific fact!"

Siggy nodded rapidly. "You just have to pump a little white phosphorous fluid from the fire-making glands behind your fangs into your saliva before you spit. Lucky told me."

Rachel sighed. "Sigfried, you're a human being. You don't have glands like that."

"*Yet!*" said Siggy stubbornly. "You told me people can't turn into dragons—but look at Dr. Mordeau! If she can do it, I can do it. I have great hopes for alchemy class. I can't wait to perform alchemical experiments on my head!"

"It'll work out great!" Lucky added loyally. "You'll overcome many naked monkey boy handicaps! When have horrible experiments with unknown magical forces ever gone wrong?"

Siggy put down his hotdog on the dirt. He smacked his palm against Lucky's catlike paw with a high-five. Picking up the dirty hotdog, he wiped it haphazardly, and put it in his mouth.

"The crazy arsonist boy who eats dirt is telling me not to go into danger?" objected Joy.

Siggy shrugged, unimpressed. "Plants eat dirt. They're healthy!"

Rachel listened without weighing in, for two reasons. While she knew that she could do some things as well as boys could, many even better, she thought that the world where men tried to protect women was likely to be a finer one than the world where they did not. Things would have been much better for Valerie Hunt had someone taught Jonah Strega that girls should be protected. Rachel was not as keen as the other two on talking the unusually-strong, super-magical boy out of his chivalric beliefs.

The second reason was, while Joy was a member of the Inner Circle, it was only because she had barged in, and they had been forced to share their plans with her. If they were going to bring in someone else, she would rather have had it be Zoë.

The others continued arguing. Rachel sighed. The time had come to resolve the matter.

In a calm voice, she said, "Sigfried, it's ridiculous for it to be safe enough for us and not safe enough for Joy. It's detention, not monster-hunting. Besides," her face became solemn, "your roommate, Enoch, was sitting in alchemy class when he got attacked. How dangerous does that sound? Wherever we are *is* the front line."

"Enoch Smithwyck is dead," Joy announced. They all gaped at her. She shrank back. "M-my sister Hope told me. He died this morning, from his injuries."

The princess lowered her head respectfully.

"Then...I didn't save him." Rachel felt an odd floating sensation, as if the bottom of the world had vanished, but she had not yet fallen. She wished very much that Gaius were nearby.

Siggy blinked three times. "You mean dead-dead, like dead forever? Like Neeley at the orphanage, the time Punker swung the fire poker wildly and accidentally impaled Neeley through the eye, so that when Banger pulled the poker out, Neeley's brains fell out onto the floor, all gray and squirmy? That kind of dead?"

All three girls became paler. Siggy was quiet for a time, blinking and scowling.

Finally, he turned to Lucky. "All the girls are against me! Miss O'Keefe thinks I broke a promise, which no man alive dares to say; and Her Highness thinks my words are unbecoming of knighthood; and the freaky, genius, dwarf girl thinks there is no point in keeping the women back at camp with the luggage, because the camp is where the foes are! I can't fight O'Keefe. I can't disobey royalty, and I can't argue with the brainy girl! What do I do?"

Lucky rippled his body in an elegant shrug. "They're your harem. Can't you control a doe or three?"

"Harem?" Joy stamped her foot.

The princess frowned severely.

Sigfried crossed over to where Joy O'Keefe stood, and solemnly went down on one knee. Her eyes grew wide. He pulled the hot gooey marshmallow off the knife point. Holding the marshmallow behind his back, he laid his Bowie knife down on the dirt before her. "I, Sigfried Smith, solemnly vow I will not leave O'Keefe behind when we go on adventures."

Joy looked extremely pleased. Her cheeks turned bright pink.

The princess sighed and opened her purse. "If you must come, you had better hide in my bag. That way, there will not be any fuss about whether you are allowed along or not. You better hurry, the proctors are on their way over to investigate the burning roses."

Gratefully, Joy climbed inside. From within, her voice trailed out, calling, "Hey, this is where I left my hat!"

Lucky, who was warming his whiskers near the burning bench, asked, "Boss, are you going to eat that whole marshmallow?"

• • •

The Gardener, Mr. Burke, met them by the garden shed. He was a young man with curly, light brown hair, who had aspirations of joining the faculty as an alchemy tutor. He had a gentle disposition and a ready sense of humor. Rachel liked him immediately.

Mr. Burke explained that the assistant dean had given him the task of presiding over their detention. They would leave school grounds to collect herbs for the Alchemy Department. He handed each of them a pair of work gloves and a satiny black bag. Rachel took them and thanked him. As she prepared to depart, she caught a glimpse of two of the proctors putting out the burning bench with a cantrip. Rachel noted that one was the handsome young Mr. Fuentes, who had helped her the time the beastly Drake girls attacked her. She was grateful to see that he had recovered from the geas cast upon him by Dr. Mordeau.

Mr. Burke gave brooms to the princess and Siggy, and the four of them—five including Joy in the bag—flew across the commons, over the lily pond, down the tree-lined path, and out through the ruins of Frances Bannerman's castle onto the docks. From there, they circled north and east around the island, toward Stony Tor and the rolling hills beyond, following the path Rachel and Siggy had taken the first time they met.

The wind caught at their hair and chilled their ears. Rachel rejoiced to be up in the sky again. The weather had been so oppressive the last two days; she had missed her early morning flights. Breaking away from the others, she pinned her square black cap in place with bobby pins from her pocket. Then, she soared upward, celebrating her good fortune with a series of twirls and loops.

Mr. Burke called cautiously, "Miss Griffin! Do be careful."

Siggy stuck a thumb in her direction. "Don't worry about her. She's an ace in the air! We call her the Broom Goddess."

"I see why," the young gardener murmured, his eyes still concerned. His light brown curls flew every which way. "That is some flying, Miss Griffin, but perhaps you should play it safe and stick with the rest of us, rather than do these daredevil tricks."

Rachel smiled. She had not yet begun anything dangerous. Mounting upwards, she dived down in a rotating spin, the move she had come up with when Siggy asked her to imitate a butter churn. It was much easier when she was not carrying a second person. The wind whipped through her hair. She gained speed. The exhilaration made her shout with joy. Then, laughing gaily, she evened out. By the time she flew dutifully into formation with the others, the gardener's face had become so pale that it was almost green.

They flew upward. The brown water of the Hudson stretched out beneath them. To their left, Storm King rose, a pyramid-like peak, its blunted top stark against the steely gray sky. To the north, the faint line of the Newburg Bridge was visible crossing the brown waters of the river. To the right stretched the Breakneck Ridge and the Hudson Highlands, rolling green-clad peaks, dotted here and there with bright spots of yellow and red. Behind them, at the bend in the river, glittered West Point Military Academy.

Directly beneath them lay Pollepel Island, the false obscuration cast to hide Roanoke from the Unwary. It consisted of a ruined castle, a short stretch of forest, and an abandoned white brick mansion that Rachel had seen from the air on her first day.

"What is that place?" the princess inquired, pointing.

"The mansion of Francis Bannerman the Fourth," Mr. Burke said. "He is the one who set up the obscurations that protect the island. He was the Grand Inquisitor until his death in 1918. His successor, Herodotus Powers, was murdered by the Terrible Five in 1999. The Powers twins, Napoleon and Sebastian— maybe you saw them at the Bonding Ceremony?—are Herodotus's grandsons."

"Since Power's death, the Grand Inquisitor has been Cain March," intoned the princess. "Mr. March is a family friend."

Mr. Burke looked impressed and, perhaps, slightly nervous.

"The Grand Whoha?" asked Sigfried.

"The Grand Inquisitor is the member of the Parliament of the Wise who represents law and justice," explained Rachel. "He is the head of the Obscurae and the Wisecraft—which means he's my father's boss."

"The justice you called swift and terrible?" asked Sigfried. "Sounds like a man to avoid."

"It's better not to cross him," Rachel agreed quickly. She added, "Two of March's children are students here: Evelyn and Joshua. They are both in the Knights of Walpurgis."

"I would be careful of socializing with them, were I you," the gardener spoke warily.

"How so?" asked Rachel.

"The Grand Inquisitor is parano..." The gardener glanced at the princess and pressed his lips together. "He is very protective of his children. Everyone who becomes friends with them gets grilled by their father—under the *Spell of True Recitation*."

Recalling the discomfort of being under the effects of the spell that had caused her to blurt out her thoughts without filtering, Rachel flinched.

She added, "Joshua March was the one Xandra Black told the princess not to touch."

"Was that the guy who made her faint?" asked Sigfried. "The one the princess's brother slugged, who was being tortured by the Lightbringer in her vision?"

The gardener gave him an odd look. Rachel nodded.

"If Miss Black should offer any more advice," the princess opined, as she flew gracefully beside the gardener, "I shall be inclined to listen."

"Bannerface's mansion looks spooky." Siggy's voice had a nervous edge to it, as he glanced to the left at the partially ruined cement and brick house with its crenelated turrets and empty windows.

"It is," Mr. Burke assured them with a scholarly cast to his voice. "Every Halloween, the Dead Man's Ball is held there."

"What's that?" Rachel leaned forward eagerly.

"The shades of the drowned—all those who have died in these waters, killed by the storm goblin and his lightning imps—gather there to dance and remember."

Rachel gazed curiously at the mansion. Ghosts fascinated her. Who knows what secrets they might possess? Several haunted Gryphon Park—a white lady who appeared in a window in the West Wing; an ancient ancestor who died in some horrible calamity; and Thunderfrost, a beautiful black-and-silver horse with a huge flowing mane who was said to appear as a warning when the family was in need.

Rachel had seen the second one, her ancient ancestor, twice in the main library, though he would not speak to her. Thunderfrost, on the other hand, she knew well. He used to canter beside her and her pony Widdershins as they sped across the fields or up the slopes of Gryphon Tor. Sometimes, a ghost boy in dark Victorian garments rode on the back of the magnificent steed. Rachel mentally referred to him as Thunderfrost's Boy.

"Ghosts!" Siggy shivered. "That's awfully creepy!"

"Wouldn't that be exciting! To attend the Dead Man's Ball!" Rachel gazed at the old dilapidated mansion with a strange sense of longing.

Siggy shook his head, his face pale. "Not interested in seeing ghosts. Thank you."

"What, really?" Rachel glanced over in surprise. Siggy looked a bit pale. It had not occurred to her that anything could scare the erratic orphan boy. "Huh."

Siggy murmured in a low voice, "I hope my dead roommate doesn't come haunt us."

Mr. Burke dived down. As the other three followed, the obscuration broke. They could see the real Roanoke Island spread out beneath them. Behind them, they could see the spires of the school. To the left, the mansion was still there, but beyond it stretched several extra miles. Ahead, a bare, stony peak loomed above the five green hills beyond.

"Oh! I can see the real island," the princess called, as they descended. "And Stony Tor."

"How do they do that?" Siggy gawked. "Make a bigger space fit in a smaller one?"

"Kenomancy," Rachel replied.

"Keno...like the gambling game?" Siggy asked.

"No," said Mr. Burke. "*Keno*, like the Greek word for *void*. It is the sorcerous art of adding space."

Nastasia added, "Kenomancers are the people who manufacture the bags that are bigger on the inside than on the outside."

Directly north was Dutchman's Cove, a large inlet, with cliffs to the left and an island in the middle. To the right, the barnacled ribs of an abandoned man-o-war jutted up above the brown waters. Only one of the massive sailing vessel's three masts rose from the wreck.

They landed on the southern shore of the cove, in a field of tall dried grass. Forests surrounded the fields. A river leapt down the side of the closest of the northern hills ending in a waterfall. Its distant roar mingled with the tweeting of songbirds and the soft rustle of the wind. Now and again, a loud rumbling, like that of an approaching storm, came from the tor.

Mr. Burke gestured to the forest stretching to their west. "We are looking for three herbs. These are magical plants that are hard to grow in our gardens: moly, royal yarrow, and honeymint." He held up a long slender stalk with a puff of flowers at the top; a lacy-leafed plant with a metallic glint to its purple flowers; and a square-stemmed herb with a sweet minty scent, which he let the students sniff. It reminded Rachel of pennyroyal with a hint of honey.

"By no means cross any of the stone walls," Mr. Burke continued. "They are wards against the greater dangers out here."

"Greater dangers?" Sigfried asked intently.

Rachel wondered if this was the first time the boy had ever given a tutor his full attention.

"Many unsavory things are drawn to Roanoke by the extraordinary amount of sorcery gathered in one place."

"Like what?" Sigfried pressed eagerly. "The Storm Goblin? If we cross the stone wall, will he get out?"

"No, but there are worse things than Storm Goblins."

"Worse! Lucky, do you hear that?" Siggy cried excitedly. "There are monsters! What kind? Are there dragons?"

"No..." Mr. Burke frowned, flustered. Apparently, this was not the response his admonitions ordinarily provoked. "I don't know them all. The head of the proctors, Mr. Maverick Badger, could tell you more, but..."

He turned towards the river and pointed his arm, sweeping from left to right as he spoke. "Each-Uisge in the marshes. A type of kelpie. Very dangerous. And folks have spotted Wilis on the cliff. Wilis are the ghosts of women who died of a broken heart after being jilted by their lovers. They tend to be vindictive. What else? See the caves along the west side of the cove? Near the shoreline? Two years ago, an ogre emerged from there and ate three kayakers."

"Wicked!" Siggy cried, high-fiving Lucky.

Rachel cringed inwardly at his callousness, but her face betrayed no reaction. The princess rubbed her temples and sighed.

"Men died, Mr. Smith." Mr. Burke frowned severely.

Sigfried entirely failed to look chastened.

"There are spriggans on the slopes," Mr. Burke continued. "Not as dangerous but troublesome enough. Spruce trolls on the hillsides, their cousins, the trow, in the rocky valley beyond. Phookas have been spotted on the meadow by the northeast lake, which is said to contain a water panther. Recently, a herd of selkie moved in hereabouts. Oh, and it is said that a *Mexaxhuk* lives in the lake on the island in the Cove. I had forgotten that one." He pointed back at Dutchman's Cove where an island was visible beyond the hulk of the Man-O-War.

"What is a *Mexaxhuk*?" the princess asked.

"A horned serpent that eats human beings. It and the water panther lived here before Roanoke Island floated into these waters. As did the Storm Goblin."

"Double Ace!" Siggy peered out fiercely, as if the fervor of his gaze would force the creature to emerge.

Mr. Burke ran a hand through his curly hair and sighed. "The point is, ordinarily, the wards of the school keep us safe.

You are not behind those wards. This area has been protected for the purposes of gathering herbs. Do not cross the stone walls. Do you understand?"

"Indeed," said the princess.

"I guess." Siggy shrugged.

Rachel did not speak. She did not even nod. She just stared steadily back at the gardener, her eyes large and dark, hoping he would interpret her silence as assent. She had no intention of obeying his instruction. She was here to find the Tree. Where it was, there she would go. But she preferred not to break a promise. To her relief, it worked.

As Mr. Burke turned away, Rachel noted with mild surprise that it did not trouble her to disobey a direct order from an adult. She felt no sense of resistance, no rebellion. Rather, it was as if the words were not meant for her.

During her wild ride to warn her fellow students of Dr. Mordeau's wickedness, whatever had made her so obedient throughout her previous life had broken beyond repair.

Chapter 19:
The Magnificent Tree of Roanoke Island

"King of the Big Rock!" Siggy shouted. He leapt atop a lone boulder in the middle of the field. In the gloom of the overcast sky, the rock gleamed with a silvery sheen. He swung his clasped hands to the left and right over his head, like a champion prize fighter. Lucky zipped around him, crowing his victory crow.

Nastasia shook her head and headed for a nearby little pond to search the shore for royal yarrow. Tickled by the enthusiasm of the boy and his dragon, Rachel watched a bit longer. Then, she, too, set out to collect herbs. She left the tall grasses and moved into the trees. Smooth leaves brushed her cheek, and dead ones crunched under her feet. Inhaling deeply, she luxuriated in the scent of forest.

She found a few sprigs of moly growing in a sunny patch. As she bent to pick the long stalks, a strange feeling came over her—of hush and exhilaration. It felt like the mounting excitement before a storm, like the dawning of a long-awaited morning, like the sudden realization that anything truly was possible.

Rachel straightened slowly, brushing aside stray locks of hair. She knew *that* feeling.

Fairy folk were near.

With eyes honed by hours of wandering through the forests of Gryphon Park and over the Dartmoor, she surveyed her surroundings. Signs of the fey abounded. A ring of toadstools grew just beyond the glade. A faint scent of hyacinth filled the air, despite being out of season. Beside a mossy stone, acorns and thorns rested where wee folk had left their helmets and lances. A tree knot had a hole in it. The Unwary thought such cavities in trees developed by some natural process. Rachel knew better. If a tree contained a hollow, some elfin creature dwelt in it.

Rachel peered into the knot. The hole was filled with water. Three tiny she-pixies with glittery dragonfly wings bathed within, kicking up a spray with their shapely legs. They squealed when they saw a giantess peering at them and scrambled backward in terror. But they flashed bright smiles when Rachel put her finger to her lips and backed up, winking.

She crept farther into the woods. She could feel the Folk of the Forest watching her. Between the knobby roots of a huge oak, she spotted a foot-high cavity splitting the trunk. The edges of the hollow area were thickly rounded where the bark was attempting to grow over the break. Squatting down, Rachel peered inside. Bits of twisted bark littered the sawdust-covered floor, and tell-tale traces of thistledown floated in the cavity. This was the home of a wood sprite. Pressing her lips together to keep herself from making a sound, she took a toffee from her pocket and left it inside the tree for the wee one.

Ahead, a large outcropping of rock jutted up among the trunks. Beside them, a birch grew sideways for three feet before rising skyward. Rachel looked left and right. No one was watching. She crept closer and laid her hand on the smooth bark.

"Are you a riding tree?" she whispered.

The trunk shivered beneath her hand.

Rachel climbed onto it, a feat easier to accomplish here, where she wore sweatpants under her robes, than at home, where she wore skirts. She leaned her cheek against the bark and put her arms around the tree. But it did not move again.

Not that she expected it to. Riding trees only pulled up their roots and ran through the forest at the cusp of twilight, those few precious moments before nightfall or daybreak when it was too dim to see clearly. To anyone lucky enough to be granted a ride, the trees became transparent, and the dryads became visible within, waving their branch-like fingers.

Slipping down, she gave the trunk one last pat. Then, she stopped. Speaking of trees, where was it—the great Tree the Lion had shown her? Slowly, she turned around, looking upward. When she had come full circle, she closed her eyes and recalled what she had just seen—expecting to suddenly recall a large trunk towering up above its fellows.

But there was nothing.

No obscuration.

No huge tree.

Had she been wrong?

She walked on, but the magic had gone out of the forest for her. Disappointment weighed so heavily that she could no longer feel the presence of the little folk.

She walked until she reached the waist-high stone wall. Pale green moss and paler lichen grew upon the rocks. Beside it was a patch of honeymint. Kneeling, she donned her work gloves and diligently gathered herbs, striving to dispel her growing fear that the gardener had brought them to the wrong place. As she worked, she imagined Gaius kneeling beside her, their fingers accidentally brushing as they reached to pick honeymint. It pained her that the princess did not like him. She so wished the people she cared about would all get along.

And what was she to do about Peter? She so hated fighting with her brother.

Rachel sighed.

• • •

"Hey!" Joy's voice called from where she was hiding in Nastasia's open bag. "Weren't you all supposed to stay on the other side of that stone wall?"

Rachel raised her head and looked around. She, Siggy, and the princess stood in a little glade of clover and tiny purple flowers. The stone wall was behind them.

"Wait." Rachel stared at the lichen-covered stones ten feet away. She felt strangely disoriented, as if she were in a dream. The tassel of her hat hung in her eyes. Brushing it aside, she walked to the wall and peeked over it, hoping to discover that she had gotten turned around. But no. On the far side lay her patch of honeymint. "Wh-when did this happen?"

"Don't remember." Siggy shrugged.

Pulling an apple from his pocket, he took a huge bite. Bits of it fell to the ground. Juice dribbled down his chin. He threw the rest into the air. Before it could hit the ground, Lucky darted over and swallowed it whole.

A rumble of thunder shook the forest. Rachel straightened her scholar's cap and replayed her memory of the last ten minutes. She was picking honeymint along the stone wall. Then, she...

Then she...

Then she...

"I-I can't remember!" Rachel's voice came out as a shriek. She took a stumbling step backward and grabbed her head. "I *can't remember* how we crossed the stone wall!"

"I can't either." Nastasia clambered over the stones, back to safety. "I guess we didn't notice. But we must hurry back now."

Rachel spun around, holding her head in confusion. "No...*I* can't remember. I...I *never* can't remember! I..." Then her voice cut off.

Ahead of her, rising above the forest, was an enormously wide tree truck that went up...

And up...

And up...

It towered above the forest, above the hills, above Stony Tor. It was gigantic, colossal. Twenty men standing with outstretched arms touching fingertip to fingertip could not have surrounded it. Rachel's lips parted in awe.

She had not realized the Tree would be *that* big.

Taking a few steps back, she turned her head this way and that in an attempt to glimpse the whole thing. High above, the trunk divided into seven great branches, each bearing a different type of leaf: oak, beech, birch, ash, elm, hickory, and maple.

A jolt of recognition shook her from the soles of her feet to the crown of her head. The Roanoke Tree—the seven-branched tree pictured on the Roanoke coat-of-arms, each branch of which represented one of the Seven Arts of Sorcery...*it was real.*

Or was it? Her heart beat faster. Maybe this was an obscuration, and the true tree was smaller. Rachel closed her eyes, remembering. In her memory,...

That could not be right!

Her eyes flew open. Amazed, she closed them a second time, recalling what she had just seen a second time. In her mind's eye,

the tree blazed with a glorious light that curled, flame-like, around the great branches. It was as if the sun had come down to roost like a hawk in the crook of the trunk. Just perceiving this radiance lifted her spirits. It filled her with a kind of sacred joy that she had no words to describe. As if drawn by a string, she walked toward it.

"Rachel, stop!" Nastasia put both her hands atop the wall and leaned over it. "We must not cross this. You must come back."

"But this is the Tree! Don't you see? The one the Lion showed us in our visions. It's the Roanoke Tree!" Rachel breathed in awe. Her limbs still felt weak from the horror of not remembering, but fear was muted by awe. Eagerly, she waved her friends forward. "Come on!"

"No!" The princess cried fiercely. "We were strictly instructed not to cross the wall!"

"That's some tree. A tree that big...maybe there's treasure hidden among its roots!" Siggy's eyes glittered the way Lucky's did when the dragon talked about gold.

"Mr. Smith. If you are my knight, you must stay here."

Reluctantly, Sigfried backed up and joined Nastasia. He sat down on the stone wall, crossing his arms and scowling. Rachel saw him make a slight gesture with his head. Lucky the Dragon snaked forward, rapidly disappearing among the lesser trunks.

"You should come back, too, Rachel," said the princess.

"But the Lion..." Rachel murmured, distracted. The spot in her memory that would not yield its secrets troubled her. Her mind kept poking at it. It felt strange, unfamiliar.

"We cannot disobey a direct order because of Kitten's familiar." The princess frowned severely. "Beside, I am not yet certain what side that creature is on."

Rachel's eyes returned to the Tree, her gaze resting on the seven great branches. She recalled the feeling of peace that had come from the tiny Lion—as if she were standing in a meadow surrounded by sweet-smelling wild flowers, and all the troubles of the world had blown far, far away—the same Lion who had later, impossibly, seemed larger than the universe.

Breathing a ragged breath, Rachel replied very softly, "Whatever side the Lion's on, that's the side I want to be with."

She walked toward the tree.

"Come back, Rachel!" the princess called, anguished. "Mr. Smith, I fear she has been affected by a spell. You saw how strangely she acted just now."

"No spell," Rachel called back over her shoulder. "I just want to see this Tree."

"Shall I go after her?" Sigfried asked, starting to move forward.

"No!" Nastasia commanded. "I forbid you!"

A figure flying a racing broom shot over the trees and landed on the clover. It was the assistant dean, Mr. Gideon. The princess hurried along the stone wall until she was across from the true history tutor, but still on her side.

"Thank goodness you are here, Sir," the princess called. "I told them we were not to cross the wall. They will not listen! I fear they are under a spell."

Mr. Gideon wore the black and gold robes of the Scholars of Dee Hall. He was a rather good-looking man, slender and trim, with dark brown skin, a mustache, and gray at his temples. His voice was always tinged with wry amusement.

"Your highness," he said, "you may cross the wall. That's why I brought you here."

"Wh-what?" The princess drew back, startled. "Mr. Burke instructed us not to cross."

Mr. Gideon chuckled. "It did not occur to me that students who left the infirmary to go *fight* Dr. Mordeau, *of their own will*, would be cowed by a little warning of danger. I did not think to explain to him why you were really here."

"We are here for detention, to make right our transgression," the princess insisted primly.

He shook his head kindly. "That was merely an excuse to allow you off campus. A friend of mine wishes to speak to the three of you."

"You mean, this detention was a trick?" The princess looked horrified.

"Not a trick, Miss Romanov. I thought you understood."

"I understood," Rachel murmured. It felt so nice to know that, for once, she had been right about something. "It was to see the Tree."

"You did not make your intentions clear," Nastasia spoke with stiff formality. Her regal expression broke. "I thought...that we saw eye to eye, you and I."

The princess looked so woebegone that Mr. Gideon had not assigned detention because he shared her strict honor code. Rachel's heart went out to her.

Mr. Gideon bowed toward the princess. "I am sorry, your highness. I did not realize that you were strict beyond your years. The woods are safe here. It is to protect what is on this side that our staff has been instructed never to go farther than the stone wall."

The princess, her voice tight from the sting of betrayal, continued to argue with Mr. Gideon, but Rachel did not stay. She hopped on her steeplechaser and zoomed forward.

• • •

The Tree rose, a vast gray-black and knobbly wall of bark. Rachel eagerly breathed in a sweet smell. The air was filled with a perfume like wild flowers mingled with the most aromatic of spices. The scent was glorious.

Then she felt it again, only ten times stronger. The hush; the anticipation; the undercurrent of rising excitement, like an electrical charge searing the air.

The Folk of the Forest were near.

Every nerve alert, Rachel slowly moved her bristleless forward. Her gaze flickered here and there, taking in everything. She replayed her memory constantly, to be sure her senses were not ensorcelled. The farther she went, the stronger grew the presence of fey. Never, even near the dryad who lived in the old oak behind Gryphon Park, had she felt anything like this.

Something amazing was near. Amazing or terrifying.

Huge roots stretched from the bottom of the tree, big snaking lengths of wood as high as her knee. Near where they met the trunk, they rose even higher than her head. Between these living fences grew herbs—though not in rows, like a human garden—meandering, wild.

Rachel's hands tightened on the handlebars. She recognized the plant with the frosty pattern on its lacy, moon-pale leaves. It was *manahrim*. Only in the secret *Compendium of Arcane Wisdom* her grandfather had kept hidden, even in his private library, had she seen mention of it. She flew lower, peering at the herbs. There was *mavričin koren*, also called rainbow root, whose existence was debated, even among the most learned scholars, and...

Her brow furrowed as she looked at the plants. She did not know that one.

Or that one.

Or...

Floating over great wall-like roots, Rachel gazed across the gardens. Dozens of plants bloomed here that she had never seen—not in all the encyclopedias and botany books she had perused in the many libraries she had visited, not even in her grandfather's secret compendiums.

What did this mean?

Everything was so lush, so alive. As Rachel breathed in again, exhilaration rushed through her trembling limbs. She felt wide awake and, yet, as if she were dreaming. Walking through the dreamlands with Zoë Forrest had felt a bit like this. Happiness burst within her like a fountain. *What manner of wonderland had they stumbled upon?*

Then she froze.

In the Tree was a hollow.

Not a little crack, like the den where she had left the toffee, this crevice sank deep into the Tree. It was nine feet tall, its edges rounded with thick bark. Rachel hooked her feet onto the brass footholds on the back of her steeplechaser, and darted back a good ten feet.

If all tree hollows were home to the fey, what lived in this one?

"Siggy! Nastasia! Come quickly!" she shouted in great excitement.

"Coming!" Sigfried's voice echoed in the distance.

Out from the giant hollow stepped a being. Its face was turned away, but the shell-like ears that poked through the long fern-green hair ended in delicate points.

An elf.

But not any earthly elf.

Chapter 20:
The Exiled Daughter of Idunn

The elf stood seven feet tall, more glamorous and voluptuous than any mortal. Her skin was a luminous gray, like the smooth bark of a beech. Her eyes glowed warm as polished wood, and starlight shone where mortals had pupils. Her features were upswept, high cheek bones, slanted eyes, and fern-green brows. Long, fern-green hair floated about her like a leafy mantle.

Rachel had seen earthly elves. Once, she had accompanied her parents to a Moth wedding. The Moth family kept in contact with their supernatural kin. During the ceremony, doors had opened in the hillside, and the fey branch of the family had glided forth to join the festivities. Somber and gracious, yet filled with spiteful glee, members both tiny and tall had danced with the guests and given blessings to the happy couple. The next day, the cows throughout the county produced purple milk.

But Lord Moth's kin, as amazing as they were, had not been like this woman. They had not had hair the color of ferns. They had not glowed, as if standing in moonlight. They had not had stars instead of pupils.

"Greetings, children, come forward." Her voice was as sweet as the sound of bells. When she moved, her iridescent gown, which looked as if it had been woven from light reflected off of the sea, rustled like aspen leaves. Turning, Rachel saw Nastasia standing uneasily on the far side of the nearest root-wall. Siggy sat atop the same bark-covered wall, one knee bent, his foot resting on the bark. Lucky's head and whiskers peeked over the edge beside him.

"Can...we help you?" Rachel asked haltingly. She slipped from her broom and took a step or two forward.

"No, but I can help you." She smiled. "The three of you."

"Four!" Joy's face peered out of the princess's bag.

"What have we here? A stowaway?" The elf smiled, but a terrible sorrow haunted her eyes.

As if in a dream, Rachel recalled the last time she had seen such sorrow. It had been on the face of her grandmother, Amelia

Abney-Hastings Griffin, the time the deer ate the roses she had brought with her when she became the Duchess of Devon. It was the only time Rachel had seen her stern grandmother cry.

Rachel's heart constricted. Roses were the holy flower of the vestal virgins. Those rosebushes must have come from the *Atrium Vestae* in Rome, a memento of the life her grandmother abandoned when she wedded Blaise Griffin. Rachel could see them so clearly, smell their sweet, sun-soaked, rosy scent.

The roses grew until they were as tall as men, as tall as houses. Distant towers, that were actually trees, loomed majestically above ice-capped mountains. Oddly, these trees grew atop other trees, one forest perched on the canopy of another.

Rachel shook her head, and this strange vision popped like a soap bubble.

Free of the grip of roses, tree-towers and sorrow, Rachel struggled to remember why she was standing in a glade of herbs in front of an enormous tree hollow. It was like trying to recalling a dream. If she deliberately thought about her dreams upon waking, she recalled them thereafter. If not, they vanished with the day, her memory never having made a record of them. That feeling of waking, of something ephemeral slipping through her fingers, was how she felt now. She was again reminded of the feeling of seeing Zoë Forrest step out of nowhere.

"Who are you?" the princess inquired politely of the elven woman.

The elf's voice rang like chimes. "I am one who wishes to help."

"Help us do what?" Sigfried looked both skeptical and eager.

"To learn, to grow in your gifts, to be ready to face the perils you will soon face."

"Perils?" the princess asked stiffly.

"Perils!" Sigfried exclaimed enthusiastically. "What kind of perils? Will it involve bombs? Explosions? Horrible dismember-ments? Disasters? Disembowelments?" He turned to the dragon. "Lucky, quick! What other perils begin with 'dis?'"

"Dark powers grip your world, and darker still are waking," said the elf. "Harsh is the path that lies before you. You will need all of your gifts, if you are to triumph."

"Dark powers! Wicked!" Siggy jumped down from where he sat atop the root-wall and clapped his hands together once. "Let's go slaughter baddies! Lucky can breathe fire on them, and I can stab them with my knife. Or maybe magic them? Only I don't think opening a door at them is going to do much. I need to learn more magic. Especially, kick-butt destructive magic. You, Weird Elfish Tree Person, can you teach me to throw a fireball? What about a lightning bolt?"

"We'll learn to throw lightning in Music," Rachel murmured.

"Someday, shmumday." Siggy waved a hand at her dismissively. "I want to know what this extremely..." He stared at the inordinately-curvaceous, seven-foot tall elven woman for an uncomfortably long time before blinking twice. "Er...generous...tree lady can teach me now."

Siggy strode toward the elf as he spoke. A few feet from her, his eyes lost their focus. His expression became confused. Lucky darted forward and wrapped around him, opening his mouth, as if to breathe fire on the elf.

Siggy backpedaled with a quick indrawn breath. "That was...weird. I thought I saw armies marching through darkness...ugly blokes with horns. A dark man with eyes of fire and wings of smoke glared at me."

"That happens sometimes," the elf said kindly. "Come walk with me, and I will tell you of your gift." She reached out to Sigfried.

Rachel took her own slow step backward, for she had remembered something important.

Elves were dangerous.

The Unwary did not grasp this. Rachel's older sister Sandra, who loved all things mundane, had explained to her how the Unwary thought fairy folks to be supremely natural, at one with forest and streams, like Lenni Lenape braves or Maori tribesmen. They believed the risks in dealing with elves were mainly from the tricks fairies liked to play on mortals.

They did play tricks, true, but that was not from whence came the true danger.

The most perilous thing about elves was that they were *not* natural. They were native to the other world, the world of fey. They clothed themselves in magic, the way humans clothed themselves in cotton and wool. Where they walked, the material world awoke. Trees grew eyes. Tables picked up their legs and scuttled like spiders. Knives turned on their wielders and slashed them. Elves breathed the atmosphere of dreams and enchantment. It was not an atmosphere beneficial to humans.

Elves were dangerous, in and of themselves.

Rachel swallowed with some difficulty. "Maybe you shouldn't go, Sigfried."

"And miss out on a gift?" Siggy charged forward. Lucky snaked suspiciously beside him. "Lead the way, weird tree lady. I fear nothing."

"Except ghosts," Joy murmured from the open bag. Siggy shot back a dark look. Despite her trepidations, Rachel could not keep her lips from quirking in amusement.

The girls waited in nervous silence. Sigfried walked with their hostess. Her steps gracefully avoided the tender plants, while his stomped forward heedlessly. Marvelous fragrances rose from the herbs, as he crushed them underfoot. Here and there, snaking through the garden, they caught a glimpse of the golden and red glitter that was Lucky the Dragon.

A deep frown marred the princess's perfect brow. "I don't trust her."

"But Mr. Gideon vouched for her," said Rachel. "She must be the friend he mentioned."

"Mr. Gideon disappointed me deeply," intoned the princess. "I believed we had a meeting of minds, but I was mistaken. He may not be reliable either."

Rachel started to object that *she* had understood Mr. Gideon but demurred. That would only make the princess's back stiffer. Instead, she turned and examined the glade. Her eyes lingered on the hollow in the tree. What was it was like inside? Wild and rugged and dripping with sap? Neatly-appointed chambers carved into the living wood? This was the very kind of place her hero, Daring Northwest, wrote about in his books. She longed to peek inside.

She could not wait to return to school and tell Gaius everything. If only she could tell him about the inside of the tree, too.

Sigfried came rushing back, waving a small bag and a leather-bound book. "She said I'm destined to be a great Alchemist! These herbs? Each one improves the effects of certain magical essences, when added to talismans and elixirs. See this one?" He held up a silvery-green sprig with waxy silver-blue berries. "It's moonberry. And this," he held up a plant with an orangey sheen, "is scarpelhoar. Here's a little book that explains how to use them. And here is a bag of seeds, so I can plant my own. But, until they grow, the Tree Lady said I can gather all the herbs I want." His grin could have blinded the charioteer of the sun. "Me! A great Alchemist!"

"I have a destiny," Joy piped up from the bag. "There's a prophecy about me and a girl my age. We're supposed to stop a terrible evil. I only know this because I heard my mother and father talking once late at night. I am pretty sure they didn't want me to hear. Was one of you born early in the morning on the winter solstice fourteen years ago? That's part of the prophecy. The other is about the seventh daughter of a seventh daughter. That's me."

"I was born on the summer solstice," observed Nastasia. "Not the winter."

"Huh. That's close...but not it," Joy pouted. "Weird."

"Weren't you born in Australia, Nastasia?" Rachel asked.

The princess nodded.

"Then, your summer solstice is our winter solstice, right?"

"Miss Griffin, I believe you are correct." Nastasia inclined her head toward Rachel. "Perhaps, I am the other girl in your prophecy, Miss O'Keefe."

"You!" Joy let out a squeal of delight. Sticking her head and shoulders out of the bag, she squeezed the princess's hand. "I knew we were meant to be friends. You're the greatest. The best person in the universe! You're better than peanut butter! Better than salt! Salt could take lessons from you in how to be savory."

Nastasia did not yank her hand away, but she looked uncomfortable.

"Whatever." Sigfried rushed back into the garden, where he began picking the mixed herbs by the handfuls and stuffing them in his pockets. "I'm collecting loot!"

"Miss Romanov?" The elf's bell-like tones rang like chimes in the breeze.

The princess took a deep breath. Then, with supreme dignity, she climbed over the root-wall and joined the elf lady. Rachel watched with longing as the two of them disappeared into the Roanoke Tree. Sighing, she went to help Sigfried gather plants.

The pale silver-green herb and the metallic orangey one grew amidst stalks of other plants. One, a golden plant with a flame-like design on the leaves, bore many tiny pink flowers. Another had a small reddish leaf that exuded a strong, spicy perfume. Rachel used one of the bags she had been given for the royal yarrow and moly. The scent rising from the severed stalks was glorious, though she had no words to describe the fragrances.

As she breathed in the exotic herbs, she wondered suddenly what the elf would tell *her*. What would her gift be? Would she like it? Sigfried was delighted to discover he had the potential to be a great Alchemist. She could hear him boasting about it to Lucky. Rachel was glad for him, but she feared she might have found that destiny disappointing.

She chewed thoughtfully on her lip. All three of her friends were chosen ones with some great fate or task they were destined to perform. Did she have a prophecy, too? If she did not, was that bad?

Sigfried, Nastasia, and Joy were super sorcerers—the best young sorcerers anyone had seen in generations—while Rachel was just...Rachel. Thinking about it, she decided she would rather not have a prophesied destiny. Being compelled to carry out some pre-designed plan did not appeal to her. She wanted to be free to find the future that best suited her.

Rachel picked herbs and breathed in the amazing fragrances. The more time went by, the more her thoughts wandered back to the gap in her memory. How had she climbed over the stone wall? When had she done it? Why had she gone? Her mind worried at the missing moments the way the tongue worried the tender gum left behind by a lost tooth. She did not want a magic gift or a destiny.

What she wanted was to make certain that nothing *ever* interfered with her memory.

Nastasia emerged from the tree and glided back to where she had left her bag and broom.

"What about me?" cried Joy. "Do I have a gift?"

"Let us see, child." The elf stood again in the garden. "Come along."

Joy scampered from the bag and ran inside.

Siggy returned, his arms laden with cuttings. "Um...can I put some in your house-bag, Princess? I've run out of room in my pockets."

Nastasia gave him a weary but kind smile. "If you must. But you must remember to remove them, when we return to our dorm."

"Oh, I will...the giantess-tree-lady told me how to spread them out to dry. I'm hoping Griffin will give me a ride to the roof."

"Of course." Rachel added what she had gathered to Siggy's supply. "Nastasia, what did she tell you? Are you an alchemist, too?"

Nastasia shook her head. "She taught me how to control my visions...so that I don't need to go places when I touch people, unless I wish to. Or rather, she taught me the first step. She has promised to come into my dreams at night to show me the rest."

"Truly?" Rachel cried. "Did she give you a proper explanation? Why do you have them?"

Nastasia frowned thoughtfully. "She said I had inherited a power to travel, but that this power required a ritual in order to use it properly—a ritual I have not completed. At the moment, all I can do is travel in dreams. She says I am traveling to a dream of the place that the people I touch come from. Not to the real place."

"If you took Zoë Forrest with you," Rachel's mind worked furiously, "could you step out of the dream and visit the real place? That would be…"

She could not finish for the violence of the longing that seized her. To see other worlds! To walk on their distant soil! There had to be a way Nastasia could take all of them!

"Perhaps," the princess spoke diffidently.

Rachel stared at her friend, unable to comprehend Nastasia's lack of enthusiasm.

"Did you touch her?" Siggy asked eagerly. "The Tree Lady, I mean?"

Nastasia nodded. "We traveled together to the dream of her past."

"So you can take people with you?" cried Rachel, almost too breathless with joy to speak.

"If I go from the dreamlands, yes."

"What did you see?" cried Rachel and Sigfried together. Their gaze met, burning with mutual wanderlust. They nodded at each other, an unspoken promise.

"We saw another her, a younger version," said the princess, "from before she suffered some kind of disaster and came to our world. Her younger dream-self did not understand who we were. I am not certain the dream-her could see us properly."

"Who was she?" asked Rachel curiously.

"A queen among the Lios Alfar, in a world called Hoddmimir's Wood, an endless forest with more than one layer to it."

"More than one layer?" Siggy frowned, puzzled.

"Trees grew out of the canopy of other trees. It was beautiful, yet strange."

"I saw that!" Rachel cried. "Just a few minutes ago, in a dream or something."

The princess continued, "The current version of our hostess seemed—amused, perhaps?—by the past queenly version, who was more imperious."

"So she's from another world," asked Siggy, "and she remembers? What's it like?"

Before Nastasia could answer, Joy came out from the hollow, pouting disgruntledly.

"My gift was stupid." Joy stomped across the garden. "Your turn, Rachel."

The elf turned to Rachel. "And you, little one. I saw in my dreams that I could help you, but I could not see what form that help would take."

Rachel bit her lip. "Do I have a special destiny?"

The elven woman shook her head, her face both radiant and tremendously kind. "I am sorry, child. Only a few are chosen for special prophesied destinies."

Rachel nodded. A quiet happiness filled her. She liked the idea that her future was free.

"Is there something you desire?" pressed the elf.

"I want to remember," Rachel blurted out. "I want to be protected against having my memory changed ever again. As it was today…when I approached this tree."

As the elf woman gazed at her, Rachel felt suddenly vulnerable, as if she were standing on the edge of a cliff in a strong wind, as if her heart were laid bare before this woman who now had the power to hurt it.

"My mother is Idunn, the caretaker of Yggdrasil," said the elf. "I spent many long years in the shadow of the World Tree. Wandering among its roots, I gleaned a few of its Runes: *'I know a twenty-first. All those who seek to remember should cherish it. If I wish to recall events that have come to pass, no power shall deter me.'* It can even protect you against what made you forget your approach to this great Tree."

"Can you…?" Rachel breathed.

Hope gathered within her chest, burning like a glowing star.

"Yes, I can." The gracious elven lady extended her hand. "Come, Rachel Griffin…"

Rachel woke with a start. Nothing had changed, but the sense of hush, like a breath she had caught but not yet released, vanished. The stars in the elven woman's eyes dimmed, and her skin lost some of its luminescence. She looked like a mundane elf now, if such a concept made sense. Lucky growled and darted off into the distance.

Siggy swore. "He's gone dumb again!"

A jet black Raven flew over the Tree. It landed on a low branch and cocked its head, eyeing the small gathering. His blood red eyes fixed on Rachel. A shiver ran through her body.

The Raven opened its mouth and croaked in a hoarse rasp, "Is this how you repay my kindness, Illondria? By helping these children destroy my world?"

Chapter 21:
The Raven and the Elf

The graceful elf's voice rang like a bell, "Guardian, I am trying to help you."

"Help me?" croaked the Raven. "By weakening the already fragile Walls of my world?"

The great black bird drew itself up until it seemed twice as large. Its blood red eyes glared at them. Rachel and the other girls huddled together. Siggy pulled out his knife.

"I have no such wish," said the elf.

"I could have left the gates sealed, Illondria, and watched as your delicate form melted into the chaos beyond," croaked the Raven. "Instead, I granted you shelter. Nor have I forced my will upon you, to change your memories. Was this not a great gift that I bestowed?"

"It was, dear one," she bowed her head.

"Then why do you seek to impede me?"

"You need help," the elf insisted. "I know you fear your world's destruction. Every time refugees are dragged here, you lessen the harm by integrating them. In doing this, you have wiped out all traces of the damage—including the clues as to who caused the damage. If you continue, without assistance, this world will break. And soon. I have foreseen it."

The Raven made a cawing noise that sounded unpleasantly like dark laughter. "Little Elf, you have seen nothing but dreams. This world will remain safe, so long as the Walls are repaired. The only tool I have to repair them is Oblivion. Yet, you would take even this from me?"

"Your own people began it, Guardian, and they will have to stop it. But, they cannot end the cataclysm, if they cannot see the traces left by their enemy."

"Already, people here are moving against those responsible," the Raven replied. "They do not need to be given the keys to the gates to do it."

The elf did not seem daunted. "I see otherwise, dear one."

"You speak of what you can see," the Raven croaked grimly. "Have you told these children what you see of yourself? Tell them what happens to you now—since they brought too many this day. Will you be honest with them, and let them make their decision, knowing all?"

The elf looked away. Rachel smelled roses and sorrow. "My fate does not concern them."

The Raven flew off the branch and landed on the ground. It hopped a few times. Then, an eight-foot-tall man with immense black wings stood in its place. He was beautiful, the way the most perfect of statues were beautiful—pure and holy and pristine. He wore black slacks but no shirt or shoes. His eyes were a brilliant scarlet. A blinding ring of light hovered above his head. Reaching up, he pulled it from the air. In his hand, it turned into a golden hoop.

A strange joy seized Rachel, tingling up and down her arms and legs. A man with the wings of a bird: it was like her statue— the statue of the winged woman that had so inspired her.

Then, a shiver down up her spine. The statue had been wingless, when she returned to see it a second time. Worse than wingless. When she returned, there had been no evidence that wings had ever been there. How had that happened? Had this Guardian-being removed the evidence of the statue's wings, the same way that, according to the elf, he removed the evidence of those who were dragged here from Outside? And, if so, why?

The eight-foot-tall, winged figure, whom Rachel still thought of as the Raven, turned to the princess. His voice rang out like a trumpet.

"Princess Nastasia Romanov," he said, "this woman endangers her life. The more people who know she is here, the more certain the chance of her death. There were only supposed to be three of you. Three would have been safe."

The princess considered this carefully, her head slightly inclined. "What can we do?"

"Vow that you will tell no one of her existence."

Rachel's chest constricted. She clenched her fists. *Oh, no!* First the Raven showed up, right when she was about to receive the gift for which she yearned. Now this, right when she had been so looking forward to telling Gaius about meeting an elf. She swallowed twice, as if by doing so, she could somehow gulp down her regret.

"I disapprove of secrecy," the princess spoke with quiet dignity, "but if it is for reasons of security, then it is a necessary evil. I will agree."

"I hate keeping secrets," Siggy scowled. "It means I have to remember what not to say."

Rachel's thoughts flew rapidly. She hated breaking her word. She did not want to give it unless she was certain she could keep it.

"What about Valerie?" she asked slowly. "She's a member of the Inner Circle."

"We cannot keep this secret from the sleuth of our operation," Sigfried announced. "Miss Hunt cracked the Dr. Mordeau case wide open. She puzzled and puzzed until her brain bled out her nose. It would be an ill turn to repay that kind of moxie with a brush off—especially now that we've found a real live, um, silvery-gray woman with pointy ears, who seems to know something of what's going on in the bigger picture."

Rachel nodded. "That's why I brought it up."

Sigfried continued, "If we are going to be a gang, and I mean a real gang, like the Purple Gang, or the Daltons, or the Merry Men, or the Short Tails, or the Knights of the Table Round, we have to stick up for each other through thick and thin. We've talked over who to keep in the inner circle, until we were blue in the face. Now that we found and plugged the main leak—Geased Hunt—I suggest the inner circle consist of Romanov, Griffin, Me, Hunt, and O'Keefe."

"Maybe we should include Zoë Forrest," suggested Rachel. "She is the one who took revenge on the Drake girls for me. And, she can walk through dreams. Very useful."

"That is useful!" Sigfried exclaimed. "She could be our wheelman! Which brings me to code names! I suggest Princess Perfect, Dragon Boy, Memory Lass, Fearless Reporter Girl, Keefster, and Wheels."

"I'd rather not have a code name that gives away my secret power!" squeaked Rachel. She glanced nervously at the supernatural creatures, to see if they were impatient. The elf looked infinitely patient. The Raven looked annoyed. Of course, the Raven always looked annoyed.

"You make some good points, Mr. Smith," agreed the princess. "On the other hand, this elf woman's life is at stake. And she did just help us, asking nothing in return."

"Mr. Gideon knows, of course," said Rachel.

"Give this no thought," the elf's bell-like voice was soft as distant chimes in a faint summer breeze. "I have lived a long, long time."

"How long?" Siggy asked. "Are you older than potato chips? Older than sliced bread? Everyone's always saying 'the greatest thing since sliced bread', so there must have been a time before it. Older than cheese?"

"I am older than spoken language." She gave him a gentle smile. "I chose my path willingly, knowing the possible conesquences."

Siggy looked impressed. "Is spoken language older or younger than cheese?"

"Please," Rachel spoke softly, not sure if she addressed the elf or the Raven, "explain so we can understand. Why are you in danger? Who is damaging our world? What Walls?"

The Raven said, "Behold."

Rachel fell into a dream. She could smell the exotic herbs, but instead of the garden, stone walls rose around her. Five sorcerers in gray robes stood around an altar. A man was tied upon it, blood running from the slit across his throat. Beyond the altar, a shimmer formed in the air. The shimmer coalesced into a dark man with eyes like burning coals and wings of smoke.

"Hey, I saw that guy before," Sigfried said, "when I first approached the Tree Lady."

Rachel started. She had not realized that her friends were in the dream with her.

The princess stated, "His wings look like those of the being I spoke with when I touched Joshua March. The one calling himself the Lightbringer. But this is not the same creature."

"Behold the demon Azrael," said the Guardian. "The sorcerers who worked for the German leader, Bismarck, used a spell known to their foremost member, Johann Faust the Fifth, to summon him. Their intent was to send the demon against the British sorcerers in an attempt to wrest Egypt away from Great Britain. However, they picked their target badly. The intended victim bound Azrael with a great spell that locked him into a human host.

"While in this state, Azrael is bound to the laws governing human beings. I do not mean the laws of men, but the natural and supernatural laws that govern the relationship of human beings to the universe. This is well, as it limits his capacity for evil. However, as long as he is within a human being, the rules allow him to remain. I cannot oust him from my world.

"The goal of his human host was to resurrect the dead. This became the goal of the composite. This is, also, the goal of his human servants—the Morthbrood."

"Is that the goal of the Veltdammerung, too?" asked Rachel.

The Raven shook his head. "The true Veltdammerung are from Outside. They seek the destruction of the world."

"I knew it!" Siggy cried. "I knew those idiots were Metaplutonians!"

"But...why?" Rachel cried. "What have we done?"

"They seek the destruction of *all* worlds."

Rachel's mouth fell open. "*Oh.*"

"Excuse me, Mr. Raven?" The princess raised her hand. "I have a question."

The Raven regarded her. "Yes, Nastasia Romanov?"

"What is a demon?" asked the princess.

"A denizen of Hell," he replied.

Copying the princess, Joy raised her hand. "You mean the goddess Hela's kingdom?"

The Raven shook his head. "Hell is a place of horror and torment, where those who have not lived good lives are punished after their deaths."

"Like Tantalus and Sisyphus being punished in Tartarus?" asked Rachel.

"A bit like. In the mythical Tartarus, the punishments had a certain poetic justice. Those in hell are tortured and tormented by creatures motivated by barbaric cruelty."

"That sounds...terrible," murmured Rachel.

"It is," the Raven spoke gravely, "the most terrible thing."

Siggy raised his hand. "Um. I have a question. If he wanted to raise the dead, why didn't he just raise an army of zombies?"

"They wish for true resurrection."

"Is true resurrection...bad?" Rachel asked curiously.

"Demons always act so as to cause the most possible harm," the Guardian explained. "Azrael knows a spell that rips a person from another world, causing disaster and carnage on the far side. He used this spell again and again, telling his human servants that it would summon someone who could raise the dead for them—if they performed it often enough."

"This spell..." Rachel's voice faltered, "it involves slaughtering families?"

The Raven nodded. "Slaughtering a family before the eyes of one survivor—usually the weakest and least self-reliant member."

A deep growl came from inside Sigfried. "This Azrael is an orphan-maker?"

The Raven inclined his head. "You could call him so."

"I wonder if that's what happened to your family, Mr. Smith," mused the princess.

Sigfried yowled like a wild animal and jammed his knife into the root of the great tree. As the blade sank into the wood, the elf flinched.

Rachel turned back to the Raven. He towered above her. His hair fell around his head and shoulders like dark feathers.

She asked, "You said their spell brings someone here, right? But when the person comes, you fit them in. So, no one notices they are from Outside. Is that right?"

He nodded gravely.

"So," Rachel mused, her thoughts whirling furiously, "they are trying to bring about an effect they've already accomplished. Only they do not know, right?"

He nodded again.

"And the Wall, you mentioned? What is it?"

"The Wall is the barrier that keeps the Outside at bay. It is both a thing and an idea—the thought in the mind of the citizens here that their world is a definite, solid thing. Each time someone is dragged in from beyond, the Wall weakens. When people talk of the Beyond, or of things not in keeping with the Laws here, it grows weaker."

"And if we suddenly told everyone the truth about Metaplutonians?" asked Sigfried.

"The Wall would crumble away," replied the Raven. "The world would dissolve back into the chaos of Outer Dreaming."

"What if we just told the Unscary about the World of the Wisecrackers?" asked Siggy.

The Raven was undaunted by Sigfried's non-standard terminology. "The sudden change in what mankind believed would be too great. The Wall would fail. The world would be lost."

"That's not fair!" Siggy kicked the pommel of his knife, driving it deeper into the tree. The elf lady flinched again. "What happens to this Azrael if we kill his host body? Does he die?"

Rachel reached over and tapped Siggy lightly on the shoulder. She pointed at the knife and shook her head. He looked puzzled, but he shrugged, pulled out the blade, and wiped it off.

"No. He cannot die, per se. Under the current confines of the spell, he moves into the closest appropriate body. Or he might conceivably get free. This would be even worse, because there would be no force restraining him from causing as much damage as he desired."

"Wait!" Rachel cried, "This Azrael. He ended up inside someone from Bismarck's era?"

The Raven inclined his head.

"Aleister Crowley?"

He nodded yet again.

"And when Crowley died, he went into a boy who was nearby: Mortimer Egg."

The Raven cocked his head. "You know a great deal."

"I pay attention."

"Apparently, you do."

"But, Guardian," the elf insisted gently, "the binding on Azrael grows weak. Any day now, it might break. What then?"

"What does this mean?" Rachel looked back and forth between the elf and the Raven.

The Raven stated, "The spell that binds Azrael was expertly cast. It consisted of two parts. The first and greater part confined the demon to a human form. The second confined his powers to the latent abilities of his human host. Were this second binding to break, he would still be trapped in Egg's body; however, he could bring to bear the full force of his infernal powers. The carnage he could commit would be far greater. In a single day, he could kill more victims than all the wars of the past two centuries. He could destroy the Wall."

"And this second binding is the one that is weakening?" Rachel's heart hammered in her chest. *She knew it! She had known the world was in imminent danger.*

The Raven inclined his head. "It has grown weaker, but it remains. Mortimer Egg is still in control of the body the majority of the time. His love for his family—his son and particularly his wife—keep him human. So long as he can maintain this humanity, the bindings will hold."

Siggy stepped forward, glaring. "You make Lucky into a stupid animal! Why?"

"That is not my intent." The Guardian bowed his head. "This world is flexible. It can adjust to new powers. As I bring people here, I fit them in as best I may—I strive to keep what is unique about them, even if it is at odds with our current laws of nature. It can take time for the world to learn to obey the new laws."

"That's why there is so much new magic!" Rachel cried triumphantly.

The Raven turned his head, staring off into the distance. "I must go."

"Go where?" asked Princess Nastasia.

"I watch the Walls," he replied. "I have not mingled with people since...before there were people."

With a last nod to them, the Raven turned into a bird again and flew away. A rumble of thunder from Stony Tor, now only a short ways east of them, rolled across the glade.

Joy shivered, hugging her arms. "Boy, that guy was creepy!"

The princess's eyes narrowed. "I do not trust him."

Siggy shrugged and turned to the elf. "You're a Metaplu-tonian? How did you come here?"

"There was a terrible calamity on my world, and I fell physically into dreams. I could not navigate, as I normally did. Ordinarily, I traveled in my dreams, but my body stayed safe at home. This time, I was lost. I would have perished had your Guardian not saved me."

"And you cannot return to your home?" asked Joy.

"I can see the place I left behind in my dreams, but I cannot move my body to return."

"Are you a..." Joy waved her hand, "whatever that bird guy is, too?"

"No. I am a Lios Alfar. He is a god." The elf paused. "He is the brother of my mother."

"Enough! Back to important things!" declared Sigfried.

He stepped forward and began pestering the elf with questions about his destiny as a great alchemist. The princess and Joy lowered their voices and discussed their suspicions about the Raven. Nastasia pointed out that the Raven had seemed friendly with the Lightbringer and had allowed that smoky-winged being, whom she had first come upon torturing a grown-up version of one of their fellow students, to trouble her dreams. Rachel listened, but her thoughts were elsewhere.

She wanted to concentrate on the threat, but the blind spot in her memory absorbed her attention. Her mind worried at it. Nothing of any import had happened. She had climbed over a stone wall and walked toward a tree. Yet, she could not seem to drag her thoughts away from it.

The idea that such a thing could happen again terrified her.

The elf concluded her discussion with Sigfried and extended her hand toward Rachel. "Now, your turn, dear one. Come."

Rachel took her hand. They walked together toward the cleft in the Roanoke Tree. As they entered the hollow, Rachel's heart beat rapidly with joy. Inside, she turned slowly in a circle. Her lips parted with delight. It was every bit as wonderful as she had hoped. A chamber had been carved from the living tree. In the soft glow of the will-o-the-wisps, everything shone like warm gold, bringing out the grain of the wood. On the far side, a spiral staircase wound its way upward and out of sight.

Rachel ran her fingers over the glossy surface of a cabinet and a chair, both still part of the trunk. She stared up at the swirling grain of the living wood. Breathing in a wonderful scent, wintergreen and fresh sap, she twirled in a circle, her arms outstretched, her head tilted back. Here was something truly marvelous—a fairy dwelling.

The elf's lovely, silky gown rustled softly. Rachel stopped spinning and beamed at her.

"You're still willing to help me?" Rachel asked tentatively. "After what the Raven said?"

The elf's smile was kind yet sad. "I cannot give you that for which you asked. You will have to pick new gift."

A feeling like the ripping of a priceless tapestry occurred inside her. Her mind poked yet again at the missing spot. Now, its absence would torment her for the rest of her life. Worse would be the knowledge that it could happen again. She knew this must be a problem other people faced—those who had not grown up with perfect memories. But they had had years to get used to forgetting things. They did not seem entirely paralyzed and unable to concentrate when they could not remember something. They continued their lives without a fuss. Neither

Sigfried nor Nastasia had seemed particularly troubled that they had forgotten what happened at the stone wall. Sigfried forgot things constantly and thought little of it. If anything, he was proud of it.

Her mind, on the other hand, did not seem to work correctly with a hole in it. She felt adrift, as if someone had tossed her over an abyss and left her there, spinning with no hand-hold.

"B-but...you said you knew a..." Her voice failed, her mouth too dry to speak.

"That was before the Guardian came, child."

"Oh...He..." She paused and took a ragged breath. "When he spoke of Oblivion, he meant the ability to rob us of our memory."

The elf nodded. "If I gave you the Memory Rune, he would no longer be able to make you forget. Nothing would."

"You mean...if someone new came, and the Raven changed things...a person with this Rune would still remember the original version."

The elven lady nodded again.

"Oh, my!" Rachel stood entirely still, her fingers pressed against her mouth.

So great was the longing in her heart for this Rune that no part of her was left for frivolous things, such as speech or movement. To be free from having her memory changed. Ever. By any power. How painful that such a thing existed, and yet would never be hers. Her chest felt numb, as if a hole gaped where her heart should be.

"What gift would you like instead, child?"

"No gift." Rachel lowered her head humbly. She swallowed but could not seem to dislodge her heart from where it was stuck in her throat. "I...don't need anything." She looked up, meeting the elf's gaze. "Maybe you could give something extra to one of the others?"

They stood in silence; no sound except the rustling of the elf's gown, which moved as if it carried its own breeze. Finally, Rachel drew a ragged, painful breath. Her voice sounded low and strained from her effort to control it.

"I suppose you think it is childish of me," she choked out, "to be pained so by losing something others cannot ever have. To complain about forgetting a few things, when everyone else forgets so much. I am sure my friends must find my request... pathetic.

"I will go now, and try to be more grateful for what I have. I...thank you for letting me see your house. For a brief moment, I felt..." She covered her face and could not continue.

The elf's gown rustled beside her. Rachel heard it move in front of her and then move lower to the ground. When she peeked between her fingers, the elven woman was kneeling before her. She took Rachel's hands in her own, chafing Rachel's cold fingers with her warm ones.

"Oh, child," the elf's face glowed as if illuminated by the reflected light of joy, "what a hard path I see before you. If you choose to tread it, great sorrow awaits, and yet even greater joy. Not only for you, but for all those who would never leave the darkness, were you not willing to travel it."

Rachel's lips parted, but no sound came out. With crystal clarity, she remembered the little Lion in the infirmary telling her: *"If you meet a man, and he is lost, take his hand...You see the path and walk it already. Some just need to hear the sound of their footsteps upon the path to know it is different than the woods."* He had been talking of Gaius. Or she thought he had. Was that what the elf meant, too?

"I..." She paused and drew a deep breath, calling on her mother's dissembling techniques to help her regain her composure. She spoke calmly but with studied deliberation. "Whatever path that is—the one that brings others joy—I want to walk that path."

"And you will, dear one." The elf squeezed her hands.

"I will accept a gift." Rachel's voice was quiet yet fierce. "Give me whatever, in your judgment, will best help me to reach that future. The future you see where even one more person walks in the light. That's what I want. To help others leave the darkness."

Kneeling before her, the elf stared up into Rachel's face. She gazed at her for what seemed like a very long time. Then, she tipped her head back, her eyes half closed.

Finally, she rose. "Child, where would you like me to put your gift? Do you have a ring or a trinket that you carry with you?"

"Does it have to be on an object I could lose?" Rachel looked around her uncertainly, patting her robe and her pockets. "Would my broom do? It's outside."

"Hmm. You could lose a talisman, couldn't you? Would you like me to put it directly onto your body? That might hurt a bit."

"That's...okay, I guess."

"Pick an out-of-the-way spot. It will look like a silver tattoo."

"Um..." Rachel patted the side of her head. "Could you put it here? Under my hair?"

The elf woman smiled. "Yes. I can. Come."

She led Rachel to the center of the room, the will-o-the-wisps whispering their soft song overhead. She placed her hand on the right side of Rachel's head. Then, the elf woman stood straight and seemed to grow mightier.

In a voice that rang through the chamber, the daughter of Idunn cried, "*I know a twenty-first. All those who seek to remember should cherish it. If I wish to recall events that have come to pass, no power shall deter me.*"

A burst of joy exploded inside Rachel. "But...You said you couldn't give me that one! I thought..."

Tremendous pain seared the side of her head.

Rachel screamed.

Chapter 22:
Of Brooms and Iron Filings

"Are you sure you're all right?" Joy asked for the fifth time. "You screamed really loud."

The four of them stood in the broom closet, amidst the racks of floating harnesses. It smelled of sweat and polish. Rachel held onto Vroomie, while Sigfried and the princess returned their borrowed Flycycles. Mr. Burke had paused outside the gym to speak with another tutor.

"I am fine," Rachel insisted. "It only hurt for a moment."

She rubbed the right side of her head. It felt normal, but the memory of the searing pain lingered. It had been frightening. She had never experienced such pain. Still, it was worth it. Just the thought of the silvery rune hidden under her hair—the elf had let her examine it in a mirror—made her tremble with joy. She did not know why the elf had changed her mind and given her the memory-protecting Rune after all, but she was tremendously grateful.

"So," Rachel leaned forward conspiratorially, "what do we do now? How do we use the information we've gained to protect the world and catch Egg?"

"Catch Egg?" Joy sputtered. "We can't catch Egg! We're only fourteen!"

Nastasia wiped down her bristleless with a cloth intended for that purpose. Her golden curls bounced as she worked. She said, "We've had quite a bit of adventure lately. I recommend we concentrate on our studies. We *are* here to attend school. I let the dean know about Azrael, and she will tell the appropriate people."

"Oh," murmured Rachel dejectedly.

The thought of helping to save the world had ignited a fire within Rachel. It burned like a steady flame. The princess's practical words extinguished it as rapidly as one snuffs a candle. Nastasia was right. What could a handful of children do against demons and threats from Outside? It was time to turn the matter over to the Wisecraft.

The thought made her feel empty.

"Studies, muddies! The grown-ups don't know anything. They won't do anything. They don't know about Azrael. They don't know about the Elf. They don't know about the Metaplutonians," Sigfried declared as he hung up his borrowed broom. "It's up to us!"

That made Rachel smile. Siggy could be relied on both for his enthusiasm and for his distrust of leaving things to adults. She feared Nastasia was right that there was nothing they could contribute, but the tiniest spark of her old resolve rekindled.

A group of older girls walked past the open door. Joy cried, "Oh! There's my sister, Hope. There's something I need to talk to her about. I'll see you later." She rushed off, following the older girls. Sigfried and Lucky wandered after her. This left Rachel alone with Nastasia. Rachel took a breath. The time had come to confess.

She blurted out, "I promised Dread we would swap information."

"What?" the princess exclaimed. "What about keeping secrets in the Inner Circle!"

"You're telling the dean."

"I am reporting to the legitimate authorities," Nastasia replied regally. "This is not a game, Rachel: I tell someone, you get to tell someone else. As you are so fond of repeating, the world may be at stake—if we believe that Raven, which I, for one, do not. He let the Lightbringer come into my dream, after all. I do not trust him. So, my telling the dean does not give you carte blanche to share secrets with Vladimir Von Dread."

"I'll write out everything. You and Siggy can veto whatever you don't want me to share," Rachel spoke hurriedly. "But he has information we lack. Information that might prove crucial."

"I hardly think so," the princess said haughtily.

"He knew the Raven was our world's Guardian. No one else knew that. Not even Maverick Badger or the school's Master Warder, Nighthawk."

Nastasia frowned imperiously. "Have you forgotten he forced me to disobey my father? After I strictly told him not to touch me! Dread is a villain. I want no dealings with him."

"You don't have to come, if you feel uncomfortable." Rachel tried to keep the hope out of her voice. It was important to speak privately with men like Von Dread. She had learned that from her grandfather. If her friends chose not to accompany her, it would make her task much easier.

"No. It is best if we are all there," the princess replied simply.

"Yes, of course," murmured Rachel.

"Hey," Siggy's voice drifted in from the hall, "why does this door go nowhere?"

The two girls joined Sigfried in the hallway. He stood before an open door. Beyond it was a blank wall. The princess tilted her head to one side and pursed her lips, frowning.

Rachel asked, "Did you ask for anything before you opened it?"

"Ask for something?" Siggy gawked at her as if she were bonkers. "I opened a door."

Rachel stepped up and shut the door. "Swimming pool, please."

The door opened into an Olympic-sized swimming pool. Girls frolicked in bathing suits. A boy jumped off the high dive. A group of young women walked out of the locker room. Rachel recognized some of the girls who had walked by with Joy's sister.

"Bah..." Siggy's eyes bulged. He covered his face with his hand. "Mustn't look! Loyalty to Girlfriend! Argh, the bikini cuteness!"

Rachel slammed the door.

"That's..." Siggy gawked. "And you can get anything? Mansions? Xylophones?" His eyes glittered with gold lust. "A new fortune?"

Rachel shook her head. "Only gym equipment."

"Gold gym equipment, please!" Siggy shut the door and yanked it open again. Inside was a small room, empty except for a set of golden golf clubs.

"All conjured," explained Rachel. "It will vanish tomorrow."

"Great! Twenty-four hours in which to spend it!" cried Sigfried.

Nastasia arched a perfect eyebrow. "Sir Knight, you would not rook the peasantry?"

"Er...of course not!" Sigfried frowned and whispered, "Lucky, this being a knight thing is harder than I expected."

The princess gave Sigfried a long look, her lips pressed together, barely containing her mirth.

Lucky replied loyally, "That's what makes it worth doing, Boss. Or so you tell me."

"That's how the gym works. It's a very complicated spell, the most sophisticated of its kind in the world. It uses a mixture of conjuring and kenomancy to create temporary spaces and gear upon request," Rachel explained, pushing the door shut on the golden golf clubs in spite of Sigfried's whimper. "Practice room." She opened the door a third time. Beyond lay a room with dueling strips, dummies on wheels, and other simple gear. "See."

"Quite clever." Nastasia nodded in approval. "Since you have so thoughtfully provided the room, shall we make use of it? We lost much study time due to our false detention."

"You mean studying?" Sigfried asked suspiciously. "Or spell-slinging?"

Rachel giggled at the term *spell-slinging*. "She means the latter."

They moved into the practice room. Sigfried dragged the practice dummies into the center of the room. Rachel spun in a circle, her robes floating about her. She felt so happy. She wished to share her happiness with her friends. If only she could do something for them.

"I know!" Rachel cried eagerly. "I can teach you the paralyze spell I used on Mordeau!"

Sigfried was not paying attention. He and Lucky were wrestling with a practice dummy. The princess looked dubious. "You mean the one you failed to use on Mordeau? You cast it down the hall, and she threw it back at you, freezing you, if I recall."

Rachel pressed her lips together. She had not told her friends about how she had helped Dean Moth during her final battle with the dragon. Ordinarily, she would have shared this secret with the Inner Circle; however, Nastasia had already demonstrated that her loyalty to the dean was greater than her loyalty to Rachel. Telling Nastasia would be the same as telling Dean Moth.

"Yes, that one," she said. "And, obviously, it works, as it froze me."

"On top of all the other cantrips and enchantments we have to practice?" the princess frowned petulantly. "I think not. We should first master what we have already been taught."

"But..." Rachel's voice cracked with disappointment. "I-I thought you were upset that I learned that spell without you?"

Nastasia's reluctance caught her entirely by surprise, leaving a hollow feeling where her overflowing joy had been. The princess had looked so envious when she discovered that Rachel knew an important spell she did not. Rachel had assumed her friend would be eager to learn it.

"Let us stick to the curriculum," the princess sniffed disapprovingly. "I am certain our tutors know what they are doing when they issue assignments."

Rachel hid any further reaction beneath her mask of calm. The princess took her calmness to be agreement. Reaching into her bag, Nastasia retrieved her violin and played the notes to summon a wind.

A blast of air, accompanied by silver sparkles and the scent of a spring garden, hurled the practice dummy against the far wall, where it bounced against the cement and rebounded a good two feet. Beside her, Sigfried blew his trumpet. A second wash of silver sparkles accompanied a second wind as a second dummy slammed into the wall with a tremendously loud *bang*.

Rachel felt heat creeping up in her cheeks. She had been practicing so hard, hours and hours and hours. But she still could not produce a wind a tenth of the strength of Nastasia's or Sigfried's. She was not sure she could even move the dummy, much less send it all the way to the wall. The idea of having her friends watch her feeble attempts filled her with shame.

"Um...you guys practice," Rachel backed toward the door. "I'm going to bring my broom back to the room."

Reaching the outside hallway, she hopped on her steeple-chaser and fled.

• • •

Rachel did not go to her room. Instead, she headed to her favorite practice spot. Arriving in the abandoned hallway, she gave the suit of armor a pat and went to the small table with the rock on it. Taking a deep breath, she whistled. Enchantment tingled at her lips, tickling. Wind, accompanied by a swoosh of silvery sparkles and the scent of vanilla, pushed against the rock.

The rock did not budge. Her heart was not in it. Instead of concentrating, she kept picturing Nastasia and Sigfried slamming the dummies against the wall. Ashamed, she pulled herself together. She did not practice to be better than others. She practiced to be the best she could be. She whistled again. Silver sparkles pushed the rock. It sailed through the air, landing ten feet from the table. Using the lifting cantrip, she raised the rock and levitated it over to the table. Then she did this again and again and again.

To her disappointment, Gaius did not come by.

• • •

Rachel kept going until her lips went numb from the tingling of the magic. Picking up her broom, she jogged downstairs to the third floor, the uppermost floor that extended around the hollow rectangle of the main building. The empty hallway stretched away from her in both directions, beckoning. Her hand tightened around her broom. Her lips quirked into a tiny smile. Mounting the steeplechaser, she zoomed down the hallway.

Rachel loved flying. Even the euphoria of sudden under-standing, her *eureka* moments, did not compare to the joy of flight. With a shout, she threw her weight to the side and jerked her broom, so that she spun horizontally—a move she called a star spin.

Hair whipping around her, she twirled down the center of the corridor, her face shining with happiness. Then, bending down low over the broom handle, she grinned with glee and flipped down and up again, straightening herself out in the process.

Now she barreled down the hallway—five miles an hour, ten, twenty, forty-five, faster. She raced around the great square that made up Roanoke Hall, the wind whipping through her hair. Abandoned papers flew up behind her, stirred by the broom's enchanted wake.

Each corridor of the square of Roanoke Hall was more than a hundred meters long. This provided plenty of room to race and to practice cornering at full speed. Through the windows to her right, she could see students playing soccer on the field of the inner courtyard. To her left, classrooms flashed past in a high speed blur. She knew that the back leg was the home of school clubs with signs like: *Treasure Hunters, Cook's Broth, Saturday Night Probabilities Study Group, Roanoke Seers, Chess Masters.*

As she continued around the square, she noticed out of the corner of her eye that many classrooms were empty. No books on the shelves. No tutor's file cabinet. They contained nothing but a table, chairs, and dust. Thirty years ago, in her parents' time, the academy had been full to brimming-over. Thousands of students had attended Roanoke. All the dormitories and classrooms had been in use.

Then came the Terrible Years.

The entire staff, except for art teacher Jacinda Moth (now dean of the school) and proctor Maverick Badger (now head of security), had fled when the Terrible Five seized the school—those who had not been killed in the initial conflict. The students had been left behind, prisoners of the Veltdammerung. After the enemy's defeat, Roanoke shut its doors for the first time since 1624. When it opened again three years later, most of the tutors who had fled were not invited to return. The first new class had consisted of a handful of students with a very small, hand-picked staff. The staff had been expanded greatly in the last two decades, but it was still less than a third of what it had been twenty-five years ago, before the Terrible Years.

With a last sorrowful glance at the abandoned classrooms, Rachel turned her attention back to flying. The third floor was deserted on this nice Sunday afternoon. The long stretches of open hallway provided little challenge. She was never happy sticking with what she had successfully mastered. Always, she wanted to strive for more, pushing herself to expand her abilities, to try something more daring, more difficult.

As she zoomed along, she considered how best to take the spiral staircase that led down to the lower floors. At home, the spiral staircases had an open area like a tube down the middle. Rachel had mastered the art of bending low over the shaft and shooting up or down through this hollow center. Here, the large steps circled around a solid column of marble. This would allow for new banking techniques. As she flew, she calculated different paths and effective avenues of attack.

She went up and down the stairs three times—first slowly, then twice as fast, and then finally at what she gauged to be about twenty-five miles an hour. She still was not happy with her approach. She was not negotiating the curves as well as she would have liked. She could not decide if she should fly in a curving spiral or in short straight bursts followed by sharp turns. She would have to do research to figure out which approach produced the least drag.

As she came up the stairs the third time, she saw that the doors into the third floor of the library were open. The library was unlikely to be crowded on the first Sunday afternoon of the school year. She recalled that it had a wide open area with a balcony that looked down on the lower levels. If she went through it, she could try a trick she occasionally used in the ballroom at home, when she wanted to move quickly from one floor to another.

Rachel zipped down the hall and into the library. She darted out over the open area, looking down at the lower floors. Then, she deliberately stalled out her broom—a move that would have been impossible on a modern bristleless, such as a Flycycle. On the old-fashioned Steeplechaser, it was easier than perhaps it should have been. The broom, with Rachel on it, dropped like a stone. The second story whipped by. The instant she was below it, she shifted her weight. The steeplechaser came to life and zoomed forward.

Bursting through the stacks, she shot out into the open. The wake of her broom sent books fluttering and papers flying across the study desks. Rachel winced. She had forgotten about the wake. The librarian, a very tall man with gray hair but a youthful face, dressed in the owl-feathered robe of a monk of Athena, looked up, startled.

As he began to frown, she threw him an apologetic shrug over her shoulder. "Sorry! Very sorry! Won't do it again!"

The librarian's scowl turned into a bemused smile. "See that you don't!"

Picking up a dog whistle, he blew. Soundlessly, silver sparkles left his instrument. The spilled books rose up into the air. Rachel smiled and sped onward.

• • •

Tired yet happy, she put her broom away and went to dinner. Coming out of the serving line with her tray, she stood searching the dining hall for the face she longed to see.

Salome Iscariot sashayed up behind her. "He's not here."

"Who's not here?" Rachel asked in a rush.

"Val-iant," Salome broke the name into two parts. Rachel tensed, fearing that she was about to be mocked, but Salome's smile was cheerful.

"What makes you think I was looking for him?" Rachel asked casually, heat slipping through her false calm and onto her cheeks.

Salome rolled her eyes. Before answering, she paused to shoot a smoldering glance at a passing boy. The young man stumbled and nearly dropped his tray. "Oh. Come. On. What girl—having just acquired a new boyfriend—would not look for him?" She swayed toward Rachel, her huge luminous eyes dancing with mischievous delight. "Especially such a *cute* boyfriend."

Rachel's face grew pinker. "How do you know he's not here?"

"He's down in the Summoning Vault, putting charges in his new wand. Von Dread has a whole horde of people helping him. I escaped because, as a freshman, I know nothing."

Rachel chuckled, but underneath she felt a wrenching sense of loss at not having been asked to participate. She wished she had been invited—even if there was little she could do.

An idea struck her. She inclined her head closer to Salome's and whispered, "Hey, could you do me a favor?"

"Depends on what it is," Salome whispered back. "Annoy somebody? Yes. Wear my bra as a hat? Probably not."

Rachel paused. "Why would I want you to wear your brassiere on your head?"

"No idea. You're the one asking the favor."

"But...I didn't..." Rachel puffed out her cheeks and blew, sending a stray wisp of hair flying. "That wasn't what I was going to ask you."

"Probably wise. What can I do? Please make it be to annoy someone. Please. Pretty please with a brownie on top...and I don't mean a supernatural bakery worker."

"Er...sorry. No. I just wondered if you could ask around Drake Hall, discretely, and find out a little bit about Gaius."

"Ooo. Spying and gossip! Right up my alley." Salome pantomimed pulling out a notebook and taking notes. "What do you want to know?"

"Um..." Rachel blinked. "Oh, I don't know. What do other kids think of him? Who were his previous girlfriends? What kind of stuff did he do during the last three years? Don't pry. I'm just curious what's publicly known about him...and I can't ask my brother. He'd go ballistic."

"I imagine so." Salome pursed her lips with suppressed delight. "My brothers would go ballistic, if I were dating a sixteen-year-old. My boyfriend is only a year older than me— he's my brother Carl's best friend—and my brothers still give me a hard time."

Rachel blushed.

Salome leaned toward her. "He is a cutie, though! This boy of yours."

"Yes," Rachel murmured, her eyes dancing, "that he is."

As they approached a table, Rachel noticed an atmosphere of suppressed excitement, the sort that often accompanied disasters.

"What is everyone talking about?" she asked.

Salome, always delighted to be the bearer of ill news, blurted out, "You didn't hear? A truck struck the Wisecraft building in New York. Dr. Mordeau escaped from her cell. The entire building is on lockdown. No one goes in. No one goes out."

"Oh, no!" Rachel breathed.

"How do they stop prisoners from *jumping*, I wonder?" Salome mused. "Can't she turn into a beam of light and, wham, she's out of there? Do Wisecraft offices have no-*jump* zones, similar to Roanoke?"

Recalling how Vladimir Von Dread had *jumped* on school grounds, she wondered if anyone thought to check whether Mortimer Egg had the password to the Wisecraft's wards.

Aloud, she said only, "That's rather scary. My father and my oldest sister work for the Wisecraft. I'm ever so glad they're safe in London!"

• • •

After dinner, the others took off to study, leaving Rachel, Nastasia, Joy, and Sigfried at the dinner table with Valerie, who had come over to join them. She was reading a history book.

"This is amazing," Valerie murmured, her nose in the book. "Did you know that it was once legal to mail children? A couple put fifty-three cents in stamps on their daughter, and the mailman delivered her to her grandmother's house. Boy, can't help wondering how different the world would be if they had not outlawed that."

"Is this World of the Wise history?" asked Joy.

"Nope." Valerie turned the page with a flourish. "Regular, mundane, Unwary America."

"Thought so," Joy giggled. "The World of the Wise is a lot less safety-conscious than the Unwary. We probably still ship kids by mail."

"I thought you all sent your posts by owls." Sigfried surrepti-tiously wrapped a slice of pizza in a napkin and slipped it into his pocket. "Or was it vultures? Flying rodents?"

"That's fictional," Valerie smirked. Her head snapped up from her book. "Isn't it?"

"There's no such thing as homing owls, though that would be fantastic!" Rachel laughed. "But we do still have a loft at Gryphon Park from back when we kept homing pigeons."

Valerie glanced at the princess's Tasmanian tiger who sat chewing on a bone beside its mistress. "Please tell me there are still passenger pigeons in the World of the Wise."

"No. Sorry." Rachel's face fell. "They really were killed off."

The girls were all quiet for a moment, their expressions a chorus of sadness.

Sigfried looked around, as if counting who was present. "Ace! The uninitiated have departed. Valerie, you won't believe what happened today!"

"Mr. Smith!" the princess cried, shocked. "We promised not to tell!"

"You can tell me. I won't tell anyone," Valerie assured him with a big smile.

"I didn't promise anything." Sigfried dismissed the idea with a gesture of disdain. "I told them I wouldn't keep secrets from Goldilocks, here."

"I order you not to tell her!" the princess commanded. "Are you my knight, or not?"

"But..." Sigfried drew himself up, "what kind of knight would I be if I were not loyal? Could I be your knight, Highness, and betray you? The one order you can never give a knight is to be unknightly. Leaving my girl in the dark is unknightly." He took a bite of food and continued, his mouth full. "It's also foolish. We have to pool our information to puzzle it out."

"I confess to being tremendously intrigued." Valerie looked back and forth, her eyes bright with curiosity. "I'm in the Inner Circle, right? Didn't we agree to share all information?"

"We did!" Sigfried and Lucky nodded at each other. Lucky was under the table munching on a pile of leftover pizza crusts he had collected from other tables and some student's left shoe. "So today, during our detention, we met this—"

Rachel cut him off, her voice urgent. "Siggy! We were told that if we tell even one other person...someone dies."

"I don't care if someone I hardly know dies! They have no right to command me to silence! Valerie is my girlfriend. A guy has to be loyal to his girl! What loyalty do I owe a stranger? Right, Lucky?"

"Right, Boss!" chimed the dragon.

Siggy continued, "The way Romeo was loyal to Juliet. Or Pyramus to Thisbe. Or Tristan to Isolde. Or...blimey! Aren't there any loyal lovers who didn't bite the dust?"

Rachel bit her lip, torn. She hated keeping secrets, too. It weighed upon her like a heavy yoke. The idea of keeping the matter from Gaius was even more painful, and Gaius wasn't even a member of the Inner Circle. She already had to keep things from him. Siggy did not have to keep anything else from Valerie. And yet, she could not bear to think that she might contribute to another's death, especially that of the Elf who had given her such a noble gift.

Reluctantly, Valerie held up her hand. "You can't tell me. Not if someone is really going to die. That would make me an accomplice to murder."

"So?" Sigfried frowned angrily. "You're my girlfriend! I tell you everything!"

"No!" Valerie insisted. "I won't participate in a felony!" She reached out and squeezed his hand. "I appreciate your loyalty, Sigfried. I really do."

Scowling with annoyance, Siggy puffed out his cheeks and blew.

• • •

As she lay in bed that night, Rachel played back her memory of the day, recalling the Elf and the Raven and all that they had revealed. She could now remember the missing part. She had crossed the stone wall on an impulse without thinking clearly. It had been a bit like being in a dream, rather like what happened when she stood too close to the elf—remembering roses and trees growing on trees and the rest. Once on the other side, she had seen the Tree and walked towards it.

Thinking back, she could remember other things that were different, too—little things. There was no pattern that she could discern: a name in a history book, a landmark that was slightly to the left of where it had been when she was a child, a silver rattle in her mother's jewelry box with an *A* engraved on it. Why those things and nothing else? She could not guess.

An idea occurred to her. She searched her memory more diligently, examining dictionaries and encyclopedias. She could find no new information about the orphaned words—the words everyone used, but no one knew what they meant, like *friar*, *saint*, and *steeple*.

She did find one forgotten thing. Once, in her grandfather's library—the one in the highest chamber of the tower of the old castle around which Gryphon Park mansion had been built— she had come upon a very old bestiary. It was a leather-bound book illustrated with delicate, hand-drawn illuminations of fanciful creatures. When she reviewed her memory of having read it, there was one additional page she had forgotten.

On it was a picture of a bird-winged woman. She looked much like the Raven in his man form or like the statue she had found her first day at school. The word above the picture was one Rachel had never encountered before: *angel*.

Nothing was making sense. She wanted so much to speak to someone about it. In particular, she wanted to talk to Gaius. She could not tell him about the Elf, but she could share what she had learned, so long as she did not identify her source. Perhaps he could help her make sense of it all. She could not help smiling as she anticipated how impressed he would be.

Gaius credited her with his return to his true shape. Perhaps he was right. It had taken great courage to confront Dread. She replayed her conversation with Von Dread and concluded that she was pleased with how she had comported herself. While recalling the conversation, however, she noticed something she had missed at the time. The gold, silver, and bronze disks hanging on the wall beside his bed were *Olympic medals.*

Sitting up in the dark, she pulled her knees to her chest and drew the memory into the foreground, examining the awards. He had taken golds in fencing, skiing, skating, and the sorcerous sport of septathlon. There were also silvers for swimming and shooting, and a bronze in fulgurating—a sport of the Wise involving striking targets with lightning. Even in the World of the Wise, winning so many metals in so many sports was a feat of legendary proportions.

Holy Jove! He must be good at everything!

Rachel had known Vladimir Von Dread won these events. She recalled having heard that he took time during his senior year at the upper school to compete in the Winter Olympics. Yet, hearing it was somehow different from seeing the medals with her own eyes.

Her impression of him, reading on his bed, altered. He seemed more impressive, more majestic. The awareness that she had been in his *bedroom*, while he was clad only in his sweats—which totally failed to hide the firm muscles of his upper thighs—seemed palpable. Her lips felt dry, her body strangely hot.

Despite his casual dress, he had been regal, imperial. He had radiated...Rachel pressed her fingertips together, searching for the word. What had she felt when she looked at him? Intimidated? Impressed?

Desire? Rachel shivered. She had never felt desire for a boy, not real desire, such as appeared in romances. The thought that she might feel such toward Von Dread dismayed her. She did not want to desire anyone but Gaius.

Besides, desire was the wrong word. It implied something coming from her toward him. What she needed was a concept that described an effect that drew her towards him. It made her feel as if she were aware of him, even when he was not present.

Magnetic.

He was magnetic—as if he were a magnet, and she an iron filing.

Trembling, she lay down, closed her eyes, tried very hard to think of something else, anything other than the dark penetrating eyes of Vladimir Von Dread.

Chapter 23:
Adventures with Elf Herbs

For the next four days, Rachel attended classes without interruption, except for the assembly on Tuesday, during which the faculty attempted to soothe fears over Friday's events. Not a single wraith supped on a student. Not a single tutor transformed into a flame-belching dragon. Not a single world-guarding Raven glared at her with blood-red eyes.

The only downside was that she saw very little of Gaius. He spent all his free time closed away in the summoning vault adding spells to his new wand, though, he seemed happy to see her whenever they met. He would stop and smile and make an amusing remark and even kiss her lightly on the lips. He also arranged a meeting between her group and Dread for late Thursday night in the gym, after the main activities of the Knights of Walpurgis.

Despite waiting eagerly for Thursday, she enjoyed her classes. The subjects fascinated her. She loved the things they were learning: the structure of language, how to draw a perfect circle, the ancient origins of the Wise, the tune for summoning domestic will-o-wisps, how ash, cedar, and juniper were best for warding knives, and Euclid's Postulates. She asked many questions, some even made her tutors smile.

Math class was conducted by substitutes—mainly other staff members who temporarily took on an extra class—while the school searched for a new tutor to replace Dr. Mordeau. Normally, that class would have been Rachel's least favorite, since she shared it with the girls from Drake. Their recent adventures, however—being geased and told to kill other students—had left them subdued. They hardly spoke to one another, much less anyone else. Even Cydney Graves, who previously had been so mean to her, left her alone.

The downside was that classes went so slowly. Unlike at home—where she had studied at her own breakneck pace—the tutors aimed their instruction at students who did not have perfect recall. A great deal of each period was devoted to review, repeating the same idea over and over. Some classes contained so much repetition that it caused Rachel physical pain. Her head throbbed. Her eyesight blurred. She could not force herself to pay attention. She wished she had something else to do in class, something that could keep her mind busy without her appearing disrespectful.

Now, sitting at her lab station in science, staring out through the tinted windows—which had been repaired since she crashed through them on the previous Friday—Rachel tuned out Mr. Fisher's fourth reiteration of the preferred methods for placing essences into objects. Instead, she recalled the conversation between the Raven and the Elf. It worried her that the Elf had been so concerned about the weakening of the spell that bound the demon Azrael. Illondria had made it sound as if it would be only a matter of days before the fiendish creature broke free. According to the Guardian, once this happened, terrible events would follow.

What would happen if Azrael broke free? Rachel's mind replayed the details of the conversation, seeking clues that might help stop Mortimer Egg from killing more families. Alas, nothing presented itself. She hoped that the Wisecraft, informed of the matter through Nastasia's report to the dean, was having better luck.

After half an hour of spinning her mental wheels, Rachel's attention drifted. If cleverness could not help her save people, maybe old-fashioned heroics could. She pictured the dangers: the failing Walls, the demon Azrael. In her imagination, all this looked like tornadoes of black whirling nothingness rushing the campus, accompanied by smoke-winged minions shooting cruel spikes. She imagined herself leaping in front a spike to protect her friends.

The idea that she might be hurt, or even killed, did not trouble her.

She did not even think about it.

Gazing out over the hemlocks at Stony Tor, rising bare and rocky in the distance, she dreamed of courage and sacrifice. She wanted desperately to do something noble, something of worth:

to save her world; to save her friends; to save even a single stranger.

She dreamed of a chance to be brave.

• • •

"We won't begin our athames until next week," Mr. Fisher's words broke through the haze of her daydream. "Today, for a change of pace, we're going to make a chameleon elixir."

The students stirred. Hands-on science classes were far more interesting than a lecture.

Their tutor was a pleasant man with sandy hair and glasses, who dressed in the black and orange of the Alchemists. Like Agent Darling and Agent MacDannan, he was one of the Six Musketeers—the leaders of the students who had defeated the Terrible Five— making him a great hero.

"Some of you only recently joined the World of the Wise," Mr. Fisher said, "and do not know anything about alchemy. So I will start with a basic principle: never transfer magical essences directly into a living creature. Never take the strength of an elephant and put it directly into your body. Not unless you want to end up looking like the Elephant Man. Anyone here know who that is? The young Victorian man whose body had huge lumps all over it?...Good. That's what comes of improper use of alchemy."

"So...putting magic into my arm is bad?" Zoë drawled. Her hair was bright scarlet today. The feather perpetually stuck in her braid was magenta with blue speckles.

Mr. Fisher nodded emphatically. "Putting magic directly into a living body produces unexpected and unpleasant side effects. Never, never do it. Never."

Ameka Okeke, the soccer ace from Kenya, raised her hand. Her skin was a creamy brown but her eyes were slanted like Rachel's, courtesy of her Chinese mother. "Sir? At home, I saw airomancers at the fairs—or even down at construction sites— lifting amazing amounts of weight with their bare arms. They claimed they did it with the strength of an elephant."

"And you are wondering how they can do that without turning into elephant men?" Mr. Fisher turned back to the class. "Miss Okeke, I'm here to tell you, those men—or occasionally you see tiny female airomancers—are either using a talisman, such as a belt of strength, or, more likely, they have drunk an elixir."

The tutor wrestled several large jars from the shelves to the table. His charm bracelet jangled. All the alchemists Rachel knew wore such bracelets. Charms made excellent talismans, and it was easy to add more to a bracelet.

One of the jars contained dried skins of frogs; another held lizard tails; a third some kind of scaly lizard hide. He gathered test tube holders and some crystal vials with cork stoppers. Next to these, he put a large bag of rock sugar. Filling a vial with water from the sink, he lit a Bunsen burner. Rachel caught a whiff of gas.

Mr. Fisher set the vial above the flame on an aluminum test tube holder. Then, he turned back to the assembled class, which consisted of Rachel's core group from Dare, and a core group of students from Raleigh Hall. "Everyone divide into pairs and move to the lab stations. Send one member of each pair up to the front to gather your ingredients."

• • •

As they left the central table and headed for the stations, Nastasia and Sigfried converged on Rachel. Nastasia was smiling so sweetly that Rachel's spirits lifted. She smiled back at her friend. Being the princess's lab partner was going to be such fun.

But Sigfried, too, was grinning with eager anticipation. He wore his crisp new robes and a pair of black running shoes that Rachel called trainers, but most of her new friends called sneakers. His new ruby-tipped wand had arrived, too. The length of cherry and gold hung from a lanyard around his neck. He even had on a proper square mortar board cap.

Siggy seemed to assume Rachel would be his partner. She hated to turn him down, especially after she had vowed to herself that she would be there for him. Maybe Mr. Fisher would allow the three of them to work together?

Before Rachel could open her mouth, Joy O'Keefe arrived, grabbing Nastasia's arm.

"This is going to be great, princess!" Joy turned to some of the other students, waving the princess's arm in the air. "Hey, everyone. I've got the best lab partner! The princess is the most amazing girl alive. Did you know she invented chocolate? That's right. All the chocolaty goodness you've experienced in your life,—it was the princess's doing!"

People laughed. Zoë shot them a thumbs-up. Poor, shy Nastasia struggled to look calm, but Rachel could tell she was terribly embarrassed. Rachel paused, conflicted. She could save the princess from Joy, but that would mean abandoning Sigfried.

The princess had betrayed her. Siggy never had.

Rachel slipped her arm through Sigfried's and pointed at a lab station. "Let's use that one. We'll take one side. Nastasia and Joy can use the other. Then we can all work together."

Nastasia threw her a look of gratitude.

Feeling guilty, because she could have done much more, Rachel winced.

• • •

They retrieved their ingredients and brought them back to their stations. Mr. Fisher then explained the instructions, demonstrating as he went. "According to the dictionary, an *elixir* is 'a clear, sweet-flavored liquid used for medical or alchemical purposes,'" he explained. "Elixirs are how we put magical essences or qualities into a living body. The effects of most elixirs—all the ones you will learn about in this class—are temporary. Usually, they last an hour. Now, watch."

Mr. Fisher demonstrated the entire process. At the end, he poured the contents of his crystal vial into a cup, touched it with an ice bar talisman—this particular ice bar was painted to look like an icicle—until steam stopped curling from the liquid, and drank it.

As the students gawked, their tutor's outline wavered. His hair, face, and clothing changed color to match his surroundings—like a chameleon, until he looked like the bottles and blackboard behind him. Each part of him reflected the image beyond it, so that no matter where anyone stood, it looked to them as if his body had the coloration of the scenery beyond.

Rachel could tell the difference if he moved quickly, because there was the slightest delay as his body changed to match the background. Also, she could hear him. His bracelet jangled, the charms ringing against one another.

If she looked right at him, she had trouble seeing him. If she glanced at him sideways, however, she could catch the distortion between him and his environment.

Laughing, the students eagerly set to work on their own elixirs.

• • •

"Okay, we put our ingredients here, like this, right?" Joy laid the chameleon skin, the chameleon tail, and the dried skin of a color-changing Peron's tree frog out on the three points of the triangle marked on the counter. She picked up her cube of rock sugar. "What's this for?"

Rachel tapped the center of the counter, where she and Siggy had set up their three ingredients. "You put it in the center. It's where the magic goes—into the sugar. Then you dissolve the sugar crystal into the water, by heating your vial over the Bunsen burner, and *voila!*"

"I beg your pardon?" the princess asked. "Magic into the sugar?"

Rachel took a deep breath and repeated what Mr. Fisher had told them five times in the last two weeks. It baffled her that everyone did not have it memorized. Her voice even dropped slightly in pitch, impersonating his intonation. *"Putting magic into a physical object is called alchemy. Putting temporary charges of magic into high-quality gems is called thaumaturgy. Putting magic into a living body requires an intermediate agent. Now, if we put magic in a gem and ate it that would be an expensive way to do magic. So we use sugar crystals—which resemble gems and have many similar properties."*

"That's all very well and good," Siggy interrupted, "but where do I put the moonberry? The Elf's book says that moonberry improves chameleon elixir." He held up a leaf from the supply that he had, with Rachel's help, dried on the roof, per the instructions he had received.

"Simple enough." Rachel batted the dried lizard tail over next to the piece of chameleon skin and pointed to the spot where it had been. "Put it here."

"Wait!" The princess glanced over at their tutor, where he blended into the wall as he helped Zoë and Astrid with their elixir. "You cannot seriously be planning to deviate from the instructions the tutor gave us! You don't even know what you are doing! What if putting the skin and tail together causes a bad reaction? Shouldn't you, at least, remove one of them?"

"Not at all," assured Rachel, who had watched her mother prepare elixirs for years. She had read many of the books on alchemy in the Gryphon Park libraries. She understood the basic principles. "More parts of chameleon merely represent *chameleonness* more precisely."

"Represent in what way? To whom? I don't understand!" the princess objected. "Please be careful. One of my father's Alchemists deviated from a prescribed formula one day. Afterwards, he sprouted ears like a Koala and only ate eucalyptus."

"My father says alchemy is dangerous," Joy warned nervously. "I would listen to the princess."

"And miss a chance to try out my new herbs? Never!" Sigfried reached into the leather pouch and pulled out a bit of the gray-green leaf. It crumbled in his fingers, giving off a pleasant odor. He placed it where Rachel had indicated. "What's the point of being destined to become a Great Alchemist, if I don't commit alchemy? *Commit alchemy, or be committed!* That's my new motto. No, my new motto is: *No risk, no reward for your head posted at the Post Office!*"

"*No pain, no remains burnt and screaming on the ground!*" offered Lucky in a growly whisper from under the table.

Sigfried grinned. "That's good. How about: *No dragon, no wagon full of gold!*"

"*No threat, no more gold yet!*"

"*No dumb risks, no loud explosions followed by a day of no classes!*"

Lucky said, "It does not rhyme. And there is no mention of gold."

"You can count the gold while the school's burning," Sigfried suggested.

Rachel wondered briefly if it were necessarily a good thing that she would remember Sigfried's nonsensical conversations with his dragon forever.

"I do not think this is safe," the princess frowned. Turning, she called, "Mr. Fisher?"

Rachel sucked in her breath so quickly it made her throat ache. *Was the princess going to betray Sigfried's secret herbs to Mr. Fisher?* Scowling, Siggy hid his moonberry and pushed the chameleon tail back to its original spot.

The tutor crossed to where they sat. Blackboards, specimen jars, and even students' faces flickered over his body.

"Yes, Miss Romanov?" Mr. Fisher joined them, smiling—which looked odd on a face colored like the door across the room.

"Please, sir," Nastasia asked, "what is a magical essence?"

"Ah! Excellent question!" He rubbed his hands together. "A magical essence is the quality we wish to take from one thing and put into another thing. The strength of an elephant, the stubbornness of a mule—though why you would want to make something more stubborn, I couldn't say. The quickness of a fox. Or the cunning of a fox. Whatever you wish to borrow."

A tiny furrow appeared on the princess's lovely brow. "Cunning of a fox? Why do we take cunning from foxes? They seldom score well on IQ tests. And why a fox? Why not the cunning from a cow or flamingo?"

"Because people believe foxes to be cunning, Miss Romanov. But they do not believe that of cows, who are known for demonstrating less than stunning intellectual talents. Or of flamingos—so far as I know."

"I have never seen a fox demonstrate cunning. In Magical Australia, they are routinely outwitted by our evil rabbit population."

"Evil rabbits." He blinked. "Ah...well, perhaps things are different in Magical Down Under, Miss Romanov, but here, we can take cunning from a fox."

"So, in addition to strength and speed," asked Joy, "we can take the qualities from popular sayings? Can you get wisdom from an owl? Gentleness from a lamb? Fat from a pig?"

Mr. Fisher nodded. "Very good, Miss O'Keefe."

"Why would someone want to make someone fatter?" chortled Seth Peregrine.

"Can we give our fat back to a pig?" asked Zoë, amused.

"My father's favorite saying is: 'crazy as a cucumber,'" intoned the princess. "Can I take madness from a cucumber?"

"Does everyone in Magical Australia believe cucumbers are mad?" Mr. Fisher rubbed the back of his neck. "Um...I think the answer to that one is probably: no, Miss Romanov."

"Would it matter if everyone did believe it?" Sigfried asked. Far from the bored student he had been a week ago, he was now intrigued by every aspect of alchemy.

"It might," said Mr. Fisher.

"That...makes sense," Rachel murmured, recalling the Elf's and the Raven's conversation about the mutability of the laws of nature. How much *actually* depended on the beliefs of the Unwary? The mundane world did not believe in magic, but magic was real. Yet they knew it from their fairy tales. Was knowing about it *from fiction* enough? Gaius had grown up among the Unwary. She wondered about his opinion on the topic.

The princess frowned. "If I do not make the same assumptions about foxes as other people, how do I know what qualities can be taken from which creatures?"

"Books, Miss Romanov." Mr. Fisher gestured at a far wall where a bookshelf stood. It was crammed with volumes of all sizes. "Also, my class. This is a science class, not just alchemy. We study animals, plants, and minerals and their physical and alchemical natures."

"I see." The princess frowned, unsatisfied.

"Anything else? No? Ah, yes, Mr. Volakov...?" Mr. Fisher went to help one of the students from Raleigh Hall.

"You didn't ask him about the moonberry," Joy hissed under her breath to the princess.

"Of course not!" Siggy shot back. "Because if she did, she would be a tattler, and that's a worse crime than murder or eating someone else's food."

Joy laughed, as if she thought Sigfried was kidding.

Rachel was not so sure.

Rachel met Siggy's gaze. "Are we going to try it?"

"Of course! Do I need to say another rhyme to make my point?" Sigfried looked at her as if she were crazier than a cucumber. Rachel grinned inwardly. Siggy was so reliably gung ho.

She poked at the ingredients. "Let's do two. Some of the others teams are. We can make one according to the instructions and one using the Elf's ingredients. Then, we can show Mr. Fisher the first one. And test the second one secretly, in case it has...an odd reaction."

"Great!" Siggy grinned with great anticipation. "Then we can compare the results!"

"You're kidding, right?" Joy burst out. "You're not going to drink an untested elixir?"

"It will be tested once I drink it!" said Siggy.

"Of course, he is kidding." The princess leaned over the counter adjusting her tricorne mirror. "No one would be so foolish as to ingest an unknown substance. Mr. Smith, this weekend, we will look your new herbs up in the library and discover if they are poisonous."

Siggy was not listening. He was crouching under the table, asking Lucky what rhymed with *obliterate*.

"You can look up the elf herbs," murmured Rachel, "but you won't find them. They're not from our world. She must have brought them with her."

Rachel picked up her own tricorne mirror—*the centerpiece of all alchemy*, as Mr. Fisher had stated precisely seventeen times since the school year had begun two weeks ago. Rachel could remember each incident distinctly.

A tricorne mirror was about the size and shape of a large, angular, old-fashioned megaphone. The one the school provided was a solid black device, much simpler than the ornate silver antique Rachel's mother used. They had a similar form, however: a long, slanted, triangular case with a bowl-like shape, maybe four inches deep, set into the mouth of the wide end. The bowl consisted of four mirrors. Three, orange-tinted, triangular essence glasses made up the sides. The triangles were angled at each other, with their narrow ends meeting at a fourth mirror that was round and slightly convex. On the outside of the device were toggles that changed the angles of the three triangular mirrors.

Rachel filled her glass vial with water from the nearest sink, set it in a test tube holder, and lit a Bunsen burner. She started the water heating, carefully holding back her stray hairs, which kept threatening to float too near the flames. While it sat above the flame, she retrieved a second set of ingredients. She set them up in a triangle, so that one ingredient was reflected into each of the orange essence glasses in the tricorne mirror. Then she put her crystal of sugar in the center, where it was reflected in the round convex mirror.

As she worked, Rachel thought about the Elf. Could they trust what she said about the herbs? Or was there a chance that she wished to trick them—that if they made an elixir following her instructions, something terrible would happen?

She thought of the wonderful, kind look in the Elf's eyes, of the searing pain in her head when she received her memory Rune, of the memories she could recall now that had been hidden before. If Illondria meant them ill, had she not had sufficient opportunity to harm them? Why disobey the Guardian and restore Rachel's memory, if she meant harm? Unless the visit of the Raven had been a trick, too—a good Agent, bad Agent routine.

Rachel threw up her hands. The ramifications, if everything were a trick, were too complicated to follow. She would trust the kindness in the Elf's eyes.

If harm came, it came.

Her ingredients were all in place, and the water in her vial was steaming. Now, to bring the essences together. By adjusting the toggles on the sides of the tricorne device, she manipulated

Tricorne Mirror
with essence glass

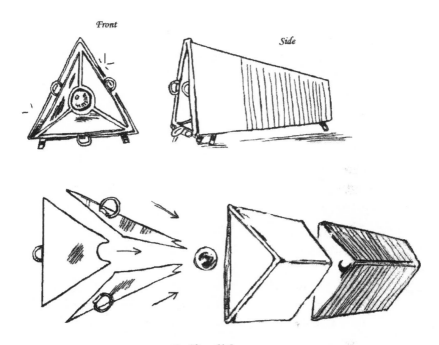

Front

Side

Top (dissembled)

the triangular mirrors. As they moved, the image of the reflected ingredient moved, sliding down the triangle. Moving the mirrors, she slid each image off the triangular mirror and onto the convex one at the center of the bowl. It was eerie to see the object present on the table but no longer reflected in the orange triangular essence glasses.

The final step of was to use the Word of Bridging to move the magical essences to the sugar. It was the same cantrip Agent Standish had used to connect her to the thinking glass. Rachel put her fingertips together with her thumb, forming a beak and spoke the cantrip.

"*Oré.*"

Nothing happened.

She looked at the others. Sigfried, Nastasia, and Joy all performed the bridging cantrip. The image in their central mirror vanished, and their sugar briefly glowed with an orangey light. Rachel tried again and again. Nothing.

Sighing, she rested her forehead on the cool counter. This was going to be like the opening cantrip all over again. If she could have done that one, she would have been spared a painful trip through a closed window. She still had not managed to get that one to work.

Now, she could not get the Word of Bridging to work, either. Finally, she had to ask Siggy to do it for her. Lucky the Dragon demanded she should pay a small but reasonable fee. Siggy aimed a kick at his familiar, saying, "Friends ride free. It is a law of nature."

When they had dissolved both sugar cubes, Rachel showed her finished concoction to Mr. Fisher. He sniffed it, cooled it with his ice bar, and offered it to her. Taking a deep breath, she drank. It tasted sweet, like dissolved sugar, but the tingle as it passed over her tongue were disturbingly reminiscent of chameleons and tree frogs.

Her hands flickered and changed to reveal her robe and then, after her robe changed as well, to reveal the lab station behind her. Rachel gasped with delight.

"Very good, Miss Griffin. Mr. Smith. Excellently done. Whichever of you conveyed the essences did a particularly splendid job. Look how clear the pattern of the floor tiles is!"

Rachel beamed at him, not that he could tell her smile from the windowpanes. She did not explain that she had not been able to complete the process. To her relief, she was not the only student to have that problem. On some teams, neither member could perform the sorcery to convey the essences.

"Okay," Siggy whispered as soon as he left, "it's now or never!"

"Wait...you shouldn't—" the princess began, and Joy squawked, horrified.

But it was too late. Sigfried had swallowed the second elixir.

He disappeared entirely.

Chapter 24:
Unrecognized Murder Weapons

"Where did he go?" Rachel glanced left and right.

The princess indicated with a gesture of her head. "He is right there, I believe." She squinted. "Yes, he is." With a smile that brightened the room, she added, "I must give credit where credit is due. The herb the elven woman gave us is quite effective! Perhaps, I was wrong to worry. He has not become an *eucalyptusvore* after all."

Occasionally, books moved, ingredients switched places, or robes suddenly twitched. But Rachel could not see Sigfried. Recalling the previous minute or so did not show her who had committed the act. Whatever hid Sigfried from her sight was not affecting her memory.

The princess could see him. Joy and Wulfgang Starkadder—the broody Transylvanian prince who could turn into a wolf—could tell something was there, though they could not make him out as well as Nastasia could. Rachel watched as Wulfgang's eyes narrowed. He reached out, but Sigfried must have moved, for he caught nothing.

No one else in the class seemed to notice Siggy at all.

"Where is he now?" Rachel asked a few minutes later.

"Front of the room," the princess squinted and then pointed. "Beside the tutor's seat."

Mr. Fisher's glasses suddenly floated off his face.

"I say! What?" Mr. Fisher lunged at the floating glasses, which were beginning to disappear as well. A moment later, they dropped into the science tutor's outstretched hand.

"Who did that?" Mr. Fisher peered around the classroom. "I don't see anyone using a cantrip. Who snitched one of the lifting talismans? Fess up! For your information, I just bought these glasses. My last pair was damaged on Friday. I would prefer not to lose another pair."

No one spoke.

Mr. Fisher sighed. He rubbed his eyes and put his glasses back on. "That's it for this period. Enjoy looking like the wall behind you. It should wear off within the hour."

Around the classroom, students, each the color of the blackboard or the sky beyond the window, bragged of the clever uses to which they planned to put their chameleon elixirs.

Joy had her hands pressed against her mouth. "I can't believe Siggy did that. He's so cute, but he's crazy! You should have seen him, Rachel; he was grinning like an imp! Or, at least I think he was. He was kind of hard to see."

The princess frowned disapprovingly. "I do not approve of mocking our instructors."

"I wonder why Nastasia and I can see through it, and you can't," mused Joy.

"It must have to do with whatever makes the four of you such smashing sorcerers," Rachel replied. "Whatever the elixir does, it's not affecting our memory. I guess it bends light."

"What makes you say that?" asked the princess.

"I can see through obscurations by remembering back," Rachel said, keeping her voice low. "I use the same trick to see the Raven."

"You can see things with your memory that you can't see with your eyes?" Nastasia asked, her voice rising in surprise. "You can see the Raven?"

Rachel nodded, cringing inwardly at the volume of the princess's voice. It made her nervous to have anyone speak openly of her secret gift.

The princess's daylight-rivaling smile faded. Frowning petulantly, she gathered her tools to put them away. Taken aback, Rachel lowered her gaze. It was almost as if Nastasia were annoyed that Rachel could do something she could not—which seemed ridiculous from someone who had so many desirable talents. After all, the princess could currently see what Siggy was doing; while Sigfried could stab Rachel in the throat with his knife, and she would never see him coming. Why would her friend begrudge Rachel being able to do something useful, too?

As Rachel cleaned up, her spirits ebbed. The joy had been sucked out of the afternoon. Gazing at her hands, which looked like the lab station counter and the sink, she felt dishonest. It was as if her chameleon colors were a lie, a claim to powers she did not possess.

Some heroine she would make. The powerful sorcerers in her class—Sigfried, Nastasia, Wulfgang Starkadder and Joy—would all be out saving people, while she would still be struggling. Her heroic dreams spiraled towards a fiery crash. She wondered if she was doomed to become a female Walter Mitty, dreaming of great things she could never accomplish.

"Miss Griffin?" called Mr. Fisher.

"Yes, sir?" Rachel ran to where the blackboard-colored tutor stood in front of the room.

"Thank you," her science tutor said simply, "for saving my life."

Rachel bowed in the manner of her Korean grandfather. "Oh, Sir. You are welcome."

As she walked away, a big smile slowly bloomed across her face.

She had saved someone, hadn't she?

• • •

Rachel walked back to her dorm, breathing deeply of the crisp autumn air. Golden leaves gilded the paper birches surrounding Dare Hall, and the maples in front of Spenser Hall glowed a brilliant, fiery red. As she walked, she replayed in her mind how she had saved Mr. Fisher—crashing through the window, spinning out of control, broken glass flying around her in a jagged spray. She remembered knocking into his attacker, leaning over her, taking her whip.

Rachel stopped short and frowned. What had she done with that whip? She remembered putting it in her pocket. Where had it gone after that?

• • •

"Psst, Rachel!" Salome waved her over fifteen minutes later, as Rachel hurried across the commons on her way from Dare Hall to the proctors' office.

Salome was sitting on a bench beside Valerie Hunt. On the grass beside them, Zoë, Joy, Siggy, and his roommate Ian sat watching the royal Transylvanian flying clipper ship—with its triple masts and massive sails extending both upward and sideways like wings—land on the southern portion of the commons.

"I got the dirt!" Salome's huge, luminous eyes danced.

"The dirt on...oh!" Eagerly, Rachel rushed over. "What did you learn? I've had the hardest time getting together with him this week. He's still working on his wand."

Salome moved toward Valerie and patted the bench beside her. Rachel sat down. Tucked under one arm, she carried the robe she had been wearing last Friday. She had found it behind her bed, where Mistletoe had dragged it—perhaps, because blood had dripped off the whip and drenched the fabric. Now it stank of old blood. Rachel held it away from her body to avoid the horrid, sickly-sweet odor.

"Peeww! That smells bad!" Salome pinched her nose. "So. I asked around. Everyone in Drake Hall loves our Mr. Valiant. He's considered an all-around great guy. Not like his bully of a boss, Dread the Dreadful, before whom everyone scurries in fear. But not me. I'm not scurrying for him!

"But back to Gaius," Salome continued. "General opinion: very good. Girlfriends? A bit more complicated. Some people think he's dated Tessa Dauntless. But I don't think so. I think she just has the hots for him. Most of the kids in Drake don't believe he is dating you to begin with. But the ones that *do* believe it think that Tess will steal him from you in a matter of days."

"Um...nice of them," murmured Rachel, blinking.

Salome tossed her tassel out of her eyes. "Anyway, everyone thought Gaius was dating Colleen MacDannan their sophomore and junior year, but there was no hard evidence of it and both denied it. So, I broke out the big guns. I asked my most inside connections, my brothers.

"Carl told me Gaius and Colleen were quite the item those two years. On the other hand, my older brother, Devon—who was actually here both of those two years—said they were just friends and not dating at all. Which goes to show that even the insiders are clueless. Sorry."

Ian MacDannan had been watching people embarking and disembarking from the huge three-masted flying clipper, while lying splayed across the grass. Now, he looked up at Rachel. "Is it true you're dating Gaius Valiant?"

Rachel nodded.

Ian blinked. Parts of his body were back to normal. Other parts were still lawn green. Where his shoulder should have been, Rachel could see Lucky dive-bombing the row boats on the reflecting lake. "Didn't he, like, embarrass your brother in front of an entire class two years ago? My brother Liam says Valiant pantsed Peter during a duel."

"He what?" Joy looked up from where she sat reading a *James Darling, Agent* comic.

"Me brothers told me all about it." Ian sat up excitedly and slipping into his Irish brogue. "Gaius Valiant blew Peter Griffin's robes over his head first. Then, while Peter was flailing, trying to get them off his head, Valiant yanked his pants down to his ankles."

A strange feeling seized Rachel. She could hear her friends talking, like a soft buzz, but their voices were so much softer than the pounding in her ears.

"You mean...the boy who humiliated Peter and blackened his eye that other time? That was *Gaius*? *Gaius is my brother's rival?* But..." she blurted out, feeling cold and clammy, "I vowed to hate that boy for life!"

"Well...that's going to be hard, if you're dating him," said Joy.

"Ooo. This is so exciting!" Salome bounced up and down on the bench. Siggy and Ian stared at her in fascination. Siggy then turned his head away, scowling. "What shall you do?"

"I...don't know," murmured Rachel. "I hadn't prepared for this possibility."

She sat very still, reeling. No wonder Gaius had not been willing to approach Peter about the new geas. No wonder Peter thought Gaius was trying to date her just to upset him.

Was he?

No. She did not believe that. He might come hang out with her in the hallway to fool her, but he would not have dueled Von Dread just to irk Peter. Still, she wished she had known before she agreed to be his girlfriend.

Or, better yet, before she fell in love with him.

Salome pinched her nose again. "Why are you carrying around such a stinky robe?"

"Oh!" Rachel shelved the horrible topic of Gaius and Peter. She would deal with that later. She leaned across Salome to address Siggy's girlfriend. "Valerie, you know about this stuff. I still have the whip I took from the possessed girl who attacked Mr. Fisher. What should I do with it? She hasn't come back to school."

"Well, I guess you could..." Valerie had been messing with her camera. Now she sat up straight, her whole body taut. "That's evidence. It should be turned over to the police!"

"Um, okay." Rachel looked around. Her favorite proctor, Mr. Fuentes, was leaning against a lamp post, keeping an eye on the people boarding and leaving the flying clipper ship. She rose, crossed the intervening lawns, and approached him. "Mr. Fuentes?"

Upon seeing her, the young man flashed his big, good-natured grin. "What can I do for you, Miss Griffin? No more pranks being played on you, I hope."

"No. Thank you." She gestured toward the clipper ship. "What is happening?"

He shrugged. "Some of the Starkadder princelings are coming or going. I'm not exactly sure. Probably something to do with Remus and Fenris getting expelled."

"Um. I have this whip, and I don't know what to do with it." She pulled part of the whip from the pocket of the robe.

"Whip?" He squatted down to be closer to her height. Then he flinched and held his hand in front of his nose. "Ugh. That smells awful."

"It's what that girl used to hurt Mr. Fisher and..." she swallowed, "Enoch Smithwyck."

All the humor left Mr. Fuentes face. "Where did you find this?"

"I...didn't find it anywhere. I took it from the girl, after I knocked her over."

"You mean...you took it last Friday?"

Rachel nodded solemnly.

"Why did you wait until now to bring it to me?"

"I...don't know. I didn't think of it."

"Didn't think of it?" He looked agitated. "What kept you from turning it in?"

Rachel blinked. "Um...nothing...I...just didn't..."

"Did anyone tell you not to give it to me?"

"N-no."

"Did something else keep you from turning it in?" he insisted.

"N-no. I...just..." she stammered, thoroughly flustered.

"But then, you wouldn't remember, would you? Scott, Stone!" Fuentes called to two of the other proctors. He put his hand on Rachel's shoulder. When the other two came over, he gently shoved Rachel toward them. "Bring her to the Watch Tower. Something fishy here. I think she may be geased. I'm going down to the glass room to call New York and fetch Darling and MacDannan."

"What...no! Please, don't leave me! Send one of them!" Rachel cried, frightened at being turned over to strangers. Mr. Fuentes had pulled a green Flycycle out of a small wallet, however, and was already flying toward the lily pond and the path off campus.

• • •

Once again, Rachel hovered in the disenchanting chamber, amidst tiny golden sparks. Most of them blew about her in a cool breeze, but a few burned hot, causing her to twitch. Her square cap flew off and floated in the air. Her dark hair spread out around her, catching the little glittering stars. Scarlett MacDannan played her bagpipes; her rat crouched on her head. James Darling leaned against the stone wall, Pyewacket sitting regally on the stone bench beside him.

The song ended. Rachel came slowly down and landed on her feet.

She shook her now unruly hair, freeing a few sparkles still trapped there. Then, she retrieved her mortarboard and placed it back on her head. Once she was properly attired, she presented herself before the Agents. She could not quite meet Scarlett MacDannan's gaze, however, as her mind kept taunting her with the memory of that other Mrs. MacDannan, the one she had seen in the dreamland with Zoë.

Agent Darling leaned on his fulgurator's staff and smiled at her. "Do you remember anything now that you did not remember before you came here?"

"N-no. Nothing."

"Why didn't you turn in the whip earlier?" asked Agent MacDannan.

"I didn't know I was supposed to," replied Rachel, brushing stray locks from her face.

The bushy-haired Agent said tartly, "You didn't know murder weapons were considered evidence?"

"I-I knew that. But it wasn't a murder weapon when I put it in my pocket. Enoch hadn't died yet."

"Why didn't you turn it in when you found out?"

"A lot happened since then. I didn't think about the whip."

"A lot happened?" Agent MacDannan pressed. "What else has happened since we last spoke that we should be aware of?"

The meeting with the Raven and the Elf rushed into the foreground of her thoughts. Rachel opened her mouth, compelled to blurt out every thought.

Then she paused.

Something intriguing was happening inside her head.

The words Agent MacDannan had spoken reverberated in her mind. They formed paths that made her remember the truth. Ordinarily, she would have had no choice but to blurt out the answer, because that would have been all she remembered.

That was how the Spell of True Recitation *worked.*

Only this time, Rachel was aware of the influence attempting to force her to remember nothing but the truth—

aware but not compelled. Thanks to the Elf's Rune, nothing could disturb her memory, even her memory of imaginary things.

She was free to lie.

Rachel did not answer the question. The two Agents exchanged looks, surprised.

"Did you hear me?" Agent MacDannan asked.

Again, Rachel did not answer.

Agent MacDannan glanced at her partner, alarmed. "How is she doing that?"

"I don't know. I..." Then James Darling grinned. He squatted down so his face was on level with Rachel's. "Miss Griffin, is this about a boy?"

Rachel nodded very rapidly.

He stood up again. "Obviously, Scarlett, this was a false alarm."

"But she didn't answer. She shouldn't have been able to do that!"

"I suspect it was the wording of your question," said Agent Darling. "She wasn't sure if boy trouble was something we needed to know or not. Right, Rachel?"

Rachel nodded again.

Agent MacDannan looked skeptical. "In that case, I will ask her more specifically..."

"Agent Darling," Rachel interrupted urgently.

They both looked at her. Rachel thought furiously. She did not want them to discover that she could resist the *Spell of True Recitation*. Searching for a distraction, she pored over what she had learned during the last two weeks,. Something she knew now that she had not known when they questioned her a week ago. Something that would not get her into greater trouble.

Three pieces of random information suddenly snapped together. A galvanizing shock ran up her spine.

"Sakura Suzuki!" Rachel's eyes grew wide. "Her family was murdered, right?"

"I'm not sure we should be discussing this," began Agent MacDannan.

Agent Darling held up his hand. "Wait, Scarlett. I want to hear what Rachel's getting at."

"But they weren't killed by the Terrible Five?"

"That's correct. Miss Suzuki's family was murdered a decade after the Terrible Years."

"They were killed by a smoky-winged man, right?" Rachel drew a ragged breath, her voice soft with apologetic sorrow. "Just like the creature that killed your family, Agent Darling."

"Wha—what?" cried James Darling, startled.

"Mr. Fisher said the thing that murdered your family had wings of smoke. Is that true?"

He nodded wordlessly, his face white. "I...have not thought about that in years."

"Agent Darling," Rachel wet her extremely dry lips, "could there be a connection between the smoky-winged man and the ritual Dr. Mordeau was involved in? Could it be that your family was not killed by the Terrible Five? Could it be that, like Sakura Suzuki and Misty Lark, you are the member who witnessed your family's deaths and survived?"

James Darling became entirely rigid. He blinked rapidly. "I...ah..." Twice, he tried to speak. Failing, he looked to Agent MacDannan, his eyes pleading for help.

"That's enough, Miss Griffin," Agent MacDannan spoke hurriedly, looking at him with concern. "You are dismissed."

Chapter 25:
Yeti vs. Wookiees

Opening the disenchantment chamber door, Rachel came face to face with Sigfried, Gaius, and Vladimir Von Dread. All three of the young men had their wands drawn and aimed at her. Joy, Valerie, and Salome crowded behind them. Lucky the Dragon swooped overhead, head drawn back, ready to blast. Payback the Norwegian Elk Hound barked.

Von Dread's wand vanished up his sleeve the instant Rachel appeared in the doorway. The other two held theirs steady. Rachel wondered if she had made it sufficiently clear to Sigfried that he had to fill his wand before he could use it.

"Um...hello?" she said.

"Rach! You're all right!" Gaius drawled, giving her a grin so absolutely adorable that her legs felt wobbly. He slid his wand into his pocket. "Sigfried here seemed to think you were in some kind of trouble."

"She was abducted by our dread enemies, the grown-ups!" announced Siggy.

"I'm okay," Rachel gazed up at the group, some of whom towered above her. "I..."

She bit her lip, not wanting to blurt out her discovery about the intriguing side effects of her new Elf Rune in front of people who did not know her secret.

"They made me answer some questions, but I am okay."

"What occurred, Miss Griffin?" Von Dread gazed down at her, his dark eyes cool and imperious.

"I turned in the whip that killed Enoch Smithwyck," explained Rachel. "The Agents didn't believe me when I explained that I had forgotten that I had it." Having a perfect memory did her no good, if she did not think to use it. "They thought someone geased me into hiding the murder weapon. So they de-geased me."

She lowered her voice. "Then I asked Agent Darling if the smoky-winged thing that killed his family was the same one that killed Sakura Suzuki's family, and if so, was this related to the ritual that destroys families in front of one member? The ritual—though I didn't add this—that sucks people here from other dimensions." She glanced briefly over her shoulder at where Darling and MacDannan were talking, huddled close together. "Now, I think the Agents are a bit stunned."

Von Dread blinked and murmured, "I hardly blame them."

Gaius grinned. "Sounds like you've found out quite a bit."

"I have a whole list of information to share with your people. We are on for tonight, right? After the main Knight's meeting?"

"Certainly." Von Dread bowed slightly. "I look forward to it."

He turned on his heel and strode toward the outer door. Joy and Valerie hurried out of his way. When he came to Salome, she stood her ground, swaying provocatively.

"I'm not afraid of you, Von Dread. You don't scare me, the way you scare everyone else. You won't see me scurrying," she wiggled her fingers, making *scurrying* gestures, "out of your way, like all your other little minions."

"That is fine, Miss Iscariot," Von Dread stated, his arms crossed. He reminded Rachel of a basalt fortress, vast and immovable. "It is not my intention to frighten you."

Salome stepped back, suddenly nervous. Von Dread strode past her and departed.

"So, you're okay?" Joy asked Rachel.

"I'm just dandy," nodded Rachel. The influence of the spell still prompted her to speak the exact truth. She ignored it. "Um, Gaius...how did you and Mr. Von Dread come to be here?"

"Mr. Smith fetched us," Gaius waved a hand at Sigfried, "for which I am grateful."

"Thank you, Siggy!" Rachel smiled at her friend.

"Von Dread's brilliant! I figured if anyone could stop evil proctors, it would be him. They can't shoot him without starting a war, right? He's almost hardcore enough to be a dragon."

"Siggy was about to rush the chamber and attack the Agents," Joy giggled. "He's crazy!"

Rachel looked up at Sigfried, his hair curling around his head like golden flames. He was unusually tall for a fourteen-year-old boy, as tall as Gaius, who was two years his senior. Rachel only came to Siggy's shoulder, so she had to incline her head upwards to smile into his eyes.

Touched by the length he was willing to go on her behalf, she laid her hand on his arm. "Thank you."

He shrugged her off. "Friends stick together. Have to. Once the grownups smell weakness, they pick you off one at a time. Remember to hide food where they cannot find it!"

"We'll burn off someone's face for a friend any day," Lucky chimed in. Siggy nodded seriously. The boy and the white-furry lizard had exactly the same expression.

Rachel struggled not to laugh. With as much dignity as she could muster, she answered, "That's very kind of you, Mr. Smith and Lucky."

"So, we're done here, right?" Gaius asked, looking from Sigfried to Rachel. "I'm not up to anything. Would you like to spend some time together?"

"More than anything in the world!" Rachel blurted out, before she could remember to keep the truth magic from speaking for her.

• • •

"Okay, hold on tight!" cried Rachel.

Her steeplechaser soared into the sky. Rachel leaned forward, Gaius's arms tight around her waist. The wind streamed through their hair. The crisp scent of autumn leaves filled their nostrils. The speed of their flight made her slightly giddy, as did the warmth of his body pressed against her back. It was not exactly a hug, but it made her heart beat very quickly.

To the west rose Storm King, bright reds and yellows dotting its slopes, where the maples and birches stood among the evergreens and sheer cliffs. To the north, patches of gold and scarlet decorated the island as well, except where Stony Tor rose, bare and lifeless. Closer at hand, the campus lay beneath them. As always, the roof of the main hall beckoned to her.

Rachel flew to Roanoke Hall and up over the roof. Two dozen turrets, some round and some square, and four of the domed bell towers, as well as myriad gables and chimneys, surrounded the central belfry and the domed observatory where the planetarium was housed. Quick as a finch, she darted in and among the turrets, buttresses, and spires, even threading her way between the narrow pillars supporting the cupolas above the bells.

She flew very fast, zipping through impossibly small spaces, diving directly at the walls, and swerving only at the last possible moment. She flew close enough to feel the heat of the late afternoon sun baked into the stone of the walls. Gaius did not scream, but he did hold very tightly. Rachel could feel the rapidness of his breathing on her neck.

A slow victorious grin spread across her face. There was something about scaring boys with her broom jockey skills that made Rachel very happy.

Eventually, she slowed. In the middle of the roof was a low flat area between two of the many towers. Rachel landed there. Gaius climbed from the broom and sat down rapidly. His expression was calm, but when she slowed down her memory and recalled the moment between when he left the steeplechaser and when he settled himself against one of the slanting roofs, his legs were shaking.

Gaius gestured for her to join him. Eagerly, she stowed the steeplechaser against a spire and scooted beside him. He moved closer, until she could feel the warmth of his shoulder. She sat entirely motionless, too happy to breathe.

"Your friend Sigfried is mad as a hatter!" Gaius gestured with the hand that she was not leaning against. "He was going to attack the Agents. Just like that! Without waiting to see what'd happened to you. He was about to blast open the doors and charge in when you appeared."

"He is a bit rambunctious," Rachel admitted, brushing away a stray hair that was tickling her cheek. Sigfried was crazy, true, but this description of his loyalty warmed her deep inside.

"Rambunctious isn't the word I had in mind," Gaius said in his casual British drawl. "Maybe barmy? Lunatic? So...tell me about this spell. It kills families and brings people from other worlds? Is that how I came to be here? A family was killed in front of some innocent kid's eyes?" He blanched and raised a hand. "On second thought, don't tell me now. Tell me at our meeting tonight. If you tell me now, I just have to remember it to tell Vlad."

"Okay. I've been dying to tell you, but," she paused, thinking, "well, it's quite grim. I'll tell you both at the same time, tonight."

"It's a date," he grinned lazily.

Rachel ducked her head, blushing.

To the west, the sun was setting. Fiery bands of cherry and purple stretched out from behind Storm King Mountain. Looking up, she stared at the colors in the darkening sky and wished she had the courage to lean against him, to put her hand on his arm, or, most of all, to put her arms around him...but she didn't.

Sighing, she said slowly, "I should explain about Sigfried."

"You can try," he quipped, amused, "but I'm not sure even you are *that* glib."

Rachel elbowed him lightly. "True, Siggy's famous, handsome, and rich...but remember, it's only been the case for a very short time. Until he fought that dragon, a few months ago, he was a lonely, scared boy with no family. He lived in a horrid orphanage where his good looks got him nowhere with the nuns and the other boys, and all his problems were solved by fighting.

"Suddenly, he discovers magic. He comes to school. He finds a girlfriend and someone..." Rachel's voice gave out. With some effort, she continued. "Horrid things happened to her. And the Agents—for obvious reasons—won't let Siggy go kill the monster responsible.

"So, he is frightened and frustrated, and he doesn't know whom to attack. Of course, he wants to assault proctors." Rachel face began to burn. She looked down at her hands, where she smoothed her robes across her lap. "Think how you'd feel if someone did to me what happened to Valerie. And there was nothing you could do about it."

"What happened to Valerie?" Gaius asked, pulling his mortarboard cap out of his pocket, where he had put it for safekeeping during the broom ride, and placing it back on his head. "The attack that first day, you mean?"

"No!" Rachel blanched. She had assumed Von Dread would have found out and shared it with him. "Dr. Mordeau...she gave Valerie to Jonah Strega, using the geas. She let him..." Rachel made some gestures with her hands as she searched for words to express the unspeakable. "Let him do...*everything.*"

Gaius grew pale. He jumped up and paced back and forth, chewing on his thumbnail. When he moved away, Rachel was startled to discover she was trembling. She watched her hands shake and then quickly stuck them underneath her. Seeing his distress, she did not wish to draw attention to her own.

"No. *No.* No!" When he finally spoke, his voice was frantic. "I saw her! Talking to Strega. They were near our dormitory. I almost said something, because I knew what he was like. I even almost mentioned it to you. I just...I should have talked to her..." He looked utterly crestfallen.

"You did tell me," she replied mournfully, using her mother's dissembling techniques to hold her voice steady. "But I thought I knew why. Valerie was interviewing people to find out more about Mortimer Egg. I even gave her your warning, but she insisted she had never spoken to Strega...and I didn't yet know if I could trust you. So I didn't know what to think.

"The point is..." she charged on, not wanting to dwell on her uncertainty about him. "You see why Sigfried is so angry."

"Yes. I understand," replied Gaius, his voice low and grim. "He must be furious."

He sat back down next to Rachel. Putting an arm around her shoulder, he pulled her close, sighing. Rachel's heart sang with joy. It was not quite a hug, but he was holding her. Cautiously, heart beating rapidly, she rested her head on his shoulder and laid a hand on his chest. He did not object.

"You can tell Von Dread, but, please don't tell anyone else. Valerie is a smashing girl—so brave and smart. She doesn't need this getting out and demeaning her in other people's eyes."

"I suspect Vlad already knows," Gaius mused. "I'm ninety-three percent certain. He doesn't give out information if it does not directly affect the fate of the world. He's a very good person to tell something to in confidence. As long as it's not: 'I'm going to destroy the planet'."

"Luckily, I am devoted to protecting the planet, so we should get along just fine," giggled Rachel. She held still, concentrating on how firm his chest felt under her palm. She wanted to move her hand across his shoulders, but she was too shy to try it.

"I don't know much about you," she said presently. "Can you tell me about yourself? How did you come to Roanoke? How many girlfriends have you had? How did you meet Dread?" Rachel said each of these things in exactly the same tone. She felt proud that she was not jealous of any possible previous girls; however, she was curious.

"I met Vlad when I was a freshman." Gaius leaned his head back against the slanted tower. "Some of the older kids were…not very kind to me. Because I was an outsider, a farmer boy. Because I was a poor kid, but in Drake.

"Vlad took me under his wing. I started training at dueling, since the other kids seemed to like to bother whomever the older kids didn't like. Turns out I was good at it. I joined the Knights my second year; Vlad invited me. I have been working with him ever since."

"Very interesting." Rachel noticed that he had not said a word about earlier girlfriends. Slid right past it. Gathering her courage, she asked casually, "Have you had other girlfriends?"

"I've dated before."

From his expression, that was all he planned to say. She sighed inwardly. What was the point of being an understanding girlfriend, if she did not get a chance to demonstrate how understanding she was?

"As to how I came to Roanoke," Gaius leaned back and gestured casually with his free hand, "I was really good at science in Elementary School. I was sure I was going to be a scientist. So much so, that I applied for a summer internship with the research division of Ouroboros Industries—which I only knew as a mundane corporation. Our dishwasher was an O.I., as was some of our farm equipment.

"I went to the interview, even though my father had already told me I couldn't take the position. He needed me on the farm for the summer."

"And they gave you an aptitude test?"

"You know?"

"That happened to a girl in my class," Rachel said, remembering shy Astrid Holywell's explanation of how she came to learn about Roanoke.

Gaius nodded. "After I scored well on the test, Mr. Poole, the librarian here at Roanoke, came to my house. He explained to my father about how the school worked and how my tuition would be paid. I am here under a scholarship awarded by O.I."

"Congratulations," Rachel smiled, delighted that her boyfriend was brilliant enough to earn one of Ouroboros Industries's coveted scholarships. No wonder he had thought he might have liked to be in Dee Hall. It still warmed her to remember that. Their love of all things scholarly was something they had in common.

"Speaking of sorcery and science," Gaius leaned forward, eyes alight, "I've been reading more of the Darius Northwest books you told me about. I'm on my third one: *Domovoi, Kikimora, and Other Denizens of the Forest.* He's terrific! He writes like a scientist! His work reminds me of Darwin and the other early biologists."

"Daring Northwest and Charles Darwin were friends," said Rachel.

Gaius's eyebrow twitched. "Don't tell me Darwin was a sorcerer, too?"

Rachel laughed. "No, but sometimes we sorcerers are friends with mundane folk." Gaius grinned so widely that Rachel wondered if he still thought of himself as part of the mundane world, rather than as a sorcerer.

"Anyway," Gaius continued avidly, "Northwest's really easy to understand. Sometimes when I'm reading Carlton Scotchbriar or Lloyd Lord Fairweather, I feel like they don't make any sense. All this talk about essences and sympathy and contagion. What does that stuff even mean?

"But Northwest writes in clear, logical terms, laying out his premises and drawing solid conclusions. I'm so glad you introduced me to his work. It's like finding a bridge between what I understand here at school and what I don't understand."

"I am so glad!" Rachel cried, utterly delighted.

Lloyd Lord Fairweather was a favorite of hers, but she could understand why someone coming from a mundane science background might find his work a bit intimidating.

She gazed at her boyfriend, her face aglow. She had known almost nothing about this young man when she agreed to become his girlfriend. He could have turned out to be a masher. Instead, he was proving both fascinating to talk with and as chivalrous as a knight of old. The overlap of their interests filled her with a secret delight. Her thirst for knowledge was matched by his love of science. And now he, too, had become an admirer of her adored hero, Daring Northwest. She felt extraordinarily lucky.

How propitious that they had so much in common!

Gaius flashed her a really cute grin. "I really enjoyed his work on Yeti and Sasquatches. Big Foot has always reminded me of a Wookiee."

"Excuse me? A what?"

"You know...Wookiee? Big walking carpets from *Star Wars*?"

Rachel stared at him blankly. "I...don't know what that is."

"You know, the movie? *Star Wars*?"

"Movie?" Rachel blinked. "You mean a moving picture film? I've never seen one."

"You haven't?" He looked extremely surprised.

Rachel shrugged. "They require a mundane device. We don't keep those at home."

"But..." Gaius screwed up his face in puzzlement. "I know some families of the Wise are backwards that way. But I thought your s—" He stumbled slightly over his words, looking both disappointed and confused, finishing lamely, "I thought your family was different."

"No." Rachel shook her head.

His comment stung. She was very proud of her family and their lack of interest in the ever-changing world of the Unwary. She would never describe this as "backward." Her cheeks grew warm.

"Oh!" said Rachel, suddenly. "Maybe you've heard of my older sister! Sandra's fascinated with the mundane world. She fancies everything Unwary. She even had Father outfit the gatehouse with electricity, so she could play with all sorts of mundane toys—a kind of a living Unwary dollhouse. But that's a Sandra thing. Not the rest of us."

"Oh." He looked so disappointed that Rachel's heart ached for him. She felt unexpectedly bad, as if she had somehow let him down.

The feeling of solidarity, for which she had just been so grateful, popped like a soap bubble—assuming soap bubbles felt a wrenching sense of disorientation as they tore apart. She pulled her hand back from where it rested on his chest and put it in her lap, feeling suddenly lost.

"I know!" He leaned toward her, grinning. "I'll teach you. I can tell you all about the things you don't know. As a scientist, I even understand how they work."

"That would be fantastic," Rachel murmured, her face a mask of calmness.

She needed her dissembling skills, or else she would not have been able to hide how uninterested she was in mundane technology. Still, she did not want him to think she did not care about things he cared about. This lack of interest took her by surprise, however. She had not known there was an exception to her thirst to learn. She was not sure why this subject held no interest for her. Perhaps because it had so little to do with the unexplored places of the world? Perhaps because technology interfered with the working of magic? She did want to know about mundane things, as she wanted to know *everything*, but she was content to leave this particular branch of knowledge for last.

Her head still rested on his shoulder; the cloth of his robe rough beneath her cheek. She breathed in his clean, soapy scent and sighed. She burned to tell him what had happened in the disenchanting chamber, but she could not do so without telling him about her perfect memory. She felt reluctant to do so. She still did not know if she could trust him not to repeat everything she said to Von Dread, and she wasn't ready to share that secret with the Prince of Bavaria.

Speaking of Von Dread, how had he resisted the *Spell of True Recitation*? Did he have a memory trick, too? She wondered if Gaius knew.

"Your friend Vladimir is rather impressive. I was..." she caught herself, realizing she was not supposed to have seen the interviews the Agents had performed the previous Friday. She changed her tack slightly. "I heard he conducted himself very well during the investigation."

"You heard about that?" Gaius asked, surprised. "Yes, Vlad is rather an impressive man. Almost frighteningly so, sometimes."

"How did he resist the enchantment? Could he actually lie?"

"No." Gaius shook his head. "I mean, I don't think he could lie. He said he could not. And I believe him. He is just a very careful thinker. He was able to interpret their questions to their narrowest interpretation. No one can resist the *Spell of True Recitation*."

"Of course, not." Rachel struggled hard not to grin. "I wonder how the spell works."

"Actually, we just went over that in class. Truth spells are a very specific type of geas. Which is funny, because they use a different mode of music, Mixolydian for the truth magic instead of Dorian, and the color of the sparks is different, too—gold versus purple. But, apparently, both spells affect the same part of the brain."

Rachel sat straight up. "You're pulling my leg!"

"No. We spent a whole class period on this. Geases affect the same part of the memory that the *Spell of True Recitation* affects."

"So, theoretically, a person who could lie under the truth spell could resist a geas?"

"No one can lie under the *Spell of True Recitation*," Gaius corrected her, "But someone who could think clearly, like Vlad, might have a chance of doing what Valerie and Magdalene did—resisting the geas."

"Interesting," murmured Rachel.

"I can think of things that are a great deal more interesting," he said lazily. He pushed her tassel out of her eyes. "To me, anyway."

Leaning forward, he kissed her.

Chapter 26:
The Fortress That Is Dread

Gaius had to depart soon after, as he had been spending all his time working on his wand and needed to study. He appeared again after dinner, however, to escort Rachel to the Knights of Walpurgis meeting. The atmosphere was subdued. Many of the members, especially those from Drake Hall who had been under Dr. Mordeau's geas, sat downcast, unwilling to meet anyone's gaze. Even Salome was unusually quiet. It was as if they were all fearful of what was to come.

Vladimir Von Dread rose slowly to his feet. The room fell silent.

"Words cannot express the depth of my disgust, when I think back upon the performance of the members of this organization during the disaster last Friday." Dread's voice was deep and stern. "The purpose of the Knights of Walpurgis is to defend the school. To guard against harm to our fellow students and our instructors. To protect the innocent.

"But that was not what occurred. No. Instead, you cowered in the dining hall or worse, allowed yourself to be used by Dr. Mordeau."

Dread remained absolutely calm. Yet, his words struck like a whip. "Why was it that two little girls—freshmen girls—were able to fight off the geas, but the Knights were not? I shall tell you why. Because you are weak. Weakness is not to be tolerated. It must be expunged wherever it appears.

"There are a few here that deserve commending. Mr. Valiant and Mr. Locke fought admirably. Miss Griffin and her friends detected the threat and moved to stop it, saving many lives, including some of your own.

"The rest of you are...pathetic. You allowed your fear to interfere with your duty to others. You are a disgrace to the name of the Knights of Walpurgis, to Roanoke Academy, and to yourselves."

Vladimir paused. The other students, except for Gaius and William Locke, trained their eyes on the table. Some traced the grain of the wood. Others played with their wands and dueling rings, or scuffed their feet against the floor.

"We shall train harder," Dread continued. "Should this happen again, we will be ready. Any Knight showing such a deplorable lack of strength in the future will be expelled."

All around her the Knights drooped like unwatered flowers. Rachel appreciated Dread's praise of herself and the princess, and yet she could not help feeling intimidated. He made weakness sound like such a truly horrendous failing. She was not sure she was as strong as Dread might require.

Did her boyfriend feel the same way as his boss? The thought made her very uneasy. She resolved to hide from Gaius any sign of weakness within herself.

Rachel noted that some of the students were watching Romulus Starkadder, as if they expected him to speak up. He did not. He sat at the far end of the table, frowning slightly and watching Dread.

She also noted that, despite his impressive performance during the attack, Dread did not praise himself.

• • •

As soon as they were on their feet, the evening improved dramatically. Rachel, Wanda, and Salome gathered in the training area. Gaius acted as their teacher again, instructing the girls in the basics of dueling. Then he advised them as they practiced, winking at Rachel whenever he passed by her. Each time he did, an ember deep within her heart glowed more brightly.

After that, they were free to duel. Rachel did reasonably well, for someone on her second week. However, she could not fire off cantrips quickly enough to compete with those who had stored their spells ahead of time. If she wanted to duel, she needed a dueling ring or a wand.

Rachel wanted a fulgurator's wand. One could not throw lightning with a dueling ring. Someday, she wanted to be the one who struck the next cursed scarab brooch with lightning.

Evelyn March flashed her a friendly smile. She had aquiline features, an olive complexion, and a mysterious yet joyful air that evoked both curiosity and sadness. Rachel nearly ran over to speak to her. Then she remembered the gardener's words— that everyone who befriended the March children was questioned at length under the *Spell of True Recitation* by their father, the Grand Inquisitor. A jab of terror paralyzed her.

She had met the Grand Inquisitor. He did not strike her as a man who could be easily tricked. She very much doubted she could lie well enough to fool Cain March.

She recalled her father had once commented that it was good that a spell as mild as the *Spell of True Recitation* was so effective. Otherwise, his boss would need to employ more intrusive methods of acquiring the information he needed. Rachel gleaned there were other, more painful spells for compelling truth by magic. The last thing Rachel wanted was for the Grand Inquisitor to discover she was immune, try something more painful, and wring out of her the Elf's secrets.

Sadly, she decided not to approach Eve March.

She did say hello to Beryl Moth, a cool college junior with steady gray eyes and short hair of a color half-way between straw and honey. Beryl was the daughter of Iron Moth, her father's cousin and one of the two owners of Ouroboros Industries (the other being William Locke's father). Beryl's grandmother was the sister of Rachel's beloved grandfather.

The two young women exchanged pleasantries. As Rachel turned away, she paused and looked around. "Beryl, isn't someone missing? How come I haven't seen your brother on campus? Shouldn't Blackie be a senior? Or did I count wrong, and he graduated last year?"

Beryl looked uncomfortable. "You didn't hear? The summer before last, while working on a research project for Father, he...had an accident."

"What happened to him?" Rachel asked, aghast.

"He lost his memory."

Rachel shivered. "How...much of his memory?"

"All of it. He doesn't remember anything before that August."

Beryl departed to duel her friend Naomi, leaving Rachel covered with goose bumps.

• • •

Rachel dueled diligently. One of the older students she lost to was Mark Williams. He did not seem a bad fellow, despite having stopped her broom, though he seemed embarrassed near her. Gaius did not help. He smirked at Williams whenever an opportunity arose.

Boys. Rachel sighed.

But she could not judge Gaius too harshly. Everything he did enchanted her. She wanted to be part of his world so desperately. She envied the way Von Dread, Locke, and their younger friend from Dee Hall, Topher Evans, interacted with him so easily. She wanted to be able to talk to him as they did, or at least to walk up to him without her heart hammering like a woodpecker on a bug-riddled tree. She wanted to duel elegantly as he did, to casually call the Prince of Bavaria by the nickname of Vlad as he did. Most of all, she wanted to be able to spend time with him without having to make an appointment.

And then, there was the matter of Peter...

"Hey, Valiant," she called teasingly, next time he came near.

He sauntered over.

Just watching him move stole her breath.

"That was some speech Vlad made, wasn't it?" Gaius lowered his voice, glancing at where the Prince of Bavaria dueled Romulus Starkadder. "I have never seen him so angry."

"I must admit, he was quite intimidating. But speaking of anger," Rachel crossed her arms and, narrowed her eyes, mock-glaring at him, "I had not realized until today that you were my brother Peter's rival—the boy whom I had vowed to hate for life!"

"Had you vowed to hate me? I'm sorry to hear that." Gazing into her eyes, he smiled directly at her, "Might I cherish the hope that you have since changed your mind?"

"Of course." She lowered her lashes shyly. The intensity of his smile flustered her. "Clever of you to sidestep my objections by winning my heart before I discovered your identity. How did you and he come to be rivals?"

He performed a fancy bow, complete with an elegant airy gesture. "What do two young men ever fight over—except a young woman?"

"Who?" Rachel leaned forward, intrigued.

"I never duel and tell."

She rocked backward on her heels, disappointed, but she could tell that he was not going to reveal any more. "Very well, Mr. Valiant, I shall forgive you. But please, don't do it again."

He laid his hand over his heart and gave her a short bow. "I would never disparage the brother of a lady whom I am courting."

A big grin bloomed across Rachel's face.

She won her next duel handily to the dismay of her opponent, a sophomore boy who was not pleased to have been beaten by a tiny girl without a wand, who had been a freshman for less than two weeks.

She could not help being curious, though. Who was this girl that Peter and Gaius had fought over? She glanced over at Colleen MacDannan, who was gazing at Gaius with big doe-like eyes. Could she be the one? Peter was good friends with Colleen's cousins, Oonagh and her brothers. Perhaps they had not cared for the friendship between Gaius and their cousin? Maybe Peter had even fancied Colleen himself? Rachel began to make a mental note to ask Peter, but then she remembered that she and Peter were not talking. The thought left her feeling empty.

• • •

At precisely nine-thirty—according to the punctual Bavarian prince—Gaius, Vlad, William, and Topher excused themselves and accompanied Rachel across the hall to another room, where they met Nastasia, Joy, Zoë, Valerie, Siggy, and Lucky. The room had several chairs and a set of gold golf clubs. Lucky was wrapped protectively around the clubs.

The time to exchange information had finally come. Rachel buzzed with excitement. It took great effort to keep from bouncing up and down. Finally, her group and Gaius's group would be together. Finally, she would have a chance to share what she had learned. Finally, she would discover the secrets Dread and his cronies knew. Maybe, just maybe, they would have the clue needed to piece together this grand puzzle of strange new things that so befuddled Rachel.

Vladimir Von Dread called the meeting to order. He motioned Topher Evans to stand beside him. "Mr. Evans has the gift of total recall. He will remember everything you tell us."

Topher, a young man with a large Adam's apple and glasses, gave her an awkward smile that was probably meant as friendly but came off as goofy. Rachel tried to smile back, but she was too surprised. She had never met anyone outside her family who had the gift she shared with her mother.

Topher winked at her.

"Um...I wrote it all down," murmured Rachel. Taking out the notes she and her friends had prepared, she handed the pages to Gaius who presented it to Von Dread.

They read:

1) Mortimer Egg, Dr. Mordeau, Agent Browne, and a red-headed woman killed Misty Lark's family. They wanted to kill Magdalene Chase, but her family did not love her enough for the spell to work. Also, a creature with wings of smoke killed the parents of both Sakura Suzuki and Agent James Darling.

2) Mortimer Egg was seen talking to Valerie Hunt's father the day Detective. Hunt vanished. It is unknown whether Detective Hunt is alive or dead.

3) Mortimer Egg and co. had a stronghold at Beaumont Castle in Transylvania, provided by two Starkadder Brothers. In return for this, Egg promised to kill Romulus Starkadder.

4) When the Raven is near, Lucky the Dragon turns into a non-intelligent creature. This is because the Guardian enforces the local natural laws, which have not yet adjusted to Lucky's presence. The Raven can also turn into a winged man with a gold hoop over his head.

5) Dr. Mordeau claimed that Veltdammerung's goal is: true resurrection of the dead.

6) Mortimer Egg and co. have been casting the same spell—a spell that requires a family be murdered—over and over for decades. The spell works and brings people from Outside, but the Guardian makes them blend in so that no one, including Egg, remembers.

7) The princess has had two visions of the future. Both began to come true...but we were able to change the outcome.

8) Sakura Suzuki cannot get the school Flycycles to obey her. This is unheard of, even for the Unwary. She also had strange things go wrong in class—spells misfiring in bizarre ways.

9) The Wisecraft is bringing in a Maori shaman to help protect Roanoke from dream magic. It may be the same shaman who gave Zoë her dream-traveling sandals.

10) A prophecy says the seventh daughter of a seventh daughter and a girl born on the Winter Solstice will stop a great evil. This may refer to Joy O'Keefe and Nastasia Romanov.

11) The P.E. tutor can move at high speeds and survive being knocked through fifty yards of earth. The King of Magical Australia called him Roland St. Michael.

12) Mortimer Egg is possessed by a demon named Azrael, who used to possess Aleister Crowley. A demon is a creature of pure malice. It chooses its actions based upon what will cause the most damage. This demon is bound by a spell that is held in place by Mortimer Egg's love for his wife and son. This spell is weakening.

Vladimir Von Dread read the document silently. Then he handed it to Gaius and William.

"Impressive, Miss Griffin and company." Vladimir's deep voice resonated with confidence and command. "You have gathered quite an array of information. I had not known about the Starkadder princes or the demon Azrael. I am afraid you have outdone us."

"Thank you." Rachel's voice was calm, but her eyes shone as if his words ignited a lantern inside her.

After discovering that he knew that the Raven was the Guardian, she had feared nothing she had so painstakingly learned would be new to him.

Tamping down her glee, so as not to betray how much his praise thrilled her, she said in a business-like tone, "The matter I am most concerned about is the binding on the demon. Our sources tell us terrible things—worse than the crimes committed by Hitler, Stalin, and Chairman Mao—will happen if he gets free. I wish there were some step we could take to keep this from occurring."

Von Dread pressed the tips of his black, gloved fingers together. "I have never heard of a spell that binds a supernatural creature *into* a human. Normally, one exorcises possession."

"I have," Rachel replied. "We use them in Devon to bind brollochan."

"Brollochan?" the princess asked.

"A British fey creature that looks like a cloud of darkness with eyes," Gaius offered.

Rachel nodded. "You can only perform a proper banishment while they are in the act of possessing someone. An ancestor of mine, the Fourth Duke, was famous for having banished three of them. He bound them into their hosts and then sent them away."

"Did the hosts survive?" Von Dread's eyes flickered with interest.

"Um," Rachel checked her memory. "The stories do not say."

"Interesting." He paused. "I will mention your concern to my father. Perhaps, he can do something to protect Mrs. Egg. Their son, Mortimer Junior should be safe here at school."

Rachel nodded.

Dread said, "You have found out a great deal, Miss Griffin—including things that it took my father's intelligence service months to learn. I must admit that you have already discovered the information I had thought to share with you."

Despite her delight at his praise, Rachel found this disappointing. She had hoped Von Dread would offer an earthshaking revelation that proved to be the key to all the unanswered mysteries.

"I do have a piece of information for you," Dread continued. "The first name of the red-headed woman who works with Mortimer Egg and Dr. Mordeau is Serena. I do not yet know more than that. But I should soon have a photo of her. I promise to share it with you."

"What I want to know," asked Valerie. She sat by the gold golf clubs, scratching Lucky behind his horns, "is why isn't the Wisecraft sharing these photos with everyone?"

"I cannot say, Miss Hunt. We do things differently in Bavaria."

I bet you do! Rachel thought wryly, gazing at the dangerous and possibly evil older boy.

The group of them spoke together for a time, comparing notes. While the others were laughing at one of Topher's jokes, Rachel stepped off to one side to consider all that they had discussed, searching diligently for connections. As random pieces of the grand puzzle snapped into place, a glorious feeling, akin to electricity, ran along her limbs.

From her memory, voices spoke, snippets of longer conversations:

The Raven: *The sorcerers who worked for Bismarck used a spell to summon him. Their intent was to send the demon against the British sorcerers in an attempt to wrest Egypt away from Great Britain. However, they picked their target badly. His intended victim bound Azrael with a great spell that locked him into a human host.*

The Raven again: *The spell that binds Azrael was expertly cast.*

The Dean speaking of Jasper Hawke: *He died a hero!*

And Dr. Mordeau's response: *Certainly he did, defeating Bismarck's sorcerers...alongside Aleister Crowley and General Blaise Griffin.*

The Germans had sent the demon Azrael against British sorcerers. They had attacked someone who had happened to know a spell for binding a creature into a human host. Who would know such a spell, except a sorcerer from a family famous for binding brollochan?

Her grandfather.

Was this the great tragedy suffered by Blaise Griffin, The Tenth Duke of Devon? Had he had to bind a demon into Aleister

Crowley, one of his closest friends? And then been unable to banish it? If so, why did Dean Moth not know about Azrael? Or had she known that a monster had possessed Crowley but not that it had transferred to Egg?

It occurred to her someone must have known Crowley was terribly evil, or, when he was finally defeated in 1947, he would have been executed.

Instead, when Aaron Marley found him, he had been turned to stone and placed in the cave that was sacred to Nemesis, along with the other members of the Terrible Five. Being turned to stone was a punishment reserved for only the most nefarious practitioners of black magic—those thought to be so powerful that it was feared mere death might not stop them.

The idea that her grandfather had been the demon's first target shook Rachel. She turned back toward where the others sat to share her revelation and paused, horrified.

Without her there to keep them in line, her friends were eroding any respect Gaius and his companions might have had for them. The princess was so frigid with disapproval that she could have cooled a steaming elixir without an ice bar. Sigfried was behaving like a crazy goon—hugging the gold golf clubs and babbling about his plans for a moon shot using a broomstick the size of a sequoia. Joy talked loudly and giggled like a six-year-old. Zoë rested her feet on a second chair, playing with her feather and paying no attention to the proceedings. Only Valerie behaved appropriately, scribbling down notes as she spoke quietly with Topher.

Rachel had hoped for so much more. She had imagined speaking with Von Dread as she might have with her grandfather—straightforwardly, without concern for the niceties of human nature. It was an approach she was certain would have appealed to Dread. But she could not do this in front of the princess. Nastasia took umbrage at the littlest impropriety. If Rachel worded her comments to appeal to Von Dread, Nastasia would take offense. As for the rest of them, barring Valerie, they were a disgrace. She felt embarrassed and worse, hurt, as if their lack of curiosity about the matters at hand were a personal slight.

How foolish Von Dread and his people must find her and her friends.

With a sigh, she decided this was not the time to voice her suspicions regarding her grandfather and the demon. They were just that, suspicions. If she made claims about her grandfather, and they turned out to be wrong, she would look even more foolish.

If only she had insisted on a private meeting with Gaius and Von Dread.

As she gazed at the others, she was struck by what a handsome couple Dread and Nastasia made as they sat near each other, both straight-backed and listening, with similarly regal expressions. If they could only overcome the princess's resentment towards him, they might make a splendid match. They were both mind-bogglingly gorgeous, he commanding and dark, she gentle and fair. And yet they were both so severe, so reserved—like two fortresses.

Rachel drew in her breath. The comparison between the two of them and a fortress seemed suddenly extraordinarily fitting. With it, however, came an astonishing thought. Perhaps, Nastasia and the Bavarian prince would not suit each other. How would one fortress earn the love of another? Rachel could imagine them standing in the same room for years, without ever interacting—each locked away behind defensive walls, closed off, never reaching out to each other. What a fortress needed was to be besieged, for someone to scale their walls, make it over their ramparts, and reach their hearts.

Someone like her.

With the same clarity that had brought the fortress revelation, Rachel knew suddenly: *she could pierce Dread's defenses.* It was as if the camera of her point-of-view had swiveled and showed her the postern door in the wall surrounding the castle that was Vladimir Von Dread. She could not have said what that meant. She only knew with absolute clarity that the same tactics that had allowed her to win the heart of her arrogant, taciturn grandfather would work on Dread.

This did not make her want to try. Well, she could not help being a little curious as to whether she could actually do it. But it did not make her wish to prove the truth of her revelation by pursuing Dread. *She just knew.*

She did wonder whether she might have insights that she could share with someone who was interested in winning the heart of the Prince of Bavaria—should such a person appear.

• • •

Only at the very end of the meeting, as they were breaking up, did Rachel get a brief chance to speak privately with Von Dread.

"Thank you, Miss Griffin," he nodded curtly, folding the papers she had given him. "You have given me much to think about."

"You are welcome." Rachel curtseyed. Then she blurted out before she could lose her nerve. "Um...may I ask you a favor? Two favors, really."

"You may ask," he replied coldly, in a tone that made her feel as if he meant anything but. "I give no promise."

"The first is for Magdalene. Gaius probably told you that her doll came alive and talked to us. She wanted to be allowed to go through the Familiar Bonding Ceremony with it, but they didn't let her. A chance to do so might comfort her—at least a tiny bit."

Dread nodded. "I will arrange it at once."

Wow. Rachel blinked. Just like that. Not even an *I will try to arrange.*

He truly was impressive.

"And your second request?"

"May I call you Vlad...the way Gaius does?"

He inclined his head a second time. "Of course, Miss Griffin."

"Thank you, Vlad." Rachel curtseyed again and dashed off to find her boyfriend.

• • •

Gaius walked her to the door of the gym. They spoke softly in the darkness while the princess waited nearby, radiating palpable disapproval.

"You gathered a great deal of information." Gaius leaned over and brushed a stray lock of hair from her face. "I'm impressed."

"Thank you." She blushed, basking in the warmth of his regard.

"Makes me feel mildly inadequate." Gaius grinned lazily. "Vlad's going to think I'm a slackard and get himself a new lieutenant."

"Never," Rachel beamed at him, approval shining in her eyes.

"You are adorable, Miss Griffin." He kissed her nose. "Till tomorrow?"

She nodded, her face aglow. He winked and walked off into the night, whistling.

Chapter 27:
Dragonsmith's Patented Crush Crusher

Two more weeks passed, and no disasters ensued, unless being apart from one's new boyfriend counted as a disaster.

Rachel and Gaius spent time together during the Knights of Walpurgis meetings. Occasionally, they found a moment to stroll, hand-in-hand, around the reflecting lake. Gaius was so busy refilling his wand, however, that he could seldom pause for more than the briefest of chats. He did promise repeatedly that they would see more of each other in the future, but so far, that future had not come to pass. Rachel wished she could help him with the restoration of his wand. After all, he had lost it on her behalf. But what help could a new freshman give?

At least, when they did find a few minutes together, he always seemed happy to see her.

So, she attended her classes and tried to absorb every smidgeon of information. The Roanoke curriculum was based on the premise that Sorcery was best taught through the works of the masters who invented each Art. While tutors did occasionally assign reading in modern textbooks, students mainly studied the original treatises, written by ancient worthies.

Each of Rachel's classes covered something fascinating. In science, they were discussing a treatise by Fu Xi, the ancient Chinese Heavenly Sovereign, called *A Debate on Salt and Fire*. It delved into the discovery of magical essences and how to remove them from objects. On the practical side, they finished making their first warding athames—Rachel made hers of cedar and the spirit-warding essence of salt—and began work on creating shadowcloaks. Siggy added the Elf's herbs to elixirs and prospered.

Language was Rachel's favorite class. She loved learning new words. The course covered both English grammar and the Original Language. Currently, they were learning basics by translating an early epic about Alulim, an antediluvian king of Sumeria, and how he passed his blessing to grant names to things to his son Iaptesh.

Language was also the class with the most practical magic. They covered *Oré* and *Obé*, the Words of *Bridging* and *Ending*. Rachel remained awful at performing cantrips, staring glumly as repeated tries brought few results. She might not have felt so inadequate had she been in another class. Many freshmen were much worse than she. But when compared to the amazing talents of Siggy, Nastasia, Joy, and Wulfgang, her efforts were insignificant.

After two weeks of substitutes, Dr. Mordeau's replacement was announced. To everyone's amazement, Scarlett MacDannan stepped down from her position as an Agent of the Wisecraft and came to Roanoke Academy to teach. Students teased Ian, claiming he was now on easy street, since his mother would be his math tutor. Ian looked glum. His pessimism was well-founded. Mrs. MacDannan proved to be a tough instructor, and she was even harder on her son.

Rachel very much enjoyed having Mrs. MacDannan as a tutor. Her range of knowledge and her exacting standards were both to Rachel's liking. It did take several classes, however, before Rachel ceased to be plagued by disturbing memories of the other Scarlett MacDannan, the one she had seen in the buff in the janitor's dream office.

If Language was her favorite class, Music was her least. Rachel was diligent about the rest of her homework, but she still avoided practicing her flute. She hated playing. Currently, she was doing well in class, thanks to her ability to instantly memorize sheet music, and her meager playing skills were still better than those of some of her fellow students, many of whom were new to their instrument. But she knew it was only a matter of time before her lack of practicing would catch up with her.

The theory part of music class fascinated her, however. The tutor explained the seven modes of music and which mode was used for which of the seven kinds of enchantment. In one of Rachel's favorite sessions, Miss Cyrene played *Twinkle, Twinkle, Little Star* in all seven modes, demonstrating the differences. The tutor also taught them songs for clearing fog and for summoning domestic will-o-the-wisps, neither of which Rachel managed to play successfully.

In art, Rachel continued to be the only student without a familiar. She finally cornered Mistletoe and brought the cat to class. He spent the entire period chasing Zoë's tiger-striped quoll and Juma O'Malley's miniature elephant, knocking over paints, and causing a general commotion. After that, she did not even bother trying to catch him before class.

True history class was fascinating when it covered new material. Alas, this did not happen as often as Rachel would have liked, as a great deal of the class was review drills. The tutor emphasized learning by reading original works but explained that this would mainly come later, as the early shamans had left few written records.

Rachel listened attentively—when the tutors covered new material. When they droned on, repeating material previously covered, her mind drifted. And when it did, there was nothing to stave off the darkness. The tutor's voice would fade, and Rachel would suddenly find herself reliving her harrowing ride across campus, as she warned her fellow students of Mordeau's perfidy. Or she would again find herself being yelled at by John Darling in front of a faceless crowd. Or her imagination would begin to picture the encounter between Valerie and Jonah Strega, or what Misty Lark might have seen while she was tied to the couch, watching Egg and his cohorts murder her family.

It was all she could do to keep from crying out in fear in the middle of class.

She tried keeping her mind occupied by rereading books from the library of her memory—her favorite activity before she came to school; however, she often became absorbed in the story and missed some important class point. The only thing she could do during review periods that successfully kept the horror at bay was to contemplate how to stop these terrible events from happening again.

So long as she kept her thoughts focused on this goal, she felt calm.

The first day after the meeting with Dread, Rachel spent her time musing about her grandfather. Had he been the one to cast the spell that bound Azrael into Aleister Crowley? If so, was this incident related to the tragedy he had suffered? And what could this tragedy be that she had never heard so much as a word of it?

Then, it struck her.

Rachel sat straight up in the midst of an Alchemy review session, startling Siggy, who was snoozing beside her. If her grandfather, the great cryptomancer, had cast the original spell on Azrael, wouldn't he have used cryptomancy?

If so, they needed only to pronounce the masterword, and the binding on Azrael would be restored to full strength!

From that moment on, during the review periods, Rachel mentally searched the journals her grandfather had kept in his tower library, looking for clues. In her memory, she could recall each crisp, yellowing page clearly enough to reread its firm, looping handwriting. She found no mention of *Azrael* or *demon*. Crowley was mentioned quite often, but always in reference to either youthful capers, or Grandfather's efforts to restrain the other magician's excesses during World War II. Crowley had fought on the side of the Allies, but her grandfather had disapproved of his methods.

When that inquiry proved a dead end, Rachel searched the same journals for the term *masterword*. She found hundreds of references, at least seventy-six of which also mentioned bindings. Unsure how to proceed, she gazed out the window, dreaming of bravery, of sacrifice, or of Gaius.

By the fourth Thursday of the school year, two weeks after the meeting with Von Dread, she had mentally reread each of her grandfather's journals three times. If he had written down the masterword to the binding holding Azrael, Rachel feared it had not been in one of the volumes he left in his tower library.

Maybe Nastasia was right.

Maybe there was nothing they could do to help.

• • •

Her next class was true history. Mr. Gideon gave a fascinating lecture on the origins of the Seven Arts. Rachel listened raptly, until he began explaining for the third time—for the benefit of those who still had not grasped it—that alchemy came from ancient China, while enchantment came from Scandinavia, where it had been taught to humans by the elves. Rachel who, by the age of four, had been able to recite from what part of the world each of the Seven Arts came, again found it impossible to pay attention.

Bored, her thoughts drifted to her friends and their romances. Siggy and Valerie seemed to be doing well. Joy mooned after Sigfried in an embarrassing way. Lots of boys stared at the astonishingly lovely Nastasia, but she did not seem to notice. Watching the princess's obliviousness reminded Rachel of her fortress notion. As she pictured the princess and Von Dread standing side-by-side, like twin icebergs, it occurred to her that she herself might have a great deal to offer a prince.

After all, the Griffins were of noble blood—noble enough for her family to be of interest to Ivan, Prince of Magical Australia. How useful it might be for a head of state to have a wife who could mingle graciously at some formal affair and then repeat back to him every word of every nobleman and diplomat she passed. True, she was very young, but Von Dread seemed like the calculating type who might decide a young girl had qualities he desired in a wife and choose to wait for her.

As she gazed out over the commons, she pictured him standing with his arms folded, curtly informing her that he had decided to make her his wife. In her daydream, she gazed back at him coolly, explaining that she preferred his lieutenant, Mr. Valiant. She pictured Dread staring down at her, his face impassive. He leaned toward her, lifted her chin, and kissed her. His mouth claimed hers. His lips left a trail of fire down her cheek and throat. His arm supported her back. His other hand slid around her front, caressing her...

Rachel made a tiny noise of alarm.

Where had that come from?

She pressed her palms against the heat of her flushed face. Never in her life had she imagined such things! She certainly did not want to imagine them between her and Dread! She tried to picture Gaius embracing her in such a fashion. This only made her more uncomfortable.

She was not ready for that.

She did not even want to think about it.

Straightening up, Rachel returned her attention to Mr. Gideon's description of how conjuring was discovered by the natives of Australia and New Zealand.

From now on, she promised herself, no daydreaming about anyone but Gaius!

• • •

Checking her mail after lunch, Rachel found three letters and a package. The first letter was from her father. Rachel's fingers trembled as she opened it. She had heard from her mother regularly, but this was the first written correspondence from her father. She hoped it might be news of an impending engagement between Ivan and Laurel but feared it would contain a command to break things off with her boyfriend.

There was no mention of Gaius, or of Ivan and Laurel. Instead, the letter contained a brief denial of her request for a wand, explaining that fulgurator's wands were only needed for dueling. He went on to say that she would, upon graduation, receive a ring of mastery, in which spells could be stored. For now, however, she should concentrate on practicing these spells, not storing them.

Sighing, Rachel quickly tossed off a reply explaining that she understood that wands were for duelists and that she had joined a dueling club. It seemed unfair that Sigfried now had a wand—picked out by her—but she did not. She wondered if Siggy would lend her the money to buy one but decided against asking him after she remembered how Lucky had named each of their coins. Besides, how could she pay him back?

The other two letters were from her sister Sandra. Both were dated well before they had been posted. The first read:

Dear Rachel,

It is so nice to hear from you. I was worried when Father told me your friends had been attacked. PLEASE be careful. If you see something strange, tell a tutor.

I am doing well. I have been working for the Wisecraft, doing some financial research. It is extremely boring. I wish I had worked on more interesting subjects when I selected college courses! Remember my words, little sister!

As to your second question...Are you kissing petrified boys? Are boys petrifying and kissing you?? I am not sure either is a good idea, but the second sounds rather inappropriate. I think if you kissed a petrified boy, on purpose, then yes, it does count. I wouldn't count a kiss stolen while I was petrified, though.

If you are kissing a boy, I should be informed of who it is! Also, you may want to avoid telling Father about kissing anyone. Just a suggestion.

Much love,

Sandra

As she read the first part of the letter, a lump formed in Rachel's throat. She tried to swallow it away but failed. She felt terrible for her sister. Bright, quick-minded Sandra stuck behind a desk bored to tears? So unfair! Her sister was so talented, so clever!

Rachel comforted herself with the thought that Sandra would not stay behind a desk for long. The Wisecraft would recognize her talents and promote her any day now.

The second was short and looked as if it had been rapidly scrawled.

Dear Rachel,

Father and I just left the Wisecraft building in New York, after being stuck inside for six days. It was not a pleasant experience at all. I have spoken with Father, and I would like to come visit you, if you would not mind. I will not, though, if you think a visit from your big sister would be embarrassing.

Please let me know.

Much love,

Sandra

Rachel gawked. Sandra and Father had been caught in the lockdown? No wonder she had not heard from Father sooner. By the time he was released from the Wisecraft Building, he had probably forgotten all about unimportant things, such as his youngest daughter's new boyfriend.

What had Father and Sandra been doing in New York? Had they been in terrible danger? Rachel took several deep breaths, assuring herself that they were okay. Then, she wrote:

Dear Sandra,

I would LOVE to have you visit. How could you even imagine that I wouldn't want to see you and introduce you to my friends?

Love,

Rachel

PS: Unless you're coming to yell about my boyfriend, in which case it's okay if you don't.

Rachel marked the letters with her post seal and slipped them in the outgoing mail slot. Then, she opened the package. Inside were the first of the calling cards she had ordered for Sigfried—six green talking glasses with gilt frames. An enclosed note explained that the second six of the dozen ordered would arrive two per week for the next six weeks. Squealing with delight, she ran off in search of Sigfried.

• • •

After class, Rachel and her friends gathered in the music room, in the cellar of Dare Hall. Sigfried handed out mirrors to Nastasia, Valerie, Zoë, Joy, and Rachel. An instruction pamphlet, written in six languages, included the cantrip for bonding card to owner. The group performed this cantrip and then tried calling one another. When a name was spoken, the green glass turned clear. It then showed an image of whatever was in front of the card of the person called.

Their group sat on the left side of the music room, in the comfy armchairs that formed a semi-circle in front of the large hearth. The fire had been dead when they arrived, but Lucky breathed it back to life. Now, the sweet smell of burning cedar perfumed the air.

Behind them, on the stage in the middle of the vast chamber, musicians practiced. The band, known as the Ginger Snaps, consisted mainly of a bevy of red-headed MacDannans, along with their cousins and a few friends. The impish Oonagh

MacDannan alternated between directing the group and playing her tuba. Rachel wondered if Oonagh planned to become a rock star, like her father. A number of Enchanters had become sensations in the Unwary world, but she had never heard of a popular mundane musician who played the tuba.

Glancing that way, Rachel could not help noticing that one of the musicians was John Darling. On the outside, she smiled and chatted with her friends, playing with her new calling card. Inside, she seethed. Since that beastly boy had humiliated her in the dining hall, her long-standing crush had turned into hatred. Part of her mind listened to her friends. The other part plotted and re-plotted young Mr. Darling's abject humiliation.

Joy sat curled up in a comfy armchair holding her card. "Nastasia. Oh! I can see you!"

Rachel said the princess's name and could see Nastasia in her mirror as well. The calling cards allowed for conference calls.

Joy bounced up and down. "So...what should I ask? I know! Have any visions lately?"

Nastasia sat regally on a wooden rocking chair, her Tasmanian tiger resting its head in her lap. She addressed her card. Her voice issued from the card in Rachel's hand, as well as from Joy's card.

"Not visions such as the one that predicted the death of Mr. Von Dread and his cronies," said Nastasia, "but I now believe that our roommate, Astrid Hollywell, is from the same world as William Locke, and Naomi Coils. The first time I touched each of them I saw the same event, though from different perspectives— a scientific experiment gone awry. An explosion in the middle of what looked like a sideways tornado. Miss Hollywell thought it might be something called a wormhole."

"Wow!" Rachel and Joy murmured.

Siggy scowled. "Wish I could see that. Collisions. Super-explosions! Wicked!"

"Other than that," Nastasia spoke with the mirror close to her face; her blue eyes looked huge in the square of Rachel's card, "my only adventure has been that I spoke to Kitten's fami-

liar. I asked him to visit the girls whose families died and those
harmed by Dr. Mordeau."

"What a fantastic idea!" Rachel cried. To her embarrassment, she had to fight down a burst of envy. She wished she had
been the one to think of that. "Do you think it helped?"

"He came to see me." Valerie experimented with speaking
into her card. She held it so far away that it did not pick up her
voice properly. "He did not speak. But I held him, and he purred.
It was very comforting! Like one of those vibrating pillows that
smell like pine needles my grandmother used to have...only
comfier."

"He truly is a Comfort Lion," murmured Rachel.

"He helped my girlfriend? Good," Siggy made a grand
gesture. "I'll spare him!"

"Spare him from what?" Valerie's lips twitched with amusement.

"From being my dragon's lunch, of course," Siggy replied.
"Lucky! Next time you go feral, eat some other familiar. Not the
tiny lion."

"You got it, Boss."

Valerie sat on the blue and purple braided rag rug playing
with the lenses for her camera. Raising her card, she spoke into
it: "Okay, next question. Princess, have you seen those red lines
in any new visions? The ones that made you bleed when they
pressed against you?"

"No. The E..." Nastasia paused mid-word. She looked
tremendously distressed. A dark, petulant storm brooded upon
her features. "No. I haven't. Excuse me." She shut the textbook
that had been open in her lap, picked it up, and quietly left the
room.

"Wait! Princess! Where are you going?" Joy looked after her,
puzzled. "Can I come?"

The princess looked flustered. "I plan to...use the facilities."

Joy perked up. "Girls go to the bathroom in pairs. My father
says it's a law of nature."

The princess's face grew pink. "Please, do not disturb
yourself." She departed.

"These walky-talky mirrors are wicked!" Sigfried exclaimed. He hung upside down off his chair, making kissy-faces at Valerie through the calling card. Valerie smirked back at him. "No payment plan. No battery to run out. Even better than the cell phones of the Unscary!"

"Unwary! The word is Unwary! By Hecate, can't you remember anything?" Joy waved her arms in exasperation. Rising to her feet, she stomped off, slamming the door on her way up the stairs. This noise caused the musicians across the room to jump.

"Well, I am not scared of them, so to me they are Unscary..." said Siggy, throwing a brown apple core he brought out from the pocket of his robe to Lucky, who swallowed it in a single gulp. How long the apple core had been in his pocket was anyone's guess.

Rachel and Valerie watched Joy depart. They glanced at each other and shrugged.

Zoë sat sideways with her feet on the armchair next to her, feeding bits of beef jerky to her quoll. Her head tilted back, she held her calling card above her and spoke into it, addressing Sigfried, who looked at her in his own card. "Sigfried, you need to talk to Joy. She's got to get over her crush on you. Otherwise she'll constantly be getting annoyed and stomping away."

"Are you daft?" Siggy gawked at Zoë as if she had sprouted a second head while singing *God Save the Queen.* "You don't walk up to a girl and say, 'Don't have a crush on me, please.'"

A muffled choking noise escaped Rachel's lips. The mere thought of a boy she fancied confronting her thus, especially if he did not return her affections, sent her into a cold sweat. She snuck a super-quick glance over at the horrid James Darling and blanched.

Zoë raised her voice to be heard over the *oom-pah* of the tuba. "It's true. You're a doofus and will probably hurt her feelings, Siggy. I'll speak to her, if you want."

"No, talking is no good." Sigfried stroked his chin, as if pondering deeply, while gazing into his calling card. "I know what you're thinking. You think I should ask Valerie," he gestured at his girlfriend, "to go pull her hair, slam her head into a table top, and grind a lit cigarette into her ear? That's what the older girls did in their dorm at Sister Rahab's Home For Unwanted Tramps, when they had an argument over a boy-friend."

"Sister Rahab's..." Zoë blinked.

Siggy shrugged. "Rahab was the sister institution to Brother Dismas's Asylum For The Criminally-Inclined And Mentally Meager Waifs And Foundlings, where I grew up. Both were facilities run by the Nuns of Hestia—there wasn't any Brother around, Dismal or otherwise. Sometimes, on Punishment Day, the two establishments would have assembly together."

The girls all stared at him, not sure how much of his ravings they should take seriously.

"I do not mean to disappoint you, Zoë," Siggy continued, "but I must say it is a bad idea. Two reasons. First, Miss Hunt, here, has been in the infirmary, so it might not be a fair fight. Second, Miss O'Keefe's a member of the Fire-breathing Tutor Hunting and Vigilante Retaliation Club—or whatever we call ourselves. A fight between members might hurt group spirit.

"No, talking is no good in a case like this, nor is fighting. I shall ponder. I shall ponder it and ponder it until my ponderer is sore!" Sigfried ate a linty pancake from his pocket. "An elixir!"

"A...what?" Zoë squawked, sitting upright in her armchair.

"Alchemy can solve all problems!" Siggy still spoke into his mirror. "Either I can drink some semi-lethal concoction to give myself a loathsome smell. Or better yet, I can concoct an elixir to alter the delicate chemical balance of Miss O'Keefe's brain, so she doesn't have extra love-juice, or whatever it is that causes girls to be so girly. Is there a textbook around here somewhere I could look at? I will talk with my hero and mentor, Mr. Fisher. I am sure he knows the elements involved in altering a victim's brain structure and basic personality..." A look of hungry scientific zeal was beginning to form on Sigfried's features.

"Love-juice?" Valerie poked Sigfried in the ribs. "Siggy, you're too much!"

"You're a girl, Miss Hunt." He asked, in a mock-scholarly tone, "What's the active chemical involved?"

"Zoë, Joy knows Siggy's my boyfriend," Valerie said firmly.

"But we aren't ruling out the emotion-distortion elixir as Plan B, are we?" Sigfried asked. "I've already made up a name: *Dragonsmith's Patented Crush Crusher.*" Turning to Rachel, he announced, "When I graduate, I have decided that *Smith's and Lucky's* is not the best name for an alchemy shop. I'll call it *Dragonsmith's*—which will also be the name of my rock band."

"Sigfried, are you even slightly capable of being serious?" Zoë rolled her eyes. "Joy's my roommate and my friend. No, you cannot use an elixir on her. Yes, *Dragonsmith's* is a good shop name. Now focus. How are you going to deal with this situation?"

"I'll talk to her," Valerie tossed a pencil into the air and caught it, spinning it around her fingers until she ended up with it grasped firmly in her hand, as if she were wielding a knife by its hilt. "When I am done, matters will be *very* clear."

Sigfried meanwhile looked at Zoë, as if she were from another planet, and not an earth-like planet around a G-type star, either. "Miss Forrest, the idea of talking to her is cuckoo, crazytown, nutso-riffic, bonker-maniacal, super-goofisonic. If that is the way you Wiselings do things, you are stone-cold freakazoids. And not just because you can shoot sparky-sparks while wiggling your fingers.

"If you don't want to set up a cat-fight between Miss Hunt and Miss O'Keefe," he continued, "and you don't want to solve the problem with magic, then we do nothing and wait for her to find a boyfriend on her own. She cannot have me because Miss Hunt has me."

The calling card in Rachel's hand lit up. In it, the princess appeared with her finger pressed to her lips. She beckoned, indicating that Rachel should come to her. Rachel nodded.

"Fine, Sigfried. You win." Zoë crossed her arms. "No more crazy suggestions from me. So, what were we talking about before? Was it saving the world?" She rose to her feet. "If not, I'm going to study in my room, where there is distinctly less tuba."

"Let's go, Zoë." Rachel rose as well. "We can put off saving the world until after dinner."

Chapter 28:
Saving the World Before Dinner, After All

Rachel and Zoë walked through the foyer that led to the theater and up the sweeping staircase to the girls' dorms. Zoë invited Rachel to join her in the room she shared with Joy, Brunhilda, Wendy, and Sakura. Rachel assured her she would as soon as she was done in the loo.

To her relief, Zoë did not offer to accompany her. Rachel ducked around the corner into the bathroom and pulled out her calling card. Nastasia's face, framed by her golden curls, was still visible in its surface.

"Yes?" Rachel whispered.

Nastasia's face was pale. "Rachel. I cannot abide this secrecy. I do not wish to take responsibility for slaying the elfin woman, but it is not right that we should have to deceive our friends. I am…quite distraught."

"I am ever so sorry, Princess!" Rachel said. "I completely agree. It's maddening. I want to tell…" she paused, saddened at the thought that the princess would not sympathize with her desire to tell Gaius. "…to talk about this, too. I don't know what to recommend."

"I wanted to tell you," Nastasia whispered, "since I cannot tell the others: those lines? The ones that made me bleed? They also cut the Lightbringer when he pressed against them in his effort to trap me where he was. Though he seemed more amused by the injury than harmed.

"Anyway, what I wished to tell you," she continued, "was that these red lines were our Guardian's doing. He was trying to keep me from becoming lost in other worlds. Now that I know how to control the effect, he has promised to stop."

"Really?" Rachel cried, intrigued. "How did you come to know this?"

"The elf woman told me in one of our nightly dream sessions."

"So she has been teaching you!"

The princess nodded. "I am sorry. I meant to tell you that. I've been...preoccupied."

"That's okay." Rachel smiled back at her. "We've all been a bit overwhelmed."

"I wanted to answer the question, but I couldn't tell the others how I found out," Nastasia sighed glumly. "I'm off now to practice with my siblings. Today we're covering the history of dueling. I wish they'd just admit they're babysitting me to keep me out of trouble."

"Good luck," Rachel said wistfully.

The history of dueling sounded fascinating. Rachel was delighted to hear that Ivan had taken up her suggestion that he and his other siblings train Nastasia, so that when the next disaster came, she would be ready.

Nastasia passed her hand over her mirror. Rachel's card turned green again.

• • •

As Rachel walked into the other girls' room, Zoë was kicking off her sandals, which clattered to the floor. Zoë scooted back, picked up her language textbook, and started reading. Rachel sat down beside her, clutching her own textbooks. She pretended to look at one, but she had already glanced at all the early chapters. She held the book, but she read the memorized text in her head.

Joy came into the room and plopped down on her own bed with an exaggerated sigh. Her gaggle of Witch Babies—brightly-colored, collectible, bobble-headed rag-dolls that were currently all the rage—bounced against her pillow. Witch Babies were strewn haphazardly across Wendy's bed as well.

From behind her book, Zoë muttered, "I changed my mind, Joy. He's all yours."

"What? Who? Siggy?" cried Joy. "Aww! That's no fun! I wanted to beat you fair and square. Not have you just give up!"

Zoë, still behind the book, murmured, "No, you win. I even tried to cheat and get him to come up and talk to you about not liking you. He shot down the idea. Big time."

"As would have any sane being," murmured Rachel.

Joy jumped off her bed. She tried to feign rage but amusement fought to take over her features. She shouted, "Zoë! How could you?! That is dirty pool!"

Still not glancing up from her textbook, Zoë responded mildly, "Well, that's just the sort of girl I am—underhanded and evil."

Joy giggled. She dodged left and right, trying to look at Zoë around the other girl's book. Zoë kept moving the book to block her. To Rachel's surprise, as Zoë ducked to avoid Joy, Rachel saw that Zoë's eyes were a bit shiny, as if she was in danger of crying.

Rachel blinked, astonished. *Zoë? Crushing on Sigfried…for real?*

Joy hopped into the bed and sat on Zoë's other side. "You still like him, Forrest. I know you do. I still like him, even though he's an impossible chore of a boy."

Zoë put down the book and leaned her head on Joy's shoulder. "Yeah, he's a jerk."

Joy smiled at Rachel around Zoë's head. "So, Rachel, tell us. What is it like to like a boy who you actually have a chance with?"

"Well," Rachel laid her textbook on her stomach, "I don't quite know what it's like yet. I haven't had much time with him. But…it feels nice. Safe and warm. So, don't give up. There are lots of other cute guys out there."

"Other cute guys?" shouted Joy, waving her arms and nearly braining Zoë. "Other cute guys? Would you offer a starving dog a rubber bone? Cruel, Griffin, so cruel."

Rachel giggled, pressing her fingers over her mouth and nose.

"Doesn't matter how many there are," quipped Zoë, "no cute boy is going to be interested in a doofus like O'Keefe."

"Yeah?" Joy shot back. "Boys don't like pink-haired weirdos with big butts either."

Zoë looked as if she had been slapped. She laughed out loud, punching Joy on the arm. "Mean! No telling Rachel about my big butt issues!"

"Come on," said Joy, "Rachel won't tell a soul. Right, Rach?"

Rachel blinked at the two girls, baffled. This was a subject she had never contemplated. Without looking at either girl, she pulled up memories of what they looked like from the side or back. Zoë was a bit rounder in back than some. Joy looked normal, too. Neither girl looked unattractive to Rachel. She wanted to turn around and determine what kind of rear end she had, but she was too embarrassed.

Considering the size of the rest of her, it was probably also tiny.

Which kind did boys like, Rachel wondered, big or little? She did not know, but she had a vague notion that they liked girls to be curvy, both in front and in back. Zoë's had certainly stood out in Sigfried's memory.

"Zoë doesn't have a big bum," Rachel said finally. "She's really cute."

"See?" Zoë punched Joy's arm again. "And Rachel can't lie. It's like a rule or something. Notice how she didn't say you're not a doofus?"

Rachel thought of the hot sparks of the *Spell of True Recitation* and winced. The distance between her and truthfulness seemed to be steadily increasing.

"So, Rachel," Joy giggled. "We're probably a huge disappointment right now. You guys, in the other room, talk about saving the world. Zoë and me? We talk about our butts. Or I do. Usually, it's impossible to get her to say anything. She must actually like you!"

Zoë blushed slightly.

Rachel wished she and Nastasia spent their time discussing saving the world. More and more, it seemed as if she spent her time feeling as if she should be apologizing for her strengths, while resisting the longing she felt for the princess's unappreciated talents. True, Nastasia was having a hard time adjusting to school life. But the growing number of times that the princess seemed resentful—of her of all people—was baffling to Rachel.

"Um...can I ask you a question?" she spoke in halting tones. "Is it my imagination...or, does the princess act as if she's jealous of me? She has so many gifts and strengths. But, if I can do anything she can't—such as see something, or cast a spell she didn't learn first—she acts petulant." Rachel appealed to the other two plaintively. "Am I imagining this?"

Zoë shrugged. "I don't think I've been around enough to notice."

Joy said, "No, Rachel is right. Nastasia gets all miffy any time Rachel does anything. It's kinda weird. I bet she's just too used to getting everything she wants."

"What should I do?" Rachel asked. "I don't want to upset her. I try to hide what I know...but I'm not very good at that."

"Maybe the princess needs a boyfriend," Joy giggled.

"She wants her family to pick her husband," Rachel sighed. "At first, I thought the princess and Vlad...er...Von Dread would be perfect for each other. They're both regal and place a high value on law and order. But now that I know a bit more about romance, I've changed my mind." Rachel told the other girls her theory about the princess and Von Dread being like two fortresses. She ended with, "For there to be love, someone has to put a fortress under siege."

Joy lay back, staring at the ceiling. Sighing happily, she said in a dreamy voice, "I wish Siggy would lay siege to my fortress."

Zoë almost choked. She rolled Joy out of her bed. Joy fell to the floor with a *thump.* All three girls started laughing.

A tall Japanese girl with bells ringing in her long pigtails walked into the room. Sakura was dressed in the subfusc style: white blouse, black skirt, and black half cape. She looked at Joy, getting off the floor, but said nothing. Walking to her bed, she pulled the bells from her hair, and put them on her end table. Then she curled up on her bed with her back to the other girls.

Rachel heard her take a deep breath and exhale. It was not a melodramatic sigh, but the sound someone made when breathing was painful. With a shock like a blow to her solar plexus, Rachel remembered that she had not saved everyone from Mordeau. According to the princess's visions, Sakura Suzuki came from the same world as Siggy's dead roommate,

Enoch Smithwyck. Slipping off Zoë's bed, Rachel went over and silently hugged her.

"Get off me, Joy!" shouted Sakura. She spoke with a Japanese accent.

Rachel jerked away, embarrassed.

"Um, not me this time. But it can be." Joy crossed to Sakura's bed and climbed on. "And I am going to squeeze you twice as hard, since Zoë is too proud to come over and hug you."

Zoë got up off her bed, came over, and slipped in beside Joy, who looked deliriously happy. The four girls hugged one another. Rachel felt a bit squashed, since she was underneath, but the presence of the other warm bodies was comforting. She felt snug and happy, almost as if she were at home again. Even Sakura giggled a bit. Then she started to cry softly.

Sakura whispered, "Can I tell you a secret?"

"Of course," replied Rachel.

The other two nodded.

"Enoch died saving my life," Sakura said in a small voice. "That girl with the whip crashed through the door nearest to my lab station. Enoch jumped in front of me, pushing me out of the way. I ran away, and Mr. Fisher came forward. The girl went after him. Only Enoch jumped in front of him, too." Sakura choked and cried a bit harder. "Then he was down. And that girl with the whip—she looked so blank. Like it didn't mean anything to her. Enoch glanced at where I was hiding with that stupid little grin on his face, and he told me not to worry. It would be all right. But it wasn't. Oh, Naoki!"

Zoë mouthed, "Who's Naoki?"

"We should let the professors know," Rachel said firmly. "A plaque should be put up in the Memorial Gardens in memory of his heroism."

Sakura said, "I told Mr. Gideon. He's really upset. He's friends with Enoch's dad."

"I'm so sorry," Rachel cried, "Sakura. I never even spoke to him. I know you knew him...better than you might remember."

Sakura pulled away from the others and studied Rachel. "W-why did you say that?"

"Because someone told me that you and he used to know each other," Rachel said seriously. "A spell cast by that horrid Mr. Egg led to you forgetting." She left out that the spell had led the Raven to save Sakura, and that it was the Raven who had turned her into a child and made her forget her old life.

It seemed better not to talk about the Raven.

"No, I didn't know him before my family was killed." Sakura gazed across the room, her face haunted. "When I remembered seeing my parents die...it hurt so much. But when I met Misty. She saw her parents die, too—much more recently. I felt worse for her. Like my parents dying right in front of me wasn't even real. Like I had just read about it.

"But when Enoch died, it was so much worse. Like I had lost something, and I didn't even know what it was. I loved him— more than my parents. But I had only spoken to him a few times! How that even possible?" she cried, her grasp on English slipping as she became more distraught. "What person feel that way?"

The sight of Sakura suffering tore at Rachel's heart. Knowing that Sakura and Enoch had known each other and not being able to say anything made her feel terrible. Rachel resolved to tell her only enough to bring comfort without doing harm.

"No. I don't mean before your parents died." Rachel shook her head fiercely. "I mean you used to know Enoch, but after Mr. Egg's spell, you forgot that you knew him."

Joy chewed nervously on her hair, but she did not interrupt. Sakura stared at Rachel. "Egg changed my memories? Why? How do you know this? How do I get them back? Will Enoch still be alive if I do? Who I was? Who Enoch was? Were we married?"

"I don't know," said Rachel, "but I suspect his name was really Naoki."

"I want my memories back!" Sakura's expression slowly transformed from sorrow to fury. Her body tensed. Her fists clenched. "It's not fair!"

A buzzing filled the room, like a mundane radio unable to get a signal, and her eyes began to shine with a golden light. Rachel realized that she was not hearing the buzzing, she was remembering it. Two parallel versions of the scene existed in her memory. One was being changed to remove the buzzing and the light in Sakura's eyes. In the other, they remained.

Sakura's skin began to shine. The old memory chains, without the shining, lost ground. It failed and ended. Joy and Zoë hopped out of the bed and gawked at the glowing Sakura.

Joy cried, "Sakura, what are you doing?"

"Something is trying to change me," Sakura's voice rang out, fierce and commanding. "I won't let it. I will not be forced to be someone else!"

With a *crackle*, her body shifted. She grew taller and curvier. Her white blouse grew tight. She looked liked an adult.

"Enkai did this!" Sakura cried fiercely. "He put us here, Naoki and me. Enkai must have rewritten history, turned the world into this ridiculous place. Oh God, Naoki really is dead! I wasn't able to protect him!" She blanched, shocked.

"I knew Mr. Gideon in my old life. I've got to speak to him. He'll know what to do." She turned to leave but paused, looking down at herself. "My clothes don't fit anymore. Stupid spell turned me back into a fourteen year old. Being a teenager once was more than enough. Do any of you have anything bigger I could wear? Could I borrow…"

Sakura froze mid-sentence and stopped moving. Zoë and Joy stopped moving, too. Startled, Rachel looked around. Her heart froze in terror.

The gigantic, red-eyed Raven was flying directly at her.

The Raven flew through the closed window. It landed on the floor and hopped a few times. Then it transformed into a man. He was eight feet tall with enormous black wings and a blinding circle of light above his head. In this light, Rachel felt an impression of extraordinary diligence, as if her mind were focused upon completing the tasks set before her and nothing else. A determination to persevere took hold of her, a very familiar feeling. It was the feeling that possessed her when she was flying or pursuing knowledge. It felt…

Just like her.

The Raven reached up and pulled the ring of light off his head. It turned into a large gold hoop. Rachel's personal determination to do her part remained, but the outside inspiration that had temporarily reinforced it vanished.

The Raven in his man-form was wearing black slacks but no shirt or shoes. He looked at Rachel sadly. "So, little one, tell me what I should do."

"I'm so very sorry," Rachel whispered. Now that the outside emotion imposed by the golden hoop was gone, she felt so frightened that her chest was resisting the order to breathe. "I thought I was helping. I thought I was being careful. Is there some way to move backwards and make it forgotten again?"

"I cannot move time backwards. I can change the memories of these children. But I must also change the gift within this one," he pointed at Sakura, "or it will happen again."

"Gift?"

"When I rescued her from the darkness Outside, I tried to leave her as close to her original self as possible. This was hard because her essence is very orderly. Her gift is one which suppresses sudden changes and chaos. I did not realize it would also break carefully-constructed changes. It must be removed and remade so as not to interfere with what I do."

"You mean she interferes with magic, don't you?" asked Rachel. "That's why her spells have such odd results. And why the brooms would not work correctly for her?"

He nodded solemnly.

"Does it matter if she suddenly grows up? I mean, she's just one person."

"Will she keep the matter quiet? Allow me to provide an explanation that is understandable by the laws of this world? Not try to find out more about her life Outside?" the Raven asked gravely. "The illusion that the world is safe is difficult to maintain. There are forces without battering at the Walls, trying to get in. They wish to rip apart this world and destroy everything within it. They will use any excuse to enter."

"Then why don't you stop Nastasia's visions?"

The Raven glanced upward. "They come from One with whom I shall not interfere."

"Who?" asked Rachel curiously.

The Raven said nothing.

"Can you change Sakura's gift without hurting her?"

"I can, but that is not what worries me."

"What..." Rachel's mouth suddenly felt terribly dry. "W-what is worrying you?"

He gazed at her with his blood red eyes. "It would be wisest for me to change you as well, Rachel Griffin. But, to do so would be a great injustice. Unlike these others, your perfect recall is part of who you are. To alter it, after you have learned so many things, would be the same as making you into someone else. Someone new. Do you understand what I am saying?"

Rachel understood exactly. Her memory was woven together like an intricate web. To change her memory, he would need to remake her mind—which was essentially the same as killing her and putting a new person in her place.

Rachel swayed on her feet, feeling faint. The entire universe seemed to tremble with her heartbeat.

Her voice cracked as she begged, "Can't you leave me the same? Please, I'll be quiet about—everything. I won't say anything...to anyone!" She rushed over to him, pleading. "I don't want to not be me...*oh!*"

Rachel's body went rigid. Her pupils slowly widened.

What was she saying?

Wasn't this the moment for which she had been wishing?

A chance to sacrifice herself for her world?

"I take it back." She lowered her lashes humbly. "I want to help. I wish to save the world more than I wish to be me."

The room was utterly silent.

No clock ticked. No bird called. No rumble of thunder came from the tor. All she could hear was her own breathing and the rustle of his feathers. He regarded her more closely.

With fierce determination, she raised her head and met his gaze, though tears blurred her vision. "Go ahead. Change me, too.

Unless—" she tried to swallow but could not, "unless I could serve the world better by remaining myself."

The Raven's eyes shone as he regarded her. They were not scarlet anymore. They were gray and very, very steady.

"Child," he lay his hand on her cheek, "I would sooner rip the sun from the heavens than change you from who you are."

"Are y-you sure?" Rachel barely recognized her own voice. Looking up at him towering over her, she searched his face. "I don't want to be the one who destroys the world."

"I know you will protect the world," the Raven replied gravely. "I will find another way. These are not your mistakes. They are mine. I let these people into the world to save them from the chaos Outside. I had to change them. If I just let them appear, with their old memories, it would disturb all the people on this world. Such disruptions draw great attention to the chaos outside of the barrier. That chaos would begin to batter down the Walls. It thrives on attention."

He looked immensely sad. "If the Walls break, this world will end. I will not be able to save everyone. I will only be able to save a few. It is not something I want to see happen again."

Rachel nodded wordlessly, but her fear had evaporated.

The Raven, who had so terrified her, now seemed inexpressibly dear.

The Raven pointed at Sakura. "I will alter her so that her power cannot undo my changes. I am sad to have to reduce her gift, but I will give her something to lessen the loss. Then I shall change their memories, all of them, so they remember falling asleep after hearing of Enoch's brave sacrifice. I will not lessen her feelings for him. It is painful for her now, but I would be loathe to take away even more of her previous life."

He reached into Sakura's chest and pulled out a glowing sphere of light. It glittered with many colors, some bright, some muted, all dancing and sparkling inside the sphere. The Raven ran his fingers through the glittering globe. Then he frowned.

He reached into Joy's chest and drew out a similar sphere. It, too, danced with many colored lights, predominately purples and greens. He ran his hand through it, catching some of the purple light. Putting Joy's shining globe back, he moved the purple light through Sakura's ball, making slight changes to the dominant colors.

"What are you doing?" Rachel asked, fascinated.

"Joy's gift is to alter memories. I am borrowing it to help Sakura forget again. This way, I do the least damage to her."

"Where did Joy get this gift?" Rachel asked. "Did you give it to her?"

"I did not. I will not speak of He who did. These gifts you each have been given are great things. I cannot make them. I can only diminish them and replace them with something less elegant," said the Raven. He thrust Sakura's sphere back into her chest.

"As for you, Rachel Griffin, I can see many paths stretching into the future, some more likely than others. When I interfere with the world, it can make these paths come to be or, as now, disrupt them. Then my vision of things to come grows dim.

"I ask that you tell only one person of what transpired here. My vision of the future is clouded, but I believe I know who that person will be. I will shield his mind and yours from the tampering of others, enough that no one who walks this world will be able to draw the information from you without your consent."

Rachel curtsied. "Thank you, sir."

The Raven cocked his head. "I have spoken to you more today than I have spoken to any mortal in many centuries. And the previous conversations were not very stimulating."

An idea seized her, a ridiculous desire that would probably get her killed for her hubris. But she had just faced death and been reprieved. Rushing forward, she threw her arms around the towering figure and hugged him.

Above her, the Raven let out a sigh. Resting his hand on her head, he gazed down at her with the faintest, ghostly hint of a smile.

Then he was gone.

Chapter 29:
The Unfortunate Wife of Mortimer Egg

Nothing had changed.

Yet, everything was different.

That night, at the Knights of Walpurgis meeting, Rachel was unusually quiet. The next day, when Sakura showed up for flying class, her broom neither refused to work, nor flew off at breakneck speeds. As she circled the track, Sakura clapped her hands with excitement. The bells in her hair rang merrily. Rachel, in her roll as the assistant instructor, cheered encouragingly.

After class, Rachel slipped away into the Oriental gardens. Finding a grove of thick bamboo, she hid within. Amidst the dimness of the leafy green stalks, she wrapped her arms around her knees and wept, mourning in secret the loss of the gift that had kept Sakura from flying.

• • •

Later that evening, Rachel and her friends gathered at the Storm King Café. She was dying to tell them what had happened in Joy and Zoë's dorm room, but she could not. Nor had she had a chance to talk to Gaius. The secret pricked at her like burrs in her clothing, never giving her a moment's peace.

How was she going to find the strength to keep from telling people?

The answer, of course, was: *by remembering*. Her blabbing of secrets to Sakura had sparked yesterday's disaster. With one brief phrase, spoken out of a desire to comfort, she had nearly destroyed the very thing she so yearned to protect. The Guardian had been right when he warned the Elf that giving Rachel the memory-protecting Rune could end the world.

It nearly had.

She wished she had asked the Raven more questions. If he removed memories, was he responsible for what happened to her second cousin, Blackie Moth? She also wished she had asked about the statue in the forest. He was there when she found it. Had he removed its wings? And what about angels? Was he the one who had hidden from her the picture she had seen in the book in her grandfather's library?

Was he an angel?

As she sat lost in thought, her friends chatted and laughed. Rachel tried to follow what they were saying, but their words seemed so trivial, so frivolous. It was like trying to follow the logic of a dream. She could not put into words why everything was so different. But it was.

Something had happened inside her. Confronted by death, she had chosen saving the world over her own life. Her life had been given back to her, and, yet, she felt transformed, almost as if he had altered her. She knew she would never again be the same.

Every moment, henceforth, was a gift from the Raven.

In the depth of her heart, she vowed that *he would never regret that gift*.

Xandra Black brought their drinks to their table, her little, blue-trimmed white paper hat perched atop her black hood. Rachel absently sipped her egg cream. Beside her, Nastasia, who had again chosen cream tea, offered her a scone. As Rachel turned to respond, Nastasia made a slight noise. Her head jerked, and her eyes rolled back, only the whites showing.

Rachel jumped up. "Nastasia's having a vision!"

"Better her than me," murmured Xandra Black, where she stood behind the marble counter, wiping it with a sponge.

Nastasia swayed in her seat. Sigfried lunged forward and caught her shoulders, steadying her. Her head slumped. Then she straightened, herself again.

"Quickly!" The princess leapt to her feet. "We must alert the dean!"

• • •

The dean gathered proctors, who gathered Flycycles, Mr. Chanson, and the student members of the Brotherhood of the White Hart. This group flew off for the docks. Rachel wanted to run and tell Gaius, but the princess insisted that Von Dread and his cronies were not to be trusted. For Rachel to explain why it would have been sensible to tell Dread would have required

revealing that he knew the secret of opening the school wards—
a secret even the proctors did not know. Dread could jump
directly to the source of the trouble, while the proctors first had
to cover the half mile to the docks on brooms. Not knowing how
serious the matter of the vision was, Rachel was not willing to
spill his secret to Nastasia.

Once the proctors were under way, Nastasia returned to the
café and shared the details of her vision. "I saw an apartment in
New York City—high up and very posh. A woman was standing
by the window, blowing her hair with a mundane device. The
door opened. Two Agents let a second woman into the
apartment. She was wearing a shadowcloak. I could not see her
face.

"The first woman put down her device and said, 'Serena, so
kind of you to come by.'"

"Wait...Serena, as in the fourth member of the murderous
quartet?" asked Rachel. Chills traveled up and down her body.
No. No, no.

"Very possibly." Nastasia replied. "This Serena woman
stepped closer to the first woman and said, 'My apologizes,
Mattie, I've always liked you, personally, but I have learned that
you are in our way. You're keeping our master from reaching his
full potential. If Mort is not man enough to do what needs to be
done, I shall do it for him.'"

"What did she do?" Rachel's words came out in a hoarse
whisper.

"She made a gesture. A silvery distortion surrounded the
hair blower, which sparked and smoked. The first woman, the
one named Mattie, cried out and crumpled to the floor. The
second woman, Serena, leaned over and snapped her neck. It
made a very ugly sound."

Rachel's breath caught. "Oh!"

"The last image was of Serena screaming that Matilda Egg
had been electrocuted."

"Does this mean..." Joy whispered, her face a pale green,
"that the demon Azrael will escape his bonds and kill us all?"

"Most likely," Rachel whispered back. Her head felt light, as if she were swimming through the thick air of the suddenly blurry cafe. She drew a deep breath. "*If* it happens. We stopped the other two visions, right? The dean and the proctors will stop this one, too!"

That was the purpose of Nastasia having these visions, was it not? To give them sufficient warning? But what if they failed to stop it? Would the existence of Mortimer Junior be enough to keep his father from losing control? Would that smiling boy, with his freckles and his phooka, be the next target? She pictured an Agent informing him that his mother was dead, and his father was wanted for the murder.

Her mind shied away. The thought was too painful.

Yet, the fate of Mortimer Egg, Jr. was nothing compared to what would happen to everybody else, if the demon inside his father broke free. Squeezing her eyes closed, she mentally begged: *Please don't let her die. Please don't let her die. Please don't let her die.*

Rachel paced back and forth across the black-and-white checkered floor of the café, clasping and unclasping her hands repeatedly. Oh, why had Nastasia not told them sooner? She would not have hesitated to reveal Dread's secret, had she known the direness of the situation.

Returning to her friends, she found them looking drawn and frightened, except for Siggy who sat sharing a hamburger and fries with Lucky, looking utterly unconcerned.

"I was afraid of this," Valerie stirred her elderberry cordial with a pink straw, "ever since Siggy told me that you told the dean what you learned, Nastasia, I've been worried. Egg and Browne both worked for the Wisecraft. The Wisecraft is where I got attacked. We don't know how many more leaks might exist in the organization. Agents might still be geased."

The princess frowned sternly. "It is far more likely that the King of Bavaria is the weak link. He openly encourages practitioners of black magic to move to his country. His son stated openly that he planned to share the information we gave him with his royal father."

Rachel dropped into her chair, cold shivers running through her limbs. If the vision came true and Mrs. Egg died, and the demon got free and destroyed mankind, it would either be her fault or Nastasia's.

She had told Dread. Nastasia had told the dean.

"Should we go to the Memorial Gardens and say a prayer at a shrine?" Joy asked.

"To whom would we pray?" the princess asked.

"Hera, maybe?" suggested Valerie. "Freka? Or Isis? The goddesses who protect wives. That's who the cops who work for my father pray to when they have domestic violence cases."

Salome interrupted, "My evil mother adores Isis, so naturally, I'm inclined against her."

"You should not call your mother evil." Siggy looked up from his fries to scowl blackly at Salome. "At least, you have a mother."

"You don't know my mother." Salome ate the cherry off her sundae, unperturbed.

"Or maybe," Valerie continued, "I don't know...who is in charge of keeping the world from being destroyed? Odin?"

"My father does not approve of invoking the gods," the princess stated. "He says we are better off without their interference."

"That's...an odd thing to say." Without really paying attention, Rachel had spread clotted cream on the scone the princess had given her. Some part of her noted that what she was spreading was Double Devon Cream, from her home county back in England. She wondered absently if any of it came from cows that lived on the tenant farms of her family's estate.

"My father says a great many odd things," the princess confessed.

Footsteps came down the stairs. The handsome young proctor, Mr. Fuentes, staggered in, dirty and exhausted. He crossed to Nastasia and sank into a chair.

"We fought the red-haired assailant, Miss Romanov, but she got away," he said apologetically. "Your brother Ivan did well, but he's been hurt. He's at the Halls of Healing." Seeing Nastasia's white face, he added, "He should be fine. His injuries were not serious."

"And Mrs. Egg," Rachel's mouth was dry, "did you arrive in time to save her?"

Mr. Fuentes shook his head. "We arrived too late. Mrs. Egg was already dead."

• • •

It seemed strange to attend class the next day. Their fellow students argued and chatted, unaware of the impending disaster. Rachel walked through the crisp chill of the late September air, bright red maple leaves swirling among the golden birches. Overhead, the sky was a perfect cerulean blue.

How could the day be so beautiful, when such a horrible fate loomed?

When she reached art class, Mortimer, Jr. was not there. When Rachel casually asked Juma where his friend was, he shrugged and said that a proctor had come to get him, something about a call from home. He thought perhaps Mortimer's aged grandmother had died.

Rachel nodded wordlessly and took her seat.

Her luck finally ran out this morning. Mrs. Heelis announced they would begin the practical portion of their curriculum today.

"Our class is more than just an opportunity to learn to draw," old Mrs. Heelis explained as they concluded a discussion of the Greek sculptor and mathematician Phidias, whose statues of Athena, Poseidon, and Apollo were still the models used for these deities by most temples. "We strive to bring to life the loveliness that the ancient Greeks saw when they comprehended the Golden Mean and its relationship to beauty in art. This is why our study of the history of art starts with the Greeks, and not with the Egyptians, with cave paintings, or any of the earlier peoples who committed acts of art upon the world, but who did so without the symmetry and elegance that proper proportion and the Golden Ratio brings to artistic expression.

"We will cover earlier peoples later in your scholastic career. Now, we wish to develop our artistic eye."

Mrs. Heelis smiled kindly at the class. "Speaking of artist's eye, we have worked to master drawing the three basic shapes: circle, triangle, and square. We have learned how to shade them, and we have made physical versions out of clay. As of today, I am sufficiently satisfied with your progress to allow you to begin conjuring real objects."

A great cheer went up from the students. Even Rachel cheered, until she realized that this was the fundamental activity at Roanoke that required a familiar.

Valerie raised her hand, waving it. "I heard conjurations vanish at midnight."

Mrs. Heelis shook her head. "Not at midnight, twenty-four hours later."

"Then they disappear? Like Cinderella's dress?"

Mrs. Heelis nodded again. "Assuming that her dress had been conjured the previous midnight. Yes."

"All conjurations?" asked Valerie.

"All conjurations, Miss Hunt," Mrs. Heelis replied firmly. "The talismans one makes using alchemy are temporary, too. They last a month. There is a process for degossamerizing them—for making them permanent—but that is not a matter for this class. Shall we begin?"

The assignment was to hold the image of a twelve inch hoop in mind, clearly, and then conjure it. All around the room, students performed the *muria* cantrip, and then—with the help of their familiars, who reached up with their silver paws or wings or talons and pulled it from the dreamland—produced hoops of a pale white substance that reminded Rachel of ceramics.

Or rather, that is what was supposed to happen.

The princess and her Tasmanian Tiger produced a circlet of such pure gold that it reminded Rachel of the hoop above the Raven's head. At the sight of it, Mrs. Heelis clapped with joy. Siggy and Lucky conjured a live alligator that had to be dispelled by Mrs. Heelis before it could eat Juma O'Malley's tiny elephant. Fortunately, the tutor got it right away. If conjured items were not dispelled immediately, they remained real for twenty-four hours.

"Your elephant seems to be the target of choice," Zoë observed wryly. Her hair was a pale jade color today. The feather was teal with dark green spots. "First, a cat. Now, an alligator?"

Juma shook his head of shaggy copper curls. "They must know Jellybean's a tasty guy."

"I guess that's what you get when you name your familiar after candy," Zoë snorted.

Juma shrugged. "What's the name of your...whatever-that-is?"

Zoë held up her spotted, orange creature. "It's a tiger quoll, and his name is Aardvark."

"But...it's not an aardvark?" Juma wiggled his eyebrows. Rachel noticed that he wore gold rings in his ears, like a pirate.

"Is yours a jellybean?" Zoë quipped back.

"Still, 'tis odd to name one animal after another." The princess looked up from her second golden hoop. "Would you call a cat 'Dog'?"

"I would," Zoë grinned. "Nor am I the only one. Seth's family had a cat named Dog."

Seth Peregrine nodded from where he and his tortoiseshell cat were trying to manifest a hoop that looked more like a circle and less like an industrial accident. "It's true. Though, in my defense, I was not one who named it."

"What is the name of your current cat?" Rachel pointed at his feline familiar.

Seth grinned. "Turtle."

Mrs. Heelis walked around the room, checking each student. Soon she would reach Rachel's seat. Embarrassed to fail in front of everyone, she resolved that she would conjure something without a familiar to help her. She could hardly do worse than Seth Peregrine, and he had a familiar.

She tried very hard to picture the ring she had drawn, but she was not entirely sure what this ring should look like in three dimensions. As the tutor approached, Rachel hurriedly pointed her fingers upward and then pulled her fingertips together as she drew her hand downward.

"*Muria!*"

A white ring appeared, but it was only three-quarters solid. Mist billowed up from the inner section that she had not properly pictured. The mist smelled of plaster-of-Paris and lilacs.

As she breathed it in, Rachel felt unexpectedly sleepy.

The world tipped sideways.

Chapter 30:
I Don't Remember That Cup

A breeze blew across her face.

Hands lifted her. Rachel opened her eyes and shrank away from the gray snake with two hollow eyes hovering over her. Then, her mind's eye readjusted, and she recognized Jellybean's trunk. The tiny elephant blew air into her face, fanning the mist away with its big ears.

Siggy and Juma leaned over her, too. Their hands were under her arms, lifting. Lucky flew around her, his gold eyes wide with concern. Embarrassed, Rachel shook off the boys' hands and climbed to her feet.

Class was ending. Mrs. Heelis gave their next assignments and then said, "Very well. Everyone please put your hoop or facsimile thereof into the vanishing bin." She finished with, "Miss Griffin, will you please remain? I wish to speak with you."

Rachel's heart dropped so far that she feared those in the classroom on the floor below would be sending someone up to complain. As the other students filed out, Rachel approached the art tutor with great trepidation. Mrs. Heelis's ordinarily kind face had taken on a stern cast.

"Miss Griffin, we must never have a repeat of today's events. Conjuring without properly comprehending the object is *very* dangerous. The mists of dream are not to be trifled with."

Rachel lowered her head meekly. "I am sorry."

She thought, but did not say aloud, that her chance of repeating such an offense was low, because *the earth was about to be destroyed by the demon Azrael*!

"I cannot emphasize this enough, child," the art tutor continued. "Not only does this mist cause sleep, but also if you are injured while surrounded by it, no magic can heal you."

Rachel nodded numbly.

"This is a great danger for conjurers, especially performers who use the mist as part of their act. Every decade, a few are permanently crippled. 'Tis very sad. There's a girl in the Lower School who lost her family in such an accident. Poor dear is in a wheelchair. This mist is so potent that Agents use it for catching particularly odious monsters. You do not want to breathe it on purpose."

Feeling hardly as tall as Thumbelina's baby sister, Rachel nodded.

"It is our familiars' task to make certain that no portion of the conjuration is unfixed before we draw it down. Where is your familiar, Miss Griffin?"

"I..." Rachel hung her head, tears pooling in her eyes. "He won't come."

"He won't...come?"

"You saw him the day I brought him. Even when he comes, he's useless."

"He's not a familiar quality creature, is he?" Mrs. Heelis asked shrewdly. "He's a pet."

"He comes from a long line of illustrious familiars." Tears warmed Rachel's cheeks. "I love him! I don't want to give him up."

"You must, if you wish to continue studying conjuring. And you must take this class to pass your freshman year. Would you like to borrow a loaner familiar from the menagerie?"

The idea of giving up on Mistletoe was unbearable. She knew, for certain now, that he would never be a familiar. He was not a wonder cat in disguise. She had picked badly.

Yet, her stubborn loyalty made her balk at the idea of replacing him.

Rachel gazed at the tutor imploringly. "Isn't there a way to conjure without a familiar?"

"Certainly, but to do that, you must be able to hold a perfect image in your mind. Perfect in every way." Mrs. Heelis picked up a mug, gesturing at it. "The color, substance, size, shape."

Rachel straightened, suddenly intent. "I can do that."

"How so?"

Rachel took the cup from her and ran her hands over the sides. It was a blue mug—cold, shiny, and smooth. She looked at it from all sides: above and below. Closing her eyes, she recalled it exactly. Without opening her eyes, she performed the cantrip, drawing her hand down.

"*Muria.*"

Rachel opened her eyes. In the air before her, a puff of mist solidified into a blue mug. She caught it and ran her fingers over it, awed. It looked and felt exactly like the original.

The art tutor's old face lit up. "Oh! That's...very good! Very good!" She clapped her hands. "Now, make one that is red and taller."

Rachel balked. She stared at the mug.

Finally, she said haltingly, "I-I don't remember that cup."

Mrs. Heelis's brow beetled. She gazed at Rachel in confusion. Then, realization dawned across her kind, crinkled face. "Oh my. You're Ellen Kim's daughter."

Rachel nodded.

"Your mother was one of my most beloved students," the art tutor said, her face aglow. "I had her the first time I taught at Roanoke, before I departed to teach at the Montana Institute of Conjuring Arts," she explained with a wry smile. "After the Terrible Years, I was asked to return, because there were so few tutors. Ellen was amazing. She could do the most advanced conjurations so quickly. She had a very reliable familiar, if I remember."

"A black-and-white cat named Calidor?"

"Yes, that's right! Oh what a sweetie that cat was!"

Rachel sighed. "What can I do? Only conjure things I remember? Memorize other student's successes?" Her voice trailed off. How pathetic that sounded.

Mrs. Heelis looked up at the walls of her classroom. On them hung the figures the art tutor had created in her famous youth: Peter Rabbit, Jemina Puddle-Duck, Squirrel Nutkin. The old woman smiled faintly. "Well, my dear child, you could always try the old fashioned way."

"Old fashioned way?" Rachel asked, intrigued. "What is that?"

"Learn to draw. When you can draw an object from every angle, you can conjure it."

Rachel gazed at the characters, beloved from her childhood: mice wearing glasses and reading newspapers while seated on thimbles; foxes in waistcoats beguiling lady ducks; young rabbits getting their jackets caught in fences. The idea of learning to draw grabbed hold of her. Not only would it help her conjure, but also it would solve her problem of what to do while tutors reviewed previously-covered material. Drawing would take just enough of her attention to keep her from growing too bored, without absorbing too much.

Her own artwork was currently not worthy of notice, but even as Rachel contemplated this, ways to use her memory to improve her drawing occurred to her.

She itched to try them.

As Rachel glanced at the walls, Mrs. Heelis gazed around the classroom as well. Smiling, the old tutor took a silver picture frame from one of the low cabinets that housed supplies and held it out toward Rachel. "You might enjoy seeing this, child."

Normally, Rachel enjoyed old photos, but the thought of learning to draw had set her imagination aflame. She was dying to get to work at once. To be polite, however, she gave the old picture a cursory glance.

What she saw caused her to cry out in surprise.

It was an old daguerreotype, creamy with faded blacks. Five people, three young men and two young women, stood side-by-side. The men wore military uniforms from the Crimean War. The women wore Victorian gowns with large bustles. As in many old portraits, they looked rather serious, except for one of the young women, who was smiling, and one young man, who had a dashing gleam in his eye. Between the two women stood an extremely handsome soldier with deep bushy eyebrows and an imperious gaze—a very familiar imperious gaze.

"Grandfather!" Rachel peered closer. "And that girl who is smiling..." Rachel gasped. "I say...could that be Grandmother!"

"This was before Amelia took her vows," Mrs. Heelis recalled. "She was a brainy girl with great moral strength. Your grandfather was so in love with her. That was before he met Estelle, of course."

Rachel had no idea who Estelle might be. She examined the face of the youthful Amelia Abney-Hastings. The young woman looked so joyful. It was almost impossible to imagine that she could have become the strict disciplinarian Rachel had known. Of course, Vestal Virgins lived extraordinarily disciplined lives. Perhaps her grandmother had come to expect that same level of devotion from others

The thought of her grandmother abandoning her duties as a Keeper of the Eternal Flame to marry her grandfather sent a shiver through Rachel's body. The elderly duchess had valued keeping one's word above nearly all other things. It must have taken something extraordinary to convince her to break her sacred vows.

"And on the other side. That's you! You were both so beautiful!" Rachel glanced at the rest of the photograph. She poked a finger excitedly at the dashing figure on the far right. "It's him! I've seen his picture a thousand times, in all my favorite books! Only he's a bit younger here. That's Daring Northwest!"

"Yes. What a charmer he was. What an intelligent and driven man." Caught in memory, Mrs. Heelis face filled with sadness. "How I loved him, but he never noticed."

"He's been my hero for years!" Rachel shook her head in amazement. She felt both delighted that she and her art tutor admired the same man and envious of the time Mrs. Heelis had spent in his company. "I had no idea Grandfather knew him." She paused. "Maybe that's why he had so many of Northwest's books in his private library!"

Mrs. Heelis reached for a tissue and dabbed at the corner of her eye. "I was so sad when he died."

"I'm sorry." Rachel bit her lip, wishing for a better way to express her sympathy. "Had you known him long?"

"Since we were children. We had all known each other since…" Mrs. Heelis pressed her lips together and glanced warily out the window.

"Who is this?" Rachel pointed at the last figure, a fierce-looking young man with pale hair and an olive complexion.

"You would not have heard of him. He died in the fight against Bismarck's sorcerers."

"Jasper Hawke!" whispered Rachel.

"Yes!" Mrs. Heelis cried, surprised. "Did your grandfather tell you about him?"

"No...Dr. Mordeau mentioned him while she was fighting the dean." Rachel would have said more, but it occurred to her that, finally, she had found someone who might know the answer to the question that consumed her. "Mrs. Heelis, do you know...about the tragedy my grandfather suffered? The one that caused my grandmother to break her sacred vows and marry him?"

A terrible sorrow came over the old art tutor's face, far worse than the sadness of remembering the death of the young man she had once fancied. Icy chills, like the grip of a cold hand, constricted Rachel's heart.

"Yes, child. I do."

"Wh—what was it?" Rachel's voice was barely audible.

"Are you sure you want to know?" Mrs. Heelis asked gently. "If your parents haven't told you, I am not sure I am the best..."

"Please!" Rachel begged. "I must know!"

The art tutor gazed at her, her face full of pity, but she said nothing.

"Please!" Rachel cried desperately. "No one will tell me. Loving someone and not knowing...the horrible things that occur in my imagination. It is worse than knowing the truth!"

"It might not be worse," Mrs. Heelis whispered. She covered her face with her hands.

After what seemed like a long time, she pulled them away again. "I know what that's like, child. No one knows how Darius died. He just went into the Glass Hall in Castle Beaumont and never emerged. We kept expecting he had popped through some travel glass and would appear again from some odd corner of the earth...but he never did. That was over a hundred and fifty years ago."

Rachel swallowed with some effort, nodding.

"Very well, child." Mrs. Heelis seemed frailer. She made her way to her chair and sat down. "Bismarck sent a monster to attack your grandfather. I never learned the full details, but Blaise...got there too late."

"Too late?" Rachel asked confused. "Too late for what? I thought it attacked him."

She shook her head, a slow and creaking motion. "The creature slaughtered his family."

"His...*his family*?" Icy fingers gripped Rachel's heart, constricting until she thought she might faint. "What *family*?"

But the words made horridly terrible sense.

In Grandfather's library, eternal candles burned before three paintings: King Alfred the Great, the Second Duke of Devon, and a portrait of a woman and five children dressed in Victorian garments. Grandfather had been over two hundred years old when he died. He had lived through the entire Victorian age. Why had Rachel always assumed the six people in the portrait were ancient ancestors?

Mrs. Heelis whispered, "His beautiful wife, Estelle, his three lovely daughters, and his two sons—the heir, Lord Falconridge, and a babe in arms. All murdered."

Azrael.

"Before his eyes," Rachel's voice spoke on its own, without permission from her mind. It sounded distant and flat in her ears. "They were murdered before his eyes, weren't they?"

"Yes." Mrs. Heelis looked faintly surprised. "Your grandfather's friends, Hawke and Crowley, were present, too, but they arrived too late to help. Back then, Crowley had not yet been lost to the path of black magic. The three of them, your grandfather, Crowley, and Hawke, cast a spell. They bound the creature in some manner. But the harm was already done. And Jasper died in the process."

The sound of her own heartbeat echoed oddly in Rachel's ears, like thunder.

It *had* been Blaise Griffin who had cast the spell that bound Azrael, but at a more terrible price than she had imagined. He had lost his own family. *Her family.* He had sacrificed his companion-at-spells, Aleister Crowley, who had gone on—while possessed by Azrael—to become one of the blackest sorcerers of all history and, later, one of the Terrible Five.

And Grandfather's other friend, Jasper Hawke—the beloved of Jacinda Moth, now the Dean of Roanoke Academy for the Sorcerous Arts—had given his life to complete this spell. Rachel reached out and touched the fierce-eyed Jasper Hawke in the daguerreotype. In her mind's eye, she recalled the happy mother and children in her Grandfather's painting.

So many people, lost.

As she recalled the painting, her lips parted in astonishment. It had been some time since she had studied that portrait closely. Calling it to mind now, she recognized one of the figures—the serious young heir in black clothing. His face and garments were the same as the ghost boy who rode beside her when she raced her pony across the moors.

Thunderfrost's boy.

Her uncle.

"Mrs. Heelis," it took her two tries to speak audibly, "my grandfather's son, Lord Falconridge—the original one, before my father and, now, Peter. Do you recall his given name?"

The art tutor tipped her head back in thought. "Myrddin. His name was Myrddin."

Rachel smiled very slightly: Blaise, Ambrose, Emrys, and Myrddin. Her Arthurian-loving brother Peter had always regretted that their parents had broken with the family tradition and failed to name their son after one of the magicians associated with the Court of King Arthur.

"Thank you," she whispered. "Um, would you have any books on drawing?"

• • •

Rachel attended math, ate lunch, and went to music. Or rather her body went obediently to those locations. Her thoughts were entirely elsewhere; so much so that, later, she was not able use her perfect recall to remember what the tutors had said. She had not even heard their voices.

Six family members, dead. Six relatives she had never had the chance to meet killed by Azrael. Bismarck's sorcerers had feared Blaise Griffin more than any other sorcerer in England. They had summoned a fiend from the underworld to dispatch him.

The Griffin family had been the demon's first target.

No wonder her grandfather had become so grim and imperious. What had he been like in his youth, before this tragedy? Had he been kinder? More like Father? Would Father become grimmer and colder, if she, her siblings, and her mother were killed before his eyes?

She could not even properly imagine such a thing.

What had it been like for Grandfather, who lived through it?

She had told Mrs. Heelis that guessing was worse than knowing the truth. She had been wrong.

The truth was even more horrible.

She almost wished she could go back to this morning, when she had not known.

Rachel straightened, startled. Were there some things she did not want to know? If so, how could she accomplish her goal of knowing *everything*?

"Rachel!"

Coming back to herself, Rachel realized she was standing on the commons. Music class must have ended. On Fridays, it was followed by a free period. She was reasonably sure that it was Friday. It had definitely been Friday that morning, before she talked to Mrs. Heelis.

"We have it!" Gaius rushed up to her waving a photo. "I wanted you to see it right off."

"Um...it?" asked Rachel.

She looked around, vaguely wondering where she had been heading. Her dorm, maybe?

Gaius held a picture of a smiling red-headed woman. "That Serena woman—the murderess who killed Mrs. Egg. This is what she looks like."

Rachel leaned forward and examined the photograph.

Ice ran through her veins.

She had seen that woman before—standing on the dock beneath Storm King on the first day of school. The woman had been among the parents waiting for the ferry that would take their children across the Hudson to Roanoke Island.

She was Juma O'Malley's mother.

Chapter 31:
Leaving on a Jet Plane

Rachel and Gaius pelted across campus, hand in hand. They found Vladimir Von Dread on a bench among the trees near Drake Hall, studying. He closed his book as they approached. Gaius bent over, trying to catch his breath, as he gasped out what Rachel had told him.

"We should speak to Master O'Malley," Von Dread stood up, "and then to the dean. You discovered this information, Miss Griffin. Would you like to take the lead? I must be present, though, because I have questions. I cannot afford to lose him to the Wisecraft before I ask them."

Rachel was so surprised to have an older person treat her with respect, instead of pushing her aside and ordering her not to get involved, that it took her a moment to compose her thoughts. When she replied, her voice was steady.

"We should bring Nastasia," she said. "If she touches him, we may learn something useful. She would probably like to be involved in telling the dean. They are friends."

Vladimir nodded and set off. Gaius and Rachel tried to keep up, but Von Dread's strides were far longer than theirs. He spoke out loud to no one in particular, "Locke, Evans, meet me in front of Dee Hall. Miss Griffin, Princess Nastasia, Valiant and I will meet you there. Bring Miss Westenra. Tell her we have a boy with whom we wish her to speak."

There was no answer, but Gaius did not stare at Dread as if he had flown off his proverbial rocker, so Rachel assumed magic was involved.

She pulled out her new calling card and asked for her friends. Nastasia and Joy promised to come right away. Sigfried had chosen to spend the free period between music and science in the alchemy lab. The way he held his card, she could not see him. She saw instead a lit Bunsen burner and the ingredients for Chameleon Elixir spread out in the proper triangle pattern. His voice came from the card, promising to join her as soon as he could get away.

• • •

They waited outside the dormitory for Nastasia, Joy, and William Locke. When the others arrived, Rachel showed her two friends the picture. Topher Evans, who lived in Dee, met them at the door and welcomed them inside.

Dee Hall was everything Rachel had dreamed of, back when she had kept a photo of the impressive edifice under her bed in hopes of someday living in its hallowed halls. The moment she stepped into the foyer, she felt the hush of readers deep in concentration. The wonderful scent of leather and old paper filled her nostrils.

Books were everywhere.

The walls of hallways were covered with books. The risers between the steps on the staircase had been replaced with books. Walking down a corridor lined with volumes on every side, they passed two alcoves containing comfy window seats, both occupied by readers. Around a corner, a small spiral staircase led up to a private reading nook above the ceiling.

Even the doors had bookshelves built into them.

Rachel gazed longingly at a display of old tomes, wondering what fascinating tales these volumes contained. Occasionally she recognized a title, but many were new and filled with unknown promise. She would have liked so much to have lived here. She wondered wistfully if it were too late to switch dorms.

"This is quite impressive," remarked Nastasia, looking around with interest. "I do not believe Dare Hall has a single library."

"Each dorm's designed to help with the activities associated with the study of the Art it supports," replied Gaius. "Scholars study, so Dee's a library. Thaumaturges summon supernatural entities, so Drake has summoning vaults. Enchanters play instruments, so Dare has a theater and practice halls—or so I've been told. I've never been in Dare Hall."

Topher led them to a common room, which was indistinguishable from a library. The room smelled of lemon-scented furniture polish. Long narrow windows let sunlight into a book-lined chamber with brass-cornered oak shelves and leather chairs. Golden curtains hung beside the windows. Set into alcoves, above head level for Rachel, were seven marble busts.

"Who are these esteemed gentlemen?" the princess asked, as she strolled along the long narrow chamber, gazing up at the busts.

Rachel's eyes flickered across the familiar marble faces. "The seven Elizabethan sorcerers after whom our dorms are named: Edward de Vere, Sir Frances Drake, Sir Walter Raleigh, John Dee, Edmund Spenser, Kit Marlowe, and Virginia Dare, the founder of our school."

Gaius glanced at William and Topher, his eyes twinkling with amusement. William smirked slightly. Topher laughed outright. Von Dread watched the three of them impassively.

Gazing up at the busts, Gaius gestured from himself to his friends. "We have long been of the opinion that the school should build an eighth dorm and name it after the great Elizabethan Alchemist, Francis Bacon."

"And why is that?" Nastasia asked politely.

"Bacon Hall?" Gaius drawled. "Who wouldn't want to be able to say, 'I live in Bacon?'"

"Oh, that sounds delicious! I adore bacon!" Joy giggled. Her voice brimmed with enthusiasm. "Maybe the building itself could be made of bacon!"

Gaius grinned at her. "I can see you're on board with our idea."

"Definitely!" Joy grinned back.

The princess tilted her head, frowning slightly. "What would be the purpose of this eighth dorm? What kind of magic would be practiced by its residents?"

Gaius shrugged expansively. "I'm sure we could find another kind. Maybe all these new magics could be studied there. Or it could be used for overflow from the other seven dorms."

"But the dorms are half-empty, as it is." Nastasia's frown deepened. "I fail to comprehend why a new dormitory would be desirable."

"If the dorms are half-empty," Joy asked, "why do we freshman live five to a room?"

"Tradition," Von Dread replied gravely.

"Bacon..." Gaius peered at Nastasia's face, as if searching for some sign that she had caught on. "As in the most delicious food on the face of the planet? That bacon?"

"I am aware of what bacon is, Mr. Valiant. We do raise pigs in Magical Australia," she replied primly. "But I fail to see how a reference to it would improve our dormitory experience."

Gaius blinked. Leaning close to Rachel, he whispered, "Is she really this way? For real?"

Rachel bit her lip to keep from laughing and nodded solemnly.

"Oi," murmured Gaius.

A young woman from Dee joined them. She looked about Gaius's age. She might have been pretty, if she had not been so extraordinarily pale. The only color of any kind on her face was her wine-red lipstick. When she opened her mouth, her incisors were as sharp as a wolf's.

Von Dread introduced the newcomer as Lucy Westenra. Rachel recognized the name, though she did not know if this individual was the infamous Lucy Westenra, who had once been proposed to by three men on the same day—before her unfortunate encounter with a Transylvanian Count—or a younger member of the same family. The Westenra family were all said to practice the same dark arts that led to Lucy's current affliction. Rachel wondered how Miss Westenra and Abraham Van Helsing, the young man from Dare Hall who led the vampire-hunting club, felt about attending school together.

Topher left, returning with Juma, who was carrying Jellybean tightly in his arms. His shaggy curls bounced around his head like coils of copper. He seemed nervous, though he gave Rachel a very friendly smile.

She smiled back reassuringly.

She would not have done so, had she known what was coming.

Lucy Westenra walked up to Juma and gazed into his eyes. Speaking softly, she explained that they just wished to ask him a few questions. The tension drained from Juma's face, but his gaze became vague.

Rachel's stomach knotted. She did not care to see her friends hypnotized, even for a good cause. Glancing up at Von Dread, who stood to one side, his arms crossed impassively, she decided to say nothing.

William Locke stepped forward. "Mr. O'Malley. What is your mother's name?"

"Sasha O'Malley." Juma's voice was flat and expressionless.

Rachel and her friends exchanged glances.

William asked, "Who is Serena O'Malley?"

Even under the hypnotism, Juma's pupils widened in fear. William repeated the question.

"That's what Mom calls herself when she's evil."

"Your mother turns evil?"

"She had an...illness." Juma's voice had the flat quality of someone talking under the influence of magic, but it trembled slightly. "It's called dissociative identity disorder. Normally, she's really nice. Gentle and sweet. We have so much fun together. She makes wonderful treats for Jellybean." He absently petted his tiny elephant, who snuffled his hand fondly. "But sometimes, she ch-changes. Then she...does really bad things."

"What sort of bad things?" William's expression was calm and dispassionate, as if the matter were a scientific inquiry into the atomic weight of an element. Von Dread, however, was frowning slightly and glancing at the freshmen, as if he was not certain that they should hear whatever Juma might say next.

"When I was little, Evil Mother would hurt me. But Mom got me Jellybean. When he is next to me, Evil Mother won't touch me. She just scowls and goes and does other things. Mom told me that it wasn't magic. Just an agreement she and her evil self made.

"Evil Mother breaks things. She steals stuff. She causes arguments. She goes into stores and knocks groceries off the shelves and then accuses someone else of having done it. She likes to put out food for stray animals and then kill them.

"And she misuses her gift. She stands on overpasses and makes cars slam into each other. She made the garbage truck run over our neighbor's puppy—in front of their three-year-old daughter. She once made a school bus full of kids drive off an embankment. I think she does much worse things, too, but she doesn't let me find out about them."

William exchanged glances with the rest of Von Dread's posse. "Is she responsible for the truck that struck the Wisecraft building?"

Juma said flatly, "I don't know."

"These are serious allegations," William said. "Why didn't you tell anyone, Juma?"

Juma's expression did not change. He made no sound, but tears spilled over his lashes and ran down his cheeks. "I did tell. Many times. No one believed me."

"I believe you." Von Dread leaned forward, his face as impassive as ever, and laid a comforting gloved hand on the boy's shoulder. Juma's tears slowed.

William proceeded to ask Juma a series of additional questions about his mother and her whereabouts. Even under the hypnotism, Juma did not know the answers to these questions.

"Miss Romanov?" Von Dread inclined his head to Nastasia.

The princess drew off her gloves and touched Juma's arm. She gave him an encouraging smile. Juma held Jellybean up for the princess to inspect. The tiny elephant snuffled her golden ringlets with his trunk. The princess blinked and then stepped to the side. Rachel, Joy, Gaius, Von Dread, and Locke all joined her a little distance away, beneath the bust of the dorm's patron, Queen Elizabeth's personal sorcerer, John Dee. Topher stayed behind, speaking to Juma. He squatted before him, letting Jellybean sniff his hand. Lucy sat to one side, her nose in a book.

"What did you see?" Joy squeaked.

"Very little," the princess frowned. "A scene of him at home—an Unwary house with mundane appliances. His mother was definitely the red-headed woman in the picture. She was very sweet when she spoke with him. When she turned away, however, her expression became fiendish, wild. She looked like two different people. Also, there was a shadow behind her, like a winged figure, but I could not make it out. It went by too quickly."

"That matches his story," William said.

"Perhaps she's also possessed," Rachel mused.

Gaius, who stood close to Rachel, smiled at her. "They must come from another world, too, if you saw a vision, Miss Romanov. That's how it works, right?"

"We think so," nodded Rachel.

Rachel tried not to stare at Gaius. He was *so* cute. The tiny distance between them gaped like a great chasm. She could imagine energy crackling between them, trying to bridge the gap. To Nastasia, however, the older boy was standing far too close to Rachel.

The princess frowned disapprovingly.

Von Dread straightened and flexed his black dueling gloves. "The boy seems to know very little. Let us take him to the dean."

• • •

They escorted Juma to the dean's office. Clouds were rolling in, hiding the previously perfect blue sky. When they reached Roanoke Hall, the princess went into the office, along with Juma, Von Dread, Locke, Lucy Westenra, and Gaius. Topher, Joy, and Rachel were left in the hallway. The other two departed, but Rachel remained, glum at the thought of having been excluded.

But standing outside a door bearing a brass plaque that read: *Dean*, while all her friends were inside, did not make her feel any more included. Sighing, she left Roanoke Hall. Standing on the bridge over the reflecting lake, she stretched her hand toward Dare Hall, barely visible behind the brightly-colored trees to the west.

"*Varenga*, Vroomie!"

She waited, hoping no one had closed the window she had left open for this purpose. Cantrips did not work through glass. The steeplechaser came soaring out of the trees, across the common, over the reflecting lake, and into her outstretched hand. As she caught it, someone tapped her elbow. Rachel jumped and turned.

No one was there.

"*Psst.* It's me," hissed Sigfried's voice. "*Behold!* My latest Chameleon elixir— or, actually, if you can behold me, it is not working."

"It is working...quite well." Rachel grinned. She peered hard at where he must be but could not make him out. She could barely see a distortion of distant objects when she stared right at where she thought he was. "Too bad we're not both invisible. We could hover outside the dean's window, and you could tell us what they were saying."

"Put out your hand," ordered Siggy.

Rachel did so. Fingers touched hers and pressed a vial of elixir into her grasp.

Sigfried said, "This moonberry stuff is so good, it makes your gear disappear...I bet it will make it so no one can see your broom. It is not as dangerous as some of my other horrible elixirs. You might survive. Bottoms up. Down the hatch."

"What other elixirs, Siggy?" Rachel asked. "Isn't this the only kind you've ever made?"

"A guy can dream."

The two of them jumped on the broom, with only a small amount of confusion caused by Sigfried's unseen state. Then Rachel drank the contents of her vial. It tasted like sweetness and the slither of a chameleon. Her body and her broom faded from sight.

Luckily, she did not need to see the steeplechaser to fly it.

They flew around Roanoke Hall and hovered outside the dean's office. Inside, Juma sat in a chair reading a book, with Jellybean's trunk hugging his leg. Von Dread was still in the room, his arms crossed. Next to him stood Westenra, Locke, and Gaius. The dean sat behind her desk.

No one was talking.

Rachel and Sigfried waited, though Sigfried complained repeatedly that he was bored and wanted to blast something.

Lucky flickered back and forth above the reflecting lake. A short time later, two figures in Inverness capes carrying fulgurator's staffs strode into the office. Rachel recognized her friend, Agent Dorian Standish, his shoulder-length hair done up in a multitude of braids, and the lovely, mysterious Agent Melody Briars with her pixie-cut black hair. Her heavy black eye-liner nearly hid the shape of her eyes, which Rachel knew to be almond-shaped like her own.

Agent Briars knelt before Juma. When she moved, the dozens of charms on her bracelet danced around her wrist. Gemstones on a little chain separated each charm. Rachel guessed that these were low-grade gems, each able to hold maybe ten spells.

"Okay, she's asking him about his mother," reported Sigfried. "He says he hasn't seen her since she helped him put his bags in his room, on the first day of school. Now the Agent's saying that he has to go with her to the Wisecraft offices in New York City. He doesn't want to, but he says he will, if he can keep Jellybean with him."

A nervous Juma departed with the two Agents. Rachel could no longer see them, but Sigfried reported that they had left Roanoke Hall and were heading for the docks. Rachel turned her broom and zoomed around the building. Unseen, they followed the two agents and a frightened Juma, who clutched Jellybean tightly. They flew across the commons, around the lily pond, and down the tree-lined walk toward the docks. Agent Standish put his arm around Juma and Jellybean, and they disappeared in a column of light. A second flash, and Agent Briars jumped, too.

The sky was a dove gray now. Mist hung low over the campus, drifting in clumps. It clung to their faces, as Rachel flew them back and peered into the dean's office. Von Dread and his companions were still speaking with the dean. Nastasia sat to one side, quiet and composed. Rachel wanted to know what they were saying, but Sigfried declared the conversation too boring to repeat.

"Well," complained Sigfried, crossing his arms, "that was bizarrely anticlimactic."

"I want to go somewhere and see something." Rachel gazed up at the spires of Roanoke towering above them. "Are there attics in the school we could fly up to and investigate? If you go back to class, I'm going to do that...unless you have a better idea."

"GO BACK TO CLASS?" Siggy bellowed.

Several students approaching the main building from De Vere Hall stopped and looked around, puzzled at the source of the noise.

"And waste the superlative moonberry chameleon elixir? Never!" exclaimed Sigfried. "There must be something we can break into!"

Rachel laughed, her spirits rallying.

Rrrrrrmmmmm.

A noise like thunder rumbled over the campus, only it did not end, as thunder ordinarily did. It grew louder. Nor was it coming from the tor. The sound grew alarmingly loud. Rachel looked up. Overhead was a roil of gray and mist-white. Behind this foggy curtain, something moved, ghost-like and indistinct. She squinted, trying to make out what it was.

With a tremendous roar, an enormous metallic object burst from the low-hanging clouds. It had a huge glittering eye and a snub nose like a dolphin. Bird-like in shape, it hung in the air without flapping, like a bristleless. It took Rachel a moment to realize it was a mundane airplane. She had never seen one this close.

"Holy Jove!" Sigfried shouted eagerly. "That's a jumbo jet."

"Juma's mother! She must be doing this!" Rachel shouted back. "She's a technomancer."

The jet was still several miles away. Rachel's thoughts became crystal clear. Using the same three-dimensional matrix of vectors that she pictured in her head when maneuvering at high speed, Rachel calculated its flight path and speed.

It was flying directly at them!

The distance was rapidly diminishing. News glass pictures of balls of fiery death caused by plane crashes exploded in her thoughts. If it struck the hall, everyone in the plane would die, as well as Gaius, Nastasia, and all the other students and staff on the upper school side of the building.

"Sigfried! It's going to hit the school. We have less than a minute until the collision!" Rachel shouted, turning the broom and flying at the plane.

"*Tur lu!*" She shouted the cantrip that Mark Williams had used to stop her broom.

The plane did not slow in the least. Behind her, Sigfried had pulled out his trumpet. A blast of silver sparkles swept from it at an unbelievable speed and danced around the plane's nose. Alas, the accelerating jumbo jet was significantly heavier than the muskrat.

It plowed forward, unaffected.

"Why don't they pull up?" Siggy shouted.

"I don't think they can see the school," Rachel called back, as she sped toward it. Her heart pounded rapidly. Her hair flew everywhere, threatening to blind her. She gritted her teeth and concentrated. "The obscurations protecting Roanoke from Unwary eyes are hiding it. They might not know they're about to crash!"

"There's a weird distortion around the nose of the plane, a silver shimmering," Siggy shouted rapidly. "I can also see it inside, on the engine. Lucky says it's a spell or something. Should I have Lucky breathe on it, killing everyone aboard the plane?"

Could he do that?

"Not sure if that will help," she called. "It would still crash."

No matter how quickly she flew at the plane, if she hit it straight on, it would not budge. It was too massive. But even a large object could be tipped, if enough pressure were applied at the right spot. The nose only needed to rise a tiny bit for the vehicle to zoom over the top of Roanoke Hall. If she dived at high speed and struck the edge of the tail, would it tip the plane upward? That was how a broom worked.

If she flew high enough and dived fast enough, the weight of the two of them together might be enough to tip the plane. However, there was a major downside to this plan.

Neither she nor Sigfried would live through it.

If it worked, however, everyone else would live.

Rachel searched relentlessly for another way, some less final option.

Nothing came.

Briefly, she considered dropping off Sigfried—so that he, too, could live. Without him, however, the maneuver would surely fail. She was not heavy enough.

She would kill herself while gaining nothing.

"Sigfried! We're going to have to ram it. Even though we are small, if we hit the very tip of a wing or the tail fin, at a fast enough speed, we might be able to alter its course." She paused and then added, "I can't put you down. Won't have enough weight. I'm going to have to kill us both. Sorry."

"Fly! Fly like the wind, Griffin!" Sigfried grinned maniacally, without any hesitation. "We'll die heroes! Hit the tail assembly."

"The what?"

"The big thing that sticks up like a fin in the back," Siggy directed. "But first...magic! Did I mention I'm a sorcerer?"

His bravery made her heart soar. Rachel angled her broom and flew upward.

"Siggy! Let's fire every cantrip we know!" she called. "If it swerves, fantastic! If not, we dive in fifteen seconds."

Letting go of the handlebar, she shouted every cantrip she knew, gesturing accordingly. Behind her, Sigfried shouted cantrips as well.

"Tiathelu."

"Argos."

"Obé."

"Bey-athe. Nothor. Libra. Legaré. Do."

They soared upward, so high that the oncoming jet was now beneath them. Was this high enough? If she calculated incorrectly, she would accomplish nothing. Or worse than nothing.

She would kill herself and Siggy for no reason.

"The shimmer! It's breaking up!" Sigfried shouted suddenly. "I think it was the third one you tried. Right after I tried the golden bands...that did nothing."

"That was the Word of Ending," she called back. "Let's try it again."

She dived. The wind blew their hair straight back. It ripped off Rachel's mortarboard cap, in spite of the bobby pins with which she had secured it. The cap sailed into the distance, tassel waving wildly.

"*Obé!*" They shouted together, gesturing.

"*Obé!*"

"*Obé!!*"

"The pilot sees the school!" Sigfried shouted excitedly. "He's terrified. He's pulling up!"

With a deafening roar, the enormous jet sailed up and over the top of Roanoke Hall. It passed so close to the roof that the wind from its passing rang the bells.

Chapter 32:
Hiding in the Couch

Below, students and staff cheered.

Rachel saw Zoë and Seth Peregrine, Eve March and her brother Joshua, the P.E. Tutor Mr. Chanson, and Mr. Badger, among others. Looking behind her, she noticed that Siggy's elixir was wearing off. He must have drunk his some time ago, which explained why she had not seen him when she had called his card.

She landed her broom a short distance from the gathering of students. That terrible shyness that overwhelmed her in front of crowds threatened her. The air itself seemed to close in around her. Her insides twisted uncomfortably.

"Quick, you take the credit," she whispered.

"Are you certain?" He stared as if she had lost her mind. His eyes tracked her face, even though she still could not see her own hand. "All that delicious, delicious credit, all for me?"

"Yes."

"Ace!"

Grinning like a hyena, Siggy climbed off the broom and bowed, accepting the praises of the growing crowd, as Lucky snaked around him. Above, windows opened, and students in upper classrooms along the east side of the building, who had seen the plane heading directly for them, shouted and cheered. Sigfried clasped his hands over his head in a gesture of victory. As the people below rushed toward him, Rachel slipped away.

Flying upward, she circled the pristine, happily un-smashed spires and towers of Roanoke Hall, waiting for the pounding of her heart to subside.

She had been cool as ice when called upon to sacrifice herself and her best friend. Now, her limbs shook. Her heartbeat thundered in her ears. Her stomach tied itself into a permanent knot. She felt strangely lightheaded.

Feeling her shaking hands and trembling legs, she wondered if it were safe for her to fly.

She peered into the windows of the myriad towers and belfries, searching for an unused attic. In the top of a six-sided turret to the northwest of the main belfry, she spotted a little hexagonal room that contained a couch, an end table, and a throw rug. She tried the Word of Opening on the window.

To her delight, it *finally* worked.

When the pane slid open, stale air assailed her nose. Ducking sideways, she flew into the room and collapsed onto the old springs of the cream and rose sofa. Dust puffed around her.

Rachel tried to cover her face but in their super-chameleoned state, her hands did little to prevent the glare of the afternoon from reaching her eyes. Turning over, she buried herself in the crevice where the cushions met the back and waited for her heartbeat to stop racing, for the tremors in her limbs to cease.

For the second time in less than a day, she had been called on to face death. It was hard to comprehend how little time had passed. If she had conjured something in Joy's room when the Raven appeared, it would not yet have vanished.

Yet those two experiences were nothing when compared to the terror of watching the plane head directly toward her boyfriend. This fear mingled within her with the horror of her grandfather's tragedy.

Her mother had warned her repeatedly that there was a price to pay for being able to suppress her emotions. When the emotions she had suppressed finally came back, they did so with a vengeance—as if they hit harder on the back swing than they would have had she not ducked the first time.

They were striking back now. As she tried to relax, she grew worse. Her body felt weaker, rather than stronger. Fear hammered her, doubt clawing from within. She felt overwhelmed, lost—a tiny piece of flotsam caught in a tsunami.

If only there were someone she could go to who could make her feel safe—with whom she would not have to keep up her false mask. She would never dare let her boyfriend see her like this. Dread's voice rang in her ears, denouncing weakness.

Rachel shivered.

Boys did not like girls who were not cheerful.

The roar of excitement outside waxed and waned. Rachel lay motionless, longing for the comfort of Mr. Muffin or Torture the Penguin. A terrible lethargy crept over her, a reluctance to move ever again. Her eyelids fluttered closed. She wondered if she could stay here forever, safe from interference. No one knew where she was.

This fantasy was dashed almost before it had begun. Lucky the Dragon darted in the window and sniffed her, reporting aloud to Sigfried that she had been found. Rachel felt keenly disappointed to lose the anonymity of having a place only she knew, but at least Sigfried would not be worried. After he had behaved so bravely when she informed him that she planned to kill them both, she owed him at least that much.

"Boss wants to know if you are okay," Lucky asked in his growly voice.

"Yes." Even saying a single word took a tremendous effort.

"She's okay," the dragon announced. "She's just moping."

Reducing the gravity of her state of mind to "moping" seemed exceedingly cruel.

Rachel could not find the wherewithal to object.

The dragon flew away, leaving her alone in the sunlit silence. She rested on the couch, face down, her mind drifting. She fell into a fitful dream, scattered with nightmares about demonic planes that blasted through Gryphon Park mansion, killing Rachel's entire family, while her grandfather looked on, shaking his head sadly.

The dream grew more turbulent. Darkness swirled around her. Rachel found herself unable to move. Beside her, Laurel, Peter, and Sandra struggled. A grinning man with a knife stalked toward them. Laurel screamed, but Rachel could not turn her head. Blood splattered, striking her cheek. She fought to turn, to go, to help, but it was like being stuck underwater and fighting seaweed. The grinning man raised his knife and moved toward Rachel's throat.

She screamed.

Moonlight shone everywhere. The nightmare vanished. Rachel stood on a meadow of purple and silver flowers. Above her, the source of the silvery light, stood the Elf.

"Fear not, little one," Illondria smiled down at her. "'Twas but a nightmare. It is gone."

Rachel ran to her. "I've found out such horrible things! My family! My poor grandfather! And there was a plane and the Raven—why do these things happen to me?"

The Elf knelt and smiled into her eyes. "Because you can bear them, dear one."

A hush came over Rachel, something kindred to happiness.

She whispered, awed, "Can I?"

"Can't you?" smiled the dream Elf.

Rachel stood blinking in the silvery elf-light. Was the Elf really here, in her dream? Or was this just another dream? The Elf claimed to be able to travel in dreams. Rachel decided to assume it was the real Elf, until she found out otherwise.

"B-but the world is going to end!" Rachel cried, her body trembling. "Mrs. Egg is dead. The demon will slip his binding and destroy the Wall. Everyone will be lost!"

The Elf looked at her with eyes as deep as the roots of the World Tree, bottomless pools of infinite wisdom and sorrow. "That may be, dear one. And yet I still see hope. I see a path by which we are all saved. I see you saving us."

"Me?" Rachel gaped.

"Is there something you have learned that could help?"

Rachel's eyes grew wide. "I found out my grandfather cast the binding on Azrael."

"Truly?" Illondria knelt on one knee, bringing her head closer to Rachel's. She gazed at Rachel raptly. "Did he leave any instructions? Any clues as to how to renew the binding?"

"No, I don't think..." Rachel paused and tipped her head back.

Or had he?

Rachel had found no reference to *Azrael* or *demon*, and none to Crowley that seemed apropos, in her grandfather's journal. Suddenly, she did recall a single reference to another word—a word she had not heard in reference to her grandfather until today.

The entry was written to Rupert Tennyson, a relative of the current Tennyson, the butler at Gryphon Park. This earlier Tennyson, whom her grandfather had always referred to as his squire, had died in April of 1942, during Operation Myrmidon. While aborted by the Unwary troops, Operation Myrmidon had been carried out by a cadre of the Wise, destroying the Adour River base of a cabal of French sorcerers who had been supporting the Nazis.

This earlier entry read:

8ᵗʰ September 1940

Squire:

The binding on E. A. grows weak. It must be refreshed. Should I not return, you must carry on for me. You must confront him, fix your gaze upon his eyes, and pronounce the masterword. This will rejuvenate the spell. The rest I have already done.

The masterword: Myrddin.

The sorrow of her grandfather's loss cut her anew, opening a gash in her heart. Grandfather had never mentioned Myrddin, told Rachel of his existence, or written the boy's name elsewhere in his journals.

Yet, he had cast a spell using as the masterword the name of his dead son.

Might that mean this spell was particularly associated with his son? This fact and the description in the journal made it sound as if it might be the clue Rachel had been seeking. But there was no mention of Azrael or Crowley.

Who was E. A.?

Searching her memory, Rachel found a reference, this one from an encyclopedia. The title of the article was: *Aleister Crowley, né Edward Alexander Crowley.*

Finally!

The masterword to renew the spell binding Azrael was *Myrddin*!

Perhaps the world could be saved, after all.

• • •

"Rejoice."

Rachel opened her eyes.

She lay on the couch in the hexagonal tower room. Something loomed above her, silhouetted in the setting sun. She could not see it directly. Rays of sunlight, too bright for her eyes, spilled around it.

Startled, Rachel twisted and shaded her eyes.

A tiny Lion stood on the arm of the couch, regarding her steadily.

"Leander!" Rachel brushed her hair from her face. "Why do such horrid things happen?"

"Fear not," the Lion regarded her with a gaze more steady than the sun, *"for they that be with us are more than they that be against us."*

"Really!" Rachel drew herself up into a sitting position, and stared at him curiously. "How so? Do you mean the Raven? The Elf?"

The Lion gazed at her unblinking. "Your friends need you."

"Wha-what?" Rachel fumbled for the green mirror in her pocket. "My friends? What…"

The little lion was nowhere to be seen.

• • •

Rachel sped on her steeplechaser toward the docks, her hair flying every which way. Joy, Valerie, and Zoë had all responded to her call. They were safe in class. Neither Sigfried nor Nastasia had answered; however, she had been able to catch a glimpse of the scenery visible to the calling card peeking from Sigfried's pocket.

She had seen trunks, branches, and sky.

Rapidly, she had checked that particular glimpse of branches against her memory of places on campus. After several seconds, she had found a match. Sigfried's mirror was showing her the trees lining the path that led to the docks. She and Sigfried had just been down there—right before the airplane came, spying on the Agents who took Juma.

Why had he gone again?

She dashed across the commons, over the lily pond, and along the path to the docks. As she flew, she heard music— hauntingly beautiful music. It called to her, promising the answer to all her questions.

Rachel slowed her broom.

Something was not right.

Ahead, between the two lines of stately trees, purple sparkles danced along the path. Purples sparkles, Gaius had said, were the color of *a geas*. The swell of the music called to her, urging her forward.

Rachel resisted.

Ahead, she could see Sigfried, Lucky, and Nastasia. They walked beside a woman dressed in a voluminous shadowcloak. Her hood was down, revealing hair the same pale red as Serena O'Malley's. She had her wand pointed at Rachel's friends.

Music and purple sparks flowed from the gem at its tip.

Serena O'Malley must have been the one controlling the jumbo jet. Rachel guessed that one of Egg's contacts inside the Wisecraft—either voluntary or geased—had alerted her when Agents came to question her son. A shiver ran down Rachel's spine: possibly the same contact whose indiscretion led Ms. O'Malley to murder Mrs. Egg?

Rachel looked over her shoulder. In the far distance, she could see two proctors standing near Roanoke Hall, the blond one and a tall one with curly black hair who wore a cowboy hat. Could she reach them and get back in time? Her geased friends were nearing the end of the tree-lined path. They needed only to walk through the archway in the ruined castle and down the stairs, and they would be at the docks—where jumping worked.

Once there, they could be kidnapped and taken anywhere.

Pulling out her calling card, Rachel leaned over it, whispering, "Joy! Zoë! Valerie! Someone's kidnapping Siggy and the princess. Get help!"

She landed and hid her broom behind a bench that stood beside the path. Creeping forward, her eyes locked on the sparks of purple light. Gaius had told her that geases worked by the same principles as the *Spell of True Recitation*. If so, the Elf's gift would protect her from the effects.

If she continued forward, and the Rune did not protect her, she would be entirely helpless. Yet, in her mind, she saw the golden eyes of the little Lion. He would not have sent her, if there was nothing she could do.

Taking a deep breath, she walked bravely into the music and the sparks.

Chapter 33:
Held by the Collar While Everyone Else Fights

"Rejoice!" Mortimer Egg declared, raising his arms. "The world ends today!"

Mr. Egg stood upon a stone dais, surrounded by a sea of hooded figures in long deep purple robes. He wore a gray suit, his dark hair pulled back into a ponytail. Two women in voluminous shadowcloaks, Serena O'Malley and another, flanked him. Behind them were Rachel and her friends. Nastasia, Sigfried, and Lucky stood in the places Serena had told them to take, after she had jumped them here. They waited motionless and glassy-eyed.

It was hard to imitate glassy-eyed.

Rachel's eyeballs felt dry.

Around them were the rock walls of a cavernous, vaulted chamber. Light streamed in through arched windows twenty-five feet above the floor. From the odor of wet earth and the moistness of the air, Rachel guessed that the majority of the chamber was below ground level.

From the center rose a forty-foot-tall crystal lighthouse bulb, much like the one in the belfry of the Watch Tower, only eight times larger. To the left of the bulb was an altar, the surface of which was stained dark from years of use.

"My followers, with your own eyes," Mortimer Egg's voice rang, "shall you see the Twilight of the World! To perform this final act, we have a special sacrifice. Two of the seven prophesied Keybearers! We shall strike a dire blow against Heaven. All Hell shall praise us!"

As Egg harangued his followers, Rachel considered how to carry out her purpose. His back was to her. To use the masterword, she had to catch his eye. To catch his eye, she needed to be in front of him.

She considered breaking her masquerade and running forward but decided against it. There was no guarantee that she would get in front of Egg before somebody stopped her. Even if she managed to paralyze one of the women flanking him, the other one would be free to capture her…or worse.

Better to bide her time, and hope for a more propitious moment.

"Who is to perform this great sacrifice, O Master?" called Serena O'Malley.

"That honor shall go to our newest initiate." Mortimer Egg's voice rose in anticipation. "It will make this act all that much more potent."

Why? Would this be the new initiate's first murder? Did the corruption of such innocence add spice in the eyes of the demons, the way cloves and cinnamon did for humans?

"The time has come!" Mortimer Egg gestured to the feminine figure on his right.

She nodded and turned. As she moved toward the three students and the dragon, Rachel saw five rings of mastery flash on the slender fingers protruding from the sleeves of the robe, familiar-looking slender fingers.

A tremor of terrifying uncertainty gripped Rachel.

The approaching figure drew back the hood of her shadowcloak. Underneath was a lovely young brunette. Her extremely dark eyes had a mere hint of a slant, giving them that exotic look that had catapulted several famous Hollywood actresses to stardom.

It took every ounce of Rachel's dissembling skill not to scream.

Sandra!

Rachel's oldest sister glided toward them with swan-like grace. Her lovely face was calm with the slightest curve of a smile. Rachel's mind reeled. Her heart stopped beating.

Surely, not…

Sandra's left pinky was rigid and vibrating slightly. Relief ran through Rachel's body. The Griffin Girls could hide their feelings from the world, but they could not fool each other. Her sister was not calm and serene. She was extraordinarily nervous.

Sandra was undercover.

Her sister was not an accountant. She was an Agent! And to think that Rachel had felt so sorry for her sister's *fake* boredom!

Sandra raised her hands and formed the same gesture Mr. Fuentes's had made, the time the geas had been forcing him to cast deadly black fire. Rachel's heartbeat echoed oddly.

Sandra would not kill her little sister to protect her cover.

Would she?

Sandra spoke in a clear voice, "*Pyr Tur*...Daddy come save us!"

Crash!

The window over Mortimer Egg's head shattered.

Through the shards of broken glass leapt Agent Ambrose Griffin. His Inverness cape billowed about him like the dark wings of an avenging falcon. His steady hazel eyes were fixed on Egg, his fulgurator's staff aimed at the dark sorcerer's heart. Crackling white-gold flame leapt from the fist-sized gem at the staff's tip, striking Egg in the chest.

Mortimer Egg bellowed in pain, screaming and writhing. He tried to draw his wand and fire back, but the agony was too great.

Crack. Crash. Crack.

More Agents came through other windows. Rachel recognized Darling, Standish, and the dark-skinned Templeton Bridges, her father's closest associate. They, too, pointed their staffs. Glepnir bonds encircled many of Egg's hooded followers. Agent Standish's cheetah leapt through a window, landing on the back of a man who cried out and crumpled.

Ambrose Griffin hung in mid-air. Then he landed lightly on his feet, firing continuously. Blue sparks danced across Mortimer Egg, who froze, mouth wide from screaming. Agent Griffin turned to Egg's followers. Blue sparks played across the robed crowd. The first dozen froze.

Pillars of light flashed. More Agents arrived, fulgurator staffs firing. They all wore Inverness capes and tricorne hats, with medallions bearing a lantern surrounded by stars around their necks. These medallions immediately surrounded their wearers

L. Jagi Lamplighter

with glittering shields. Spells fired by the robed sorcerers harmlessly bounced off them.

Tall white flashes ignited as some of the hooded followers fled.

Agent Briars, the Asian woman who had escorted Juma to New York, landed as lightly as a cat. Placing a coin on her hand, she shook her charm bracelet. The coin shot from her palm faster than Rachel could see and smashed into the giant lantern. It shattered with a resounding *crack*. Large sheets of glass crashed down on top of robed followers. The scent of lamp oil filled the chamber. The noise was deafening, drowning out Serena's screams of outrage.

Six Agents jumped in at strategic points, holding tall cast-iron candelabras, which they placed on the floor. A spirited young woman and a dapper gentleman, Agent Vicky Armel, her father's prime warder, and Agent Miles Caldor, the warder for the New York office, placed their hands on the cast-iron and spoke aloud. Golden sparks formed a hexagon between the six candelabras.

Fleeing pillars of light coalesced back into people.

No new pillars formed.

Unable to jump away, most of the followers raised their hands, surrendering. A few shot spells out of wands or dueling rings. Sparks and cantrips splashed harmlessly against Agents' glittering shields.

It was over as quickly as it began.

The Veltdammerung followers dropped their weapons. Mortimer Egg and Serena O'Malley were paralyzed. Agent Miles Caldor bowed elegantly to Rachel and her friends. Then, he performed the Word of Ending. This freed them from the compulsion of the geas, though to Rachel, it had been more of a suggestion.

His big, shaggy sheepdog trotted forward and licked her face.

Smiling, Rachel wiped her cheek.

Nastasia, Sigfried, and Lucky blinked and moved. Rachel, meanwhile, eyed the frozen Egg. Would the masterword work while he was paralyzed? Or did he have to actively look her in the eyes? She ran forward and stood before him, but his eyes were frozen gazing upward.

"What is occurring?" Nastasia was asking, confused, when Rachel returned to her side. "Why are we not in class?"

"I've released you from a geas." Agent Caldor was a thoughtful man with a close-cropped beard. "You'll need to be disenchanted to be free of its long-term effects."

The princess curtsied, thanking him. Rachel would have curtsied, too, but, with a cry of joy, Sandra grabbed her and hugged her tightly, engulfing her in warmth and honeysuckle.

Rachel hugged her sister back briefly and then pulled away. "Egg! I've got to stop him! The demon. I've got to look him in..."

"It's all right," Sandra laughed, hugging her again. "It's over now. We've got..."

"Fools!" Egg shouted, shaking himself free.

Wings of black smoke opened behind his back. He gestured. An unseen force yanked a surprised-looking Agent Caldor into the air. With a second gesture, the Agent sailed across the room, falling directly atop one of the tall candelabra. His body sank. The cast-iron tip emerged from his ribcage.

Caldor made a gargling noise.

The sheep dog let out a sound Rachel hoped she would never hear again. Yowling, the Agent's familiar raced across the room to his fallen master. Blood was everywhere. Rachel's heart leapt up into her throat and stayed there. She turned away. Her legs felt weak.

Even in the battle against Mordeau, she had never seen anything so terrible.

Three other Agents converged on the spot, music and green healing sparkles issuing from their wands. Before they could reach Agent Caldor, however, the weight of his body brought the candelabra crashing to the floor.

The hexagon of golden warding sparkles winked out.

Immediately, hooded Veltdammerung turned into columns of light and disappeared. Others crouched. Grabbing their dropped wands and rings, they fired at the Agents.

Egg raised his index finger and moved it horizontally. "*Obé.*"

Those among his followers who had been dazed, paralyzed, or otherwise enchanted moved again. Those caught with Glepnir bonds remained bound in glowing golden bands.

Of those set free, some fled, some reentered the fight.

"Wicked! A battle!" Sigfried cried. Immune to the recent tragedy, he grinned and pulled out his knife. "Who's on our side? Robes or cloaks?"

"The Agents are in Inverness capes," replied Rachel. "The Veltdammerung are in robes."

"Cloaks good, robes bad. Got it." Sigfried nodded.

He raised his knife and ran forward, shouting like a Zulu.

"Robes, bad. Right." Lucky zipped after him and began spewing out flames onto the nearest Veltdammerung followers, who screamed horribly.

Sigfried paused, mid-yell, and looked up at his knife. "Hey! I'm a sorcerer!"

Sheathing the blade, he pulled out his trumpet and blew. Concentric rings of silver sparks flowed from it. Four robed figures, who were rushing the dais, were lifted into the air and thrown backwards, knocking their fellows down like living nine pins.

Nastasia was slower to act.

She blinked uncertainly, her face unnaturally pale. She kept glancing back toward where the healing squad worked tirelessly to save Agent Caldor. Rachel dismissed her for the moment and looked to Sandra, who was firing spells from her five rings at Egg and the O'Malley woman. These two were also fighting her father and Agent Standish. Serena O'Malley was screaming in fury as she fought, but Mortimer Egg casually parried the incoming spells, as if he had nothing better to do.

Rachel considered charging into the battle with Siggy. She was so short, she probably could slip among the enemy and whistle, without anyone noticing. However, that would mean leaving the dais. Rachel had no intention of leaving until after she tried the masterword on Egg.

Maybe, this was a good opportunity to get his attention.

Rachel darted forward.

"Oh no, you don't!" Sandra caught her by her collar.

Rachel's forward motion brought her throat up sharp against the collar of her own robe. Gasping and gagging, she tried to explain to Sandra what needed to be done, but she could not get enough air to speak.

Still holding her collar, Sandra hauled Rachel back to where Nastasia stood. Forcing her robes away from her throat with her thumbs, Rachel struggled to regain her breath. She shouted to Sandra, but her sister was intent on conjuring balls with dream mist inside them and tossing them at the enemy. With all the shouting of cantrips and blares of enchantment music, her sister could not hear her.

Rachel tugged at her robes, trying to break free of Sandra's vise-like grip.

"Rachel, keep still!" Sandra shouted. "I can't cast if you are yanking on me!"

Overjoyed to finally have Sandra's attention, Rachel cried, "I have to get to Mr. Egg! I know how to stop him!"

"Your friend should not have run off," Sandra shouted back, apparently unable to hear over the din of the battle. "That's no reason for you to run after him!"

"Not Sigfried! Egg! Sandra! The whole world is in danger! I know the…"

"*Tur magos,*" Sandra cast the cantrip for silence at Rachel's mouth. Rachel kept talking, but no noise came out. "Sorry, little sis, but this is very serious. Very dangerous. Now you can't cast, so you won't think that you, who has been at school only one month, are the equal of professional sorcerers! Wait here with your girlfriend. If you try to run off again, I'll have to paralyze you. Mother and Father would never forgive me if I let something happen to you!"

Sandra released her and ran back to cast more mist grenades at Egg and O'Malley, pulling them down with the *muria* cantrip and throwing them at astonishing speed. Rachel tried to whistle, but that also made no sound. Terror grew in her chest like a blossom of fire.

If she could not talk, how could she say the masterword to bind Azrael?

How ironic if the earth were to be destroyed because of a well-meaning attempt by Sandra to protect her little sister?

Rachel searched frantically through her pockets for paper and pen. Finding them, she wrote. *Masterword to bind demon into Egg: Myrddin. Look in his eyes and say it.* She held the note toward the princess, who was drawing her violin from her bag.

Looking curious, Nastasia reached for it.

A blast of silver sparkles struck both girls, sending them flying. The notepad with her message flew from Rachel's hand and floated upward, vanishing amidst the swirling, multi-colored sparks overhead.

Lying flat on her back, gasping for breath, Rachel fought back against despair. If only she had shared the masterword with someone! She could have told Joy and Valerie over the card.

If she did not survive this battle, there would be no one who knew the word.

Dragging herself back to her feet, Rachel could find no sign of her paper. She thought of running to look for it, but the moment she moved, Sandra glanced in her direction.

Being paralyzed would be even worse than being mute.

She stayed where she was.

Rachel glanced over at the battle. Everything was happening at once, but she could slow down the scene in her memory, recalling one skirmish and then another. The fight had become a raucous conglomeration of music, multi-colored sparkles, and magical scents. The smell of Fresh-baked bread mingled with brimstone, evergreens, and coconut. The Agents were defeating Egg's followers handily. Many of the Veltdammerung were young, barely out of college.

Siggy and Lucky blasted and burned everything that came near them. Fortunately, the chamber was made of stone and not flammable. However, the fuel from the broken lantern had seeped across the floor. Lucky's breath ignited it, producing a swath of multi-colored flames. Rachel's old friend, Agent Dorian Standish, pointed all the fingers of his right hand at the fire.

"*Tur pyr.*"

The flames sputtered and died.

Near him, the lithe Agent Armel blew black dust into the face of the enemies. Those she struck continued to cast, but their spells had no effect. She tried this on a tall woman who pointed a purple ring in her direction. A blast of silvery sparks from the ring blew the dust back at the Agent, causing her to cough and sputter.

Agent Armel backed up until she was behind her partner, Agent Garbarino—an Italian selkie who worked for Rachel's father in what she now knew was the Shadow Agency. The young man with penetrating eyes pointed his staff at Armel's assailant, causing blue sparks to swirl around the tall, robed woman. She began to move slowly. Garbarino stepped forward and relieved her of her wand, which he added to a growing collection in his pocket.

Across the wide chamber, Rachel's father's friend, Agent Bridges, parried incoming spells with a *taflu* cantrip while casting with his staff. He turned a man into a toad, a woman into rabbit, and a third figure into a wombat. He did this all with a cool, impassive demeanor. He kept his deep brown, oval head close-shaved. So intense was his gaze that one smaller robed figure ran screaming, merely from the force of his glare.

Behind him, Agent Briars shook her charm bracelet. She began to move twice as fast as those around her. She twisted a second charm, and a blue glow enveloped her hand. Everyone she touched clutched his head and screamed.

At the far corner, Agent Darling's staff hovered beside him, firing on its own while he himself cast cantrips. Rachel recalled that he had been the Canticler of the Six Musketeers. Watching him was awe-inspiring. He commanded a much larger effect from his cantrips than Rachel had previously seen. His Glepnir bonds encircled a dozen people at a time.

"*Tur magos!*" he shouted, moving his hand across his mouth and gesturing outwards. A fifth of the robed followers lost their ability to speak. He cast this cantrip again. This time, however, a hooded figure caught the spell and slung it back at him so quickly that Agent Darling was nearly muted by his own cantrip. At the last minute, he managed to parry.

The hooded figure stepped back into the pack. At that moment, however, Sigfried blew his horn in his direction. Silver sparkles knocked over three of the enemy and swept Darling's opponent's hood from his face. Underneath was an older man with salt and pepper hair and angular Eastern European features that, oddly, reminded Rachel of the princess and her brother Ivan.

"Dietrich Faust!" shouted Darling.

Rachel's eyes went wide. Dietrich Faust was one of the last remaining leaders of the Morthbrood known to be at-large. He was also the younger son of Johann Faust the Fifth, the man who had sent Azrael against Blaise Griffin.

All the Agents turned and fired at the man. He deflected the first seven attacks. Then Rachel's father caught him from behind with a spray of blue sparks. Faust froze, arms raised in a deadly attack.

A moment later, Faust was held fast by six Glepnir bonds.

Rachel opened her mouth to cheer their success, but no noise came out. Her enthusiasm was cut short by the cold shiver that ran down her spine. Rumor had it Dietrich Faust had been hiding in Bavaria. Could he have learned about Egg's weakness from Vladimir Von Dread's father and passed the information to Serena O'Malley, leading to Mrs. Egg's death?

Was all this havoc her fault?

The thought was daunting.

It frustrated her not to be able to help in the battle. The wheels of her mind turned rapidly, seeking some action she could perform, some way she could aid the Agents. But she came away with nothing. Turning to Nastasia, she gestured wildly, repeating the hand motion for the Word of Ending over and over, in her effort to communicate her desire for the princess to free her from the cantrip.

The princess, who was busy playing her violin, merely frowned at Rachel's antics.

It was worse than all those times, as a child, when she had been stuck waiting for someone to say her name, after having been jinxed for accidentally pronouncing the same word as Laurel. That had been frustrating, but the fate of the world had not been at stake. Unlike the mundane version, when Children of the Wise played such games, people were actually jinxed.

Mortimer Egg had been standing with his arms crossed, watching the mayhem. Gazing down at the immobilized Faust, he scowled and gestured. Around the chamber, the medallions around the necks of the Agents started to emit blue-white sparks. They glowed, growing red-hot. Rachel watched as her father and his companions were forced to tear the protective talismans from their necks and toss them aside. Agent Briars screamed in pain as she fought to yank off her charm bracelet and other alchemical talismans she wore.

They all glowed red-hot.

Rachel had never heard of a spell that could do such a thing. She wondered if this were demon magic. As she watched the man with reddish eyes and smoky wings, a shiver ran up her spine. The human man Mortimer Egg was no longer in charge of the body.

This was Azrael.

The battle turned against the Agents.

Without their defensive talismans, they had to pause in their spell casting to parry incoming attacks. They moved closer together, fighting back to back. But there was little they could do against Egg's overwhelming, superhuman power. His eyes were tinted reddish now. He laughed as he fought Agent Standish and Agent Griffin, repelling their attacks with contempt.

Just in front of Rachel, Sandra stopped moving, paralyzed. Rachel struggled to speak, hoping to put up a *bey-athe* shield to protect her sister, but no words came. She wished fervently yet again that she had a wand. She started to make plans as to how to get one; however, the realization that there might not be a

tomorrow in which to carry out such plans sapped her enthusiasm.

Darling's voice cut across the general noise, shouting
something about calling for backup. Standish shouted back,
asking who was left at the office.

To which Darling's reply came, "No, I mean *real* backup!"

Moments later, a flash at a broken window illuminated the
chamber. Music and crimson sparks swept through the opening.
Outside, a tall man dressed in a blue and red silk jumpsuit played
the violin. He had spiky red hair and gold safety pins for
earrings.

Below, everyone began to dance, even Azrael.

The music was spectacular, with a driving, rowdy Irish beat.
Ruby sparks swirled about Rachel, tickling her and making her
laugh—though her laughter made no sound. She swayed in time
to the music. It did not seem to her as if she were compelled to
dance, but rather, as if she could not bear not to join in while
listening to such an exuberant reel.

"Hey...that guy looks like Red Ryder, the lead singer from
the band *Bogus*!" cried Sigfried, from where he danced not far
from the dais, his foot stomping rhythmically on the face of one
of the robed followers.

"That *is* him," Agent Armel called as she danced beside him.
"That's Finn MacDannan."

"My roommate Ian's father is a rock star?" Siggy gaped.

Agent Armel grinned, her feet dancing a complicated jig.
"He's said to be the best Enchanter alive today."

Beside him, a short figure with bushy red hair played a bagpipe. Former Agent Scarlett MacDannan—Finn's wife and now
their math tutor—joined in the fray.

Sigfried cheered.

"I think we've won," laughed Agent Armel.

A bellow of anger drowned the music. With a wave, Azrael
lifted Rachel's father and smashed him against a wall. Agent
Griffin's eyes rolled back.

Blood ran down the wall.

Rachel's scream made no sound.

Chapter 34:
Tearing Down the Walls of the World

"There is still time to perform the sacrifice, Serena," Azrael called as he danced, surrounded by red sparks. "Kill the children."

Oblivious of all else, Rachel ran toward her father, pelting across the stone of the dais. Fear clawed at her ribs. Was he going to be okay? Was he breathing? Was he…

Before she could reach him, something grabbed her upper arm. Serena O'Malley lifted Rachel from her feet, even though the red-haired woman was waltzing. Rachel writhed and screamed in silent frustration, but she could not escape the vise-like grip.

Serena displayed Rachel to Azrael. "Will this one do, Master?"

Azrael glanced directly at Rachel. The dead look in his reddish eyes made her skin crawl. She shouted but made no sound. Tears of fury stung her eyes.

He was right here!

"That one will do nicely." His smile was like a snake's. Putting his hand around her throat, he began to squeeze.

"Unhand my companion, fiend!" cried the princess.

Despite her fancily-dancing feet, Nastasia drew her bow along her violin.

A swath of silver sparkles lifted Azrael and carried him twenty feet.

Freed from the demon's choking hold, Rachel gasped gratefully for breath. She rubbed her neck. Across the room, where he rose from the floor, Azrael looked shocked.

"She must be the one of the two from that prophecy!" Serena shrieked, still gripping Rachel's arm painfully. "The one who can hurt you!"

Rachel recalled the prophecy about Joy and the princess. She started to cheer, but again, no noise came. Terror gripped her, clenching her chest like a constricting Glepnir bond. Her father was hurt—possibly worse, and her sister was paralyzed.

How was she going to get free of Sandra's cantrip in order to stop Azrael?

Finn's music changed from a jig to a lullaby. Blue sparkles danced from his bow. Two-thirds of the Veltdammerung followers fell asleep. Finn MacDannan was so skilled and precise an enchanter that only the enemy was affected. Rachel suspected that he had spent the time while they all were dancing studying the battlefield and preparing for this enchantment.

Freed from dancing, Siggy ran at Azrael, shouting, "Lucky, get him! Save Rachel!"

Siggy blew his trumpet. A strong wind whirled from his instrument in a swirl of silver sparkles.

His attack did nothing. Azrael brushed it aside.

Lucky the Dragon swooped forward and breathed his brilliant red-orange fire on Azrael's face. Azrael's flesh melted and burned. He issued a high-pitched scream.

Nastasia cheered and played her violin again. Again, Azrael was thrown backwards. The silvery sparkles of her wind blast picked him up and slammed him into the stone wall. He slumped to the floor, his arm sticking out at a strange angle.

"Fry that Egg!" shouted Sigfried, jumping up and down.

Azrael jerked suddenly and rose to his feet. His arm straightened with a loud *pop*. His melted flesh flowed back into his proper face. His eyes were now blood red.

"Pathetic little fools," he laughed. "All you have done is to burn away the last remnants of the weakling Mortimer Egg. At last, I am free!"

Rachel's heart lurched.

Was she too late?

"Serena, we must complete our ritual," he continued. "Let us take the children somewhere we will not be disturbed. They are friends, are they not? We shall have one kill the other two."

"You do not wish your enemies to witness our victory?" asked Serena.

Azrael snarled. "Darling and his friends have caused trouble for me too many times. Let us bring down the Wall first. Then we can wipe out Darling and his Mouseketeers."

"Very well, Master."

"Besides, the lantern has been shattered," Azrael added. "We must repair to the backup location."

"I will gather the children," Serena promised.

"Let us bring Devon's progeny, too. I will enjoy sacrificing them." Azrael extended his hand, and Rachel's father's body flew through the air to hover beside him. Ambrose Griffin's chest rose and fell in ragged gasps.

Rachel's shoulders sagged, her knees buckling, as relief coursed through her body. Her father was alive! She did not fall, however, because Serena held her. With a wave of Azrael's other hand, the paralyzed Sandra rose and floated toward him.

By Devon, Azrael meant Rachel's grandfather, The Late Duke of Devon.

He wanted to kill Father and Sandra!

"Get him!" Siggy cried in alarm. "Stop him!"

Nastasia, Sigfried, Lucky, and Rachel converged upon Azrael. Rachel was not sure what she would do when she got there, maybe kick him in the shin long enough to distract him.

"*Ve Vargo Derenti*," Serena announced triumphantly.

Sigfried, Nastasia, and Lucky's eyes all went blank. Rachel felt the geas inside her head gently suggesting that she await orders. She also remembered that phrase.

Those were the words Dr. Mordeau had said to her geased students in Nastasia's vision.

Serena called to the geased students. The others walked obediently to her side. Rachel let her face go blank and joined them. Serena O'Malley reached out and touched them.

The world went white and sped away from her in all directions.

• • •

Moonlight flooded formal gardens, creating stark shadows. The gurgle of a fountain broke the stillness of midnight. The night air smelled of late-blooming roses. Above, a full moon hung in a black sky dappled with silver clouds. As the clouds parted, silvery light illuminated the vast edifice rising at the edge of the gardens.

The castle keep was draped in shadows, its blind windows obscured by crooked ivy. Moonlight revealed that carvings had been gouged into the wall over the top of older, more innocuous bas-reliefs; carvings of vultures defiling corpses and serpents swallowing children.

Around the formal garden and the ominous keep loomed an encircling outer curtain wall with tall round towers. A gatehouse built around a large arched doorway stood in the distance, guarding the way against whatever lay beyond.

Rachel and the others stood in front of a stone altar that rose from the middle of a circle of rose bushes, where other gardens might have had sundials. Azrael laid Rachel's father and sister across the altar, sideways, so that their heads and feet stretched beyond the stone surface. Her father's head lolled against the stone, but Sandra's paralyzed body remained rigid.

Beside the altar stood a bonfire piled as high as a second-story window. Azrael pointed his wand at the gathered wood, and it burst into flames. He pointed again. The flames changed, becoming the red, blue, green, and purples of an obscuration lantern.

A shiver ran down Rachel's spine.

Something very bad was about to happen.

Serena pulled back her voluminous hood. She resembled her son Juma, except that her skin was pale rather than the color of caramel, and her shoulder-length hair was red-gold. She had dark brooding eyes and very red lips.

"I should have known she was a spy!" Serena spit on Sandra's face.

"No time for that." Azrael gestured at the two Griffins on the altar. "Quickly. Before we are interrupted. The *tenebrous mundi* require payment. Put two of the children on the altar. Have the third commit all four murders."

"I have Griffin's littlest daughter here," purred Serena, pushing Rachel forward.

Azrael smiled down at her, his face bathed in purples, greens, and blues from the bonfire. His eyes were entirely scarlet, no white or pupil remained. Rachel gazed back at him blankly.

It took all her training to not betray her fear.

Or her frustration.

He was right there, looking into her eyes, and she could not speak the word.

"Good girl!" Azrael patted her on the head. Rachel's skin threatened to crawl off her body. "This is a find."

Serena instructed Sigfried and Nastasia to climb onto the stone altar and lie down, which they did. Rachel realized Lucky had been left behind at the first location.

"Shall we wake her father and sister?" Serena asked eagerly. "So their pain and horror add fuel to the spell?"

"No. They are Devon's kin," Azrael scowled. "They might know his secrets."

Azrael knew.

That made her task harder.

If she did anything unexpected, he might guess she knew the secret, too.

Of course, if she could not speak, it hardly mattered.

"Very well. Griffin child...oh, what is her first name? You... there," Serena commanded, "Walk forward."

"Ruby, I think," Azrael clasped his hands behind his back and stared down at her father. "No, Rachel. That is Rachel Griffin."

Cold fingers walked down her spine.

The demon knew her name.

"Well, Rachel Griffin," purred Serena, tweaking her cheek. Azrael handed her his wand. "Take this wand. Now, go forward and stand where you can point it at your father. Good girl."

A wand!

Relief washed over her. If they wanted her to use a stranger's wand, they would have to restore her voice.

The geas urged her body forward. Rachel did not resist. Like someone in a dream, she took the wand and walked to the altar. Her face was placid. Underneath, all her nerves blared. She waited, hoping the thunderous hoof beats of her heart would not give her away.

What if it was too late?

What if Azrael had burned away Egg's humanity? What would happen if she said the masterword, and it did not work?

He would probably kill her.

Or worse.

"You know what is happening, don't you, little geased girl?" Serena continued. She sounded so pleased, as if the greatest pleasure came from destruction and moral degradation. "You're going to kill your father! Then you are going to kill your sister. And then, your two little friends. Isn't that fun? After that, maybe I'll snap your neck."

"Oh, we need to let her live, Serena." Azrael's gaze was fixed on her the way another man might eye a tasty hors d'oeuvre. "Otherwise, she would be denied the torment her guilt over today's actions will stir in her tender soul. Think of the rest of her life. How she will suffer."

Azrael raised his arms. "*Come forth, O Vigilant Ones, Keepers of the Wall. Tenebrous mundi, I summon thee! I summon thee! I summon thee! It is my will you desert your post and tear down the Barrier that guards this world. Come accept your sacrifice and perform my bidding!*"

Dark shapes rose slowly from the garden bed, living shadows of solidified darkness. Up they rose, higher and higher, until they towered over Azrael, over the bonfire, over the turrets atop the castle. Nor were they human in their shape, such as the *tenebrous obscurii* Sigfried had accidentally summoned in the belfry.

These were the shadows of dragons.

Serena watched them apprehensively. Red, blue, and purple light danced over her face. The redheaded woman leaned over until Rachel could smell her overly-sweet perfume. "Now, point the wand at your father and say the words: '*Pyr Turia*.'"

Rachel took the wand.

It was a length of oak and steel. The ruby at the tip glinted dark as old blood in the moonlight. She pointed it at the altar, where her family and friends lay, their prone forms almost festive in the dancing colored flames. It took great concentration to keep her arm from shaking. A sudden fear seized her that, even spoken silently, these words might set off the cantrip. She extended the wand and mouthed two random words.

"What?" Azrael bent over. "What's wrong with her?"

Serena glanced nervously at the brooding presence of the *tenebrous mundi* and gave the instructions again. Rachel made the same response.

Serena frowned. "Child, tell me what is wrong with your voice?"

Rachel made the gesture for the *Tur magos* cantrip.

"Oh. Is that all?" Serena gestured, relieved. "*Obé tur magos.* Can you speak now?"

"Yes." Rachel let the geas speak for her. Her voice sounded flat in her ear.

"Good girl," Serena purred. "Point the wand. Say the words: '*Pyr Turia!*'"

Azrael watched in fascination as she prepared to kill her father. Rachel held her arm steady and took her cue from Sandra.

"*Pyr Tur...*" she looked up, gazing directly into his eager eyes. "*Myrddin.*"

"What did she say?" Serena leaned over, puzzled.

Slowly, Azrael's expression transformed from smug fascination to horror. "No! It cannot be. I am free of that now. No..."

Black sparkles, barely visible in the moonlight, spun around his body, lifting him into the air. They formed bands that moved around his limbs, rushing like the pictures scientists drew of the orbits around an atom. Serena scowled and took a step back, clearly confused.

Rachel stared, her jaw open. She had no idea what kind of magic produced black sparks.

In a burst of fireworks, red, gold, and purple sparkles joined the black. The purple twinkles rushed into his eyes, ears, and mouth. The red and gold ones swirled together, like a will-o-the-wisp sculpture, forming an image. A huge gryphon of tiny glowing stars hovered in the darkness above Azrael's head, its eagle wings arched, its claws extended.

The gryphon of red and gold dived, attacking Azrael, who screamed.

Rachel laughed and clapped. Her grandfather never failed to put his own stamp on things. She applauded his style. Between the gleaming sparks and the light of the multi-colored flames, it was as if the garden rejoiced, celebrating the demon's defeat.

Farther away in the darkness, between the dark dragon-shapes of the Keepers of the Wall, Rachel spotted a motion inside the arched doorway of the towering gatehouse that led from the castle grounds to the countryside beyond. A young man stood among the fig trees, dressed in dark, old-fashioned clothing.

She recognized him immediately.

Thunderfrost's boy. Her uncle Myrddin.

The ghost boy watched as the gryphon made of red and gold sparkles mauled the demon who had been responsible for his death, so many years ago. Through his body, she could see the moonlight shining on the outer curtain wall. The sparkling gryphon ripped away the demon's smoky wings. It raked his face. The red ran from his eyes. Then the sparkling gryphon embraced Azrael in a bear-hug and sank into his body.

Azrael screamed a horrible, bone-piercing scream.

"What have you done?" Serena O'Malley cried. "I will kill you for this, you little..."

The earth shook. Hoof beats rumbled. Serena shrieked. Something massive galloped across the gardens, as if moonlight and shadows had coalesced into the form of a great stallion. It had a shaggy mane of mingled snow and black hoarfrost and silky white feathering hiding its hooves. Like a divine wind, the enormous steed bore down on the red-haired woman.

Serena O'Malley screamed and fled, vanishing in a blinding flash.

Thunderfrost!

Rachel had the briefest glimpse of the horse rearing, and the ghost boy tipping his hat from where he rode upon its back.

Then the ghostly duo was gone.

Rachel turned back to where Azrael writhed and yowled. He looked in fear at the towering solid-shadows of the *tenebrous mundi.*

"Child!" He clawed frantically at the last of the sparkles encircling him. "Give me the wand!"

Rachel looked down at the slender length of oak and steel tipped with a hundred-and-thirty carat ruby. She thought of the hours and hours of time she had lost with Gaius, due to his efforts to refill his tiny sapphire. Imitating Vladimir Von Dread, she dropped the wand and stomped on the gem, grinding it with the heel of the boots that had been a gift from Sandra.

It shattered.

"No! My spells! My life's work! Noooooo!"

With one last burst of demonic power, he gestured from the stone altar toward the castle. Then he fell to his knees, wailing. With the slightest of smiles, Rachel whistled. Blues sparks danced around his body, paralyzing him.

Rachel's joy was short-lived.

Azrael's last gesture had lifted her father and thrown him violently through the air again. Ambrose Griffin flew toward the stone wall of the castle, hurtling at tremendous speed. Rachel's mind threatened to replay the death of Agent Caldor, and the horrible keening of his sheepdog. Cutting this off, she made her mind become as clear as a mountain lake.

"*Tur lu!*"

She performed the cantrip that Mark Williams had used to stall her broom. It had not slowed the jumbo jet at all, but her father's body froze in mid-air. He hung motionless for a moment and then began to plummet downward.

"*Tiathelu!*" cried Rachel.

Ambrose Griffin was too heavy for her to float, but she was able to slow his fall. He struck the ground head first, but he did so gently.

The *tenebrous mundi* shifted ominously. Joyfully, Rachel spun around and faced the bonfire, imitating the gestures Agent Standish had used to put out the burning lantern oil.

"*Tur pyr!*" she cried.

The bonfire of crimson, emerald, violet, and sapphire flames sputtered and flared again.

"*Tur pyr! Tur pyr! Tur pyr!*" She shouted over and over again, until she was lightheaded from the rush of magic that passed through her.

Finally, the bonfire sputtered and went dark.

Without pausing, Rachel turned to the gigantic *tenebrous mundi* and repeated the words she had spoken in the belfry.

"*Oyarsa! Taflu! Obé! Obé! Obé!*"

Slowly and ponderously, the great dragon-shades sank back into the earth. Dizzy with relief, Rachel dropped to her knees and cradled her head in her arms. The soft grass was cold beneath her legs. She forced herself to breathe evenly.

A flash of white illuminated the gardens.

Finn MacDannan appeared, holding onto his wife and Agent Darling. Immediately, the three of them started casting spells at Azrael, who became the center of a whirlwind of sparkles, scents, and sounds. Rachel wondered briefly why it had taken the Agents so long to arrive. Then she realized that if Azrael had brought them from New York to a place with a castle, and it was night here, it must have been a great jump indeed. Few people could jump such a distance.

Finn MacDannan was one of the few.

Rachel looked up at the castle, just as the moon came out from behind a translucent cloud. In the silvery brightness, she recognized the stark towers rising above them—Beaumont. Her hero Daring Northwest had died here. This was the hideout Remus Starkadder had traded to Azrael and his cronies, in return for the promised death of his older brother Romulus.

She was in Transylvania.

• • •

It was over soon after that. Mortimer Egg was apprehended. Darling freed her two friends and Sandra. Scarlett MacDannan played a lilting bagpipe piece that sent a flurry of green healing sparks swirling around Rachel's father. Then, Finn took the group of them back to the cavernous chamber where a crazed Lucky awaited.

With a shriek, the dragon wrapped around Sigfried and would not let go. The two of them put their heads together. It was inexpressibly adorable, though Rachel would never have repeated that to Sigfried.

Everywhere Rachel looked, she saw Veltdammerung followers encircled in glowing Glepnir bonds. The place was full of Wisecraft, both Agents and support personnel, taking these folks into custody, as well as white-clad Nuns of the Order of Asclepius, busily at work helping the wounded. Some knelt, performing first aid or administering elixirs. Others played healthful enchantments on flutes, clarinets, and violins.

Everything sparkled with green healing sparks.

The place smelled like a bakery.

"Rachel!" Sandra rushed to her, dropped to her knees.

She pulled Rachel close, hugging her ridiculously tightly. Rachel cried out with delight and hugged her back. To her shock, her big sister started to cry. Rachel gawked. She could not recall the last time Sandra had cried.

Choking through her tears, Sandra said, "Oh, Rachel, I was so worried."

"I'm fine," Rachel murmured into her sister's shoulder, relaxing. Sandra's shoulder felt warm and safe. The fear and terror Rachel had ducked in Transylvania swung back and hit her now. Her body trembled, and she fought against tears of her own, sniffling. Sandra swayed her back and forth and rubbed her little sister's back, cooing gentle, though hiccuppy, words of comfort. Rachel stayed there for a long time, swaying in her sister's arms, breathing sweet honeysuckle perfume in perfect contentment.

She had done it.

The Wall was not going to come down. The world was not about to fall apart. Her father and sister were not going to die. Lily-of-the-valleys, and the smell of autumn, and little children laughing—and all the good things of the Earth—were not going to pass away, reduced to but memory of a lost dream.

All was well.

They had won!

Somehow, winning was doubly wonderful, when it involved Sandra. Sandra continued to hug her tightly. Rachel's ribs began to feel a bit tender.

"Sorry, I don't mean to be so dramatic," her sister smiled at her finally, wiping away tears. "It's just, well, our time trapped in the Wisecraft offices in New York was blastedly hard. Father and I went to New York for a routine meeting, and suddenly everything went pear-shaped. We were stuck there for days. And that woman...Mordeau. She is an evil thing! She said things to Father. Things to upset him. And it worked."

"I...had no idea," Rachel whispered faintly.

Sandra nodded. "Even with James, Scarlett, and Dorian assuring us that you were okay—that Veltdammerung had not taken control of Roanoke again, we were both still afraid. Father visited your school, after we were finally released, and spoke to the dean. He even had someone check on you while you were sleeping. He was so worried about you."

Rachel blinked in astonishment. Dr. Mordeau had threatened her? Father had come by?

Rachel considered all this. She remembered how relieved she had been when she thought her family was in London, and how apprehensive and confused she had been to hear they were in New York during the lock down.

Suddenly, her eyes narrowed to slits. "You lied to me! I thought you were bored out of your mind working a deadly dull job. I felt *sorry* for you!"

Sandra gave her the cutest cat-with-cream grin. "I couldn't very well tell you the truth, could I?"

Yes. You could have, Rachel thought, but she did not say this aloud.

Sandra asked hopefully, "But you are proud of me, right?"

"Of course," Rachel's resentment melted. "Very, very proud! How did you come to join Veltdammerung?"

"The Wisecraft knew someone at the school was recruiting new members for Veltdammerung. A year and a half ago, Father asked if I would go undercover. Our initial suspect turned out to be a false lead, but eventually I contacted the right people—or the wrong people, if you prefer," Sandra laughed gaily. "And here I am."

"So that's what Mordeau was up to!" Rachel cried, as a number of pieces suddenly clicked into place. "She wasn't there to kill the dean and Mr. Fisher. She was recruiting from the student body!"

"Exactly!" Sandra stood up and brushed off her knees. She kept her gaze locked fondly on Rachel's face. "The Grand Inquisitor had done such a good job of wiping out the old Morthbrood that Veltdammerung can no longer find supporters among the adult population. So they target up-and-coming sorcerers. They have agents at schools all over the world, but their main target was Roanoke Academy, because our graduates are the most accomplished."

"If their purpose was recruitment, why did Dr. Mordeau attack?" asked Rachel.

"Her plans unraveled," replied Sandra. "I believe a student remembered something she had been geased to forget? Dr. Mordeau panicked and escalated to a long-term goal."

"Which was take revenge on Mr. Fisher, Maverick Badger, and Dean Moth—those who had stopped Veltdammerung the first time?" asked Rachel.

"Yes, exactly," Sandra's voice rose in surprised. "You know a great deal."

"Yes, I do." Rachel beamed with pride. "Information loves me. It comes and finds me!"

Sandra shook her head, smirking at her fondly.

Rachel's smile faltered. "Did you...know about Agent Browne? That he was a traitor?"

"Daniel?" Sandra's face clouded over. "Yes. He is the one who introduced me to Mortimer Egg. I told Father and Cain March. They were tracking his movements. But they could not move against him without compromising me. When Jim Darling discovered his treachery independently, they were able to move in and arrest him."

Across the crowded room, Scarlett MacDannan called, "Miss Romanov, Miss Griffin, Mr. Smith. Let's remove those geases, before they are used against you again, hmm?"

"You better go." Sandra leaned in and kissed her on the cheek. "I'll come visit you soon..." She gave Rachel a pretty grimace. "After I've been debriefed."

Rachel crossed the room and waited patiently, until it was her turn to undergo the *Spell of True Recitation*. For the third time in four weeks, she floated in mid-air, amidst a swirl of golden sparks. A few more scorched her than the previous time, but mainly the tiny twinkles stars felt cool and tingly.

This time, she spread her arms and twirled.

When she landed, her mind was free of the cobwebby traces of the geas. Scarlett MacDannan then asked Nastasia a great number of questions. When the princess finished describing the little she remembered, it was Siggy's turn and then Rachel's.

"Nastasia explained the gist of what took place. O'Malley grabbed you. Egg placed you on an altar. Finn and the rest of us saved you. Do either of you recall anything else significant that happened after you arrived in Transylvania?"

Sigfried shook his head. "Nope. Not a clue. I think I remember some stars. Or maybe dragons. I think there were dragons."

"You always think there are dragons," scoffed Nastasia.

"No dragons, Boss. I was here," whispered Lucky.

Under the influence of the *Spell of True Recitation*, the real memories in Rachel's head screamed to be heard. She opened her mouth, eager to blurt everything out.

Then she froze.

She could not explain what happened without explaining that she was immune to geases. The Agents would be able to deduce the corollary, that she was immune to their spell. The Grand Inquisitor would not like that. He would look for a different spell with which to interrogate her. What if he found one and then asked her something that would force her to explain about the Raven and what happened to Sakura? Or to betray the Elf?

Rachel looked the Agent in the eye and lied. "No."

Of course, this meant no one would know about her part in stopping Azrael. Finn MacDannan would get the credit. She did not mind this, but she did not like to mislead her father. Silently, she promised to tell him the truth when he came to ask her what had happened.

As if he had heard her thoughts, Rachel's father appeared beside her in a flash of light. He gave her the kindest smile, gazing at her as if she were the most important thing in the world.

"I am so glad you are all right." He bent low, his steady hazel eyes filled with wisdom, warmth, and love. "I cannot even begin to tell you how worried I've been."

Rachel beamed, so happy to have saved him. She fairly jumped up and down with eagerness. She yearned to tell him everything, but she kept stumbling in her attempt, uncertain how to begin.

"Ambrose," Agent Bridges's voice cut across the general hubbub, "can you give us a hand with this one?"

Rachel's father glanced reluctantly over at where some other Agents were rounding up some of the more experienced of the hooded followers, including Faust. He sighed.

"I am afraid I must go. Duty calls." Solemnly, he leaned forward and kissed her on the forehead. Then, he was gone again.

Rachel's heart deflated like a popped balloon. Regret coursed through her. Oh, why hadn't she spoken up more quickly? Sighing, she comforted herself with the thought that there would soon be another opportunity.

Rachel watched her friends and family. Sandra and Father helped with the round-up. Nastasia spoke with the Agents. Siggy and Lucky whooped and laughed, performing a war dance that might have been a reenactment of their part of the battle. A feeling of joy filled her. She recalled how bravely her friends had come to her defense when Azrael was about to kill her.

"Rachel Griffin."

Standing on one side, unnoticed by anyone else, was an eight-foot tall man with enormous black wings. Crying out with delight, Rachel ran and stood before him, smiling.

The Raven bent over and picked her up. He held her easily, as if she weighed nothing. He smelled of the wind off the ocean and summer rain. Over his shoulder, she saw nuns of Asclepius helping Agent Caldor onto a stretcher. His sheep dog stood guard beside him, wagging its tail eagerly and licking its master's face.

"He's alive!" gaped Rachel. "Agent Caldor lived!"

"By calling upon his true nature, Azrael created a certain amount of uncertainty. I took advantage of it to make sure a few things went our way," said the Guardian.

"You mean...*you* saved him?"

"Not just him. I have something to show you."

The world around them changed. Red-orange curtains hung over a dark green marble floor. The planets of a mechanical orrery clicked away overhead. The air smelled of cinnamon and chicken soup. The décor looked familiar and yet she had never been in this place before.

"Where are we?" asked Rachel.

"The Healing Halls of the Order of Asclepius, in New York City. As I mentioned, there was enough ambiguity in the possible probabilities to save another."

A nurse arrived, accompanied by a female Agent with very green eyes, whom Rachel recognized as the conjurer, Alyssa Follows, one of Darling's people. The nurse drew the curtain aside. Behind it, smiling as he looked up from his book, sat Siggy's supposedly dead roommate, Enoch Smithwyck.

The Raven said, "They remember that they kept him hidden here, pretending he was dead—because it was not known whether Mordeau's allies might be targeting him personally."

"That's...fantastic!"

The Raven inclined his head. "It was a dangerous thing, and I was fortunate that it did not go badly. But it was the least I could do for Sakura Suzuki, after I robbed her of her gift."

"Thank you," murmured Rachel, her eyes growing moist.

"Thank you, Rachel Griffin," the Raven replied, "for saving my world."

The End

To be continued in:

Rachel and the Many-Splendored Dreamland

To be kept up to date on all things Roanoke and *Unexpected*, as well as the further adventures of Rachel Griffin, subscribe to the **Roanoke Glass Newsletter** by sending an email to:

arhyalon@gmail.com

For more information, or to enroll, please see the website of *Roanoke Academy for the Sorcerous Arts*:
http://lampwright.wix.com/roanoke-academy

Glossary

AgentsMagical law enforcement. Agents fight magical foes, both
    human and supernatural.

AlchemyOne of the Seven Sorcerous Arts. It is the Art of putting
    magic into objects.

BavariaA country that exists in the world of the book but not in
    our world. It is known to both the World of the Wise and
the Unwary. It is ruled by the Von Dread family.

CanticleOne of the Seven Sorcerous Arts. It is the Art of
    commanding the natural and supernatural world with
the words and gestures of the Original Language.

CantripOne word in the Original Language, *i.e.* a canticle spell.

Cathay The Democratic Republic of Cathay, a country that exists
    in the world of the book but not in our world. It is known
to both the World of the Wise and the Unwary. It is ruled by an
elected council.

ConjuringOne of the Seven Sorcerous Arts. It is the Art of
    drawing objects out of the dreamlands.

Core GroupA group of students, usually from the same dorm,
    who attend all their classes together.

Dare Hall The dormitory at Roanoke Academy that is favored by
    enchanters.

De Vere Hall The dormitory at Roanoke Academy that is favored
    by warders and obscurers.

Dee Hall The dormitory at Roanoke Academy that is favored by
    scholars.

Drake Hall The dormitory at Roanoke Academy that is favored
    by thaumaturges.

EnchantmentOne of the Seven Sorcerous Arts. It is based on
    music and includes a number of sub-arts.

Fulgurator's wandA wand with a spell-grade gem on the tip
    that is used by Soldiers of the Wise to throw
lighting and to hold other kinds of spells.

GnosisOne of the Seven Sorcerous Arts. It is the Art of
    knowledge and augury.

Heer of Dunderberg

Storm Goblin locked up with his Lightning Imps in a cave in Stony Tor on Roanoke Island.

JumpingA cantrip that allows the practitioner to teleport.

Magical AustraliaA country that is only known to the Wise. It is ruled by the Romanov family.

Marlowe Hall The dormitory at Roanoke Academy that is favored by conjurers.

MorthbroodAn ancient organization of practitioners of black magic. During the Terrible Years, the Morthbrood served the Terrible Five.

MundaneWithout magic. Refers both to the modern technological world and to those who cannot use magic. It is possible to be mundane and Wise, if one has no magic but is aware of the magical world.

ObscurationA subset of Warding. It allows for the casting of illusions that hide things and trick the Unwary.

Original Language The original language in which all objects were named.

Parliament of the Wise The ruling body of the World of the Wise.

Pollepel Island The name the Unwary call the island they see in place of Roanoke Island. It is also called Bannerman Island.

Roanoke Academy for the Sorcerous ArtsA school of magic on a floating island that is currently moored in the Hudson near Storm King Mountain.

ScholarsPractitioners of the Art of Gnosis.

Sorcery The study of magic.

Spenser Hall The dormitory at Roanoke Academy that is favored by canticlers.

Terrible Five The leaders of the Veltdammerung, who terrorized the World of the Wise during the Terrible Years. They consisted of: Simon Magus, Morgana le Fay, Koschei the Deathless, Baba Yaga, and Aleister Crowley.

ThaumaturgyOne of the Seven Sorcerous Arts. It is the Art of storing charges of magic in a gem.

Thule

A country that is known only to the World of the Wise. It occupies the section of Greenland that is, in our world, occupied by the world's largest national park (larger than all but 32 countries).

TransylvaniaA country that exists in the world of the book but not in our world. It is known to both the World of the Wise and the Unwary. It is ruled by the Starkadder family.

TutorThe term used for professors at Roanoke Academy.

UnwaryOne who does not know about the magical world.

VeltdammerungTwilight of the World. The organization that served the Terrible Five during the Terrible Years. It consisted of the Morthbrood and of supernatural servants.

WardingOne of the Seven Sorcerous Arts. It is the Art of protecting one's self from magical influences.

WiseThose in the know about the magical world (as in the root of the word 'wizard').

WisecraftThe law enforcement agency of the Wise. The Agents work for the Wisecraft.

World of the Wise The community of those who know about the magical world.

Acknowledgements

Thank you to Mark Whipple, John C. Wright, and William E. Burns, III who breathed the life into the original story.

To Virginia Johnson and Erin Furby, who helped iron out the bumps, and to my sons, Orville and Justinian for playing along and particularly to Juss, for wearing a lightning imp under his cat.

To Erin Furby, Ginger Kenny, Deanna Quiterio, Kirsten Edwards, Laura Tayler, Theresa Murphy, Kiara Lingenfelter, Mark Thompson, and to April, Jubal, and Jeremiah Freeman, for slogging through the early drafts.

To Anna Macdonald and Don Schank, for making it readable.

To my brother, Law Lamplighter, who listened, and to my mother, Jane Lamplighter, for making dinner on Thursdays, so I could write.

About the Authors

L. Jagi Lamplighter is also the author of the *Prospero's Daughter* series: *Prospero Lost*, *Prospero In Hell*, and *Prospero Regained*. She is an assistant editor with the Bad-Ass Faeries Anthologies, and she maintains a weekly blog on writing called Wright's Writing Corner. When not writing, she switches to her secret identity as wife and stay-home mom in Centreville, VA, where she lives with her dashing husband, author John C. Wright, and their four darling children, Orville, Ping-Ping, Roland Wilbur, and Justinian Oberon.

Or visit the ABOUT page on her website:
http://ljagilamplighter.com

On Twitter: @lampwright4

Mark A. Whipple grew up in Croton-on-Hudson, which is not far from Roanoke Island. He then attended St. John's College in Annapolis, the mundane sister school to Roanoke Academy. Until recently, he has spent his free time, when not busy torturing Rachel Griffin, protecting the world from video game threats. Now, however, he volunteers with Stillbrave, a charity devoted to helping the families of children with cancer.